"This is Kristie's best book yet and I look forward to more books in the Soul Savers series." – Michelle Gregory, author of *Eldala*

"I never thought that any other book could make my heart pound like *Promise* did but I was wrong. *Purpose* exceeded all expectations and presented a story that kept my emotions on high-alert. A true masterpiece that will appeal to all paranormal romance fans."
– Jessica at Confessions of a Bookaholic

"Cook has totally outdone herself . . . . With emotions running high from *Promise* to *Purpose* . . . it's thrilling, fast paced, sexy—with moments I found myself shaking my head, my heart breaking a little, gasping or laughing out loud."– Lisa at A Life Bound by Books

"I have never cried, laughed, and been so emotional while reading a book. Ms. Cook really did a number on me. While the first book blew me away, this one left me in the dust." – Books With Bite

"Kristie Cook did such a fantastic job relating the character's emotions and making them jump off the page. I just love how easy it is for me to sit down with one of her books and realize hours later that I have actually been reading that long! It is climatic, action-packed, and fulfilling." – Extreme Reader Book Reviews

"In *Promise* we meet Alexis and are introduced to the world of the Soul Savers and in *Purpose*, everything is taken to another level . . . . I can't wait to see what Kristie Cook has in store for the next book." – Paranormal Haven

"I love when a sequel blows me away. You know, when you enjoyed the first book in the series, but then you hit the next book and it's like 'Whoa, this is some great stuff!' Well, that's what happened when I read Kristie Cook's second book in her Soul Savers Series, *Purpose*."
– Lavender Lines

Books by Kristie Cook

— SOUL SAVERS SERIES —
www.SoulSaversSeries.com

Promise
Purpose
Devotion (February 2012)

Genesis: A Soul Savers Novella (October 2011)

Find the author at www.KristieCook.com

DEFENDING SOULS IS HER PURPOSE...

BUT CAN SHE SAVE HER OWN?

Purpose

KRISTIE COOK

BOOK TWO

Ang'dora Productions, LLC
Naples, Florida

Published by
Ang'dora Productions, LLC
15275 Collier Blvd
#201-300
Naples, FL 34119

Ang'dora Productions and associated logos are trademarks and/
or registered trademarks of Ang'dora Productions, LLC

Cover design by Brenda Pandos

This book is a work of fiction. Names, characters and events
are either products of the author's imagination or are used
fictitiously and any resemblance to actual persons, living or
dead, is entirely coincidental.

ISBN 978-0-9845621-5-2

First Edition December 2010
Second Edition August 2011

Printed in the United States of America

For Yvonne Clark and Gertrude Perguson

And in honor of

Sheree Cook Chestnut

Acknowledgements

This is truly the hardest part of a book to write. There are so many people who made this book a reality, including you, the reader.

Thank you to my publishing team at Ang'dora Productions for your dedication and support. Chrissi Jackson, you have been my lifeline to reality, keeping me on track through all the insanity. Thank you for everything you've done . . . especially for the word "dictate." Thank you, Lisa Adams, for your positive energy, beautiful spirit, keen eyes and willingness to enter and support the chaos. You are both real gifts from the Angels.

Thank you to my writing buddies who helped me build and polish this story into what it is today. Meredith S. Wood, I appreciate your challenges and camaraderie. Judy Spelbring, thank you for being real in your critiques, for pointing out my weaknesses and for helping me move beyond "it." Michelle Gregory, I so love that you are as invested in my characters as in your own, helping me to see where I have not done them justice. Thank you, as well, for being my indie partner-in-crime. I appreciate all of you and what you've done for the story.

Of course, none of this would have happened without the patience, support and love of my family. Thank you to my boys – Zakary, Austin and Nathan – for being so freaking awesome that I sometimes can't breathe because I'm so proud of you. You've really been amazing throughout this process and I can't thank you enough. Thank you, Shawn, for your continued encouragement and commitment. Thank you, Mom, Dad, Keena and Terry, for all that you've done, past, present and future. And thank you, Grandma Yvonne, for passing down the love of words, reading and writing.

Finally, once again, thank you, the reader, for your love of Alexis and Tristan and their story. I sincerely appreciate your reviews, advocacy and support. You've motivated me to keep going, when I really just wanted to sleep. I appreciate your devotion and patience and I hope you enjoy this next part of the tale of the ultimate warrior and the fierce protector.

Prologue

Living with half a soul is like living forever in the hour before dawn, when the sky is no longer black, but a dark, charcoal gray, waiting for the light. It's like clinging to the hope of a new day lingering just beyond the horizon. The new day that never comes. The light that never brightens the world.

I live in varying shades of gray and with each shade, I feel like a different person entirely . . . but always only half a person. Always half empty. Except when I'm with my son, when I feel the most like the real me, the old me. When I am Almost Alexis. Dorian pushes the darkness away and brightens my life. With him, I actually feel half full.

But then there's Swirly Alexis, who disorients my thoughts to the point where I don't know what is real and what is fiction, swirling my world into confusion.

And Psycho Alexis is blind to everything but rage, lashing out with a heart and soul black as ink.

Foggy Alexis, however, rules most of the time, allowing

me to live in a dense fog, with no clear edges to my life, my thoughts, my feelings. She numbs the pain so I can survive without screaming.

The only sure thing I know is the rope of hope I hold so tightly to—the hope that Tristan still lives. That he will come back. Just as he promised.

Over time, however, the rope has thinned and now begins to fray. I have tried to strengthen it by making a promise of my own. That I will rescue him from his hell after I go through the *Ang'dora*—a promise he may never know but I will nonetheless keep. If the *Ang'dora* arrives before it's too late. As time passes, I don't know if I can continue hanging on. What remains of the rope is now just a thin thread. If it breaks, I will plunge into an abyss of complete darkness.

For now, the thread still remains intact. And as long as it does, I will hold on. I will hold onto that hope. Even if doing so means living in a fog. Even if it means living with just half a soul, as half a person. Because I am reminded nightly that I need to, that our souls are worth it.

For a short time every night, I allow myself to remember, if only in my subconscious. And then I know again what it feels like to have a whole soul. To feel loved. To be complete. To live in a world of beautiful color and light. To know that he lives. And so does the Real Alexis. Somewhere, we cling to each other, our souls still united. Somewhere, we live together in the light.

But then the sun rises and life goes dark again . . . .

Chapter 1

March, Present Day

We sat side-by-side on white sand, gentle waves sliding onto the beach with just a whisper and the sun low, about to tuck itself behind the horizon. Pink, purple and gold streaked the sky and reflected on the water. The mixed smell of salt and cocoa butter wafted on the warm air. I closed my eyes and inhaled deeply, trying to pull the whole scene in so it would become a part of me. His tangy-sweet scent filled my senses. Fresh mangos and papayas mixed with lime and sage and just a hint of man. I would never forget that smell.

I opened my eyes to find his exquisite face only inches from mine. My heart skipped a beat—or three or four. The gold flecks in his hazel eyes sparkled brightly. His full lips lifted at the corners in an enticing smile. He lifted his hand to stroke my cheek. His fingers lingered, his palm gently cupping my face. He leaned forward, still holding my eyes. He hesitated. My heart stopped beating. My breathing ceased, too. And the rest of the world melted away as his lips met mine and he kissed me for the first time.

In a heartbeat, we rode his motorcycle along the causeway to Gasparilla Island. The engine rumbled underneath me, the sound loud but comforting. I wrapped my arms tightly around his waist and pressed myself into his powerful body. We stopped at our favorite place on the beach and just sat on the bike, watching the dolphins. I closed my eyes and leaned my head against his. His lovely voice murmured, "I love you, *ma lykita.*"

When I opened my eyes again, Rina had her hands pressed to our hearts at our wedding, binding our souls into one. Then we were at our beach house in the Florida Keys, the one he built for my wedding present. The white leather bodice of my dress fell to the floor. He lifted me to the bed and we made love for the first time. Then we were in the shower. Then the motel shower in North Carolina. It was our last time. Ever.

I closed my eyes, wanting to hold onto him because I knew what came next. When I opened them again, we were at the safe house and I begged him not to leave. Then he led the others out the front door and into the battle. Scenes flashed quickly— shooting lights, mangled body parts, spurting blood. They were suddenly somewhere else, another field, the safe house nowhere in sight. Daemoni attacked the powerful warrior, once theirs. He fought, but there were too many. Dozens of dog-like creatures. *Hundreds* of them. Their fangs sank into his flesh. The scene changed again, now to a foreign place. A desert valley or some kind of cavern, stone mountains or walls reaching out of sight. He could no longer fight back, but writhed on the ground, his beautiful face contorted in agony. And then he went still.

"*NOOOO!*" I screamed.

My eyes flew open and I gasped for air. I looked around

wildly as my eyes adjusted to the abrupt change. Darkness surrounded me. My fists clamped the bed sheet to my chest. The duvet hung off the edge of the bed, kicked to the side. I forced myself to pull in a long, controlled breath, and then let the air out just as slowly. My breaths eventually became even and my heart finally settled. I looked at the clock, already knowing it was around 3:45 a.m. The blue lights glowed 3:51.

Every night was the same as the one before. Regardless of what time I would finally fall asleep, around 3:45 I would awake screaming and gasping for breath. My imagination created the last part of the memory-dream, but the rest was real and very precious. Some nights, when my subconscious knew my soul needed more, I relived some of our other times together.

I threw myself back on the pillow and squeezed my eyes shut, trying to remember in my conscious mind what my subconscious could so easily play back. I struggled to pull his image back into clarity. The edges blurred, as if an oily film coated the lens I looked through. *I'm losing him.* The image had become dim, faded with time. *I can't forget. I can't forget, damn it!* But remembering had become so hard. My dreams showed Tristan perfectly, but my waking mind had lost the clarity, unable to focus on the details.

I tried to recreate the scenes—the good ones—in my mind, focusing on the background, the feels, the smells, hoping my wandering mind could bring his face into view naturally. My scheme began to work. The blurry edges started to sharpen, the light on his face grew brighter, the hazel eyes came into focus . . . .

My consciousness drifted off as I held onto his face. And then I heard his lovely voice, distant and muffled: "I'll come back. I promise."

My dream-self felt surprised and confused. *This is new.*

Then clear and close: "Alexis."

It wasn't the same voice.

Evil! Daemoni! Evil!

The alarms of my sixth sense rang in my head. The stunning face disappeared as my heart nearly jumped out of my chest. I shot up and realized I sat on my bed again. I glanced around the darkness for the source of the gravelly voice.

"Who's there?" I asked, my voice thundering through the silence.

A shadow shifted in the corner. Two small, red lights glowed from about two-thirds up the wall. I realized they were eyes. *It can't really be Daemoni—can it?* We hadn't been bothered for over seven years. Not a single visit or even a threat. Nothing at all. They had what they wanted.

"Don't you know?"

The shadow moved forward, just enough for the light from my clock to slightly illuminate a face—pale, bluish-white in the clock's glare, glowing eyes and . . . *fangs.* The light reflected off his glimmering teeth, bared in an evil grin, if that's what you could call it, and I knew for sure those were fangs. And I knew immediately what he was. From what I could see, he favored some of my characters, as if he'd stepped out of the pages of the books I wrote.

Such a strange feeling—to feel as though I'd awakened in my usual way but know I was dreaming again. I had to be. Monsters were real, but vampires were not.

"C-Claudius?" My voice shook. I knew this dream was about to become a terrible nightmare. With his dark hair floating around the sides of his face, this visitor looked similar to my Claudius, leader of the evilest vampire nest in my make-believe world.

"Ha!" the shadow barked. "So you do see the resemblance."

I didn't respond. I stared wide-eyed at the barely visible

face, wondering what would come next. My heart pounded in my ears and my lungs seemed unable to pull in any air. I wanted to scream myself awake. But I couldn't. I was frozen.

The vampire came closer, almost near enough to touch . . . if I dared to reach out.

"I am *not* your dim-witted Claudius," he growled, "but my world and my ways are very similar. In fact, *too* similar. You are bold—and foolish—to tell the humans."

In a strange way, the dream made him more *real*. More frightening than any of my characters, even Claudius. The timbre of his voice held promises of horror, the sound more terrifying than I ever imagined when I wrote.

But his words made no sense.

"I-I d-don't understand."

"I am not stupid, woman, and I know you are not *entirely* ignorant. I know who you are. You know what I am. You have crossed the line in revealing our truths. You must stop writing and exposing us, Alexis. Or we will stop you ourselves."

The flaming red eyes narrowed. The nostrils flared.

The vampire cocked his head and growled again. "No more, Alexis, or we *will* come for you!"

Pop! The overhead light suddenly flooded the bedroom with brightness. I was sitting bolt upright in my bed, my heart hammering again, wide awake with the sound and light. I blinked at Mom's figure standing at the foot of my bed.

"Are you okay?" she demanded.

My eyes adjusted and now I could see her looking anything but vulnerable, though she only wore a short, baby-doll nightgown. Petite, but tough. She stood with her body tense, coiled and ready to fight, as her narrowed eyes scanned the room. Then she rushed to my side and braced her hands against my face. She seemed to appraise every inch of me.

"I'm fine," I muttered, pulling my face from her grip.

"You don't sound or look fine."

"You scared the crap out of me." I lay back down and closed my eyes. "And I had a bad dream. That's all."

She stood there for a long moment and I could feel her eyes still on me. I never heard her footsteps, but the light switched off and the door clicked softly in the latch when she left. Mom was used to me having bad dreams. She had no need to question me.

☙

When I awoke again, sunlight streamed under the blinds, creating narrow lines of light on the boring beige carpet by my bed. I lay on my stomach and stared at the floor for a while, not wanting to be awake. Then I remembered the dream— not the usual memory-dream, but the new one. I turned over and looked around the room. Of course, no evidence of the vampire. He was just a dream, but it had felt so real and was just so uncharacteristic. Last night was the first time I'd dreamt of anything but those memories since the day my husband disappeared into enemy hands.

Then I remembered the other anomaly of the night. The whispered promise. But neither the lovely voice nor the memory-dream had returned the rest of the night. *Damn vampire.* I closed my eyes and tried to pull the face I wanted to see into my vision. A pointless effort. Only a vague image appeared. I was forgetting.

As time had passed on, as the conscious memories faded, the feeling Tristan was still alive weakened. For the first few years, I'd felt his presence and the grief of living without him nearly consumed me. Eventually, a fog drifted in and settled, dulling the pain . . . and the memories. Foggy Alexis arrived and I liked her. She kept me numb during the day, allowing memories only at night, when I slept. But now the dullness seemed to be permanently obscuring my conscious memories and dissolving our connection.

Forcing myself to let it go, I focused my mind on the only things I'd been able to focus on for the last seven years: my son and my writing. Dorian served as the bright spot in my otherwise bleak life. He lit my path, keeping me from straying away into the complete darkness of insanity. If his father hadn't already set precedence, it would be hard to believe I could love anyone as much as I loved Dorian.

I sighed heavily and made myself stand up. I already felt today was not a good day. I felt all wrong. Something inside ticked, like a time bomb.

I had a warped sense of time, but I was sure it had been a while since I'd had a really bad day. It had to have been months, probably last July on our anniversary, since Psycho Alexis or anyone but Foggy had made an appearance. Our anniversaries were always tough. The middle of March, though, had no meaning—even the anniversary of our engagement was two weeks away—so I couldn't understand why I felt so . . . messed up this morning.

Suck it up for now. Need to say good-bye.

It was after eight and Mom was probably getting Dorian ready for school. I wanted to say good-bye to him. Then I could lose myself in my writing.

"Hi, Mom!" Dorian greeted as I trudged into the kitchen. His face lit up, his mouth stretched into that all-too-familiar, beautiful smile and his eyes sparkled. He pulled his jacket on, getting ready to leave. I almost missed him. If I had and with the mood I was in, Psycho might have taken over immediately. But since he was still here, brightening my morning, I could enjoy a few minutes of being Almost Alexis.

"Hey, little man." I ruffled his hair—the snow-white color had been unexpected, but I had a feeling a similar-looking towhead had been running around a couple hundred years ago—and gave him a big smile, too. Only Dorian could elicit a real smile from me. "You ready for school?"

He shrugged. "I guess. Just today and tomorrow and then it's Spring Break. And Uncle Owen's coming!"

"No fighting at school, okay?" I warned. "I really don't want to make another trip to the principal's office this week."

"I'll try." He gave me the same promise every day . . . and rarely followed through on it. When it came to protecting loved ones, he had control of his anger about as much as I did. Usually, he fought kids who teased him about me, his weird mother.

"You said the same thing yesterday," Mom reminded him.

"That stupid Joey! I hate him, Mimi! He said my dad's a no good shithead who didn't want me."

"Honey, that's a bad word. You are too young to be using such language," Mom said.

"I didn't say it! Joey did!"

I fought back a laugh, but the anger at the memory flashed in Dorian's eyes—tiny sparks in the gold flecks around his pupils—and I suddenly felt renewed irritation, too. Once I became "America's favorite young author," the media quickly discovered I'd been pregnant at the tender age of nineteen and the father was nowhere to be found. People made up their own stories from there. So when Dorian didn't feel a need to protect me, he defended his so-called deadbeat dad. Because he knew better.

"Good for you!" I said, giving Dorian a squeeze. I would have done the same thing—punched the kid in the face. In fact, the lunatic in me this morning wanted to hunt down the little brat right now. The not-so-crazy part of me at least wanted to find his parents.

Mom shook her head disapprovingly. I ignored her.

"Don't you *ever* let anyone talk about your daddy that way," I said. "He's a wonderful man and he loves you very much. It's not his fault he's not here. You know that, right?"

He nodded, his cupid-bow lips quivering with sadness. I held my arms out and he gave me a bear hug—as big of a hug as a six-year-old can. He knocked me to the floor and I gave an exaggerated cry. He laughed and showed me his guns, flexing his biceps. I ooh'ed and aah'ed over them. They were actually impressive. He had his dad's strength.

Then he crossed his arms over his chest and looked at Mom and then me, his eyes lit up with mischief. "I'll stop fighting if you get me a dog. Then I'll have a friend and I'll ignore everyone else."

I bit my lip, not knowing whether I would laugh or cry. I knew how Dorian felt to want a friend so badly. I also knew he would promise anything to have a dog, which he'd been begging us for since his last birthday. I had a hard time believing, though, that he would stop fighting. It was just part of his nature.

I'd wanted to put him in an Aikido class to teach him self-control, but Mom wouldn't allow it—his unusual strength would draw attention we didn't need. So I had Owen work with him whenever possible.

"I turn seven in twenty-eight days," Dorian said when we didn't respond. And then I did chuckle.

"We'll see," I finally said.

"How about no fighting between now and your birthday and then we'll discuss it?" Mom suggested.

I looked at her with surprise. She was the one usually against adopting a pet. A dog would be another responsibility to worry about if we ever had to go on the run again. Then I realized she must have figured Dorian wouldn't be able to hold up his end of the bargain.

"Deal," he said and I cringed. I agreed with Mom on this one.

I gave Dorian another hug, then Mom took him to school. Since my book sales could support us and probably the entire Amadis, Mom made it her job to tend to Dorian and the house so I could work. Even before my career took off, my writing had always remained high on her priority list.

As soon as I was alone, I poured a cup of coffee, went out the backdoor and slipped around the side of the house for a cigarette. When I heard Mom's car return nearly an hour later, I snuffed out my third one and drained my third cup of coffee, then hurried inside. I munched on chocolate-chip cookies when she came through the door and dumped an armful of grocery bags on the counter. She eyed me, her mahogany eyes filled with disdain.

"Those are healthy," she said as she placed the bags on the counter.

"Breakfast of champions."

"Alexis—"

I felt a lecture coming on and there were plenty of areas she could pick on. Normally, I wouldn't blame her, but right now, the ticking that had been in my head all morning grew louder. Then some kind of switch flipped. I couldn't control the need. I *wanted* to lash out.

Psycho Alexis reared her ugly head.

"I don't want to hear it, Mom," I snapped, marching out of the kitchen. "I fucked up by not having a girl, but I gave it my best shot. I'm writing the damn books. At least back off everything else, okay? I'm trying as hard as I fucking can."

"Alexis!" she admonished, following me into my office. She hated my language, which was exactly why I used it. "I just wanted to remind you Owen will be here later. You might want to clean yourself up."

I looked down at myself. I wore the same raggedy t-shirt and sweatpants I had slept in. Pretty much my normal attire. *What the hell do I care what Owen thinks?* I didn't. Mom seemed to, though. In fact, she seemed to care a lot about what Owen thought lately.

"I'm fine," I snarled.

I grabbed my laptop and headed outside. The early Spring morning in Atlanta, Georgia, had been a little crisp earlier, but the air quickly warmed. It would be a nice day to write outside and I hoped the fresh air would help my mood. I set up the laptop on the patio table, opened the document and then stared at the screen. For a long time. I just couldn't focus on stringing words into meaningful sentences. Giving up, I gazed absent-mindedly across the yard, thinking about last night.

I considered writing out the evil vampire Claudius, after that rendition of him interrupted my dreams last night. Maybe the time had come to kill him off. Of course, he was one of my primary villains in this last book of the series, so he was necessary until the end. But I was pissed at him now. *How dare the asshole harass me at night!* I eventually dismissed him for the time being after deciding he *would* die, a final death, by the end of the book.

Tired of thinking so much about the stupid vamp, I closed my eyes and tilted my face toward the sun, focusing on the heat of the rays on my skin, giving me paradoxical goose bumps. I felt the burn of someone watching me, but I ignored the feeling. It had to be Mom and I didn't want to deal with her yet. With the warm sun washing over me, I actually felt . . . well, not *good*, but at least no longer Psycho. Then a slight breeze came up, light against my skin and just a little cool. And with it, a familiar scent.

Mangos and papayas, lime and sage.

My eyes flew open and I sat straight up, nearly knocking my computer off the table.

"Relax, it's just me," Mom said. She placed a tray of food on the table. "Seared tuna on greens with a lime vinaigrette dressing and fruit. I thought you'd be ready for lunch."

I eyed the tray and realized the food must have given off that mix of aromas. *How could I even think it's anything else?* I slumped back into my chair, feeling the emotional wound pulling open again as if a physical gash had been carved into my chest. My body quickly healed cuts, burns and bruises, but not this most painful kind of mutilation.

I moved the laptop out of the way and took a plate from Mom. She joined me across the table. When I looked up at her, I noticed for the first time that someone stood behind her. Quite a ways behind her—at least seventy-five yards, on the other side of the pool, by the fence lining the back of my five-acre property. I froze at his sudden appearance, sure he hadn't been there just a minute ago.

Something fluttered in my stomach and I couldn't tear my eyes away from him. I stood up and took a couple steps toward him, not able to control myself. He just watched me, his arms folded across his chest. *Could it be?* I had a sudden need to see his face. I slowly moved another step or two toward him, frightened and curious and . . . hopeful. *Who are you?*

"Alexis?" Mom startled me out of my trance.

I turned back to look at her, nearly forgetting she was there. She had twisted in her seat to see what had me ogling.

"Who is that?" I asked, raising my arm toward the man.

She brushed her chestnut hair from her face and peered behind me with her inhumanly sharp eyes. "Who? I don't see anyone."

I turned back to him. He was gone.

"I thought . . ." *What the hell? Did he flash? Was it* him*? Or* *a protector? Or just my imagination?*

"Probably one of the landscaping guys," Mom finally said. "They have a different crew out today."

"No Amadis?"

"Not until Owen comes later."

"Oh. He just kind of . . . disappeared. And he was staring at me."

Mom raised her eyebrows. "There would be many reasons for that, my dear."

I looked at her for meaning. She just shrugged.

I tried to see the stranger's face in my mind, but he'd been too far away. His build, though . . . his height, the way he stood . . . so familiar . . . .

I slumped back into my chair and stared at my hands in my lap, fighting back tears. *It's not him. It's not him. It's not him.* I tried to convince myself. I'd had other instances of mistaken identities, but because this was in my own backyard, it felt different. Worse. Especially because the stranger had simply disappeared, as if he hadn't existed in the first place. As if I'd been seeing things. *It doesn't hurt. Just having a bad day, is all.*

I shoved my plate away and stood up. I had to get out of here. Because it did hurt. It hurt like hell, actually. For some stupid reason, something inside me had soared high with the tiniest glint of hope, then dive-bombed into the pavement of reality. All the pieces inside shattered into even smaller ones, if that were even possible, cutting open old wounds and making them throb and bleed again. I clutched at the pendant—my gift for our one and only Christmas together—as if it could soothe the pain.

"You didn't eat anything." Mom pointed to my plate, then gestured at me. "You eat all that junk food and look what it's done to you. I give you something healthy and delicious and you don't even touch it."

The last tick of the bomb sounded. Psycho Alexis could be suppressed no longer and a switch didn't just flip this time. The whole bomb exploded.

"*I'm not hungry, okay?*" I roared. "Why can't you just leave me the hell alone?"

The pained shock on her face stabbed me in the gut. I fled to my bedroom.

Who is he? Why did he stare at me? And what did Mom mean?

I went straight into my bathroom and, for the first time in . . . *what?* . . . probably months, I looked in the full-length mirror and really studied myself. My mouth dropped.

"How'd I get so *old?*" I demanded of my reflection, moving closer in, staring at a face that appeared to be fifty-five years old.

Dark puffy circles surrounded my bloodshot eyes that were once a deep mahogany, just like Mom's, but were now a flat brown. Deep lines permanently etched my forehead, between my eyebrows and around the corners of my mouth, which drew down into a perma-frown. My skin was pale and sickly looking, blotchy and aged. My hair, a dull reddish-brown, hung lifeless down my back in strings. *Holy shit! Grays!* I looked closer at my head and stopped counting at ten. *I'm not even thirty!*

I stepped back to see if my body looked just as bad. It was worse.

"How'd I get so *fat?*"

A round pooch protruded in front. *Where did these huge hips come from? And my ass?* No wonder I preferred sweat pants and elastic-waist shorts. My breasts were the only part that looked smaller . . . and saggier.

I crumpled to the floor, wailing a mix of sobs and screams. *What's happened to me? What did I do to myself? I'm fat and ugly and old. And alone. All alone.*

I literally looked twice my age and I never noticed I was

getting older. For me, life stopped at nineteen. I knew time had passed. Dorian's birthdays were the biggest marker another year went by. Plenty had happened, but I hadn't *lived* it. I'd just been going through the motions, barely existing in the fog. *Over seven years gone that I'll never have again.* And I looked like *twenty-seven* years had gone by. I'd let all that stress take a toll on me and my body while never realizing that *I*—the essence of *me*—was aging.

Images of the last seven years flashed through my mind like a slideshow while I lay on the bathroom floor with my eyes closed, tears still seeping. Pictures of Dorian—his first smile, his first steps, his birthdays, his first days of school—were bright. Others were dim—book launches, signing tours, buying my first house with my own money. Those experiences should have been remarkable, but I'd let them slip by barely noticed, like water through a sieve, as I wallowed in my pain and loss and loneliness instead.

How could I be so stupid? So wasteful? So fucking miserable?

I cried for some time. Then I grew mad. Mad at myself. Then mad at Tristan. The anger boiled up and exploded again.

"How could you do this to me?" My voice came raw and scratchy as I screamed at the top of my lungs to ensure the one who left me behind heard me, wherever he was. I pounded my fists on the floor, breaking the tiles. "How could you *leave* me? Why haven't you come back? It hurts so much. I am so *alone.*"

I broke down in hard sobs again.

Where are you? Come back to me! Save me from this emptiness!

I cried until my chest and stomach hurt. Then I curled into a ball on the bathroom floor, closed my eyes and pulled out every single memory I could possibly grasp, *forcing* their clarity, no matter how much they felt like daggers piercing my soul.

That first night of class, when we met. The first time he smiled that angelic grin at me. Looking into those hazel, sparkly eyes, full of love. The first time he touched me and the unusual spark. Our first kiss as the sun set that fall evening. Cooking together. Motorcycle rides. Christmas, when he gave me the pendant, explaining it was a piece of his heart. His warm laugh. The night he proposed. His strong hands and powerful arms holding me close against his hard body, feeling so safe and so loved. And our wedding on the beach. Our wedding night . . . .

Darkness overcame me.

Mom knocked once and I told her to go away. She didn't come back until much later. I didn't move from my fetal position on the bathroom floor. I no longer cried. I physically hurt from the sobs and didn't think I had anymore in me. I barely acknowledged her as she helped me up and to my bed. But I hugged her fiercely as she tucked me in, as if I were six again.

"It's okay, honey," she murmured in my hair as I held her tightly. "It *will* get better. I can feel the truth that change is coming soon."

"Mom?" Dorian squeaked from the doorway, his stuffed shark tucked under one arm. "Are you okay?"

I propped up on an elbow and held my other arm out to him. He crawled onto my bed, squirmed under the covers and snuggled against me.

"I'm okay now," I said as I wrapped my arms around him. Mom left, turning off the light and shutting the door behind her.

"Please don't be mad at Dad," Dorian whispered in the darkness. "Don't yell at him for leaving. You said it's not his fault. And he can't even hear you anyway."

I sighed sadly. I hated that he'd heard my bursts of anger.

"I love your father very much, Dorian. Don't ever think I don't. I just get mad sometimes and say things out of anger, but only because I miss him so much. Understand?"

"Yeah. I miss him, too."

I squeezed him tighter. "But we have each other right now. I love you, little man. Very much."

"Love you, too, Mom." Within minutes, his breathing settled into a quiet snore.

I fell to sleep shortly after, welcoming unconsciousness, waiting for the memory-dream to start.

But it never came.

After more than seven years of the same thing every night, my dreams were finally different. I found myself in a world where everything was a shade of what I could only call steel-blue-gray. I sat on the top of a mountain, at the apex of an arced range, with several peaks pointing to the steel-blue sky in each direction. Far below, at the base of the mountains, looked to be a meadow and a lake but they seemed small and vague from this perspective. A multitude of images hung in the air, as if projected on unseen screens. The images changed, like the slideshow of my waking memories while lying on the bathroom floor. Dorian, the beach, vampires, writing, college classes. Mom's old bookstore, werewolves, my mom, motorcycle rides, me on the bathroom floor. And the figure in the yard . . . a lot of him. In fact, I later realized, I didn't even remember seeing Tristan's face, not clearly anyway. Anytime his face would start to come into focus, the image would shift to the stranger standing in the yard watching me.

I'd always feared losing the memory-dream. Because I knew I'd lose forever the clear image of his face and perhaps even our connection . . . and my sanity along with it.

Chapter 2

I awoke slowly, not my usual gasping, upright bolt. I opened my eyes, but didn't find the expected darkness. I lay on my stomach again, my head nearly hanging off the edge of the bed. From the dim light on the floor, it looked like the sun had just started to rise. I glanced up at the clock. 6:05. Not 3:45. Not 8:00. And I felt wide awake.

I rolled over to find Dorian still sleeping peacefully, spread-eagle on the other side of the king-sized bed. He was a strange phenomenon, just like his mother. Before me, no Amadis daughter had ever given birth to a male without a twin sister. Mom and Rina had been sure I was pregnant with twins. I'd never had an ultrasound, never even went to the doctor for prenatal care. Mom acted as my midwife and her and Rina's *feelings* were supposed to be enough.

I had developed my own theory: Mom and Rina had sensed a boy and were so sure I'd follow everyone else's precedence, they simply assumed a girl accompanied him in the womb. Stupid assumption. I was always abnormal, even for us. Of course, I would be the one to screw everything up.

They hadn't given me a good reason why Dorian couldn't lead the Amadis when the time came. Instead, they clung to the hope that, because I was different in so many other ways, I might still be able to have a daughter. Mom and Rina *felt* this could happen, although no Amadis daughter had ever given birth more than once.

There was one obvious problem with this new "plan"—it required a father. And my only love was . . . *gone*. Disappeared. Not seen since that tragic battle seven-and-a-half years ago, less than three weeks after our wedding.

As I watched Dorian sleep, his face looking so much younger than his nearly seven years, the thought of him hearing my temper-tantrum last night tortured me. No kid should have to witness such loss of control by his own mother. He had his own pain to deal with; he didn't need to hear mine, too. I was supposed to be strong for him.

What had happened yesterday? What caused me to snap so horribly? Even our last anniversary hadn't been this bad. In fact, it had been years since Psycho had taken over so vehemently. The bitch even changed my dreams! Why now?

Perhaps something deep within was telling me it was time for a change. Time to truly live, instead of existing in a fog. Time to discover the Real Alexis. I couldn't entirely let go—that was out of the question—but I could surely move forward with some things. Right? I needed to, for me and for Dorian. I owed him. He deserved more than Almost Alexis. *But how?*

I thought I could start with my writing. I needed to get back on track with it. I hadn't written for nearly two days, finding it difficult to write the final chapters of the last book of the series I'd started six years ago. The series was a wildly successful—although dark—love story bringing together the worlds of humans, vampires and other creatures. I stayed out of the talks of movie deals, so they hadn't come very far. I didn't care. That's not why I wrote.

Shortly after Dorian's first birthday, my agent started harassing me for another book, since the first one did fairly well. She reminded me of my contract, but I didn't care. Writing was a part of my old life, I'd told her. That's not who I was anymore.

"Who are you, then, Alexis?" she'd asked. "You're barely alive. Your characters are more alive than you. At least they *do* something!"

I finally promised her I would try, just to get her off my back. And Mom and Rina, too, who insisted I start on the new idea I had before my world fell apart. I had decided I could use writer's block as an easily acceptable excuse when asked why I never produced anything. But no one ever had to ask. I discovered, once I sat down at the computer, I *did* still enjoy writing, and the stories came effortlessly, as if they'd been given to me by some other force and I simply served as a tool. As time went on, I found the escape to be even better than my dreams.

Apparently, I'd created a welcomed escape for my readers, too. As the normal world came into its own dark times with wars, failing economies and endless natural disasters, people looked for a fictional world in which to lose themselves. The world I'd invented became one of the most popular choices. Knowing I'd given this to readers—a little escape from their miserable lives—was one of the reasons I enjoyed writing. Because I knew exactly how they felt.

Now that I'd almost completed the entire story, however, I struggled to bring it to an end. Just two days ago, my fingers flew across the keyboard, barely able to keep up with my thoughts. But as soon as I ended the chapter and started a new page for the next one, the flow of words ceased, as if turned off at the source. I knew *how* the story ended. I just couldn't put the words together. Yesterday, I'd blamed it on the vampire dream. But I knew the real reason. I had no ideas for the next story, which meant no other world to throw myself into. Then all I would be left with was my own life of nothingness.

I needed to push past this obstacle, though. I needed to do it for Dorian. Perhaps ending this series would allow me to end this chapter of my life. Perhaps Dorian and I could move forward with a fresh start at a new story. Perhaps Psycho saw this coming and refused to go out without a fight, sparking yesterday's meltdown. Or, perhaps Swirly Alexis had stepped in overnight, mixing my thoughts into a mass of confusion.

I hated Swirly Alexis almost as much as Psycho. Nothing made sense with her. I often had a hard time distinguishing between fact and fiction when she ruled my brain. *Today will be another doozy*, I thought with a sigh. As I crept out of bed, leaving Dorian to sleep for another hour, I tried to remember the last time I'd had two bad days in a row. I couldn't remember such a time, at least, not since Dorian was born.

I stopped in the doorway of the breakfast nook, which led to the kitchen. Always an early riser, Mom sat by herself at the wooden table with a cup of coffee held between her hands in front of her. Surely she sensed my presence—even normal humans could feel when someone has entered a room—but she didn't acknowledge it. Her back faced me as she seemed to be staring out the window, watching the backyard brighten with the morning's first light. The bluish-gray of dawn still colored the sky and the birds and squirrels were already active, hopping around the lawn and fluttering among the tree branches. The windows should have muted their chatter and calls, but I could hear every note and squeak—they sounded unusually loud today.

Mom provided a stark contrast, sitting so still and looking so peaceful. A wave of remorse washed over me. I had treated her cruelly and she didn't deserve it. I lashed out at her because, well, she was here. And also because she stood next in line to lead the Amadis, but she couldn't give me even the smallest bit of information. I held a certain amount of resentment for that, but I knew she had no control over it. Until she became matriarch, she had to follow orders. And, in the meantime, she never complained, even after my bad days.

I wrapped my arms around her shoulders.

"I'm sorry I was such an ass," I whispered against her cheek. I cringed, knowing I'd just offended her again. "Sorry."

She patted my hand. "I'm sorry you're still suffering so much."

I pulled away to pour a cup of coffee, then sat down at the table with her. I played absent-mindedly with my necklace, sliding the pendant and key back and forth on the chain, rubbing my thumb over the smooth face of the triangular ruby. Usually Foggy could numb the pain, but I hadn't been fooling anyone that she made it completely disappear, especially not Mom. And not even myself. I knew the pain always lingered, under the fog, and, deep down, a part of me wanted to feel it . . . *needed* to feel it.

"I would really like to stop hurting, Mom, but then it feels like I'm . . . giving up."

"Nobody would blame you, honey," she said quietly.

I stared into my coffee cup. "I know. They'd probably be glad I was finally coming back to reality. Seven years is a long time . . . ."

"Not really. Not for us," she said, waving her hand to dismiss the idea. "I still mourn for Stefan."

My breath caught at Stefan's name. I still mourned for him, too, but . . . "He was a protector. I mean, not a boyfriend or real love or anything. It's not the same."

"Yes, but we were very close. We even talked about dating, but were afraid we'd ruin our friendship. I miss him very much." Mom sighed. "And I still mourn for my true love."

I looked up at her with wonder. She'd never mentioned her true love before.

"Yes, honey, I've lost my own true love. Many years ago." She stared out the window but seemed as though she saw something other than the backyard as she remembered. "It was 1910, a very different time, before either of the World Wars. Oliver was an English man visiting Italy, where I was born and raised. We fell in love at first sight. I followed him back to England and we married almost immediately. Barely more than a year later, he died. He'd become terribly sick and no one knew why. He probably had cancer, but we didn't know back then. I couldn't save him."

A single tear slid down her cheek. She brushed at it with the tips of her fingers and then wiped at her eyes before anymore fell.

"Mom, I had no idea."

"He was *my* soul mate, Alexis. And just like you, I had such a short time with him. As you can see, I still grieve for him. But life goes on and so do we." She smiled, just a turn of her lips that didn't reach her eyes. "So, it's not how long it's been that bothers me, honey. I understand."

"But you mourn for their *deaths*. Tristan isn't dead. I *can't* believe that. I don't mourn. I hang on!"

"Look how miserable you are. I know hanging on is part of who you are. Ever since Stefan left when you were little, breaking your heart, I realized you were given the capacity to love more intensely than even me. Once you allow yourself to even trust enough, you become so attached."

"It's more than that, though. I feel like part of me is really, physically missing, but more than a body part. Part of *me*. I don't know how to explain the . . . emptiness." An emptiness in my soul.

"You probably can't explain it. I don't think anyone can truly understand. Rina bound your souls together in a way no one alive has ever experienced. You're the only two people in the world who know what it's like." She took my hand in hers and looked into my eyes. "But, honey . . . do you really think Tristan would want you to live like this?"

Tears pooled in my eyes. This wasn't the first time she'd brought this up, so it wasn't the first time I'd thought about what he would want for me. He would want me to be happy. I knew that with my brain, but my heart didn't care. I had to hang on and wait for him, regardless of how much his absence hurt. After all, he hadn't broken up with me and he hadn't died. He was missing in action, captured in a strange and secret battle and I was left here, waiting for his return. I *couldn't* let go. She was right. That's just how I was.

"If I don't live like this, if I don't feel the pain, I'm afraid I'll forget. And I *can't* forget!" She took me in her arms and I clung to her as if *she* were the thread of hope I hung onto so tightly. "He's already so dim, fading in my mind. What if I lose his face? What if I can't remember anymore?"

Very quietly, she said, "Maybe it's time to let go, honey."

I jerked out of Mom's arms as if she'd just slapped me. *How could she* say *that?*

"No," I whispered, pushing her away and shaking my head, slowly at first and then more violently. "I can't. You just said how our souls are bound together. I can't do it. I'll *never* let go!"

Swirly Alexis jumbled my thoughts and Psycho tried to push her way in. Before I let her, before I lashed out at Mom again, I grabbed my coffee cup and stormed outside. A tumult of emotions battered at me, a hurricane suddenly raging in my mind. How could I make any changes, move forward, if I refused to let go of the pain? Letting go of the pain, of the misery, of exactly what caused days like yesterday, meant letting go of *Tristan*. And I absolutely refused to do that.

Did that mean changing would be impossible? Did I have to live like this until he returned? Or until the *Ang'dora*, which would change me, make me strong and give me powers so I could find and rescue him? Or did I hold onto something that didn't really exist? Was holding onto the thread of hope that he still lived completely futile?

Ugh! I hate you, Swirly! Stop messing with my mind!

She responded with more irrationality. An unexplainable and overwhelming need to move overcame me. I went around the corner and pulled out my stash of cigarettes from under the air conditioning unit, needing to take the edge off. As soon as I lit one, I gagged and choked. *Gross! When did I start doing this?* I smashed the butt out and crushed the pack in my fist. I took a swig of coffee. What I normally called the nectar of heaven now tasted bitter. The warmth felt thick in my mouth and coated the back of my throat. I tossed the rest out. I didn't need the caffeine anyway. I already felt wired. *What's wrong with me now?*

I was too edgy, unable to write again. My publisher would be expecting those final chapters any day now; it had been too long since I'd submitted anything. I didn't care about their deadlines as much as I did about Dorian. But despite my revelation this morning, I just couldn't bring myself to sit down and finish the story. My mind wouldn't focus and my body couldn't physically sit still.

While Mom took Dorian to school, I paced anxiously through the sprawling house, first through Dorian's and my bedrooms, as well as my office, which together made up the east wing. I picked up toys in Dorian's room and straightened the bed, though it was unnecessary. He hadn't even slept in his bed last night. I moved to the kitchen and scrubbed the counters and then the floor. Again unnecessary—Mom kept the house immaculate—but I needed to *do* something.

I even ventured into the west wing that housed Mom's suite and the guest room, which we called Owen's room. Besides Rina's visits every year or two, he was the only one who used it. Wondering why the door was closed, I cracked it open and peered into the darkness. A pillow flew at me and I jerked the door shut. *Crap.* I'd forgotten Owen had arrived yesterday. I wondered how much of my tantrum he experienced. Not that it was new to Owen. He'd seen the worst of me.

He must have had a difficult time at first. He mostly stayed away then. Being the one to return that ill-fated day and deliver the crushing news, he'd obviously felt survivor's guilt and it was hard for him to be around me. I probably didn't do or say what I should have to make him feel any better. I didn't blame him for what happened. But I did, every now and then, wonder why and how he, Solomon and the other soldier came back and not any of the others. I never asked him, though. I didn't want details . . . details that might tell me something I really didn't want to know. Owen never brought the subject up himself, either. I didn't know if he didn't like talking about it at all, or just not with me.

Although we didn't need extra protection, not even a shield, he started coming around more. Especially recently. Dorian loved his Uncle Owen. He was the closest thing Dorian had to a father figure, although I ensured everyone remembered he was *not* his father and he would *never* replace him. Mom enjoyed his company, too, and I didn't mind it.

I let him sleep, returning to the mid-section of the house. I circled the table in the formal dining room and meandered through the living room that we only used for holidays, moving around knick-knacks and putting them back the way they were. I did the same in the family room at the back of the house and eventually swept all the books onto the floor and started re-shelving them by the color of their covers. I supposed Swirly made this organizational system seem rational when I started. Half-way through, though, I realized the idiocy of it. Too impatient to put them back in alphabetical order, I just piled them haphazardly onto the built-in shelves.

At some point, Mom returned and watched me as I paced and rearranged and cleaned, trying to work off this inexplicable energy. I tried to ignore her. Once Owen woke up, they both seemed to contemplate my behavior and exchanged worried glances. I couldn't ignore that.

"What?" I demanded. They just shook their heads.

"Nothing," Owen muttered.

"For you to worry about," Mom added cryptically.

By noon, my muscles twitched and ached with the need to *move*. Cleaning and pacing weren't enough. Energy synapses shot through my nerves and muscles and the sudden urge to *run* came over me. *Run? What the hell?*

I didn't understand the impulse, but I rushed to my room to find running clothes and shoes anyway. I only found old shorts, sweats, holey and stained t-shirts and flip-flops. I didn't even own a pair of tennis shoes. Of course, that made sense. I hadn't run for the heck of it since high school gym class.

Oh! Mom runs. I found her in her room, folding laundry. "Mom, can I borrow your running shoes?"

She gave me a funny look.

"I just feel like I need to go for a run." I hopped from foot to foot with overwhelming energy, unable to explain the compulsion. She would think me deranged if I told her Swirly decided I needed to fix my fat self, the only explanation I could conceive.

She narrowed her eyes for a moment and then a strange expression flickered across her face, as though a realization had suddenly hit her and she dismissed it just as quickly as it came. "Yes, of course. They're in the closet."

I sat at the kitchen table, tying the shoes, when Owen walked in.

"Where you going?" he asked.

"For a run."

"Cool. Mind if I tag along?"

I looked at him with an eyebrow raised.

He shrugged. "I was going anyway."

"I'm sure you actually run," I said. "This will probably be more like a jog . . . or for you, a walk."

"If I get bored, I'll leave you alone to your trot." He grinned, his sapphire-blue eyes shining.

"Whatever."

We started with a jog down my long driveway. As my muscles loosened, jogging wasn't enough. My body wanted more, so I picked up the pace to a slow run. Then a faster run.

"When'd you start running?" Owen asked as we picked up speed for the third time, neither of us breathing heavily.

"Now."

He looked down at me, his blond hair falling across his face. He wore it long now, past his ears but not quite to his shoulders. He gave me a strange look. "Really?"

"Really. I'm wearing Mom's shoes because I don't even own any."

"Huh." He didn't seem to know what else to say and let the subject drop.

Once off my property, we'd taken a right and ran down the middle of the quiet, residential street for several blocks. All the homes on the street sat on a minimum of two acres, most with gates at the driveways and hedges at least six-feet-high lining the street. The neighborhood featured privacy and the people who lived here could afford to pay for it. We moved here nearly three years ago, when my books really started taking off and the media started paying attention.

We'd stayed in the safe house in Northern Virginia until a few months after Dorian's birth, when Mom deemed us healthy enough to move. The safe house was supposed to serve as a place of refuge for Amadis people needing to escape or who were newly converted. With me there, Rina refused to let anyone else come. So my presence created a few issues and we couldn't stay permanently. We moved to a house near Virginia Beach. I liked life there more than Atlanta, but we'd lived in a small town. Small towns weren't always conducive for the famous—or semi-famous, anyway. Especially when they're loony. Atlanta and this neighborhood provided a better environment for me and my insanity.

There were really just a couple of incidents that indicated to the world I wasn't quite right. But they were enough. The first time occurred several years ago at a book signing in New York City. I sat by the bookstore's window and out of the corner of my eye, I saw a tall man with sandy-brown hair walk by the store. I ran outside and took off after him, leaving a line of fans awaiting my signature. When he turned the corner and I saw the unfamiliar profile, I collapsed to the sidewalk bawling.

The second time, Mom and I were eating lunch with my publishing team when someone made a remark about the absence of my son's father and suggested I start dating. I flew off the handle. Finally, during a televised interview, my mouth open in mid-sentence, I caught a glimpse of someone standing in the shadows off-set. For a moment, I thought I'd seen Tristan, that he'd made his homecoming a surprise. Then I realized someone had set down a life-sized, cardboard cut-out of a young Brad

Pitt. I remembered the conversation of the actor's character in *Legends of the Fall* the night of my first-ever kiss and burst into hysterical laughter. I couldn't stop chortling, though the tears streaming down my face were those of grief. Someone finally dragged me off the set.

The first incident happened before I became *too* famous and the luncheon was private, so they were easily covered up. But the last one took place on live television, aired nationally. The country woke up that morning to quite a show. That was a few years ago. My publisher took me off the circuit and I didn't have to make any public appearances since. Fine by me. I hated them anyway. I preferred this private life. But that was the last impression I left, so people still thought me crazy.

We would have to move again soon. People would notice Mom wasn't aging. But, then again, maybe we could just switch places. She looked like how I should at my age—twenty-seven, rather than her true one-hundred-twenty-three years. And I didn't look exactly a hundred years older, but I did look old enough to be her mother. As I ran, I thought about mentioning this idea to her. It would at least make her chuckle. I owed her that.

Owen indicated a left turn at the intersection we approached and I followed his command. *What the hell? I don't really care where I go. I just want to* run! Though the sudden urge made no sense, the actual activity seemed like a positive action.

But then Owen had to blow it and almost make me regret the whole thing.

"Rough night last night?" he asked once we turned the corner.

"You heard?"

"Yeah. Sorry."

I sighed. "Not your fault I'm messed up in the head."

"It's just hard to see you like this. Last time I saw you, you seemed . . . I don't know, a little better, more like you used to be. I remember when—"

Damn it, Owen. I didn't want to remember. I interrupted him. "Let's not go there. Please?"

"Yeah, sure."

We ran in silence again for about half a block, the only sounds coming from our shoes hitting the pavement in a comfortable rhythm and the birds in the trees, still sounding louder than usual. Then Owen had an idea.

"See if you can keep up with me." He lengthened his stride and I kept pace with him. Then he increased his speed again. I could start to feel the push this time, but I could do it. He went even faster and got away from me.

"You're pretty fast," he said after jogging back to me. "You're sure you didn't run before today?"

"Don't you think I'd know that?" I wiped a trail of sweat from my temple. "Just look at me, Owen. Do I look like a runner?"

He chuckled and, obviously a smart man, avoided answering.

"If you want to go, go," I said. "Don't hang back here on my account."

"I'm fine."

We ran through and around a park about a half-mile from my house. Georgia pines, surrounded by brush, lined parts of the paths, giving the feeling we ran in the wilderness, and other parts took us past soccer and baseball fields. As we approached the playground, I decided I should probably turn back for home. I didn't feel out of breath—even though I'd been smoking for who knew how long (I seriously *didn't* know; I had a vague memory of someone handing me a cigarette when I felt especially stressed during a book signing)—and my muscles weren't sore. But I knew I would pay for this asinine impulse later and I saw no need to make it worse by continuing. Owen was about to head on for a longer run when I suddenly stopped as if I'd run into a wall.

There he is! He stood across the playground, about sixty or seventy yards away, and I immediately knew he was the same person who stood in my backyard yesterday. I could feel his eyes on me again. He stood a little closer now, but I still couldn't see his face. His brown hair hung way past the shoulders and it whipped around in the March breeze. The shade of the large oak he stood under also concealed his face. Something, maybe the long hair, told me he was young. *Just a boy.* But his body looked more developed than a boy's. Much more. *No, a man. Too young for me, but definitely a man.* Just like the day before, he felt . . . familiar. I started toward him again.

"Alexis? You okay?" Owen asked, after I took only a few steps. I turned and looked at him.

"Huh?" I asked distractedly.

"Are you okay? You look . . . odd."

I looked back at the stranger. He had disappeared again. *Damn it!*

"I'm, uh, fine. Go on. I'll see you at home." I started jogging again, which seemed to be enough for Owen. He took off in the other direction.

I wanted to search for the stranger. I had to know he was at least *real.* But I had no clue in which direction he'd gone. Or if he really was just a figment of my imagination. *Or wishful thinking.* I walked home, mentally and emotionally feeling like crap again.

Physically, however, I felt great. Owen ran up behind me just as I walked up to the beige-and-brick, ranch-style house. He said he'd run another three miles to add to the nearly three we did together. *Three miles? Oh, this is going to hurt.* I wanted to do it again, though, and went to the store to buy my own running wear. Of course, I would probably be over this idiotic impulse by tomorrow and would never run again, but right now, it made perfect sense that I needed my own running shoes. Which was how Swirly operated—making the most irrational thoughts seem logical.

"You're sure you want *running* shoes?" the pock-faced kid at the sporting goods store asked, his nose slightly crinkling. "I mean, we have walking shoes. Or my mom really likes these cross-trainers."

He pointed to a pair of plain white shoes that looked like they belonged on a grandma whose idea of exercise was walking around Wal-Mart. I eyed the shoes and then him. Was he serious?

"Are they good for running?" I asked, my annoyance clear. "I *run*."

He gave me a doubtful look, but led me over to the running shoes. I couldn't blame him . . . except for the part of making me feel as old as his mother. *Stupid kid. What does he know?* He couldn't have been more than five or six years younger than me.

"There you go," he said a while later, handing me a bag full of shoes, socks, shorts and sports bras. "Good luck with your, uh, running."

Maybe he was being polite. Maybe a genuine smile stretched across his face. But to me, the grin looked like a smug smirk and his tone dripped with sarcasm. Psycho flipped the switch again.

I leaned over the counter, my face only inches from his. "Who the fuck do you think you are, treating *me* like a worthless bag of shit? You don't even know who *I* am!"

He stared at me, his eyes bugged and his mouth opened wide enough to park a car. I stared back. *Did I really just do that?* A couple of customers who'd walked in the door just in time to hear me stopped and gawked. *Yeah. I did.* I opened my mouth again and then shut it. Thankfully, I wasn't so far gone to make sure they knew *exactly* who I was as I went completely whacko on the kid. I grabbed my bag and stomped out of the store before I could make a bigger fool of myself.

I stood on the gas, taking my anger out on my car, which felt bulky and sluggish. I forced myself to back off the accelerator because I already soared way above the speed limit. I aimlessly roamed the surface streets, first on the main roads, and then through a park-like residential neighborhood, but the urge to go faster overwhelmed me.

As I sat at the red light blocking my turn to the highway, my phone beeped with a text message from Mom. She worried about my uncharacteristic absence.

"Where did you go?"

I laughed out loud, a high-pitched sound that was just a little frightening, as I typed into my phone. "Crazy. Where else?"

I tossed the phone on the passenger seat, ignoring Mom's replies. Once on the highway, I moved over to the far-left lane and floored the pedal. *Speed. The faster, the better.* That's what I wanted. That's what I *needed.* The speedometer held at ninety. It felt like a crawl. The loss of control at such high speeds usually scared the hell out of me, but I couldn't go fast enough now. My Volvo sedan was designed and built for safety, not speed, which is why I had bought it. I'd wanted something practical for a mother with a small child. It had been perfect. Now I hated it. The car couldn't give me the release I needed, so I headed home.

By then, a level of rationality had returned and I wished I could hug Rina for insisting I use a pen name. Although the Amadis council originally wanted me to publish under Alexis Ames, they finally decided to use the pseudonym A.K. Emerson. I didn't know why that particular name and, honestly, didn't care much. No one but a small handful of people knew my real name, protecting my privacy, especially against incidents like today's. The clerk might recognize the name A.K. Emerson or Kat Emerson, which I'd used back when I'd made public appearances, but he wouldn't be able to match it to the name on the credit card. Otherwise, I'd be in deep trouble with my publicist and I really didn't have the mind to deal with her at the moment.

Chapter 3

Dorian, home from school by the time I pulled into the driveway, distracted me from my anxiety. I spent the rest of the afternoon and evening with him, Mom and Owen. I watched as he and Owen practiced Aikido moves in the backyard, then we all went to the park and played with him on the equipment, like kids again. Dorian and I took turns pushing each other on the swing, then he crawled onto my lap and Owen pushed us together. We both squealed with laughter as Owen did underdogs.

Unable to help it, my eyes regularly scanned the area for the young stranger I'd seen earlier. I thought I saw him once, but he was gone too fast to know for sure.

"Tell me a story," Dorian said later as he jumped onto his bed while I closed his window blinds.

"Hmm . . . about what?" I teased, already knowing.

"Dad, of course! How 'bout the boat trip?"

"Ah. Your favorite." I sat on his bed, took a deep breath to settle my insides, and started the story with his dad's thrill of fighting sharks.

At one time, telling these stories had been the hardest job of being Dorian's mom, but it was absolutely necessary. I insisted Dorian knew as much about his father as I could tell him—to know him as a real person, not as just a name of some vague entity he never met. Although telling them had become a little easier over the years, they still tore at the pieces of my heart, but not as much as stirring up memories when I was alone. The stories provided a way to remember Tristan and the precious time we had together without completely breaking down. Perhaps this was my answer—hanging onto him by sharing memories with Dorian, while letting go in other ways.

Letting go . . . my breath hitched at the thought.

"I'm going to fight sharks one day, too," Dorian promised me, not noticing the choking sound in my throat. I swallowed the lump as he wrestled his stuffed shark and put it into a headlock.

"Yes, I believe you will," I said, covering my cough with a laugh. "Now, do you want me to continue?"

"Yep!" He tossed the stuffed shark to the side and I told him about the leather-faced man who tried to rob us during our honeymoon in the Keys. Knowing the story by heart, Dorian moved his hands as if he fought the guy and shoved him off the boat.

"Okay, it's time to settle down and say good night," I said after finishing the story.

I picked up the framed picture on Dorian's nightstand. It was the only picture I had—the one Owen had taken with his cell phone at our wedding. Camera-phones were cutting-edge then, but the technology seemed old by today's standards, and the enlarged picture was grainy and unclear. But Mom's cottage and the bookstore had been torched shortly after we left that fateful August and all we had were the few belongings we'd taken with us.

The picture was mounted in an expensive silver frame. I had one just like it, lying in my nightstand drawer—if I left it out, on top of the nightstand, I could stay up all night staring at it and not get any sleep. I trailed my fingers over our beaming faces and then kissed the glass over Tristan's. Dorian kissed it, too, then embraced the frame in a hug.

"Good night, Dad," he said softly. "I love you."

I inhaled a jagged breath, my lungs feeling heavy and thick, as if liquid grief filled them.

"He loves you, too, little man," I whispered. "And so do I. Very much."

I held him until he fell asleep. I knew I should let him fall asleep on his own at his age, but holding him like this was the closest thing I had to holding his father. I would probably keep doing this as long as he let me.

Exhausted from playing all afternoon, he fell asleep quickly. As I headed for the door, two small lights in the window caught my eye. At first, I thought I saw a reflection. *No, they're outside. Two little fires.* The dream from the other night flashed in my mind—the vampire and his red eyes. A chill ran up my spine. Then my pendant suddenly heated against my skin. I picked it up between my thumb and forefinger and glanced at it, then back up. The lights were gone.

I stared at the window. I had closed the blinds earlier. I thought . . . Had I done both windows? Surely, I had. So how was one open now? I rushed to the window, my heartbeat spiking. I peered outside. Nothing there, but Owen's truck in the driveway. Not a creature stirred. No tree branches even waved in a breeze.

I let out the breath I'd been holding, checked the window's lock and closed the blinds. I watched them for what felt like several minutes. They didn't move, of course. *You're imagining things, is all.* Of course, that was all. No big deal to be seeing things. That wasn't weird at all. Not irrational or anything.

I shook my head to clear it. The lights were probably just a bizarre reflection of headlights ricocheting off Owen's truck and other surfaces. The blinds . . . I probably just forgot to close them. I held onto those sane explanations, feeling Swirly trying to creep in.

"You shouldn't tell him those things," Mom said as I stepped into the hallway, making me jump.

"What?" I asked, my brows furrowing.

"The stories about fighting. It only encourages him."

"Oh," I breathed as I shut Dorian's door. "Well, he needs to know about his dad. It's not like I have tons of stories to tell."

I turned for my room, but Mom stopped me with a hand on my shoulder.

"Owen and I need to talk to you. Can you come sit with us for a minute?"

I could hear a slight strain in her voice and I didn't think it had anything to do with Dorian's fighting. Something else bothered her. Probably my recent behavior.

I sighed. "Mom, I know I've been acting crazy. Crazier than usual, I mean. I don't know what's wrong with me, but I am really trying . . . ."

She took my hand and tugged me down the hall toward the family room. "I know, honey, which is why we need to talk. It's more important than you realize."

Owen stood at the bank of windows in the family room, staring out at the darkness of the backyard. He seemed to be deep in thought—and not good thoughts. The corners of his mouth turned down and his brows pushed together, creating three vertical lines over his nose. When he looked at me, the frown disappeared, but the smile replacing it looked more like a grimace.

Mom led me to one end of the sectional sofa and pulled me down to sit next to her. Owen sat on the ottoman in front of us as Mom took my hands into hers and studied my face. Her own expression looked concerned as she seemed to struggle with what she had to say. This was so unlike her.

"Just say it, whatever it is," I finally said.

She took a deep breath and blew it out. "Honey, the council is growing concerned."

I nodded.

"Because I'm acting like a lunatic." It wasn't a question. I was well aware of my demented behavior and now, apparently, so was the Amadis council. "Did that kid at the store figure it out and go to the media?"

"What are you talking about? I haven't heard anything." Mom narrowed her eyes. "Did you do something?"

"Um . . . no. Not really. I was just a little rude . . . ." I didn't feel like giving a full account. I was embarrassed by my actions, but right now I felt too much on the defensive. Something about their attitudes and their expressions bothered me. "Then did you and Owen tell the council—?"

Mom shook her head, cutting me off. "No, honey. We haven't said anything. Not even to Rina. We know you're going through something right now, but like I said the other night, I can feel the *truth* that things will get better. Sometimes they have to get worse before they get better, though."

I studied her face and knew then the expression she held. Owen had the same look. It wasn't the usual concern or empathy. They *pitied* me! The poor woman who couldn't get on with her life. What did I expect? I'd been wallowing in self-pity for years. I tore my eyes from hers and stared at the black windows.

"What is it then?" I asked, crossing my arms over my chest. "What has them so concerned?"

Neither of them answered at first. I finally looked back at them. Owen leaned forward, his elbows on his thighs.

"They've been asking about you," he said. "How you're doing . . . if there have been any improvements. They're actually kind of . . . freaking out, really."

"Why? What did you tell them?" Anger and a hint of hysteria edged my tone. I didn't know much about the council—nothing, really—but knew they had no problem making decisions for us. Only Rina had the power to overrule them. Only the matriarch wasn't controlled by them.

"Nothing. Nothing new, anyway," Owen said quickly. "But . . ."

He looked at Mom and so did I. She closed her eyes and pinched the bridge of her nose, while taking a deep breath. She opened her eyes and looked into mine.

"Honey . . . it's about the next daughter. They're getting anxious."

"Daughter . . . ?" I asked, the word sounding strangely foreign because it wasn't at all what I expected to hear.

"Yes. Your daughter."

"What daughter? We don't even know if I can have one."

"Rina believes you will. I feel it, too. The council wants you to start trying."

"*What?* Now?" I couldn't believe what I heard. "But how? A daughter requires a father. Surely they know it takes two!"

"Of course they do, honey."

"They're hoping . . ." Owen cleared his throat, seeming to have a hard time spitting out what they hoped. "They're, uh, hoping that you're ready to . . . to move on."

There came that phrase again, like a punch in the stomach. *Move on.* Which meant, *let go.* I flew to my feet and strode around the room. It was one thing to think about moving on myself.

It was another to hear Mom voice the idea aloud. But hearing Owen say it . . . knowing the council had been discussing it . . . this was totally different. Who were they to decide when I needed to move on?

"Why the rush?" I demanded. "Why now?"

"We celebrated your twenty-seventh birthday last month," Mom said.

I grunted. "Celebrate" wasn't exactly the word I'd use. More like "commiserated" another year gone by. Alone.

"The *Ang'dora* may only be fifteen or so years away," Mom continued. "If you're like me, though, it could be even sooner. In fact . . ."

She trailed off. I whirled on her.

"In fact what?"

She looked at me with her eyes narrowed and her head tilted, as though considering whether to tell me something. She even opened her mouth, but nothing came out. Then she just shook her head. "Nothing. Never mind. You just need to know that there really is a biological clock ticking and the council is getting anxious. Remember how even Solomon had been demanding about a daughter? And that was eight years ago. They would calm down if they at least knew something was being done."

I threw my hands in the air. "Like what? What am I supposed to do? Do they have some kind of in vitro clinic set up? Because that's the only way anything's going to happen. I won't be unfaithful!"

Mom sighed. "Just be thinking about it right now, honey. We don't expect you to do anything. In fact, you should know that Rina and I, and some others, don't support any of this. If you are meant to have a daughter, if the Amadis is meant to continue under our rule, it will happen when and how it is supposed to."

"We just thought you should know what's going on," Owen added.

I stopped pacing and leaned my forehead against the window, staring out at the backyard bathed in silver from the moon's light. I appreciated their candor. They still had to protect their secrets until I went through the *Ang'dora*, so I hadn't learned anything over the years. I hadn't even asked, since the day I realized my feeble human mind couldn't comprehend anyway. The day my world fell apart. But at least they shared this.

"Thank you," I whispered.

"Alexis . . . you do need to remember something, though," Mom said. "You need to understand this won't go away. They will eventually increase the pressure. You are royalty, honey. You have responsibilities."

Her words burned my ears, their meaning slowly washing over me, hot lava scorching my soul. I would have to choose. Stay true to my love, to my soul-mate, remain Tristan's faithful wife no matter how long it took, even if doing so meant no daughter. Or assume my responsibilities to a society that depended on me for its future, on the daughter I needed to have, even if it meant breaking my vows . . . letting go . . . moving on.

The liquid fire scalded the edges of my wounds, making them throb with pain. Regardless of how much I'd been trying to convince myself that I needed to, I just couldn't move on. I couldn't let go of the hope that we would be together again. Just thinking about doing so in such real terms felt like sharp claws ripping at my inner core, tearing at my soul. It would die with that choice . . . and so would Tristan's. After all, if our souls were bound as tightly as Rina said they were, the death of one meant the death of the other. I could not do that to him. I owed him so much more.

I turned slowly. Mom and Owen looked at me expectantly.

"We're all relying on you, Alexis," Mom murmured.

"Well, then," I said, "I guess we're all fucked."

❧

I slammed my bedroom door shut and threw myself on the bed. I knew that was the wrong thing to say. Once again, I'd snapped because of my emotions. Emotions that were tearing me apart, ripping me in two. Right and wrong no longer mattered anyway. I couldn't do anything without devastating consequences. To me. To Tristan. To Dorian. To our whole damn society. I had actually stated the truth.

That's right. You. Are. Fucked.

I startled at the thought. It didn't sound like my "voice"—the way I heard my own thoughts in my head. Though I'd just said the same thing to Mom and Owen, this was *not* me. Was it?

Who the hell else would it be?

Again, the voice sounded different, strange. But it was definitely in my head. It could only be my thoughts.

Of course it is. This is the real you. The one you've finally been letting out recently. The one who knows the truth and isn't afraid to say it.

I didn't understand myself. What the hell did that mean?

Think about it, Alexis. Who are you really? Some miserable wench who can't get over herself? Too afraid to do anything? Come on, you know what you really want to do. Why hold back?

Again, I didn't understand. Because I really didn't know what to do.

Yes, you do. You know you can put an end to all of this. No more suffering. No more choices. No more council or Amadis at all, for that matter. And you won't have to deal with any of it. You'll be gone.

What?! I covered my ears with my hands, as if they could shut out the internal voice. The thoughts sounded too much like suicide. I had *never* been suicidal. I couldn't do that to Dorian, to my mother, to the Amadis . . . to *Tristan.* Even if it were just a thin thread, I really did have hope.

Oh, give it up. There's no hope. No hope for anything. Like we just agreed, you are fucked. All of you.

I would never kill myself!

Then don't. You have other options, you know. You do have other family . . . remember?

I nearly screamed. *Holy shit!* What the hell was happening to me? This was a bigger mind game than Swirly had ever played.

Hell. That's what's happening to you. It could be your home. We hold your desires right here. You can have it all with us. With them . . . nothing. With us, everything. Your soul-mate. Your son. You don't have to worry about having a daughter with us. We'll love you and worship you anyway. You can be our queen. Your king is already here, waiting . . . .

"Stop it!" I gasped aloud.

You know this is what you want.

"No!" I said, louder this time.

But the voice wouldn't shut up. It kept taunting. The evil blood—that of my sperm donor, Lucas, the Daemoni's most powerful warrior—coursed like an icy stream through my veins. I could feel it trying to take over. I curled into a ball, my hands still over my ears, my eyes squeezed shut, my body shaking uncontrollably.

"No. No, no, *no!*"

Yes.

"This is not what I want!" An electric charge filled the air. The hairs on my arms stood on end and I heard a crackling sound around me. Again, the pendant heated against my skin.

You know it is! Let go, Alexis. Let it all go. Find comfort with us.

"No! Please, God, *help* me!"

The voice fell silent.

I trembled so hard, the bed shook under me. My pulse thudded in my ears, but at least I heard nothing else. I opened my eyes and remained in a ball, staring at nothing and praying for the voice to stay away. The energy in the room settled, as did the pounding in my chest. My blood finally warmed and the shivering stopped.

But fear still wrapped itself around me. Nothing like this had ever happened before. I was half Daemoni, but not evil. Rina assessed me every time she saw me and said the evil was repressed, virtually non-existent. *So what the hell just happened?*

Was the state of my mind bringing out the worst of me? Or was the worst in me causing the changes in my state of mind? Rina hadn't assessed me since last summer. Had something changed since then? Was something going on that my subconscious mind knew but I didn't? Could, for some unknown reason, the Daemoni blood be suddenly strengthening? I remembered the lights in Dorian's window—the two little fires. Had those been my own eyes? I shuddered again.

This afternoon and evening with Dorian had been good. Too good. Almost as if I'd swung into a maniacal state from the chaos of this morning and yesterday. And now I had to pay for it. The conversation with Mom and Owen . . . the realization of just how bad everything was . . . an Evil Alexis trying to push her way out . . . . I would really lose it at this rate, if I hadn't already. I just hoped the good side would win, that Mom would lock me up before I did anything . . . horrible.

I couldn't move. I felt drained of all energy. I lay there, with the light still on, and squeezed my eyes shut. I needed to see the beautiful face. I just wanted to go back to the way things were, when I could count on the same dream, seeing him every night. I had my miserable moments then, but I was mostly just foggy and I missed the fog. If I never found Real Alexis again, I preferred Foggy, who was a hundred times better than all these other alter egos.

The memory-dream tried to replay but even my subconscious mind couldn't focus—couldn't make his face clear. I woke up at 3:39 sobbing and my body burning. It didn't ache with soreness from the running. It actually burned as the muscles repaired themselves from the strain I'd put them through. When I finally fell back to sleep, the memory-dream didn't start again. The slideshow on the mountain played instead . . . and every time Tristan's face started to surface, Owen's pushed it away. And the images of Owen weren't really memories. They looked more like . . . possibilities.

No, no, no! I'm not only forgetting . . . Oh, hell no! He can't be replaced!

಄

Awake at 5:28. I lay in bed, though, the aberration of last night still frightening me. The state of my mind seemed to be deteriorating and the council's demands had apparently been too much for my fragile psyche. I felt even closer to the edge of that abyss—my toes curling over its lip, my body leaning forward for the fall. Only Dorian and that wispy thread, frayed and in danger of snapping, kept me from the plunge. That tiny bit of hope.

Please, baby, I need you. I need you, *not anyone else. What if they . . . ?* I couldn't bear to complete the thought . . . but then I couldn't help it. Would they force me to mate with someone else? Could I do that? Could I ever be able to tuck this part of me away and force myself? I didn't think so. Not without undeniable proof that Tristan was . . . gone, really gone. But what if proof never came? Time alone seemed to be enough proof for the Amadis. When Rina joined our souls, though, she said nothing and no one could ever sever our union. Not distance, space or . . . time.

The more I thought about everything, the less any of it made sense. Rina said we were *made* for each other. The Angels had specifically created our souls to unite with each other. How could there ever be anyone else? Such an idea went against everything the Amadis had been banking on since I was born. Were they wrong? Were our souls not really one?

Physical pain shot through my chest, taking my breath away.

The pain answered my questions. Of course we were meant for each other. Of course our souls were united. There could never be anyone else. So . . . what on earth went wrong? Why was I here, alone with no daughter and a son who supposedly shouldn't exist? Why did I feel like I was losing our connection, his memory? Why was all of this happening? Nothing made sense.

I literally rolled out of bed, nearly falling to the floor. I glanced at the bag containing my new running clothes and shoes, untouched since I bought them. They held no interest for me now. *What a waste of money.* I knew that urge to run was a fluke. Yesterday's strange burst of energy had dissipated, but my mind felt wide awake.

So I trudged into my office, turned my laptop on and plopped into my chair to wait for it to boot up. As soon as it did, my email opened. I didn't want to even look at my inbox. No one emailed me but my agent and my editor at the publishing company and right now, their emails would only be complaints or demands for new chapters. Chapters I still didn't have. I moved the mouse to click the X and close the email program, when something caught my eye. A new message from Rina.

Very strange. I couldn't remember ever receiving an email from Rina. She wasn't exactly the technological type. I knew she used email out of necessity with Mom, but only rarely. So this must be important. I double-clicked the message.

"Alexis, I understand it is difficult for you to try to move on and I truly wish your situation was different. I wish I could make it better for you, but, unfortunately, there is nothing I can do. I do hope I can help you get past this, though, because it is in the best interests of the Amadis and humankind. I believe the attached video may help you let go of your past and accept your future."

I stared at the message for several minutes, trying to understand it. The words didn't sound like Rina's and I just couldn't believe she would actually deliver such a message in an email. This was all out of character. *It must be really bad.* A lump grew in my throat with this realization. Whatever the video showed, it was something she couldn't tell me on the phone or even deliver through Mom. So bad, neither of them could even voice it. I instantly knew I didn't want to watch the video. Yet, acting on its own accord, my trembling hand moved the mouse to the file and double-clicked.

Ian, the ugly Irish ogre who'd dropped the bomb on me about the Amadis plan for my marriage, appeared on the screen. He stood in a darkened room, a spotlight trained on him, wearing black leather pants, a black trench coat and no shirt. His red hair provided the only real color to the scene. His lips pulled back, exposing his crooked teeth, whether in a grin or a snarl, I couldn't tell.

"We know ya want to go to the media," he said in his Irish accent, "to protect your lil lassie's reputation. But ya might want to think twice 'bout that. If you do, if you acknowledge Seth's existence in any way, heads will roll."

He cackled his disgusting laugh as the recording cut to another scene. This one had all the appearances of a group of terrorists with a hostage, just like those seen in the early years of the wars in Afghanistan and Iraq. Several men dressed in Middle Eastern tunics, sabers hanging from their leather belts, stood in a circle around someone unseen. Those in front of the camera moved to the side. My breath caught.

"Oh, *no*," I gasped.

The shirtless hostage knelt on his knees, a burlap sack over his head. One of the terrorists—a Daemoni, I assumed—held his saber to the hostage's neck. I had no way of knowing for sure without seeing the face, but the build seemed close to right, too close, from what I could remember. And then I saw it. My hands flew to my mouth. The blood drained from my head, coagulating into a ball in the pit of my stomach.

Just below the curve of the knife, on the hostage's chest, barely visible over his heart, a darker pigmentation against the rest of his pale skin. When our souls were joined in marriage, it had burned bright red. The Amadis mark. Choking, gasping sounds gnarled in my throat, the scream unable to pass the huge lump.

"You tell the world anything, we show them this," Ian spoke in a voiceover.

"Alexis!" a voice screamed. A very familiar voice. One I had heard only in my dreams for over seven years. It careened into a wail of tortured agony, making my heart stop.

Then the Daemoni with the saber jerked his arm. The camera's view dropped, but unlike the news producers who cut away from the gore at this point, it angled in on the round shape of the burlap sack, now rolling on the floor in a pool of blood.

Chapter 4

I felt completely numb. I sat completely still, only my finger moving on the mouse to click the Play button over and over and over again. My brain refused to register what I saw as I watched it replay, as if I watched some amateur video staged in Hollywood, fake blood and all. But slowly, the reality of it slithered its way into my mind.

And all I could think was, *It's not him.*

"Mom?" Dorian asked, running into my office sometime later and making me jump.

I slammed the laptop shut. I couldn't let him see that. He couldn't know about the video at all. Because it wasn't real. And that hostage wasn't his father.

I opened my arms and he climbed into my lap. I held him tightly against my chest, the pressure of his body like a catalyst to keep me breathing.

"Alexis," Mom called from down the hall. I could tell she rushed toward us with each syllable sounding closer. "Rina's email account's been hacked. Don't open—"

She cut herself off as she charged into my office and saw me. Something on my face must have told her I'd seen the video because her own face crumpled with what should have been my pain. I simply shook my head. She pulled in a deep breath and rearranged her expression.

"Come on, Dorian, honey, Uncle Owen's making you breakfast," Mom said. My arms fell numbly to my sides as she pulled Dorian off my lap. He ran off for the kitchen.

"It's not him," I whispered.

Mom closed the door, came over to me and swiveled my chair around to face her. She squatted in front of me, her hands on my knees.

"Honey—" she started.

"It's not him," I repeated, louder now.

"We don't know—"

"I said it's not him!" I threw my hands to my face. My body began trembling again. My head shook back and forth. "It's not him. I don't know how I know. I just do. It's *not* him, Mom. It can't be!"

She rubbed her hands against my thighs. "I know, honey. I mean . . . I don't know. I just know what you're feeling. I know it's hard to believe."

"I don't *believe*. I know!" I cried into my hands. "Don't you? Can't you feel the truth?"

She sighed. "You know I haven't been able to feel anything about him at all. And we haven't been able to find anything. We've tried to send soldiers in, but, if the Daemoni do still have him, we have no idea where."

I stopped shaking as I listened. She'd never given me so many details.

"They lie so much, we never know what to believe. And Rina's heard nothing from her other sources about any of this." She sighed again. "And this video . . . we've never been able to figure out if it's him or not. Our people examined every frame and couldn't determine if it was even real, let alone who the hostage was."

I dropped my hands from my face. "What do you mean? You've seen this *before*? You've known about this?"

She grimaced. "Yes, honey. We've had this video for a few years."

"A few *years*?" My jaw dropped with disbelief.

"When the media did that whole character bashing about your having Dorian so young and out of wedlock, we were going to make an official statement. But then the Daemoni sent this video, threatening to send it to the media worldwide if we said anything at all. We decided it best for you and Dorian that we just keep quiet. Ignore the rumors and let them run their course." She paused, then added quietly, "No one wanted you to see this."

"Until now."

"We don't know who sent it or why."

"It's obvious why! The council wants me to move on and they thought this would convince me. Well, they're wrong. It doesn't mean a damn thing to me!"

✧

The next thing I knew, I sat at the head of my bed, my arms wrapped around our wedding picture and my knees drawn up in a ball. I didn't remember if I had walked here purposely or had fled to the refuge of my room. I didn't even know how long I'd been sitting here, rocking back and forth, whispering, "No, no, no."

Mom insisted they didn't know who sent the video, that the Daemoni could have hacked into Rina's email. But the timing was just too convenient. All Owen had to tell them after our little discussion last night was that I wasn't ready to move on yet and then the council—at least one person—thought they could rush me into acceptance with this.

But the idea back-fired. Because I absolutely refused to believe my husband was beheaded in the video. In fact, with the way the camera cut away from the hostage and then the angle of the view . . . I couldn't be certain there was even a head in the sack rolling on the floor. The scene really could have been staged, just theatrics, as Mom seemed to imply. But someone obviously wanted me to see it . . . and to believe it.

How stupid could they be? Did they really think I would be so easily convinced? Our connection was too strong. *Or is it?* I froze at this thought. I'd been losing him in my memory and now even in my dreams. Our connection had actually been quite weak lately. Mom knew that. Owen had probably figured it out. They said they hadn't told anyone, but now someone on the council knew and tried to take advantage of my weakness. Tried to shred my hope, as if slashing that grotesque saber right through my thread.

I squeezed my eyes shut and saw the images in the video. It could be convincing, actually. Quite convincing. Especially with the Amadis mark on the hostage's chest. And his voice . . . beautiful and horrible at the same time . . . screaming my name.

"It's not him," I whispered again. Even I could hear the doubt in my voice. I shook my head. "No. It's not him. I won't believe it!"

I felt something inside me start to crack, about to break. Probably break me down for good. Psycho Alexis tried to work her way in, blackening my heart and my thoughts with grief and anger. Then a rough growl in the back of my mind marked Evil Alexis also wanting to take control. I shook my head again, more violently this time.

I just need to feel you again. I know you're there.

Then a thought occurred to me, rushing me to the back of my walk-in closet. I pulled out his bag, tore open the zipper and stuffed my face inside, inhaling deeply, trying to smell him, to bring back his memory, to feel him and know he still lived. The scent was so faint. After wearing his shirts every night for over a year, I'd finally packed them in here, his scent washed out of them.

But I felt his physical presence with each touch of his belongings. I rummaged through the contents. Papers and keys for the beach house lay at the bottom of the bag. The letters I'd written every year on our anniversary were in there, too. Letters where I reminded him of his promise and where I made my own promise—that I would come for him after the *Ang'dora* if he didn't come back first. Letters I could never send. I read them twice and my chest, where my heart should have been, throbbed with pain. Then I came across the envelope he'd given me at the safe house. I had never bothered to open it.

I ripped through the envelope. It contained some important looking documents I couldn't focus on and a car title—the title to his Ferrari Spider, signed over to me, as if he'd known he wouldn't make it back. *His Ferrari.* Since we'd had it in the Keys with us on our honeymoon, it hadn't exploded with the rest of his belongings when the Daemoni blew up his house. We had used it as our escape car to the safe house. He had flashed away when he left the final time, leaving it behind.

The Ferrari sat in the extra garage. Not knowing I even had the title to it, I'd never done anything with the ostentatious sports car. I could never bring myself, through all these years, to even look at it. I knew Owen, along with Dorian (he loved his daddy's car), took it for a spin every now and then and kept it maintained. Mom kept the tags and insurance up-to-date.

I tore through the house and dashed across the driveway to the extra garage. There it sat, red and shiny like new, obnoxious and beautiful as ever. Owen had taken good care of it. I circled the car, running my fingers over the horse emblem just as I had the first time I'd seen it, and stopped at the driver's side door. This was not my side. I'd never driven the thing. I took a deep breath, popped the door open and slid inside.

My hands caressed the tan leather seat and steering wheel, trying to feel Tristan's presence. I leaned back in the seat and closed my eyes, imagining that I could feel him sitting here right where I sat, his warmth and power surrounding me. And I felt even more convinced he was not in that video, his voice was edited in . . . they did not kill him years ago. I leaned forward and pressed my forehead against the steering wheel, my arm crossed over my stomach, focusing on the conviction. *It's not him.*

Then I suddenly had the incredible urge to *go* again. The need overwhelmed me. I frantically searched the workshop bench in the garage and finally found the key in a drawer. I left, pealing out of the driveway.

Driving felt good. Driving *fast* felt amazing. I sped down the highway, wondering if I drove as fast as he did. My senses felt so keen, so alert, I didn't feel like the car moved very fast at all as I weaved around traffic on the interstate. The needle on the speedometer hovered at 110. I drove for nearly an hour and headed home when the gas gauge fell to a quarter-tank . . . and only then because I hadn't brought my purse.

What is wrong *with me?* Wild impulses were taking over my life. The messed-up dreams . . . the anger and irritability . . . the impulses . . . the physical urges . . . the hallucinations . . . the voices . . . and now the fake video. Everything was crashing down on me at once. I considered again that I was finally losing it. Mom must have thought the same thing.

"Maybe you need some time away," she said when I returned. "A change of scenery . . ."

"And where do you suggest I go?" I demanded. "The demons are inside my head, Mom. I can't get away from them."

She cringed. The words had come out of my mouth before I even knew what I said.

"Actually, that's what concerns me," she said, shocking me.

Then I realized the truth—and accuracy—of her meaning. I instantly became irate, with an overwhelming urge to throw it all in her face—letting her know exactly what she'd produced with her little romp in the sack with the evil sperm donor. Her intentions may have been to save him, but she lost him . . . and now she might possibly be losing me.

"Oh, are you afraid the Daemoni inside of me is finally coming out?" I sneered. "Maybe your little miracle isn't so *good* after all."

"Alexis!"

"What does it matter anyway? They've totally mind-fucked us! The Daemoni . . . even the Amadis. They just use us! And now look. They've destroyed us instead. Him. Me. We're *useless*."

"Alexis Katerina! You *really* need to get yourself under control. I will not talk to you until you become rational."

I burst into laughter.

"Rational?" I asked between chortles. "That's a good one, Mom!"

She narrowed her eyes, turned on her heel and stomped away. The urge to run—run away from it all—came over me. So I did. I threw on my new clothes and shoes and ran for miles. I didn't know how my body survived. Just a few days ago it was a lump of old, tired lard that hadn't moved more than necessary from bed to chair to bed again. Now, on such little sleep and no food—I couldn't remember the last time I'd eaten—it felt strong and wired with energy.

But I couldn't run far enough. I couldn't run far enough

away from my shitty life. I couldn't run far enough to get to Tristan . . . to know for sure.

As I ran, I decided Mom was right. I just needed to get away for a while. Really be by myself and try to straighten my head out. And if I couldn't straighten it out, couldn't fix myself, couldn't overcome whatever was building in my system, at least I wouldn't be around Dorian and my family when I truly lost it. Went over the deep end. Became one of *them*.

Like so many irrational ideas, this one made perfect sense right now. I ran home, showered and packed.

"What are you doing?" Mom asked from my bedroom doorway.

"Packing. I'm going away, like you said."

"That's not exactly what I meant."

"Well, that's what I'm doing. I *do* need time away."

She came in and sat on my bed, watching me as I purposefully moved between closet, bathroom and bed, where my suitcase lay open.

"Where are you going?" she finally asked.

"I don't know. I'll call you when I get there." I dumped an armful of clothes into the suitcase.

"Alexis . . ."

I stopped and looked at her. "Just take care of Dorian for me, please."

"Of course. But I really don't think you should be alone right now, especially after seeing—"

"That's exactly why—" I cut myself off. I realized the video caused this pull to leave, creating a more intense need than ever to feel his physical presence. But she wouldn't understand, or, if she did, she'd never let me go. Not that I'd really be alone anyway. She'd never allow it. I took a different direction with her. "I think being alone is exactly what I need. I haven't been alone for . . . for*ever*. I've *felt* alone. But there's always been someone nearby, keeping me from completely letting it all out. Maybe being alone and facing these demons by myself . . . getting it all out once and for all . . . is what I need. I don't know, Mom. I just know I need to *go*."

I didn't wait for her response. Nothing she said would stop me. Well, nothing would stop Swirly, anyway. She was obviously in charge right now. I went into my office and packed my laptop and chargers and anything else I would need. Then I went to say good-bye to Dorian.

"Are you going with Dad?" Dorian asked.

"*What?*" I stared at him in shock.

"His car is outside," he explained with his six-year-old logic. He glanced out his bedroom window at the Ferrari parked in the driveway.

"Oh, no, honey," I said, hugging him. "I'm just driving his car. Daddy is still not home."

"Oh." His face crumpled with disappointment.

"Will you be good for Mimi while I'm gone? It'll only be a few days."

"Where are you going?"

"Just on a little trip to do some Mommy things. Sometimes Moms need to do this."

"Sounds girly." He made a face. "Yeah, I'll be good."

"Thank you, little man." I gave him another squeeze. "I'll call you later. I love you."

"I love you, too, Mom. Have fun."

Fun? Yeah, right. I gave him a smile but as soon as I left his room, I had to choke back a sob. I'd never left him overnight before, not even while on book tours. He'd always traveled with me. But I had to do this alone and I had to get out of here. Now. Before I lost it again.

I grabbed my laptop bag, my suitcase and the other bag . . . Tristan's bag. I didn't know why I felt the need to bring it but I did. *Maybe I'll just burn everything and be done with it. Maybe that would bring the closure I need.* No, I could never do such a thing. I didn't want closure. I just wanted, no, *needed* that physical connection.

"This is a bad idea," Mom said, following me outside. I threw the bags into the Ferrari's passenger seat.

"No, it's a good idea. Or, at least it *is* an idea. The first *real* idea I've had, one with purpose, anyway."

"What kind of purpose, Alexis? You don't even know where you're going."

I didn't answer her, but deep down inside, I did know my destination. After filling up with gas, the direction came automatically. Without a thought, I jumped on I-75 and sped south, then east, and then south again. As far south as the highway would go, as fast as I could go.

℘

Driving the Ferrari induced a rush of adrenaline through my veins. It purred at 120 miles per hour and it felt like no more than seventy. My senses were so highly tuned, I couldn't even believe the possibility of losing control. I would come up behind someone creeping along at eighty in the left lane and smoothly move to the right, then slip back to the left. As if I was dancing, the car as my partner, and simply gliding around another couple. Instead of the blur of green and brown streaming by, I could see every pine tree, palm and palmetto bush individually. Possibly even every needle and palm frond. I even had some kind of sense for cops, because I automatically slowed down long before I saw the marked cars. I felt so liberated. And insane . . . and maniacal . . . but I tried to ignore those theories.

The farther I put Atlanta behind me, the more this decision felt absolutely right. Perhaps because I felt a sense of release with the idea of being free—free to do what *I* wanted to do, without watching, measuring eyes. Or maybe it felt right because I headed for a place where Tristan had once been, a place with real memories, a place with his presence. Then again, perhaps I just knew I needed to remove myself from the people I loved. Before I hurt them any more than I already had, especially with this new Evil Alexis, who was even worse than Psycho and Swirly.

That thought brought Dorian's face to mind and the urge to turn around and run back to him. But something inside me knew this was more important right now. I needed to do this for him, for all of us. Whatever was going on with me right now surely couldn't last forever. Mom said things would get better, even if they became worse first. And Dorian didn't need to be around if and when things got worse. I needed to protect him. From me.

The drive should have taken over twelve hours. I approached Miami within five. By 8:30 in the evening, I came to the turn-off to our little key. I slowed down, but . . . although I'd made this trip specifically to face the beach house and its memories . . . I couldn't bring myself to make the turn. *Not tonight. Can't handle it yet.* I drove fifty miles farther, to the end, to Key West.

My hotel suite's window looked down on Duval Street, crowded with tourists hopping from bar to bar. I envied their normal lives and their ability to relax and have fun. I wanted to let go of my screwed up life and pretend I was one of them. I only ventured as far as the hotel's bar and sipped some kind of frozen, fruity concoction. The outdoor bar faced the street and the passing crowds provided limitless opportunities for people-watching. I felt bad vibes off some of the revelers. And a few set off my evil alarms. Both Tristan and Stefan had once said this was one of the Daemoni's favorite stomping grounds.

I felt their eyes on me. They surely had to recognize me. They could capture me if they wanted. I tried to ignore my sense's command to run, telling myself I wasn't the frightened young girl I used to be. *What's the worst they could do to me?* I wondered as I stirred the pixie straw around my slushy drink. Would they torture me or just outright kill me? *Maybe they'll bring me to my love.* Would they take me to him and let us at least be together? Or did they even have him? Apparently, enough doubt about the video lingered. And then I wondered if they would decapitate me, too, and send the video to the Amadis. My stomach clenched. But then Psycho Alexis told me even that would be okay. Being together, whether within their captivity or both of us dead, had to be better than what I'd lived through so far. I had a brief impulse to walk right up to one and let them have me.

And then I saw Owen across the bar, keeping an eye on me. Protecting me. Probably just as much from myself as from the Daemoni. I'd given him a job again. Actually, I realized, he was not alone. I felt the presence of several Amadis, all on guard for me. Just in case. I had been right—Mom would never let me be completely alone. Realizing this suppressed Psycho Alexis.

I wondered how these innate enemies seemed to co-exist. I'd seen the carnage both sides could produce during that bloody battle nearly eight years ago. Rina had said the Amadis only fight when necessary. But why wouldn't the Daemoni be instigating something with them? Were even they able to control themselves when so immersed in the human world? Or did they have no reason to fight? No orders to attack?

Why should we attack when you are so close to coming to us on your own? You'll soon realize exactly where you belong.

I stiffened in the bar stool. That voice again. The internal voice that was mine, but not mine. The voice of Evil Alexis that scared the shit out of me.

I ordered another drink. Then another one. I hoped to drown the voice away, along with all my other thoughts. I'd never been truly drunk before. I'd been buzzed, but never falling-down, blacking-out drunk. Why not now? I had protectors to ensure nothing bad happened, so why not allow myself that numbness? After three drinks, which should have inebriated me, I felt little effect. Probably overpriced, watered-down drinks the bartender served. In fact, Owen had probably slipped him a larger-than-necessary tip to make my drinks weak. I gave up and headed back to my room, feeling defeated. At least Owen and the others didn't bother me, for which I felt grateful.

The front room of the suite contained a sitting area with a couch, chair and walnut armoire, which housed a flat-screen television. A desk sat by one of the windows, with a view of a small courtyard two stories below. A tall, walnut sleigh-bed and another armoire with a second flat-screen furnished the bedroom, the bed made with luxurious linens and a fluffy duvet. The marble-and-walnut bathroom contained boutique-brand toiletries. The hotel was the epitome of luxury. It should have been, for the rate I paid. This would have been a nice place for a vacation . . . like a honeymoon. But not better than where mine had been. The place I would have to face tomorrow.

As comfortable as the bed looked, I knew the threat of nightmares—more replays of that video—wouldn't allow me to sleep. So I sat down to write for the first time in days, pounding on the keyboard for hours, and eventually fell asleep at the desk. The nightmare came and I awoke with a start, his scream still echoing in my head. *No! I won't believe it!*

I wished I had gone straight to the beach house now. I needed to feel him, to remember him, to keep hold of that thread. Then I thought of his bag, with his few pieces of clothes still in there—his things I could touch and feel and hold close. I started to stand up.

Daemoni! Evil! Run!

"Do not move, Alexis." The deep, gravelly voice of the vampire again. My heart jumped against my chest. "Settle yourself down. You don't want to *excite* me."

I took some deep breaths, trying to calm myself down, but not because the detestable voice told me to. I needed to be able to focus and figure this one out. Because I was pretty sure I was awake, sitting at the desk, thinking about my husband. But maybe not. Maybe one nightmare had slipped into another.

"Good girl. Nice and slow."

Yeah, whatever. I found it difficult to control my heart and my breathing because now I just wanted to scream and wake myself up. But I couldn't bring myself to do either.

"You did not listen to me, Alexis. You are still writing."

I swallowed, not answering. Real fear crept in, poking black fingers into the edge of my mind.

The vampire stood only five feet away, his red, glowing eyes glaring fiercely at me. His arms were crossed against his chest, his marble-white skin contrasting starkly with the black silk shirt, tucked into tailored, black slacks. This was the first time he'd appeared in the light and he looked very similar to the descriptions in my books. Except . . . not exactly. His lips were wrong.

I had always pictured my worst villain with full, dark-red lips, as if permanently stained with blood. This creature had white, hard lips that looked chiseled into a stone face. And he appeared much thinner, lankier, even weaker-looking than the image in my head. Finally, he wasn't exactly good looking. Most authors of vampire lore, including myself, always described the extreme attractiveness of the vampire's face as part of their lure. This creature could possibly be appealing, if he weren't so downright frightening.

"I am not here to attract you as my prey," he said, as if

reading my mind. His lips pulled back from his razor-sharp teeth and fangs. "You apparently are not taking me seriously enough, so my goal is to scare you. Am I doing a good job?"

Yes, very much so. I stared at him wide-eyed, frozen in place. The Daemoni alarms still rang in my head.

"Are y-you D-Daemoni?" I finally managed to ask.

He smiled—it looked stunning and wretched at the same time. "Ah, so you are not so stupid after all. If I answer yes, will you take me more seriously?"

I ignored his question, needing answers to my own. Even if this was just a dream. "Do you have my husband? Is he still alive? Do you know where he is?"

He glowered at me, the red eyes burning brightly, and then hissed. "You have no husband! Your baby's father left you!"

I cringed at the words although they weren't new. He'd given the public's story. Anyone could have said that.

"You're not real. You're just a dream," I muttered.

"Stupid, *STUPID* WOMAN!" he growled, suddenly right in front of me, leaning over me. His eyes changed with the burst of anger, to the deepest, darkest black of death. Just the edges of the iris still glowed red.

I could see my horrified expression in those deep-black eyes. This nightmare felt even more real than my memory-dreams. I could hear his ragged breathing, feel it on my face, smell the unexpectedly pleasant, sweet scent: strawberries covered in sugar and cream. *Is this really a dream?* My heart raced even faster. I thought my ribs would break from the pressure and my heart would just fly out, right into his hands.

"Stop it!" he hissed, stiffening, and with a blur of movement too fast to even see, he stood on the other side of the room. "Down to business, Alexis. You are almost done with your book, and I need to stop you from finishing. You have exposed *enough* of our truths."

How would he know . . . ? "Y-y-you have to be a dream. Only a few people know how this last book is going and that it's almost done."

"Think about it, foolish one. There are some of us who can fool humans, immerse ourselves into their world. You have met a few. So even you can see we could have someone working at a certain publishing company?"

I stared at him, shaking my head, trying to make it all go away. This was nonsense, Swirly screwing even with my dreams now. *Wake up!*

"This is my last warning, Alexis. *Our* last warning. Not one more word. Do you understand?"

I shook my head slightly. I didn't really mean to contradict him. The movement was more about denying this whole . . . situation.

"You're not real," I whispered. Again, not to challenge him. I was trying to convince myself. With barely a sound, I added, "Go away."

Of course, he didn't obey. Instead, he let out a dreadful, harsh bark, a humorless laugh.

"Go away? Yes, you would want that. I would, too, you know. I would much rather be spending my time on something I could *have*. But, for now, anyway, I can only play. You must know there are many ways my friends and I can torture you . . . ways to hurt you without ever providing the relief of death. You are, after all, telling the entire human race about us."

"But I'm off limits," I blurted nonsensically, my dream-self confusing vampires with the real monsters of my life. Daemoni were prohibited from killing Amadis royalty unless Provoked, as in official Provocation.

"Hmm. And you are supposed to be so intelligent." He narrowed his eyes and glared at me in silence for a moment. When he spoke again, his voice was low and his words came slowly and deliberately, as if I were too stupid to understand basic concepts. "It is simple, Alexis. Exposing us makes *anything* justifiable. One more page, one more paragraph, one more word in that damn book of yours and play time will be over. Do you understand now?"

I couldn't answer. Again, I wanted to scream to wake myself up. But this nightmare had become one of those where you can't move, speak or even breathe. I wondered if a lack of air would finally force my body awake.

"DO YOU UNDERSTAND?" He stood right in front of me again, the cold breath raging against my face, blowing my hair back. I still couldn't move, not even for a breath. His voice lowered with the next question, nearly a whisper, but more frightening to me than anything else. "You really do not want us coming after your family, now do you, Alexis?"

Then he stiffened and his head twitched. His narrow nostrils flared. He turned his head to his left, his eyes shifting over his shoulder toward the door. He let out a soft growl from deep in his chest.

And then he was gone.

I didn't know how long I sat there, how much time had passed since I'd taken a breath. It felt like hours. I didn't know where he disappeared to and I didn't know if he would come back. I still hadn't woken up, so the nightmare wasn't over.

But I'd surely wake up and not let myself suffocate. Right? WAKE UP!

I decided to take a short, shallow breath, trying not to move too much, in case even the slightest movement brought him back. The brief flow of air felt like new life to my burning lungs. I couldn't help but take another, longer draw. It was ragged, but satisfying. I focused on counting my breaths, trying to keep them slow and steady.

One.

Two.

Three.

BANG! BANG! BANG!

I nearly fell out of my chair. My breath caught again and my heart returned to its flurried pace. Someone was at the door. *Is it real or part of the dream?* It was one of those sounds where you're just not sure. If it was real, it didn't wake me up. My subconscious incorporated the noise.

The vampire had sensed something. He knew someone was coming. Was it my knight-in-shining-armor? If my hero banged on the door, there was only one person I'd want it to be. I was glad I hadn't woken up yet.

The door flew open and hit the wall with another bang.

"Alexis!" Such a beautiful voice. "Alexis! Are you all right?"

Chapter 5

As the voice came into the room, I realized it wasn't the one I wanted to hear. It sounded familiar. Nice. But it didn't belong to who I wanted.

Is this some kind of cruel joke? Is my subconscious trying to replace him? Tears welled in my eyes. *I'm not ready to replace him. This is* my *dream. Why can't it be the way I want it?*

Instead, Owen's voice rang into the room. "Are you okay?"

I shook my head, biting my lower lip to keep it from trembling. I couldn't feel the pain from the bite, though. I wished I could—it would wake me up.

I sensed Owen kneel down in front of me, trying to get a good look at my face. I squeezed my eyes tightly. *Stupid dream. Why can't I just wake up?*

"Alexis, are you okay?" he asked again. "I sensed Daemoni."

"I-I'm fine," I finally answered, my voice tiny.

"You don't look fine."

"It was just . . ." *Oh, what does it matter?* This stupid dream wasn't going anywhere now because the wrong hero came. "It was nothing."

"Well, if you're okay in here, I'll go check everything out." I felt him move away, heard his steps as he crossed the room.

Is he really coming back? Can he just turn into the one I really want? That happens in dreams. People change into other people. Please? I didn't know who I begged. I guessed my deranged subconscious, which liked to torture me and knew exactly how to do it.

Bizarrely, like a dream within a dream, I heard my mother's voice from many years ago, as we drove from some city to another. She'd just broken up with yet another man. "Don't ever let them know your buttons. If they know your buttons, they'll push them every time."

My subconscious seemed to know exactly which buttons to push. Of course, it's not like I could hide my buttons from myself. I just had to deal with the torture.

"Everything looks fine," Owen said, returning to me. *Yep, still had to deal with it.* "Do you think you'll be okay?"

I nodded and said quietly, "I'm so tired. I just want real sleep."

I lay my head on the desk. Would I simply continue sleeping here? Couldn't I wake up long enough to get to the bed? Or was I already in bed? I tried to stand up. I nearly fell back down, my legs wobbly and weak.

"Whoa," Owen said, catching me.

I refused to look at him as he picked me up. His arms were hard and strong. I kept my eyes closed and tried to pretend he was the one I wanted. *It's just a dream anyway, so it should be easy, right?* The illusion came easier than I'd expected. A slight electrical current prickled where his arms touched my shoulders and the backs of my knees. As he carried me into the bedroom, I could even imagine the scent of mangos and papayas, lime and sage and a hint of man. I wanted to bury my face into his chest. But I worried my subconscious would turn everything around and I'd end up dreaming I fell into bed with . . . *Nope. Not going there.*

"I'll stay here for a while, make sure you're okay," Owen said. He leaned over and I felt the soft bed under me.

"No, you don't—"

"It wasn't a question. I'll keep watch. You just get some rest." I felt his lips press briefly against the top of my head. I kept my eyes tightly shut, afraid my subconscious might see that button—the bright one that flashed between "Possibility" and "Nearly as Good." But I felt the movement as he stood back up and then heard his soft steps on the thick carpet as he headed toward the door. Part of me didn't want him to leave. But I was afraid of what might happen . . . of the possibilities. *Not replacing him!*

Then the memory-dream finally returned, my real hero as the star, feeling so close to me.

❧

I lay in bed at 5:15 the next morning, holding onto those memories, onto Tristan's face. The image had finally been clear enough for me to see him. And now that I was awake, back in my own gray world, I had to face reality that he wasn't with me.

As soon as the sky lightened enough to run, I dashed out the door, grateful I'd decided to pack my new running gear. I ran along the unfamiliar streets, heading south, where I knew I would eventually hit water. When I did, I paused to gaze over it. The only sounds filling the air were the waves hitting against the concrete seawall below and seagulls cawing at each other overhead. The scene might have been peaceful if my body wasn't screaming to *move*. As I turned to head back down the street, someone caught my eye.

He was still too far away and too hidden in shadows to see his face. Somehow, though, I knew he was the stranger. The same stranger who'd been in my yard and at the park all the way back in Atlanta. And I knew now he was a hallucination. I'd been imagining him all along. He took several steps toward me this time. The gait was painfully familiar. *He's not real. Not real!* Panicked by the realization, I ran the other way, as fast and as hard as I could, not paying attention to where.

I wanted to get away from that delusion because it meant I really had lost my mind. I'd been trying so hard to see him, my imagination created false images, like someone lost in the desert searching for water for days and stumbling toward an oasis that's really just a mirage. I slowed, tears blurring my vision.

And I heard footsteps behind me. I glanced over my shoulder and saw another runner following my path. He gained on me quickly. I sped up, but he ran much faster.

Daemoni! Evil! Run! Go! Faster!

Shit! Shit, shit, shit! He wasn't following me . . . he *chased* me. I cranked my legs as fast as they could go, digging into the ground and springing forward. A beastlike growl rumbled behind me, way too close. My heart pounded and my breathing came hard, the first time I'd had any difficulty running. But exertion didn't tax my energy. This was all-out fear. *This is real. Just a few more seconds . . . .*

At least I'll be with my love.

I impulsively stopped at the thought and waited. Waited to be caught and captured and possibly killed.

Just take me!

But the footsteps fell silent. I whirled around. The runner was gone. No trace he'd even been there.

I stared down the street in bewilderment and turned in circles. No sign of anyone. *Another delusion?* I swore he was real . . . but maybe not. And if not, then I really was falling over the edge, into complete madness. In fact, that was the only explanation because I'd just been willing to give myself up, leaving my son as an orphan. *How could I?* An evil snicker sounded in the back of my head.

I inhaled deeply, trying to calm my heart and clear my head at the same time. And an invisible, yet crushing weight fell on top of me.

Mangos and papayas, lime and sage.

"What are you doing here?! Get to a safe place!"

My heart and my breathing both stopped. That scent . . . that voice. That lovely, smooth, silky voice. Tristan's voice. And not twisted in pain, screaming my name. I'd never allowed myself to hear his voice in my mind, knowing it would be too painful. I couldn't control scents—they wafted in on their own from innocent sources. But his voice . . . I would purposely have to recall it. My subconscious did it for me in my dreams—just to hear his last five words I clung to so desperately. But I wouldn't allow my conscious mind to do it. I could hardly believe it still could.

The smell and the sound overwhelmed my sharp senses and crushed my fragile soul. I broke down in the middle of the street, crying, turning round and round to try to find a source. The street was residential, with big houses, old trees and fences surrounding the yards. Nobody around. *Holy hell, I'm going out of my freakin' mind!*

As I continued turning in slow circles, something caught my eye. It was so obvious. A mango tree stood not too far away, baby fruit hanging from its branches over the fence it stood behind. I took a deep, ragged breath and exhaled slowly. *At least there's a partial explanation.*

Calming myself with that thought, I began walking down the street slowly, trying to get my bearings so I could head back to the hotel. I focused on the street sign thirty yards away and almost didn't notice the runner coming from the cross-street. My heart stuttered when I saw him, thinking he was the Daemoni runner again. And then I realized who he was.

He turned down the street I walked on, running away from me. He wore black running pants and a black t-shirt and his brown hair hung down past his shoulders in a ponytail. *It's not who I want. Why would I see him as so different than my memory?* But I couldn't help it. Even knowing he wasn't real, knowing he wasn't my love, I impulsively chased after him, running as hard as I could. Though I'd gained some speed over the last couple days, I couldn't catch up to him.

"Wait!" I yelled. "Please! *Wait!*"

He disappeared down the street. I kept running, tears flowing, not able to see where I ran. So it was easy to get knocked off my feet. Someone grabbed me from behind.

"Are you *crazy*?" Owen seethed, his mouth close to my ear.

"Ugh!" I moaned. He held me tightly and I let loose on him. "Yes, I am! Actually, I'm beyond crazy. I've totally lost my fucking mind, Owen. I'm a basket case. Call the white coats. Tell them to bring the straightjacket and lock me up in a padded cell. That's where I belong!"

He kept his arms around me as I threw my temper-tantrum. When I calmed down, he set me back on my feet and stepped around so he could look at me. "Are you done?"

I dropped my face into my hands, pressing the heels of my palms against my eyes. When the pulsing in my ears quieted, I sighed and looked at him. "For the moment. I guess."

He shook his head slowly. "Come on. We need to get out of here. This is really the worst place you can be, especially by yourself."

He led me back to the hotel and waited in the front room of my suite while I showered, dressed and packed my laptop and the few items I'd taken out. He apparently wouldn't leave me alone.

"I'm going to the beach house," I said when I was ready to leave.

He nodded. "It's better than here."

"It's something I need to do alone, Owen."

He gave me a kind smile. "I understand. I'll get out when we get close. For now, I can make sure no one sees you leave or follows you there."

"You can shield *cars?*"

"Yeah, but you need more than a shield. I have to get you out of here without anyone even seeing you leave and flashing with you is impossible, so . . ." He rubbed his hands against each other, then quickly turned them palm out at me. His eyes traveled down to my feet and back up again. "There. Perfect."

I looked down at myself. As far as I could tell, nothing had changed. "What?"

He reached out and clumsily grabbed my shoulders, then led me over to a mirror on the wall. My jaw dropped with an audible gasp. Owen stood behind me, but the mirror reflected only him—his whole body, as if nothing obstructed it . . . as if I weren't there.

"I cloaked you," he said with a big grin.

I smiled with relief, although he couldn't see it. I didn't know how he cloaked me, but it was perfect. The thought had already occurred to me that I could have led Daemoni right to our safe place and I'd had no ideas for how to prevent it. They were apparently aware of my presence and would have followed. I was grateful Owen had followed me to the Keys.

He picked up all my bags and led me out of the room and down the hallway. A man and woman stood at the elevators, holding hands.

"Stay very close so they don't bump into you and don't make a sound," Owen said, his voice barely a whisper.

As we reached the Ferrari, Owen went to the front to drop my bags into the cargo space and I naturally went to the driver's side door. He walked right into me.

"Ow! What are you doing?" I asked.

"What are *you* doing?" he echoed.

"Uh . . . getting in the car."

He lifted an eyebrow. "And what happens if you pass by a cop and it looks like the car is driving itself?"

"Oh. Right." I'd already forgotten I was invisible to everyone else. Owen would have to drive me.

"I'll stop once we're out of sight of the highway," he promised.

Owen's plan worked. No one paid any attention to us, except a few guys who gawked at the car and a couple of women who smiled warmly at Owen while we sat at a stoplight. My sense felt they were plain human—not Daemoni. Either the Daemoni didn't care about me, didn't recognize the car or figured Owen was leaving by himself or just running errands or something. Or maybe we just got lucky and none were even out when we left. Neither of us felt anyone following us as we traveled the fifty miles to the beach house.

"Thank you, Owen," I said as he made the turn off the highway. He drove about forty feet, then stopped the car. From the highway, our little key, which we shared with only four other homes, was barely noticeable by passing drivers, hidden in what looked like a wild overgrowth of natural vegetation.

"That's what I'm here for," he said.

He waved his hand toward me, presumably to lift the cloak, but I paid no attention. Instead, I stared down the sandy road that led to the beach house. A lump started forming in my throat, growing larger with each heartbeat until I thought it might suffocate me.

"Are you sure you want to do this?" Owen asked.

I didn't answer, not able to talk with that boulder stuck in my throat. I finally nodded.

"I'll be close," he said and then he flashed, disappeared, leaving me alone to my task that would either lead to light and healing or push me down into the utter blackness of no return.

I heaved myself out of the car and walked to the driver's side on wobbly legs, feeling like one of Dorian's toys—the rubbery kind that could be pulled and twisted and bent into odd shapes. I folded myself into the driver's seat, took a deep breath and put the transmission into first gear.

As I turned into the driveway and the house came into view, grief slammed down on me. I hadn't been back since Tristan and I had left together. This was *our* place. I didn't want memories here without him. Yet here I was. Completely alone.

When I stopped the car at the house, I couldn't move.

Memories of pulling into the driveway the first time flooded my vision. The moon provided the only light then and our conversation had been strained. It was easy to remember—I'd been so nervous, not about losing my virginity, but about doing it right for him. The emotion was still clear, but now felt from a more experienced, older perspective. That was an innocent time, a time full of joy and love and hope. We'd been looking forward to years—centuries, even eternity—of being together. And we'd been given only a couple of weeks.

The sobs finally subsided and I wiped my face with my hands, staring at the house with trepidation. It still looked the same, as if frozen in time with the memories it held. The light gray, metal roof reflected the bright sun and the blue-gray stucco siding looked like new. The wooden stairs and deck seemed to have a fresh coat of white paint—they gleamed in the sun, too. The house hadn't changed at all.

But it was different now. Instead of promises of love and hope, the house now held guarantees of misery and loneliness. Part of me wanted to leave. A very big part.

I inhaled deeply, telling myself I could do this. I gathered the luggage and forced myself up the stairs. I rummaged in his bag for the keys, taking time to feel each of his belongings my hand came across, trying so hard to remember his face, to feel his presence. Once I stepped inside, I didn't have to try. I could barely punch in the security code for the alarm, my hands trembling and tears blurring my vision.

The memories of our unplanned honeymoon—so long ago now—flooded over me as soon as I entered the kitchen. We'd cooked so many meals here together, listening to U2, Nirvana and Smashing Pumpkins, the only three CDs that had been in the Ferrari at the time. Sometimes he'd taken me in his arms and spun me around for a short dance as we waited for the sauce to thicken or water to boil. I remembered him chasing me around the island with lobsters in his hands before he dropped them in the big pot of steaming water. My eyes traced over the crack he'd left in the granite countertop the day we had to leave and tears streamed down my cheeks.

I dropped the bags and stumbled through the unchanged family room into the master bedroom. It looked exactly the same, with a colossal bed and dresser in the main part of the room and a chaise lounge and little table in front of the sliding glass doors, which led out to the screened-in balcony. Everything was white, with splashes of jewel-tone colors in the fabrics and decorations, making it feel like a tropical island. He'd named it the Caribbean room.

My breath caught as I remembered our first night here. He was so happy I loved the place as much as he did. And so loving and gentle as he took me for the first time.

I threw myself on the bed and sobbed. When the racks of pain subsided, he swam into my vision. I saw clearly his beautiful face with the sparkling eyes, smelled his delicious, tangy-sweet scent, felt the electric pulse as he touched me, heard his lovely voice say, "I love you, *ma lykita*," as if he lay right next to me. He felt close again. *So close.* And just like that first night at the safe house, I *felt* his presence in the world. Really felt it, like a nearly tangible energy reaching into my chest, surrounding my heart and filling my body.

I knew again, really *knew* he was still alive. Any doubt had been erased. He lived . . . somewhere.

I pulled the bedding into me, clinging to it as though it were him, wishing like hell he would just come back to me.

When I felt like I had no more tears, I pulled myself out of the bed and examined the house. Mom had hired a management company to care for it and everything seemed to be in working order. I figured Mom had called to let them know of my pending arrival once she realized I'd headed to the Keys. With a push of a button, the hurricane shutters lifted and I went out to the balcony. I curled up in the chair Tristan always sat in, pretending I sat on his lap again, snuggling against his chest instead of the cushion. And I bawled.

It was a horrible, heart-wrenching day and night. But definitely not the worst of my life. In fact, I relished the agony because it made me remember. And remembering made me feel so close to him. I let the wounds open widely. I welcomed the pain when I saw the cracked headboard, a consequence of our heated passion. I embraced the burning throb as I stood at the shower door, reliving some of my favorite memories.

"Baby, I feel so close to you now. Please come to me." I moaned myself to sleep, curled in a ball on *our* bed, my hand clutching the pendant as a lifeline. My old memory-dream played throughout the night and I savored every moment, knowing how important it was to hang on, even in my dreams.

❧

The next day came easier and I knew this was the right decision, coming here. After ignoring this place for so long, it gave me what I'd needed all along—real memories, a place he had been, where I could physically feel him and his love for me. The longer I stayed in our bed, the less the memories felt like an assault shattering my heart and more like a cozy blanket surrounding me with warmth. The reassuring sensation continued everywhere in the house and on the three-acre property as I worked my way around to each special place. I sat on the little beach for a long time, just gazing out over the water, remembering how we'd swam and snorkeled and skinny-dipped in the moonlight.

Later, Owen and I left for groceries and when we came back, I didn't have to sob in the driveway. I had to admit it helped to have Owen here. His presence gave a sense of comfort, providing a link between the past and the present.

"Where do you go?" I asked him when we pulled in front of the house. When I wanted to leave, I just called his name outside and he was suddenly walking up the driveway. "I mean, when you're not right here. You're obviously somewhere nearby."

He chuckled. "I'm around."

"That's not an answer."

He shrugged. "It's true. I just hang around, keeping an eye on the place."

"Where do you sleep?"

"Where I feel like it . . . last night I slept on your balcony. I wanted to be close."

"*Really?* I didn't know . . . ."

"Well, yeah, you're not supposed to. I'm here at your beck and call. Otherwise, I'm supposed to keep my distance and just protect. But I've always been there, through everything, behind the scenes, protecting you . . . except when you were with . . . when I knew you were safe."

I knew who he was about to say. He hadn't needed to protect me when I was with the one person who could protect me better than anyone—my husband. Because he himself was the most dangerous creature on earth.

"You can stay in one of the bedrooms," I offered.

His lips formed a small smile. His eyes mixed with kindness and empathy. "I don't think that's a good idea. You came here to be alone, right?"

"Yeah, but . . ."

"Don't worry about me, okay? This is my job. And, really, I love it. You're a lot more interesting to protect than Rina or Sophia."

I snorted. "Glad I keep you entertained. You probably heard all of my sleep talking and screaming."

"Actually, not last night. You slept peacefully. Boring for me, but good for you."

"Thanks, Owen," I said quietly. "For protecting me. And for being a friend. If you need anything, like to use the shower or anything . . . ."

"Yeah, I did." He chuckled again.

I stared at him, my eyebrows raised.

"While you slept. Gotta clean up somewhere, don't I? But it's nice to have permission now. And you have fair warning, you know, in case you wake up."

I imagined finding him unexpectedly in *our* shower. "You *are* using the second bathroom, right?"

"Yep . . . but that big shower of yours is *sick*."

I narrowed my eyes. "It's off limits."

He threw his hands in the air. "Understood. I noticed you don't even use it. Your soap and shampoo are in the other one."

"Yeah, well . . ." I couldn't tell him about the memories the shower held for me. "It's just too big to get warm."

"No need to explain yourself to me."

He was too kind. "Thanks again, Owen."

"See ya 'round. Holler if you need anything." He disappeared.

I went inside and dealt with the memories again. Like this morning, it was easier, because I felt my love there with me. I didn't want to admit feeling his presence meant I was getting worse, not better. Because I just didn't feel like I was worsening. In fact, the anger and insanity seemed to be receding. *Yeah, that's a good sign I've fallen into the abyss.* Or, I'd finally found my way out. I wasn't sure which was right.

Chapter 6

"Are you sure you're okay there?" Mom asked me when I checked in with a phone call before heading to bed.

"No." I took a deep breath. "But I will be."

"I don't like you there alone, Alexis."

"I need to be, Mom. I'm sure I'm fine. Besides, Owen's been around."

She ignored the as-if-you-didn't-know-that tone to my voice. "How are you doing physically? Are you eating and sleeping?"

"No, not exactly." I shrugged, though she couldn't see it. "But I physically *feel* great."

"Like *what?*" She almost sounded alarmed. "Tell me what you're feeling."

"I don't know, just energetic, I guess. I feel like I need to move a lot."

"Like your sudden interest in running?"

"Yeah, exactly. It's exhilarating."

"Anything else?"

I debated whether to tell her how the intensity of my senses seemed to have increased exponentially. I decided not to. It seemed weird, but not my normal freakiness. Weird as in . . . maniacal.

"No. Why?"

She kept silent for a moment. "I'm sure it's nothing," she finally said. "You've been under a lot of emotional stress and I'm sure your body is just reacting to it."

"Finally in a good way, I guess. My pooch is almost gone." I rubbed my hand over my stomach. It was much smaller already.

"Just take care of yourself, Alexis. And please tell me anything that's going on. I need to know these things. I can help you through them, you know."

"Sure, Mom. So how's Dorian?" I got her to change the subject and heard all about their days without me. She handed Dorian the phone so he could tell me he loved and missed me.

Grief hit me again when I hung up and remembered I was still alone. The only other time I'd ever been alone overnight in my entire life was when Mom went out of town that one weekend . . . that one glorious weekend . . . when we became a couple. Remembering that extraordinary chapter of my life, I made my rounds to the special places in the house and let myself cry it out. I saw his face clearly as I dozed off.

Burning pain surged through my muscles and nerves, waking me up. I rolled and thrashed in bed, not able to get comfortable, my muscles and joints tight and throbbing. I got up twice to take a pain reliever, but it didn't help at all. When I finally fell asleep again, I awoke gasping from the intensity of the burn. I felt the consequences of those runs when I'd been so out of shape, physically paying for those stupid impulses. I finally fell into a more comfortable sleep just long enough to enjoy the memory-dream.

When I woke up at five, I felt completely refreshed. In

fact, I felt unusually strong, both physically and mentally. The burning in the night was a distant memory. I ran around the property several times since I had nowhere else to safely run, then I went for a long swim, pushing myself harder on each lap I made parallel to our private beach. I felt good. *It's like my body is becoming more powerful by the minute, like it's* changing.

That thought rushed me out of the water and back inside.

I stared at myself in the mirror for what seemed like hours, twisting and turning my body to study it from as many angles as I could. The woman staring back at me no longer looked fifty-something. My reflection looked completely different than it had just a week earlier. A spark of life shone in my eyes. Color brightened my skin again. Although wet, my hair felt thicker and the grays had disappeared. Even with less sleep and emotional strain, the dark circles under my eyes were hardly noticeable. The wrinkles were shallow, almost invisible.

And my body . . . I didn't understand, but the running and exercise—and forgetting to eat—had dramatically reversed the damage I'd done. The pooch had shrunken into just a shadow of its former self. My hips and butt were noticeably smaller. No wonder I had to keep hitching up my shorts. Even my breasts looked almost back to normal. And *perkier.* They were almost pre-baby.

Should I call Mom? I debated the question for quite a while. In the end, I decided not to. After all, I'd been through hell this week. My body just reacted in an unusual way, as my body tended to do. It was probably just healing itself from the long-term damage once I decided to let it. *These may not be permanent changes. Not the Ang'dora.* I had little knowledge of what the *Ang'dora* would be like, but I knew I was too young and I wasn't going to let my hopes rise . . . yet.

There was one definite difference about me: I started to feel alive again. Really *alive.*

By the next day, comforted with both sleeping and waking memories and the feeling he was close, if only in spirit, I felt real hope. Psycho and Swirly hadn't made any appearances since I'd arrived, Foggy seemed to be dissipating and I actually felt like Almost Alexis, even without Dorian. And for some reason, this made me feel like I could finally finish my book. As I set up the laptop on the screened-in balcony, Owen bounded up the outside stairs three at a time and flew through the screen door.

"It's Sophia," he said, sounding a little anxious. My cell phone rang. I looked at him and he raised his eyebrows.

"Alexis, are you okay?" Mom asked. She sounded more than just a *little* anxious.

"I'm fine. Why?"

"Listen, honey, we have some serious problems."

"What?" Panic immediately set in at the tone of her voice. "Is Dorian okay?"

"Yes. He'll be fine."

"Then what's going on, Mom?"

"Are you almost done with that book?"

What? Why is the book so important? "Actually, I was just getting ready to write. I think I can finish it soon. *Why?*"

She took a deep breath. "The Daemoni are in an uproar and some of them are out of control. We don't know the full reasoning, but part of it has to do with your last book."

"*What?* What does my book have anything to do . . . ?" My voice trailed off as the vampire dreams flashed through my mind.

"Honey, your books have to do with a lot of things. I don't have time to explain it all now, but suffice it to say that not all you've been writing is fiction."

The phone shook in my hand and I nearly dropped it with shock. "What does *that* mean?"

She sighed heavily. "The characters, Alexis. You know these creatures because of who you are, a connection you have. They're not myths."

I couldn't say anything at first. I felt as if the wind had been knocked out of me.

"Mom . . . you're saying they're . . . they're *real*? Vampires and witches and wizards and werewolves . . . they're all *real*?" I began to wonder if I was really having this conversation or if I had gone completely off the deep end. Either option was downright frightening.

"I really don't have time to explain right now, but a short answer is yes, they're real. Demons take many shapes and forms."

I sat there with my mouth open, trying to process and comprehend. "But . . . what . . . why . . . *how*?"

"Daemoni, Alexis. That's what the Daemoni are. Some are like us—closer to human than anything else—but most are the same types of creatures you write about."

My breath caught. The question came out in a whisper. "The vampire in my room . . . are you saying *he* was real, too?"

Owen whipped his head at me, a strange look on his face.

"Yes, honey," Mom said. "That's why Owen came the next day—to shield the house."

I swallowed hard as I remembered the vampire and thinking I was only dreaming.

"And in the hotel room . . . ?" My voice trailed off. I wasn't sure I wanted to know.

"I knew it," Owen muttered. I stared at him, my eyes bugging.

"Hold on, Mom," I said distantly as I held the phone away from my head. "Owen . . . the other night in Key West . . . were you in my hotel room?"

"Uh, yeah, I sensed Daemoni. Remember?"

"Holy hell, that was *real*?"

My heart skipped erratically. I heard Mom yelling my name in the phone.

"Mom, what the hell is going on? There was a *vampire* in my room! *Twice!*"

"I know, honey. I—"

"You *know*? Why didn't you say anything?"

"I didn't want to frighten you and you were protected—"

"Protected? A vampire—Daemoni—was in my room! How is that being protected?"

Owen answered, sounding defensive. "It's kind of hard protecting you in a place like Key West, with Daemoni everywhere. It's too crowded to put a shield up and useless anyway when the enemy is already inside. I came as soon as I sensed him near you."

Mom must have heard him. She added, "Owen said you were fine. Just tired and groggy—"

"Because I thought it was a dream, Mother. I didn't know there were real, live vampires roaming around. You should have said something!"

"We couldn't . . . I couldn't . . . ," Mom stammered. I could hear her take a breath and when she spoke again, she sounded calmer. More like her usual, unshakable self. "I can't get into it right now. I really need to get going. I'm trying to get Dorian packed—"

"Dorian *packed*? *Where are you taking him?*"

"That's why I called. We have to leave for safety. The Daemoni claim they have Provocation because the books are exposing them. I don't think that's the whole reason for their upheaval, but Dorian and I need to get out of here. They've given permission for attacks on *all* of us."

"Oh, no. Not my baby!"

He was our youngest generation now. I didn't know if that meant the same thing as it did for a daughter, but I couldn't imagine why the Daemoni *wouldn't* target him. I paced the balcony. I felt so far away from him. And so helpless. *How could I leave him? What had I been thinking?!*

"He'll be okay, Alexis. Just take care of yourself. Owen will stay with you and I'll be there as soon as I can."

"Please, Mom, *please* don't let anything happen to Dorian. I couldn't . . ." The thought of losing him, too, was too much. My shattered heart just wouldn't be able to take it.

"I can take care of this, Alexis, but I really need to go. I'll see you in a few days. Stay safe until then, okay? Promise me?"

"*You* promise to take care of my baby!"

"I promise, Alexis. He'll be well protected. Just hurry up and get that book done."

"*What?* You still want me to *finish* it? That's exactly what the problem is!"

Her voice remained steady, yet hurried. "You have to, honey. It's very important that you do. Just trust me. This has been the plan all along."

"*Mom . . .*"

"I can't explain right now. I need to go."

The safety of my son outweighed my need for answers . . . for now. I let her go, setting the phone down in disbelief. I took a deep breath to calm myself from hysteria to mere panic before whirling on Owen.

"*Explain,*" I demanded.

He grimaced. "I can't. I don't have the authority."

"*Owen!* You can't do this to me!"

"All I can say is the council planned all of this. I don't think they expected this kind of reaction from the Daemoni, but we're sure there's more to their anger than the books."

"They let me write—*encouraged* me to write—when they knew my stories exposed *secrets?*"

"The benefits outweighed the risks. But really, Alexis, I can't say any more than that." He looked me in the eye. "Just know you can trust the Amadis. We *always* win."

I stared at him with wide eyes, my mouth open. *What the . . . ? Who did he . . . ? How . . . ?* I could barely form coherent thoughts. When I finally could, I made my words slow, my voice low. "We *always* win? You're telling *me* we always *win?*"

He looked away from me, not answering. His jaw muscle twitched.

"I know firsthand we don't *always* win, Owen. In fact, I think I've *lost* nearly *everything!*" My voice rose in volume and octaves, barely recognizable as the last words came out in a shriek.

He finally looked at me, his sapphire eyes intense. "I was there, Alexis. Don't forget that. I was there, right in the middle of it all. I *know*. But in the end, we *do* always win."

"*Get out!* Get the hell out of my house!" I yelled. I looked around wildly for something to throw at him. Something that would hurt as much as he'd just hurt me. I picked up a chair but he was already gone.

I paced the house angrily while trying to keep myself under control. I really didn't want to destroy anything. It was all too precious to me. I pounded on the granite countertops, thinking they were sturdy enough to take my rage. I added a crack to the one left so long ago. *Damn it!*

Questions flew through my head and I had no one to answer. The only one close by said he couldn't tell me. And I'd just kicked him out of the house anyway. *For good reason!* But pacing and thinking my own thoughts—probably throwing things way out of proportion from my ignorance—didn't help.

"Owen!" I finally yelled outside. I couldn't take it any

longer. He quickly appeared at the bottom of the steps. "You *are* going to give me answers. *I* can give you authority, can't I?"

His face twisted in a grimace. "Not really. Especially while you're still . . . before the *Ang'dora*. But I talked to Rina and Solomon. Ask me questions and I'll answer what I can."

I gave him a nasty look, but took what I could get. I let him on the balcony and we sat across from each other at the table.

I leaned in and looked him in the eye. "Why hasn't anyone said anything before? About the truth of my books?"

He nodded slightly. "If you'd known the creatures were real, you wouldn't have accomplished what you did. There's a purpose for it all, Alexis. I can't tell you that purpose, but Rina or Sophia will soon. Just know it's a *good* purpose. We're *good*, Alexis."

"So even though it's putting everyone's lives in danger, they want me to *finish* it? I just don't understand."

He pushed his hand through his hair and squinted his eyes, seeming to organize his thoughts. "The Daemoni are throwing a fit, but we really think they're using the books as an excuse to push their limits. They do that sometimes and right now they're upset about something. We just don't know what yet. So they're using the books as a way to get something they want."

"And would that 'something' they want possibly be me?"

He cringed. "Probably."

I inhaled deeply as I let my mind process the meaning. *I* was the one they wanted more than anything. They probably wanted their matched set. But it was *me*, not Mom or Dorian, that they were truly after now. I let out the air, feeling almost relieved.

"Is that why I'm left here alone? I mean, no one is taking me to safety. Is it because I'll put them in danger?"

"First of all, as long as you stay on this property, you *are* safe. It's protected just as well as any safe house. But, yes, it's better you're kept away from the others. At least for now."

My brows furrowed. "What does that mean? At least for now?"

He answered with his own question. "You've noticed how you're changing recently?"

"Who couldn't notice? I'm a mess."

"I'm talking about the physical changes, too. The running and swimming, how your body's changing, you're looking younger . . . I mean, you looked terrible a week ago."

I threw him a hateful look.

"Just keeping it real."

"Sorry. You're right. Are the changes really that noticeable to you, too?"

He nodded. "Part of it—maybe a lot of it—is because you *are* changing. Actually changing over. The *Ang'dora*."

I stared at him. *I'd been right? It* is *the Ang'dora?*

"Is that what's been causing all this insanity? All of my crazy behavior these last few days?" I dared to hope it explained everything I'd been going through this past week—that I hadn't really been as mentally unstable as I'd feared, but that the *Ang'dora* caused the havoc.

"That's what Sophia thinks, anyway. Everyone says it's too early, but Sophia and I have seen you. She was planning to clear out the safe house and take you there, just in case."

"That's what she meant about needing to get away."

"Yeah, but then you took off on your own. She only let you go because she knew you'd come here, away from everyone else. Which is good because . . ." He hesitated. I lifted my eyebrows for him to continue. "Because if it *is* the *Ang'dora*, well, there are some . . . uncertainties . . . ."

I nodded with understanding. They weren't quite positive the Amadis power could conquer my Daemoni blood. I could be just as much a danger to them as any of the predators out there looking for their opportunity to attack. The sense of relief that there was a reason for my meltdown was quickly overshadowed by the memory of Evil Alexis—that internal voice, like I'd never heard it until recently.

"I see," I said quietly, falling back into the chair. "So you're not just here to protect me. You're also here to kill me, if necessary."

His eyes widened with horror. "Alexis, I could *never* . . ."

I leaned forward again and looked him directly in the eye. "You have to, Owen. You can't let me hurt anyone."

"But we only kill if absolutely necessary. That's part of being Amadis. Every soul can be saved."

"Rina told me they would've killed me when I was a baby if they thought the Daemoni blood would overpower."

"Only if there'd been no hope."

"You can't let me hurt anyone," I repeated.

The corners of his mouth twitched, as if he fought a smile. "Except Daemoni."

"Right." I sighed.

I rose from the chair and walked over to the railing, looking across the yard and over the water. I prayed none of this became an issue, but knew the truth in it better than anyone. No one else knew about the evil already trying to brandish its ugly self inside me. I realized then I had to do what I could for the Amadis, even when it made no sense to me now. I had to trust them. Although I knew we didn't *always* win.

"Thanks, Owen."

"I'm here for you, no matter what." He stood right behind me and wrapped his arms around me, strong and warm. I pulled on the Amadis power emanating from his body, absorbing it into my own. His power didn't feel strong, not like Rina's or Mom's or even Stefan's had been, but it helped. "And I'm sorry if what I said hurt you. You know . . . he was my best friend. I miss him, too."

I stiffened in his arms. We had never, *ever* discussed Tristan and that horrible day he disappeared.

Owen's voice came out husky as he remembered. "We hung out a lot, before we had to focus on you. We were pretty close, more than anyone knows. Those years he roamed alone . . . when you were still a kid . . . well, we would meet up every now and then. We both had to mainstream, but when we were together, we could be more ourselves. You know?"

"No, I didn't know." I shook my head. My own voice was thick. "Do you . . . do you really think he's dead, Owen?"

He blew out a sigh, fluttering my hair. "I don't know. I really don't. Nobody does. But that video—"

I cut him off. "I don't really care about the video. I know why they sent it, but I also know what I feel."

"No, there's something else you should know." He paused. "See, we still don't know who hacked Rina's account, but they don't think it was Amadis. It's too difficult to believe a council member—or any Amadis—would go behind Rina's back like this. They're pretty sure it was the Daemoni."

I blinked with surprise as I considered this possibility. Based on the conversation of the other night, the most obvious answer had been the Amadis council. The timing was too perfect. But . . .

Ian's mocking laugh when he told me about the arranged marriage resurfaced in my memory. He certainly enjoyed watching my pain, so it was easy to believe the rest of the Daemoni would, too. They probably wished they could have watched me as I viewed the video. They obviously didn't know anything about me. Or the connection I had with Tristan.

The Amadis council, on the other hand, did. They should have known the video wouldn't have forced me into acceptance. They would know that, if anything, the video would have pushed me into the abyss. And, from the little I did know, the council—Rina's advisors—should be the most loyal to her of all.

The Daemoni *must* have sent it.

"Why now?" I finally asked. "There's been nothing from them in so long. Why would they do this now?"

Owen's arms jerked against me in what I assumed was a shrug. "I don't know. They don't tell me everything. But . . ."

He hesitated.

"But what?"

"But the Daemoni might be sending a message . . ." He paused again, drawing in a deep breath. Before I could press him again, though, he finished. ". . . that if they hadn't actually done it before . . . they have now."

I froze. I didn't even breathe as I let this sink in, let its meaning reach into my soul. My heart thumped several times as I tried to determine what I felt. But I already knew. The feeling that he was still alive *strengthened* when I arrived at the beach house . . . *after* they sent the video.

"I still don't believe it," I said.

"I didn't think you would," he murmured.

We stood in silence for a long moment.

"Do you think I'm foolish for hanging on?" I whispered.

He didn't answer at first and I tried to ignore the interpretation I made of his silence. I told myself it didn't matter what he thought. Only my own beliefs mattered and I knew what I had felt all these years. Especially these last few days.

"I admire your loyalty," he finally said. "You do what you need to do for you. That's what he would want."

I nodded, the back of my head rubbing against his chest. I knew the truth in his statement. Tristan had once told me the same thing, a long time ago.

Owen kissed the top of my head and then he was gone.

I continued standing at the rail, thinking about Owen and what he put up with as my protector. He said he enjoyed his job, but was there more to it? I remembered how Mom had thought about setting us up, thinking he'd be a good match for me. The thought of being more than just friends had only flitted through my mind a couple times. If the Amadis was right about the video . . . if my true love really was gone . . . for good . . . Well, with Owen, life could possibly be a little more normal—as normal as it could be for an Amadis daughter, who, apparently, was enemies with creatures like vampires and werewolves. There probably wouldn't be such a strong desire to keep us separated . . . or brought over to their side. I knew Mom would approve and Dorian loved him. The council would probably be ecstatic, seeing me move on. The possibilities . . .

But it was impossible to think of Owen as anything different than a friend or a brother.

I sighed. *It doesn't matter anyway.*

Any future with Owen, or with the Amadis at all, would never happen. I knew what I needed to do—for the Amadis and for my family, especially my son.

I sat at my computer and started writing.

Now that I knew what came next—that I wouldn't need another world to escape to—the words came easily. I wrote until two in the morning. I was wide awake again at five, ran around the property a few times, then went back to the book. Just before three in the afternoon, I finished. The book. The series. Six years of writing the story. Done. *Finito.*

I stared at the last line for several moments and finally typed The End. My chest tightened with grief. Besides Mom, my characters had been my best friends, pulling me through my darkest hours, and now we had to say good-bye, never to visit each other again. Their adventure was over and so was that whole part of my life . . . or it would be shortly.

I emailed the entire book to Mom. I didn't know whether the vampire had been telling the truth about having Daemoni planted at my publisher, so I didn't send anything to my editor.

Mom could do whatever the Amadis council dictated when the time came.

I then wrote two letters—one to Mom and one to Dorian—explaining how I did this for them, to keep them safe. I wanted to call Dorian, to hear his voice one more time, but I feared what he and Mom would hear in my own voice. Mom would know something was up. So I wrote my good-byes, tears streaming. I knew I couldn't email them—she would get them too soon—and I had no way to print them at the beach house. So my fingers trembled with my sobs as I saved the two letter files on the computer's desktop, where Mom would easily find them.

I took a deep breath and focused on the rest of the plan. I hadn't figured out yet how to do it. Owen had regularly checked on me, reminding me he stayed close by. I'd tested him once, pretending I needed to go to the store. He appeared suddenly and stopped me as I sat in the car, asked what I needed and was back with a box of tampons in four minutes. I felt bad for putting him through that and since he made the trip without so much as a complaint, he clearly wouldn't let me go anywhere. However it happened, I needed to be ready to act on a moment's notice.

I showered and studied myself in the mirror, trying to see what I could do to make myself as attractive as possible. It was surprisingly difficult to do any more than what my body had already done on its own. My skin looked and felt smooth—no wrinkles or lines of any kind, no dark and puffy circles under my eyes, the light-olive tone tanned. My hair, now full and vibrant, waved down to the middle of my back and my body was small but strong. I actually looked like my age.

I eyed the sundresses Tristan had bought me on our honeymoon and I'd forgotten to pack in our hurried departure. The property management company apparently had the dresses cleaned—they hung in plastic bags in the closet. I'd seen them my first day here. Mom must have had the wedding dress shipped because it wasn't there and I knew I hadn't packed it when we left in such a rush. I was glad it was gone. Seeing it would have been too much for my fragile self of a couple days ago.

I chose a black dress with purple flowers, spaghetti straps that crossed over my back and a full skirt that ended about three inches above my knees. It was probably out of style, but I didn't care. Almost all the clothes I'd brought were dirty and the dress was better than baggy shorts and a holey t-shirt anyway. I checked myself in the mirror—the dress did the job.

"*Wow*, you look . . ." Owen was caught off guard when I called for him. I flashed him my best smile. He narrowed his eyes and said flatly, "You're not going anywhere."

I tried to act casual. "Of course not. I was just tired of looking like a frump. I feel *good*. I finished the book."

He smiled. "Great! Now we wait for it to be published and let it do its thing."

"But we can celebrate now," I said suggestively.

He looked surprised, the sapphire eyes wide, eyebrows raised. "You and me?"

"That's all we have right now, right? Why not? If you get some steaks and the trimmings, I'll cook. And we need some wine, of course."

His brows pushed together, creating those three vertical lines between them. "I don't think that's a good idea. We need to be completely alert."

I fluttered my eyelashes and stuck out my lower lip in a pretend pout. "Just a glass. Just for a toast to the Amadis and whatever it is they have planned."

He studied my face. I really wasn't trying to seduce him. Honestly. I just needed him to disappear for a while . . . just long enough. I smiled warmly at him.

"Okay," he finally agreed. "You stay here. I'll be back in ten or fifteen minutes."

I followed him out the door and watched him walk down the driveway, into the brush and disappear. As soon as he was gone, I jumped into the Ferrari and took off, my heart pounding with anxiety and fear. I'd left the keys in there earlier, knowing I needed every second I could get when the opportunity arose. I sped down the highway, clearing as much distance as possible before Owen returned and found me gone.

Guilt pierced my conscience when I thought of him searching for me. But I had to do this. At least he wouldn't be left heartbroken and helpless like I'd been when I was left behind. I just hoped he wouldn't immediately guess where I headed, but would think I went after my family. Because once he knew, he would be there in a flash.

Chapter 7

I made the fifty-mile drive to Key West in twenty minutes. I barely remembered any of it—just the gray pavement passing under the car—my mind first on Owen and then on Dorian. My son's face swam in my vision, so much like his father's. I ached to hold him one last time. *I'm so sorry, little man. Please forgive me. I love you so much.* More tears pooled in my eyes, making it difficult to focus on the road, but I reminded myself, though now with no parents, he had Mom and the Amadis. He would be well taken care of. They would provide him a security I couldn't give him as long as the Daemoni pursued me.

I forced myself to think about what lay ahead, rather than what I left behind.

My heart picked up speed the closer I came. My chest squeezed with panic, making proper breathing difficult, and my stomach rolled with anxiety. *What the hell am I doing?* This was probably the stupidest thing I'd ever done—second only to letting Tristan leave me at the safe house. But I had to do this, if it was the last thing I did for the Amadis, for my son.

My hand banged on the steering wheel restlessly and my left leg bounced with nerves as I made my way through traffic to the west side of Key West, to the old part where the tourists partied and the Daemoni . . . hunted. *Come on, come on, come on!* If this didn't happen quickly, Owen would eventually figure out where I headed. And, even if he didn't, I was afraid I would lose my nerve.

I didn't know what to expect. I thought maybe they would be on top of me as soon as they sensed me. Then I remembered they couldn't read my thoughts, so they probably didn't know I'd entered their hunting grounds. It wasn't like they expected me to walk right into their hands. Not like the last time they got what they wanted. But this was the only way I knew how to solve the problem. I didn't have the ability to recognize the best solution. Tristan did, but not me. I worked with all I knew—my heart and my soul telling me what was best for everyone.

I'd promised him I would come for him. Although he never knew that promise, I would do my best to keep it. I hadn't quite changed over, but I'd run out of time. My family needed the protection. They needed to be left alone. I hoped to give that to them.

The funny thing was, I realized, I did this as me. Real Alexis. At least . . . the closest I would know of Real Alexis, since I'd probably never make it all the way through the *Ang'dora*. But this wasn't Psycho acting out in anger or Swirly confusing me with a mix of fact and fiction. Foggy disappeared a couple days ago. I embraced this new-found purpose as *me*, clear minded, though a little frightened. Okay, more than a little. But definitely all me. Definitely Real Alexis.

As the sun began to set and darkness came from the east, I drove up and down the side streets of Old Key West, lined with ivy-covered hotels and inns and stately trees hung with moss. Avoiding the overcrowded Duval Street, I tried to decide the best way to attract the Daemoni. I hoped to find one or two on their own, separated from the crowds. And I hoped to set the scene up so I could pull them even farther away. I saw no need to involve innocent people. It took nearly an hour to find what I searched for.

I glanced down an alley as I slowly passed it and saw two men, a woman and a college-aged girl walking my way. I slowed the car. My sharp eyes recognized the dangerous situation immediately. The girl wasn't exactly walking. The others pushed and pulled her along. The Daemoni alarms sounded in my head. The group stopped about fifty yards from me, from the end of the alley, and the men started harassing the girl. I assumed they planned to rape her . . . or worse. I took a deep breath. *Here we go.*

I kicked off my flip-flops and left the keys in the ignition and the car door open behind me. I walked down the dark alley. Several Dumpsters and backdoors lined the brick walls on each side. Security lights over the doors provided pools of light between pits of darkness. The Daemoni surrounded the girl in a dark area between two Dumpsters. They pushed her around and tore at her thin, red blouse and white, satiny shorts, laughing wretchedly. Even the woman. The girl hunched over, trying in vain to protect herself. She looked taller than average and thin, but her arm and leg muscles were quite defined for a female. She looked as though she could hold her own against most normal humans. But these weren't normal humans. In fact, they weren't even human.

"Leave her alone," I said when I came close enough for them to hear me without having to yell.

"You ought to mind your own business, missy," the tall white-blond said without looking at me. He held the girl by her long, dark hair. She trembled so fiercely, the edges of her shape seemed to blur.

"You *are* my business," I replied, stepping closer.

They finally looked at me and they all froze. Even the girl, her face plastered in a grimace of pain as the first Daemoni still held her by the hair. She looked at me with pleading, fear-filled eyes, realizing she'd put herself in a bad situation. I could see why she willingly left her friends and went with them. The two men were quite attractive, dressed in silk shirts and dress pants, and they smelled nice—vanilla, freesia, rain, citrus, cinnamon . . . . Their looks and even their scents pulled her in.

They were vampires. Although subtle—they projected themselves as bait, not predators—I saw the unusually pale skin, the red tint to the irises and the slightly longer, pointy eye-teeth I knew were fangs. I wondered how she couldn't see any of it and then remembered I was specially tuned to them. The process of the *Ang'dora* had already sharpened my senses beyond her human abilities. My resolve tightened when I realized what they would have done to her.

"Well, well, what do we have here?" the woman sang. *How original.* The vampire sauntered away from the girl and closer to me, a smile spreading across her face. She looked surprisingly unattractive for a vampire, with a head of dull, pink hair that had the texture of a baby-doll's, obviously a wig, and very masculine features. And she stood quite tall, nearly as tall as the white-blond, her legs long and muscular under her mini-skirt. Her shoulders were nearly as wide as his, too, her tank top stretching across a flat chest . . . . *Oh!* She wasn't a she. She was a he. *Huh. A transvestite vampire.* I hid my mild shock behind a stoic face, trying to maintain a calm demeanor.

The third one moved toward me, also checking me out. He was shorter than the other two and not as muscular. But he was still dangerous . . . still a vampire.

The first one, the white-blond, still held the girl by her hair but had no interest in her. His red-tinted, ice-blue eyes studied me with curiosity, his full lips twitching with a smile.

"I think you know *exactly* what you have," I said. My

heart sped, as if trying to run away, as if it knew how much the vampires wanted it. The frantic pace probably excited them. But I acted as bravely as I possibly could, still trying to keep control of the situation. "So let her go and take me."

The blond let go of the girl's hair and seemed to pat her shoulder. She fell to the ground in a heap, as if shoved down by a great force. She looked up at me, her eyes wide and wild. Streaks ran down her cheeks as tears turned her make-up into little black rivers. I momentarily wondered what she would tell her friends . . . if she got back to them. Which was up to me.

"Are you *insane?*" she whispered to me.

I snorted at her choice of words. *If she only knew . . .*

"Probably," I said. "But you can go."

I glanced at the vampires. They paid her no attention, their eyes never leaving me. They walked slowly toward me, seemingly hesitant. They had to know something was coming. They surely weren't expecting Amadis royalty to simply hand herself over. *No, there are probably only two of us stupid enough to do that.* And I was the more ignorant one because I didn't even know what I was getting myself into.

I looked back at the girl and she crouched on the street, still shaking uncontrollably. If they really were anything like my vampires, they could feed off her fear. I had to make a move.

"Now!" I yelled. "*Run!*"

The girl moved awkwardly to her feet and stumbled away. I needed to keep the vamps interested in me so I took off the opposite way, toward the car. My scheme worked. They took no notice of her escape, all three chasing me. I could barely feel the ground under my feet. I ran pretty damn fast now, nearly flying. I just didn't know if I would be fast enough. I sprang into the driver's seat. They hit the car just as I slammed the door. Their fingers clawed at the convertible top. I flattened the gas pedal to the floor and pealed out. *Game on!*

The Daemoni kept pace with the car as I raced through the streets, pulling them into a darker area of town. I tried to get away from the residential area, but couldn't find a way out. Every street I turned down was lined with more houses. I rounded a corner. A brick wall rushed toward me. *Oh, shit!* I slammed on the brake and cranked the wheel, spinning the car around in a one-eighty, tires squealing. The smell of burning rubber filled the air. The three vampires rushed at me. I could see and hear people—innocent bystanders—not too far away. *This isn't good enough!*

I jumped out of the car, bounded on the back and hurdled the six-foot brick wall. I landed in the backyard of someone who wasn't home. No lights shone through the house windows, dark rectangles staring vacantly at nothing.

But I wasn't alone.

I straightened up from my crouch. I first noticed white legs that seemed to never end in a black leather mini-skirt that would have been a belt on anyone else. Her perfect breasts practically burst out of the black leather halter barely covering any of her pale white skin. Her long hair was white-blond, like the other vampire's, framing a striking face with red-tinted, ice-blue eyes that narrowed at me. This familiar blond beauty stood there as if she'd been waiting for me. And I remembered her clearly. Not just from the pub in Cape Heron the night I met Ian, although she'd been there, too. But from that Arlington street the night before we moved to Florida, when I was only eighteen and attacked by creatures I'd never known were real, until now.

She glanced up, behind me, at the other three standing on the wall, then made a face of disgust, revealing her fangs, as she looked me over.

"*This?*" she spat, looking at me but obviously talking to the others. "*This* is what he left me for?"

I stood frozen as she sauntered around me, studying me

from every angle. I tried to make my heart slow down, knowing its frenzied pace didn't help matters. I couldn't comprehend at first what she said.

"*You're* the little cunt Seth has been dying for?"

I flinched at her vulgarity. But then I realized the meaning behind her words. She used his old name, his Daemoni name, and she knew where he was. And she used present tense—not *died*, but dying. My heart sped even faster, but now with hope. And the hope gave me courage. I narrowed my eyes.

"You know where he is? Are you the cold-hearted leech who's been keeping him away from me?"

She laughed, the silvery chime both appealing and frightening at the same time. Her face was serious, her voice mocking. "If I had *my* way, I would be home with him right now, doing everything I've always fantasized about. Instead, I have to deal with *you*."

Her icy fingers suddenly gripped my throat. Not tight enough to choke me, but firm enough to communicate who was in control here. I held my ground, my eyes narrowed and my hands balled into fists at my side, trying to remain calm. After all, this is what I wanted.

"Vanessa!" The transvestite admonished. "Lucas wants her alive."

"To hell with Lucas," she hissed. "I've been waiting to tear her throat out since before she was born, when that whore of a mother of hers took my Seth."

Oh, ho, ho. Now you pissed me off.

Something horrible washed over me, penetrating into my very core. A sick, cold, hard feeling. One I'd never felt before in my life. My blood boiled with it. My head throbbed with it. My eyes saw red through it.

Hatred. Murderous hatred.

It wasn't jealousy. I knew who he loved. The feeling came from knowing she was the epitome of the Daemoni—the whole concept of everything I hated about my life, everything that had destroyed the normal life I so much desired, everything that had taken my love, my heart, my soul away—everything wrapped up in this white-blond beauty. I *hated* her and all I wanted to do was kick her dead ass into non-existence.

One of the others—the blond—chortled, the maniacal sound echoing my own madness. "He was never yours. You've never been right in the head, sis. But, hey, if you want to take her, I won't stop you."

Vanessa laughed again as her hand tightened around my neck. "You're damn right I do!"

"I don't think so, *bitch!*" I grasped her arm with both hands and yanked her hand away from my neck as I kicked her in the stomach, launching her back several feet. She landed with an ass-plant on the grass, astonishment quickly turning to outrage. I turned to the others.

"I'll go with you, but you keep *her* off of me."

She sprang from the ground and lunged at me, shoving me into the brick wall. My head and back smacked hard against it and pricks of light flashed before my eyes. She pinned me with her hand on my neck again. I pulled my legs to my chest and pushed out, driving her back. I ran for the middle of the yard to avoid being cornered against the wall. She lunged at me again.

I ducked and she flew over me, her nails grazing my back, cutting one of the dress straps loose. Then I did something I didn't know I had in me. Something I would never be able to duplicate if I tried. I went all ninja on her ass.

Bent over at the waist, I twisted my hips and threw my legs upward as if attempting a new kind of cartwheel. My feet thudded against her hard body in quick succession as she soared overhead. My torso followed the spin of my lower body, bringing me around upright, and I landed lithely on my feet. So did she.

Her eyes blazed, her stunning face screwed into hideousness with fury. She looked like the monster she was. I wondered what the hell I thought I was doing, fighting a *vampire*. But only for a moment. That's all she gave me before she charged at me again. I wasn't quick enough. I *wasn't* a vampire.

We soared across the yard and crashed through a glass patio table. *Oh, shit! Not glass!* She landed on top of me and yanked me over onto my back. Her left hand once again gripped my throat, pinning me down. The glass shards under me stabbed through my skin. I gasped for air. Pain shot through my torso and pierced my lungs. *Something's broken.* But that wasn't the worst problem.

The worst was the blood. I smelled the acrid iron of it first. Then I felt the wet warmth spreading on my face. The taste of salty rust filled my mouth. *Blood is so not good.*

The other three instantly hovered over us, their tongues swiping across their lips, pulled into maniacal grins. All four faces looked down at me hungrily, their eyes glowing red. Hissing-snarling sounds rumbled in their throats. Vanessa peeled her lips back into a detestable grin, exposing razor-sharp teeth and pointed fangs.

"She's *mine!*" she growled at the others. And I knew then, without a doubt, she was the woman in the street in Virginia. She'd said then I was always *hers.* And now she finally had me.

The others pulled slightly back but started crowding over us again, drawn to the blood. Low growls rolled in their chests.

With her right hand, Vanessa shoved my left shoulder down against the glass and cement. She moved her left hand to my right shoulder. Her knee pressed sharply into my thigh. I couldn't move. But I could breathe again. I inhaled, but it was more of a choking gasp as pain seared through my chest. My vision blurred and dimmed as her face came down to mine, her scent of lavender, vanilla and cigarettes enveloping me.

I knew this was it. She was too strong for me. Fear and pain replaced my anger, eradicating any inhuman power I'd possessed just a few minutes ago. She hovered over my cheek. Her cool breath slid against my hot, wet skin. She inhaled deeply and a satisfactory smile overcame her face, lighting it up with more beauty than she'd ever shown before. Some part of me—the human part falling for her inhuman glamour—ached for her touch. For her bite.

"Ah, at least you'll be delicious." She ran her tongue over my cheek, lapping the fresh blood. "Mmm. Tasty. Ready to join your man in hell?"

"If that's where he is," I whispered, my voice gurgling with blood.

She bent her head lower, to my throat, her hair feeling like soft wisps of silk as it fell on my face. I closed my eyes, hoping it would be fast. I felt the teeth and fangs cut through my skin, like a knife slicing into a tomato—slight resistance at first, then an easy slide through the soft flesh. Then she sucked. My blood seemed to gush through my body, rushing through my veins, looking for that outlet into her mouth, as if it wanted to be drained.

Good-bye, Dorian. You'll be safe now. Mommy loves you.

Just as everything went nearly black, I no longer felt her weight on my shoulders and thigh. *What happened? Owen?* I couldn't move, could barely see, but I could hear the fighting sounds clearly. Hisses and growls and thuds and screechy, scraping sounds, like metal against stone. It had to be Owen. And others. Too much action went on for Owen to be alone.

I wanted to yell at them to stop, to let the Daemoni have me, to not sacrifice their lives to save mine. That this was what I wanted and what they all needed. But I couldn't do anything but lay there and listen. Then the sounds and movement suddenly ceased. All I could hear was heavy breathing. I tried to move, to see what was going on, but I couldn't. My body felt numb, lifeless.

"You're really doing this?" Vanessa shrieked. "You're still choosing *her*?"

She heaved the last word.

"You're damn right. Until death." The silky, smooth voice still lovely, even in anger.

"If you think I won't kill you, you're wrong!" Vanessa screeched.

More fighting sounds. All I saw were flashes of darker black against the gray of my vision.

"Get them *both*!" one of the male vampires yelled.

"I can't!"

"He's too strong!"

Several *Pops!* And then silence.

Except for my raspy, gurgled breaths.

It was over. They were all gone. I was left here to die. And I welcomed it. I welcomed the final darkness so I would never have to feel the pain again. I was ready to sink into it, looking for the relief of death.

Blood filled my lungs and throat. My vision blurred and darkened. It went black. And there he was. My Knight in shining armor, my hero. I'd never seen anything so beautiful.

"Alexis," he said softly, his voice more sublime than I remembered. His hand lightly brushed the hair out of my face. Tiny grains of glass scratched across my skin. "My beautiful Alexis."

He bent closer, his face filling my dim vision. Through the dark blur, I saw my sweet love. The hazel eyes had the same gold sparkle, even in the anxious expression. He picked glass off my face and each time he touched me, ever so gently, I felt a small electrical pulse. Then he carefully slid his arms under me and lifted me off the ground. Everything went black.

I felt a sudden change around me. I heard the water nearby and crunching of feet on gravel. We seemed to be going up steps and then the light shone brightly. The air smelled like our beach house . . . *or Heaven.*

And I knew. This was it. I'd been wrong all along. He *was* dead. And now I had joined him. We were finally together again. He'd carried me up the stairway to Heaven.

But wait.

Something wasn't right.

It wasn't exactly his face. This one was distorted. *Wouldn't he be perfect in Heaven?*

And the *pain.* Excruciating pain shot through my ribs and back. *How come there's so much pain in death?*

Am I not dead?

But if I'm not . . .

I tried so hard to not let the pain overcome me again as I looked into the scarred face for my answer. But I fought a losing battle. I could barely breathe through the fluid in my lungs. I let my eyes close, unconsciousness tugging at me, but I wouldn't go yet. As he carried me, he bent his head down to mine, his lips in my hair.

"Ah, Lexi," he murmured. "*Ma lykita.*"

My eyes flew open and I gasped loudly, painfully. *No! Oh, no, no, no!* I tried to fight the blackness. *I have to know!*

My mind screamed, but I couldn't get any more out than a weak whisper. "Tristan?"

"Shh. It's okay. I've got you now, my love."

Blackness overcame me. The last thing I remembered was the smell of a summer's day—mangos and papayas, lime and sage and a hint of man.

Chapter 8

I ran through a golden meadow, the grass as high as my waist, the sun bright and warm on my skin. I didn't know this place and I didn't care. Snow-capped mountains surrounded me and a lake spread out before me. My body felt light as happiness filled every cell. I burst through the meadow's edge and my feet sunk into soft sand. And I couldn't stop laughing. As the image faded, one word floated lazily in my head like a feather drifting on the air: "Happy."

When the image disappeared completely and consciousness returned, I couldn't bring myself to open my eyes. The soft and plump pillows cradled my head. The sheets felt smooth and satiny against my skin. I felt so comfortable and relaxed, I was sure my body, feeling nearly numb and weightless, still slept. Or, perhaps, it just no longer existed.

I sensed bright light on the other side of my eyelids. I heard waves in the distance. I also heard someone breathing close . . . very close. A familiar, tangy-sweet scent filled my head and coated the back of my throat. *Mmm . . .* I smiled in my mind. *Am I still dreaming or am I in Heaven?*

I sensed someone watching me. *Mom? Owen? Angels? Jesus?!* I shifted slightly, wishing the feeling would go away. *Son of a witch! Ouch!* So lying still felt very good, but moving did not. And the pain confirmed I was, indeed, awake. And alive.

Then the events of last night flooded into my consciousness. The scene played out against the backs of my eyelids. Walking up to the Daemoni, handing myself over to them. The beautiful, blonde vampire. Crashing through the glass table. The *bite . . .* My hand flew to my neck.

"Am I a vampire?" I asked aloud, my voice husky so it sounded more like a croak. If I'd been turned, I wanted to be prepared. The world would be a different place for me.

A familiar chuckle nearby. *Oh, how I love that sound.* "No. Definitely not."

Ah. That silky, smooth, lovely voice, like honey mixed with butter. And I remembered the rest . . . including what he called me. My eyes sprang open.

And there he lay. Looking like an angel. Perhaps he was.

Right in front of me, on the pillow next to mine, rested the face I'd been dreaming about. The one I'd nearly forgotten and held onto so tightly so I never would. Even more sublime than I ever allowed myself to remember. But . . . not exactly the same. Ugly scars marred the perfection. Yet still breathtaking. The most beautiful sight I'd ever seen.

He couldn't possibly be real.

I squeezed my eyes shut, mentally cussing out Swirly for pulling this ultimate head job on me. Just when I thought I'd finally pulled myself away from the edge of the abyss, that I was safe from falling in, I had apparently plunged all the way to the bottom. And Swirly ruled this place, creating impossible aberrations that hit all of my senses. *But why?* Had my mind created a safe place because what truly existed was too horrible for me to handle—being held captive by the Daemoni? Or had they brainwashed me? Or was I right about Swirly playing her most cruel game ever?

I shook my head, denying it all. *I have to face this. Whatever it is, I chose it. This is what I wanted.* I inhaled deeply and slowly, ignoring the protest from my ribs, and slowly peeked out of one eye. Nothing had changed. Still in my bed in the Caribbean room. Still the beautiful face watching me. Those hazel eyes—green on the outside, gold flecks around the pupils—staring into mine with the deepest love. He lifted an eyebrow. My own eyes widened. *Could it possibly be . . . ?*

My heart skipped an unnatural rhythm as I swallowed the lump in my throat. I lifted my shaking hand, hesitated with the thought that this would kill me if I was wrong, and then finally reached for his face. I barely touched his cheek with my fingertips. Electricity sparked. My heart jumped. Tears sprang to my eyes. My whole body started trembling.

"*Tristan?*"

I barely caught his wide grin as he pulled me into his strong arms, pressing me against his hard body. My own body ached but I didn't care. It felt unreal to be close to him again. To smell his scent, to feel his strength and warmth, to be in his arms when I thought I never would be again.

"Tristan, my sweet Tristan?" I cried, wanting to believe but still afraid to. Afraid demonic magic made me believe in this moment so they could rip him away again, a part of their torture for me. Or, worse, afraid I would wake up, completely alone, nothing changed, just another foggy morning.

"Yes, my love, I'm here now." His lips found mine in a deep, loving kiss and they were so full and so soft. So gentle and lovely. So real. He wiped the tears from my face but they kept coming. "I'm here, *ma lykita*."

Nothing had ever sounded so good to my ears. And I dared to allow myself to believe. I cried as I tried to kiss him all over while holding on to him as tightly as I could. He returned every one of my kisses, covering every inch of my face. The pieces of my heart fused back together with every kiss and it swelled so large, I felt sure my chest couldn't contain it anymore. The emotions overwhelmed me and I sobbed in his arms as he held me.

"I can't believe . . . it's really you . . . I'm not hallucinating . . . I'm not *dead*?" I sputtered between tears and kisses.

"We're together, my love. It's real."

A million questions raced through my mind, but I didn't want to talk or think yet. I just wanted to hold him closely and savor the feeling of finally being together. I actually held him in my arms once again. I couldn't let go of him, still afraid if I did, he would disappear.

I finally pulled back just enough to look into his face.

"It's really you?"

He nodded. His beautiful, full lips pulled into a stunning grin. *Oh, that exquisite smile I would have died to see again.* His eyes held mine for several minutes, the gold sparkling brightly, the green like bright, shiny emeralds. I could see the love and happiness in their depths. *Has he always been this damn* gorgeous? I felt sure he had been. I remembered how he took my breath away, but he seemed just so unreal now. He looked like an angel . . . except for those scars.

My brows pushed together as I studied the scars, sadness overwhelming me. I traced each one with my fingertips—one curved down from his right temple to below his eye, another stretched across his left cheek, and a third cut across his chin. There were several smaller ones, too. Tears filled my eyes.

"What *happened* to you?" I whispered. "Where have you *been*? I've been so . . . so . . ."

I couldn't say the words. So *what*? So desolate. So lost. So alone. So *insane*.

His face darkened a shade. He put his finger to my lips.

"Shh . . . not now." He closed his eyes and tightened his arms around me. "I just want to hold you now that I can. Feel your heart beat against me. Know you're here and you're okay. It feels so . . . *amazing*."

"It feels like Heaven," I whispered, laying my head against his chest.

"This *has* been my vision of Heaven for a long time," he said. We lay in silence, staring at each other. I couldn't keep my hands away from him—over his face, across his chest, along his hair to the ponytail behind his head—needing to physically touch him.

It really felt like Heaven on Earth. The depression, the anger, the insanity already felt like a distant memory now that I lay in his arms again. I hadn't even realized how small and cold my heart had been until now. It swelled with love and warmed with happiness with every beat we lay there. He was my warmth and my light, chasing away Psycho and Foggy and possibly even Swirly.

"How do you feel?" he finally asked.

"Um, I don't know. Tremendously happy doesn't do it justice. I can't even think of the right words. It's too . . . *big*."

He chuckled and kissed my forehead. "I completely understand. But I meant, how do you feel physically?"

"Oh." I did a quick physical assessment. "Sore, if I move. And thirsty."

He reached over me for a glass of water on the nightstand. I consumed every last drop of the refreshing liquid, the cool wetness feeling like a salve on my raw throat.

"I don't feel too bad, considering. I think I had some broken ribs."

"And probably a punctured lung. But you're healing unusually fast."

He looked at me with a strange expression. He narrowed his eyes as he searched my face.

"What?" I asked, feeling self-conscious. He'd probably been watching me sleep for some time, but I felt awkward as he looked at me like that. It had been so long to even have his eyes on me.

"Just thinking . . ." He seemed to change thought processes as his expression returned to nothing but love. ". . . how beautiful you are and how much I love you."

He kissed me on the lips, the electricity charging between us. I returned the kiss with a deep hunger, not able to get enough of him.

"I've missed you so much," I breathed, as more tears fell. "I just can't believe it . . . ."

I pulled myself into him, pressing as tightly as I could, kissing the scars on his cheeks and his chin and down his neck, burying my face in the crook between his neck and shoulder and inhaling deeply.

He stiffened and a low, quiet growl escaped from his throat. I looked up into his face. Flames burned in his eyes. I pulled back slowly, not wanting to do anything rash, not knowing what this meant. At one time, such a sound meant danger—that the monster within him fought for control, fighting to kill me. Our union supposedly squashed the monster, but . . . My heartbeat picked up pace. I thought he was *my* Tristan . . . but he'd also become somewhat of a stranger to me now.

"Tristan . . . ?" I whispered hesitantly.

He blinked and focused on me, the fire controlled, and then closed his eyes and leaned back. He let out a heavy sigh.

"I'm so sorry," he finally whispered. "I don't know what they've done to me."

"Shh . . . It's okay," I told him as much as myself. "We've been through this before. We can do it again."

"I had nearly twenty years to prepare myself to be around you last time."

"But you are still *Amadis*. And you know you have our love. You have my trust. That's what it takes. We can do this."

He cupped my face in his hand and looked at me with desperation in his eyes. "God, I love you, Alexis. I love you so much. I held onto you like a life rope. Only you—my love for you—could pull me through."

My own sufferings suddenly felt insignificant. The excruciating pain I'd felt couldn't possibly equate to all he'd gone through. I knew this even without knowing the story. I heard this truth in his voice. I saw it in the scars. My heart squeezed with love and guilt and compassion and grief. He'd endured so much—for us.

"I held on to the other end of the rope, pulling from here," I whispered.

He stroked my cheek and brushed my hair back. "They told me so many different lies . . . you found someone else, they'd killed you, you'd killed yourself. But I just had to hang on anyway and if any of it were true, I would die at my own hand, not theirs."

"Tristan . . . don't ever say . . ." I shook my head. I told myself such talk didn't matter because none of what they'd told him was true. "I *never* gave up on you. I never have and never will stop loving you. I am yours. You and me together forever. Nothing can change that."

"You don't know how good it is to hear that."

He kissed me on the mouth again and our lips moved together with a desperate longing built over seven-and-a-half years. His tangy-sweetness filled my mouth and I didn't think I could ever get enough of the delicious taste. My body wanted to melt into his and I needed to feel his skin next to mine. I tugged his shirt off and pressed tightly against him, kissing his shoulder and neck. I felt the scars on his back, rigid under my fingertips. My heart contracted again. He pulled away and rolled onto his back, sighing heavily.

I turned onto my stomach so I could see his face, being careful, but the condition of my ribs had already improved. His eyes were closed and he breathed deeply for control. I studied his face, every inch, from the perfectly angled eyebrows and the long, dark lashes lying against his high cheekbones to the straight nose, full lips and square chin. Even with the scars, no creature on Earth was as beautiful as him.

And then I saw the mangled Amadis mark.

"*Tristan!* What did they *do?*"

Thick, nasty scars covered the whole left side of his chest, curving and twisting, as if snakes bored and tangled under his skin. I gingerly slid my fingertips along the gnarled ridges. Something about them made my stomach clench with the sick feeling of hatred and malevolence. He clasped his hand down on mine and held my palm against his chest.

"What did they *not* do?" he muttered, staring at the ceiling. "First, they tried torture, trying to force me to change my loyalty back to them. Physical torture, emotional, mental . . . they did all kinds of unimaginable things. But I refused. Nothing—no amount of pain or misery—could pull me away from you. Then they tried to bribe me with power and control over everything, over the world. When I still rejected them, they tried to kill me, using every technique possible. But they couldn't do it. I refused to die at their hands. They finally decided cutting my heart out would be the only way to kill me."

I gasped as my own heart nearly broke again and my stomach rolled with nausea. He continued staring at the ceiling, his hand still clamped on mine, over his heart, and the electric current flowed between us. I felt so helpless, wanting to do something for him.

"They couldn't even take my heart, though," he continued. "Regardless of what kind of instrument or weapon covered with a variety of poisons and spells they tried to use, the skin immediately healed up right behind it. Their dark magic left scars, but they couldn't get any deeper than the skin." He finally looked at me, his eyes moist and filled with a mixture of pain, appreciation and love. "See . . . *you* already had my heart."

My free hand flew to my mouth as the breath caught in my throat. I stared at him wide-eyed, more tears falling.

He closed his eyes again and pressed my hand harder against his chest. "I can feel your power. It feels *good.*"

I collapsed against him and cried into his chest. *How could I have been so angry and selfish?*

"I'm so *sorry,*" I wailed between sobs.

"Sorry? You saved me, Alexis. You *protected* me." He tried to pull me closer but I resisted, shifting so I could look him in the eye.

"I behaved horribly. Really, *really* horribly," I admitted. "I felt such anger toward you for leaving me, never really thinking about what you may have been going through. I only knew my own pain and it was nothing . . . nothing compared to . . . to . . ."

I choked on the thought of what he'd endured and buried my face back into his chest, wishing I could crawl into some dark hole and never have to show my face again. Or to be pummeled with stones or tarred and feathered or lashed with a vine whip. I deserved to be tortured by all means possible and still everything combined wouldn't compare to what he'd gone through.

"I honestly hope it wasn't 'nothing.' I hoped you missed me at least half as much as I missed you. I hung onto that hope." He kissed the top of my head as I continued crying into his chest. "I'm just sorry I couldn't get back to you sooner. I know seven years is a long time for you. You had every right to hurt and feel angry."

"I did miss you so much. And it was so long," I blubbered. "I even thought I started to forget your face, my memory fading, and with everything else going on, I thought I was losing my mind. I tried so hard to hang on to you, I started hallucinating that I saw you and heard you."

He shifted under me. "Mmm. You mean recently?"

I stopped crying. "Yeah. Why?"

"You weren't hallucinating, my love."

I inhaled sharply as my head snapped up. My eyes narrowed. "That *was* you? In the backyard, at the park, in Key West?"

He nodded. I didn't know whether to be grateful that I hadn't been quite as crazy as I'd thought or angry that he'd been back for over a week, letting the darkness get the best of me. If I hadn't been so happy to be in his arms again, anger would have definitely won.

"Why would you *do* that to me?" I breathed, pushing away from him. "How could you be here for so long and not come to me? Why would you let me go through all that?"

"Please don't be angry." He pulled me back into his arms. I let him, wanting to release the bitterness and animosity for good. "Trust me, it wasn't easy. I wanted to go straight to you and finally hold you. But I had to test myself all over again. I'm still not sure what their magic may have done to my subconscious. Seven years doesn't feel as long to me, so I could wait a few more days. Ensuring I had control was worth the delay. Unbearable but necessary." He sighed. "I shouldn't have let you see me, but sometimes I just couldn't bring myself to flash. I wanted you to run to me, into my arms. And then you gave me a real scare the other morning in Key West. They watched too closely, or I would have just taken you then."

"That Daemoni who chased me . . . ," I whispered.

"I distracted him away from you." He shrugged. "He was weak. My presence was enough to scare him away. He could have known Owen approached, too. As soon as I sensed Owen coming and knew you'd be okay, I took off, still not sure if I was ready yet."

"So . . . do you want to kill me?" I whispered.

"*I* don't. But, I don't know what's inside, what they've done. We'll need to be careful again."

The corners of his lips tugged in a sad smile and my shoulders sank with disappointment. We'd fought and won this battle so many years ago, but it had taken much time and patience.

"Do you want to kill me?" he asked.

I looked up at him in surprise. "*What*? Why would I want to do that?"

"I can feel the power building in you." He placed my hand back over his heart.

"I would never want to *kill* you. Amadis *love*. We save, not kill."

"You don't know what that power will make you want to do. And we won't know until you change over and have received the full force." He studied my face and lifted my hair away from my shoulder, twirling a lock around his finger. "And I know you're changing, Lex. I can see it. You look completely different than you did a week ago."

I groaned. "I can't believe you saw me like that."

"You'd been through a lot, my love. And you were incredibly beautiful to me." He smiled and winked. I'd forgotten the brain-fog that blanketed my mind when he winked and I welcomed it, gazing at him stupidly. He laughed. "I missed that look."

I raised my eyebrows. "You like it when I look like an idiot?"

He laughed again. I loved the sound. "You don't look like an idiot. You get this look like you adore me, like I'm the only person in your world. And I love that."

"Really? Well, I *do* adore you." I kissed him. And I couldn't control myself. I wanted him so badly. *Needed* him. And I needed to show him how much I missed him. How much I loved him and wanted him. How happy I felt to have him back. Kissing just wasn't enough to communicate all of my emotions. I needed to feel him, every inch of him, inside and out. My hands locked against his face as my body ground against his.

"Slow and careful," he murmured, pulling my hands from his face and gently pushing me back. The fire in his eyes looked controlled. I knew the look. Whatever happened to him over the years, he *was* my Tristan and he still loved me. I trusted he wouldn't do anything to me.

"You underestimate yourself," I muttered.

"Maybe. But I'm not taking any chances."

"I'm stronger now. And if you hurt me, I'll just heal."

"You know it's not about just hurting you. We know we can handle that. Remember?" The gold flecks in his eyes sparkled as he remembered our honeymoon and our few times together. We'd both had bruises from the supernatural force of our passion, even in the beginning, when I was relatively normal. I couldn't help but smile. And want him even more.

"I was ready to die last night anyway," I said with a shrug. "At least now it'd be while making love to you one last time."

He glared at me. "That's not funny."

I rolled my eyes.

"I've waited too long to see you and hold you again for it to come to such a gruesome ending," he said, making an effort to keep the mood light. He took my hand and kissed the tips of each of my fingers, then my engagement ring. He lifted the pendant off my chest and noticed the key still hanging there.

"You really waited," he murmured.

"Of course."

"Lucas said they'd convinced you I was dead."

I shuddered at the thought, then shook my head. "The only news I ever heard was just a couple days ago. A video sent to convince me . . . but I just couldn't believe it. I knew I still needed to hang onto the hope for you."

"Thank you," he whispered as he let go of the pendant, his fingers brushing lightly against my neck.

"Did a vampire really bite me?" I asked, his touch on my throat reminding me.

His face went dark and he frowned. "I'm sorry I didn't get there in time."

"You were *just* in time." I remembered the blonde bending over, her mouth at my throat, and shuddered. "So how come I'm not a vampire now?"

"You have Amadis blood *and* Daemoni blood. Vampires are nothing compared to that combination. Besides, it takes more than just a bite."

"Oh." I shivered, remembering the hatred I'd felt for the blonde. "Who is she?"

Tristan grunted. "Do we really have to talk about her?"

"You don't want to tell me." It wasn't a question. History apparently existed between them, history he didn't want me to know about. Possibly even recent history. My heart shrunk at the thought. *Did he faithfully wait for me as I had for him? Did he have a choice?* These were unknowns I wasn't sure I wanted the answers to. I just wanted to be happy he came back to *my* side—that he wanted to be here with *me* and nowhere else. But still . . .

He rolled over on his side and sighed heavily with resignation. *Here it comes.* "Vanessa is just a spoiled brat who somehow got the idea in her head a long time ago that she and I should be together and she won't give up."

My throat worked overtime as I tried to swallow the disappointment. "So you and her . . . ?"

He lifted my chin with his thumb to look into my eyes. "*Never.*"

I blew out a sigh of relief. I hadn't even realized I held my breath.

"She doesn't seem to think so. And she certainly doesn't like me."

He chuckled. "She's used to getting everything she wants and doesn't like to be told no. I've told her 'no' many times. In fact, given the choice, you are my only 'yes.'"

"So no others I should be worried about?"

"I don't think so."

My stomach rolled. "You don't *think* so?"

His voice came soft and low. "Alexis, I've been around a long time. You know I had a past, but no one else has pursued me anything like Vanessa."

I bit my lower lip and nodded. "So no one . . ." My breath hitched as I forced the words out. ". . . more recently?"

He braced my face in his hands. "Absolutely not. Only you, my love. *You* have my heart, my soul . . . my everything. I would have let them kill me before betraying my love for you."

I searched his eyes and only saw sincerity. And deep-rooted, soul-bound love.

"I remembered her from a long time ago," I said, "when she and the others attacked me before we moved to Florida . . . ." That whole night came back to me with perfect clarity and I remembered being attacked with a certainty I'd never had about it before. I had been right. I hadn't mixed up the details or confused the real events with a dream, as I had thought . . . as Mom had made me believe. There *had* been a witch and a werewolf and Vanessa the vampire . . . . "Holy hell! That was you and Owen who saved me!"

He chuckled. "I wondered if you ever figured that out. I'd been watching you that night. Owen was hanging out with me."

"So what took you so long? They would have killed me!"

"We would have never let it get that far, but, first, we had to see just how far they would go. If we stepped in unnecessarily, Sophia would have killed us for breaching the secrecy. But when Vanessa showed up, I made Owen go in. And then . . . I just couldn't help it. I couldn't just watch without helping him. It was reckless on my part—not knowing if I'd want to hurt them . . . or you." His voice trailed off at the thought, but then picked up again. "I'm sorry I couldn't tell you before. Sophia said you couldn't know. In fact, Owen was supposed to erase the details from your mind, but he couldn't bring himself to do the job completely. He didn't think it right and I thought you deserved to know enough to be aware and alert. But Sophia disagreed. She insisted that you at least thought the attack was a dream, until . . . well, until now, I suppose."

"Do you know I dreamt of you every night after that? Of course, I didn't know who you were then. And then the dreams stopped—" *Oh!* I smiled. "They stopped the night I met you, well, when we *actually* met, that first night of college. Do you remember that night?"

"How could I forget?" He smiled at the memory. "I thought converting to the Amadis changed my life forever, but I still lived in the shadows. My own shadows, not theirs anymore, but still a darkness as deep as the night. When I met you . . . it was like someone finally turned the light on. Or the sun came out. For months, I could feel something out there, an energy I felt pulled to. But I wanted to resist the draw, not knowing what it was. My darkness blinded me to the truth. It was you—your life and hope and love—pulling me and I didn't know it until that night."

We exchanged grins—along with the feeling of knowing something magical had already been in the works, long before we actually met. He kissed me and I returned it. And the passionate desire rose again. *Damn it! Damn* them*!* Before I got carried away, only to be disappointed, I pulled back and reluctantly rolled out of bed. I really didn't want to leave his side, part of me still afraid he would be gone when I returned, but I couldn't put some things off any longer.

"I can't believe you left me in this disgusting dress," I said as I headed into the bathroom.

"I didn't trust myself to undress you." He paused, then added lightly, "I might've taken advantage of you."

"Yeah, right."

I looked at myself in the mirror. He'd left the blood-stained dress on me, but it looked like he'd removed all the glass—no lumps under my skin—and cleaned up the cuts. They were completely healed now and only a few specks of dried blood remained. I wondered if he had healed me. At one time, that had freaked me out—his ability to heal other people—because he had to suck my blood. Not for nourishment, like a vampire, but to clean the wound because it couldn't heal itself. Now, though, I didn't care if he'd healed the cuts and didn't even ask. I drew in some deep breaths and I felt well, healed. Pulling the dress over my head didn't hurt at all. I tossed the ruined dress into the trash.

I stood under the hot shower—*our* shower, it felt natural to be in here now—and let the water flow over my body. It felt remarkably good, washing away years of crusted-on pain and darkness. All of my anger flowed away and swirled down the drain. I wanted to stand there forever, but I also wanted to hurry, to be back in Tristan's arms. When I turned around, though, I saw him watching me from the bathroom door. A minute later, he stepped in to join me, my soap and shampoo in his hands. His hair hung loose now and to his shoulders, falling in his face. I brushed it away and his eyes smoldered.

"Are you sure?" I asked.

He smiled. "I'm sure I can't stand it any longer."

He pulled me into his arms and we were finally flesh against flesh. The electricity jolted between us and it had never felt so good. Every touch shocked me. Every kiss on my neck, my chest, my breasts sent a current through my nerves, making my body throb desperately in anticipation. I was so hungry for him. It had been so long. So agonizingly long. I wanted to devour him, to pull him into me, to sink into him. To be one with him again. He finally lifted me to him and I wrapped my legs around his waist. My back arched and I moaned as he slid inside me.

And he growled, a deep, guttural resonance.

If I hadn't heard it before, the baritone sound might have been funny. But I knew that sound, from long ago. My heart raced faster as I looked into his flaming eyes. I tried not to panic and said what I thought he needed to hear, what he needed to be reminded of.

"I love you, Tristan," I whispered.

The flames died down as he held me still against him, one hand between my shoulder blades and his other at the small of my back. His breathing slowed a bit. He focused on me, only sparks left in his eyes. It worked.

"Mmm . . . I love you, too, *ma lykita.*"

We were cautious and reckless at the same time. Slow at first, like swimmers testing the water, making sure no danger lurked below. Then quickly giving in to our urgent hunger.

Our physical needs were so great, our bodies so desperate, the motions became fast and fervent and frenzied. And the whole thing was over in an instant with an explosive force that racked our bodies and made us both cry out. We crumpled to the floor of the shower, holding each other and panting. Our hearts pounded like bass drums, not realizing we'd already reached the crescendo.

"That was . . . necessary," Tristan muttered and we burst into giddy laughter.

Chapter 9

When I came out of the bathroom wrapped in a towel, I found a pile of sheets on the floor and Tristan, a towel around his waist, sitting on the freshly made bed. I had to pinch my arm . . . just to be sure. As he rummaged through his old bag, I picked up the sheets and took them to the washer, knowing the sooner I soaked them in cold water, the more likely the blood from my injuries would wash out. I didn't get my hopes up, though. I probably should have washed clothes first, but I thought we might need clean sheets before I needed clothes. I *would* get my hopes up about that.

I came back to the room and recognized my lavender stationery in Tristan's hand, his head bent over as he read the letters I'd written to him over the years. His hair hung in curtains, hiding his face. Sadness swept over me again. The letters, one for each of our wedding anniversaries, provided glimpses into my and Dorian's lives each year. They also begged for his return, full of raw emotion. Tucking them into his bag had been my way of delivering them, though I never really expected him to actually read them. I wasn't sure now I wanted him to know how wretched I'd been.

I crawled across the bed and knelt behind him, rubbing his shoulders as he read the last one. He didn't say anything at first. I draped my arms around him and lay my head against his shoulder. When he finally spoke, his voice came thick and heavy.

"You know, it felt like a long time only because I couldn't be with you. But seven years really isn't that long to me—feels like a year to most people. But for you . . ." He trailed off.

"It was painfully long," I finished quietly.

"And our son . . . I missed so much," he whispered. "I should have been there for him."

I moved around to sit in his lap and wrapped my arms around him. I didn't even know what to say, so I just held him. I felt his tears on my shoulder.

"I don't know if it'll make you feel any better, but I really don't remember much until I was five or so," I finally said. "You'll be there from now on and you're just in time for the good part. You missed the middle-of-the-night feedings, diapers and potty training. Now he's really becoming a little person."

"I would have loved every minute," he said quietly and I knew he would have. "The first chance I had to get to a computer, I did a search on you. I saw how the media tore you up over your so-called teen pregnancy. I almost went on a murderous rampage."

I shrugged. "I knew the truth. The people most important to me knew the truth. Including Dorian."

"Tell me about him."

I smiled automatically, my heart warming. "Well . . . he looks just like you, but he has quite an attitude, like me. Well, you, too. I think he got the worst of us both—but in a good way. He won't take crap from anyone. He's unusually fast and strong for his age and size and he never gets sick or hurt, even with all the fights he's been in. Mom says it's to be expected, with who his parents are. Otherwise, he shows no signs of abilities or powers . . . but every once in a while he gets this look on his face as if he knows something the rest of us don't."

I jabbered non-stop about Dorian and Tristan's face lit up like the sun. He asked me all kinds of questions and laughed at the stories I shared. A bittersweet conversation for us both.

"I can't wait for you to get to know him. And he'll be so excited to finally meet you." I sighed as I realized how much I missed him.

And then there was the bad news. He already knew, but I had to say the words, we had to discuss the subject. I hung my head in shame and the words came out as barely more than a whisper. "As you can see, we don't have a daughter."

He pulled me against him and grief filled his voice, too. "I'm so sorry. I've tried to forget the time I was away, pushing each day out of my mind as the next one started, but I'll never forget the day Dorian came into the world. The Daemoni celebrated. That's how they tortured me that day—celebrating that the Amadis would end with you. And it was probably the worst torture of the whole time they held me, because I needed you and I knew you needed me. It almost killed me to think of you suffering through that, and I couldn't hold you. I couldn't do anything for you . . . ."

The tears spilled over the brims of my eyes.

"I failed them," I whispered.

"No, not you. I'm the one who failed them."

I looked up at him in surprise. "How can you say that?"

"The father's genes determine the sex."

I shook my head. "I know, but we're different. According to Mom and Rina, our eggs can only accept female sperm. Once there's a forming embryo, we might drop another egg that would take a male sperm. Otherwise, males are rejected. Except for me, of course. Something happened to the female . . . or there just never was one and my egg took the male seed. I have to be abnormal in *everything*."

He held me in silence for a while. "Is there any hope?"

My breath caught as my mood suddenly brightened. The words gushed out. "Oh! There is! Tristan, there *is* hope. I'd dismissed the idea because you weren't here, but now you are and it could still happen."

"Whoa . . . slow down." He took my face in his hands and looked into my eyes. "Tell me."

I told him about Mom and Rina's *feelings* that I may still be able to have a daughter. "I suppressed that hope because you were gone and you are my only love. I couldn't—"

"You would have forsaken an Amadis daughter to wait for me?" He didn't sound happy.

I frowned and dropped my head. "Maybe not forever," I admitted. "But I thought if it ever became necessary, in vitro fertilization would have been the answer. It just wasn't something I wanted to think about too much. The council has been growing restless about it lately, I guess, and were forcing me to think about it. Thank God you're here now!"

He lifted my chin with his thumb and looked into my eyes again. "And there's still hope? Even with the *Ang'dora*?"

Right. The Ang'dora.

My bubble burst. A whimpering sound escaped my throat as I dropped my shoulders with defeat. For the first time in years, I wished the *Ang'dora* wouldn't happen yet. And what would the council do now, if it was impossible for me to have a baby? With the *Ang'dora*, there were too many odds against us.

"I don't know. I'm not even supposed to change over yet— I'm supposed to be too young. Another anomaly to chalk under

~ 133 ~

my name. Of course, Mom's the only one who had a baby after the change. But I guess it does mean there's precedence."

"So we can try." His lips twitched in a playful smile.

"Well, yeah, we can try all we want." I grinned back with understanding.

"Then we will do everything we can to give Dorian a little sister." He winked and I fogged over. He chuckled and nibbled my ear. The tickle cleared the fog.

"I need to call Dorian," I said. "I haven't talked to him in so long. I wish he could be here."

Tristan glanced at the clock. "Give them another hour or so. I talked to Sophia before you woke up and they were between flights then."

"You talked to Mom? Where are they? She knows you're back? What did she say?"

He held his hand up to stop the barrage of questions. "Your phone wouldn't stop ringing as soon as Owen saw me with you in my arms, so I finally answered it."

"*Owen*," I groaned. "I bet he's pissed at me."

"Hmph. Yeah, you could say that . . . and at me. He'll get over it." He shrugged. "Sophia sounded . . . hesitantly happy. She knows you're safe, but she's concerned."

"She thinks I might become evil."

"She thinks I *am* evil. I don't think she trusts me entirely again. She knows the Daemoni too well."

I looked into his beautiful eyes. "I trust you."

"Good. That's all that matters to me." He sighed. "Still, Sophia has every right to be concerned."

I sighed, too, and leaned my head against his shoulder. I traced my fingers around the scars on his chest, careful not to touch them. "What would you do if I did become evil? I mean, if the Daemoni blood wins."

"My allegiance is to the Amadis, so I would have to save your soul."

I mulled over this for a few minutes.

"I don't think it'll be an issue. I think she primarily worried because I'd become so *angry*. I was pretty cruel, especially to her. *I* even thought the Daemoni was coming out in me. But the anger is *gone*. All I feel now is love and happiness. I just needed you." I put my hands around his face and looked into his eyes again. "And *you* are not evil. You *are* Amadis, too. We'll be okay. No, we'll be more than okay. We're going to be *great* now."

He smiled but it didn't reach his eyes, and then he folded me into his arms. "I hope you're right. We have a lot of challenges ahead of us."

"We can handle them, as long as we're together. Just don't leave me again, no matter what the reason."

"*Never* again." He sealed the promise with a kiss and I remembered the last time he'd done the same thing . . . when he'd promised to come back. It had taken a while—way too long—but he'd made good on that one. I knew, however, there were no guarantees in our bizarre world. I leaned my head back against his shoulder.

"What happened? When you left, I mean?" I asked quietly. "Owen thought you were . . . dead . . . when he got away. They never gave me any details and I never asked. I was afraid they'd tell me something that would confirm what Owen thought and I couldn't let myself believe it."

I didn't know if he would tell me. He never spoke of his past life, of the horrors when he was part of the Daemoni. He refused to dredge up those memories. Though this was a different situation and he didn't perform the evil acts, he probably didn't want to relive those memories. But, after years of wondering and imagining my own version of the events, I felt compelled to ask anyway. And he actually answered.

With me still on his lap, he scooted back on the bed so he could lean against the headboard.

"The day I left . . . the day I made my worst mistake ever . . ." He shook his head. "I had to pull them away . . . from Rina and Sophia . . . from you. The Amadis had agreed to flash to a park in the Shenandoah Valley, away from the safe house to protect you, if needed. So I flashed there and the Daemoni followed my trail, just as planned."

"Followed your trail?" I interrupted. "When you flash?"

He looked down at me through his lashes. "You really still haven't learned much, have you?"

I shook my head.

"When we flash, we leave a sort of trail. It's like an energy signature. It can't be seen, but it can be sensed. It disappears in a second or two, but if someone is close enough to catch the trail, they can go right where you went." He paused to make sure I understood and I nodded. "The Amadis followed, too, but more Daemoni kept appearing."

"Were there dog-things?"

He lifted an eyebrow. "Dog-things?"

"Like the creature Edmund had at your house." It had been just a few days before our wedding . . . the raging wind of a tropical storm, the bulky figure of Edmund and his creature that wasn't quite dog but definitely not human, either . . . the whole fight had firmly impressed itself into my memory. Until the battle at the safe house, I'd never been more terrified in my life. The dog-thing had apparently left a lasting impression. I knew it was a stupid word, but I didn't know how else to describe the wretched creature.

"Ah, the nora."

"The *nora*?" I asked. It took me a minute to make the connection. I held an unusual amount of knowledge about mythical creatures—knowing was part of my job, after all—but the nora, bald men who ran on all fours and sucked breast milk, were rarely mentioned. I would have never thought the dog-thing to be a nora. "I didn't know they were real . . . I mean, even less so than vampires or werewolves."

"That was a real nora. And they don't just suck women's breasts. They like blood more than breast milk, but they do prefer women." He paused for a moment. "That's been your image of the Daemoni, huh?"

I thought about it for a moment before answering. Until recently, my experiences with the Daemoni had been limited to Ian, an Irish idiot who'd once been Amadis and now got his kicks out of watching the destruction of others' lives, and Edmund and his nora.

"I guess the nora scared me the most. Probably because I could see no humanity in it at all."

He rested his cheek against my head and was silent long enough, I almost asked what he was thinking. But then he continued with his story.

"Well, they are pretty rare, but there were a hell of a lot of Daemoni, so there may have been a few nora. They ambushed us. I wasn't surprised. I knew it would be the only way they could take me. I just didn't think it would be so bad. I should have known better . . . ." Remorse filled his last statement. I looked up at him when he didn't continue. He leaned his head back against the headboard, his eyes closed. "As soon as I realized their numbers, I went ahead, hoping to keep as many off of the others as I could. I knew they'd go after me. Most of them did, but not enough. Even while fighting, I kept aware of the others. They shouldn't have even been there. Stefan went down—"

I cringed and he paused. The image came clearly, very similar to the dream I used to have, the part my imagination had created of Stefan's death, followed by Tristan's disappearance. I shook my head to clear it and Tristan tightened his arms around me. His voice came even lower and quieter as he continued.

"Owen, Solomon and Micah, another soldier, were the only Amadis left standing. I had to pull the Daemoni away from them, before we lost them, too. So I flashed again, but this time they didn't know where I went. The Daemoni closest to me followed, and then the rest followed their trails, like a domino effect. They paralyzed me with their magic long enough to take me to the Ancients in Afghanistan."

I sucked my breath loudly and blew it out with an, "*Oh!*"

He peered down at me. "What?"

"Weird . . . " was all I could say at first. Then my thoughts all came out in a rush. "Every night since you left, up until last week, I had pretty much the same dream—replays of the few memories we had together. But it always ended with you in a field with Stefan and everyone, and then just you and the Daemoni, in a foreign desert, surrounded by stone mountains. I thought that part was a figment of my imagination."

"You didn't know where I was supposed to meet Lucas?"

I shook my head. "No one would tell me. You know how they are."

"Right. Hmm . . . that *is* . . . interesting." He paused again, then continued. "At first, I didn't fight. I knew as long as they had me, they'd stay away from you. I tried my first escape the day after Dorian was born and they had their celebration. Their compounds are shielded, so you can't flash out of them, but I thought I knew the location where they held me and the way out. But I was mistaken. They'd taken me somewhere new that they'd developed since I'd left them. So they recaptured me before I could get out, then took me to Siberia."

"*Siberia?*" I asked, astonished. "I planned to come find you, but I would've never guessed to look for you in *Siberia*."

What on earth had I been thinking? How would I have ever found him? And then, exactly, how would I—little me—have helped him escape against all those demons? The idea sounded ludicrous now. Tristan's humorless chuckle told me he thought the same thing.

"Trust me, I will teach you everything you need to know now. I'm going to prepare you for *every*thing," he said. "For now, just picture a large network of tunnels and caves, under the Taymyr Peninsula in northern Siberia. An underground city. All of their cities are underground, and this one is their largest—their capital, in a sense. I'd spent a lot of time there in my past life, knew it well. But they'd expanded the caves, dug down deeper. They kept me in a new part . . . far below the surface of the earth."

"Oh," I breathed. "You really were cut off from the entire world."

With the darkest of tones, he answered, "As far away as possible . . . and as close to the bowels of Hell as you can get."

He fell silent, providing no more details, but the image of a cold, dark cave blossomed in my mind. I envisioned him sitting alone on a dirt floor, the stone walls curving overhead. I could even hear distant screams of terror and pain from other caves and tunnels. I felt his dread. The dread of knowing someone or something would be coming any time to deliver his own torture. Not knowing when or even *if* there would ever be an end to it all. My heart squeezed and I fought back a shudder.

I could only imagine the loneliness he had felt. I, at least, had had Dorian and Mom and even Rina and Owen. He'd had no one. I reached my hand up and cradled the side of his face with it. He leaned his head into my hand as I stroked his cheekbone with my thumb. It felt like anything I did was so little . . . not enough for what he deserved. But he seemed to appreciate every little gesture. He'd been isolated from even the least bit of humanity, just when he'd learned the importance and joy of it . . . what it felt like to be touched and held by someone who loved him. He could only hold on to those memories, relive them in his mind.

I wondered if perhaps we had been somehow connected and that was why I had those same memory-dreams every night for the entire time he was away . . . and then they all but stopped, about the same time he'd escaped. We had both needed those memories. Perhaps we even shared them at the same time. And that connection told me I just needed to hold on to him, wait for him, although everyone else thought of me as pathetic for doing so.

I didn't know if the idea held any truth, but, I had learned in the last couple days, anything was possible in our world. And it was really a nice thought to hold onto in the midst of all we'd been through. So I shared it with him.

"Huh, it's an interesting theory," he said. We sat in silence as he thought through it. "I can see the possibility of it, especially since your blood runs through my veins."

"Like vampires?" I asked with surprise. "I mean, the connection vampires have with those whose blood they've sucked?"

"Exactly. But my body wouldn't burn through it for energy like they do. So, your theory's a strong possibility."

He just confirmed what I'd once believed to be fiction—the connection between vamps and their victims—and something about that gnawed at the back of my mind. I decided it was just lingering shock because nearly everything I'd been writing about was *real*.

"So, tell me the ending," I said, returning to his story. "How did you escape this time?"

Chapter 10

Tristan grinned but not his normal smile. This one took my breath for a different reason. It actually looked . . . *wicked*.

"I'd been planning it for a while, ever since I first heard they were coming after you. They're slow to make such decisions, which they should be, of course, especially when their reasons aren't credible. I paid attention, analyzing everything, learning the new areas as they moved me around. I hid the fact that I'd become immune to the spells they used and let them believe they still controlled me completely. So they became relaxed with me, keeping me around as they discussed their plans, still absorbed with their own pride and believing I'd change my mind about them. I learned what I needed to know to escape and when I heard they were executing their plan for you, I executed my own plan. I surprised the hell out of them—they created me, yet they still underestimate me. I took out a few of their strongest on my way. I quite enjoyed that."

Now I understood the nefarious grin. Not actually evil, just vengeful.

I didn't know what to say. He stayed with them to keep me safe and then escaped to protect me. Even while captured, sitting in the closest thing to Hell, he worried about me. And I only thought about why he hadn't come back sooner. In other words, I worried about me, too. Even now, the only thoughts coming to mind were selfish or, at least, minimal. *I wish you had come back sooner? I'm glad you're back? Thank you?*

"What are you thinking?" he finally asked after a few minutes of silence.

"About how much I love you and how miniscule that sounds compared to what I actually feel."

He nuzzled his face in my hair and murmured, "Hearing you say you love me will never be miniscule to me. It's the best thing these ears could ever hear. And I've been waiting a very long time to hear it again."

I turned to him and brushed my lips across his. "I *love* you, Tristan."

It still didn't sound like enough to me, but a glorious grin spread across his face as he closed his eyes. "Mmm . . . that's what I'm talking about."

Every little gesture *was* important to him. I needed to remember that—to never discount anything. He pressed me tighter against him and I listened to his heart, strong and steady and comforting. I slid my hand up his chest and neck, around the contours of his face and into his hair.

"Your hair is so dark," I whispered. "It used to be lighter, the color of sand. Dark sand, anyway. Now it's like caramel."

"It hadn't seen sun in many years."

I blinked back the tears at the reminder as I let the silky strands fall through my fingers. "And it's so long."

"Do you like it?"

"I don't know." I continued running my fingers through it.

"It *is* sexy."

His eyebrows jumped and a smile played on his lips. "Maybe I should have left it longer."

"It was *longer?*" Then I remembered seeing him—when I thought he was a delusion—standing in the park, long hair whipping in the breeze.

"I pulled it into a ponytail and cut it off to a more reasonable length. I hope you'll finish the job for me."

I laughed. "You want me to cut your hair? No way."

"So you *do* like it?"

"That's not exactly what I meant. I mean, I guess I like it. You kind of look like the Tristan in *Legends of the Fall . . . .*"

He raised an eyebrow. "Him again?"

I smiled, also remembering the conversation many years ago. "Yeah, but . . ."

He studied my face. "But what?"

"But you also look like you belong on the front of a romance novel or something."

He laughed. "Okay, it's definitely coming off then."

"Well, I'm not doing it. I have no idea how to cut hair and I'm not ruining it." But I did have an idea. "You want to feel something incredible?"

"I have you in my arms. What could feel more incredible than this?"

"Hmm . . . you're right. It can wait." I leaned my head against his chest.

"You have me curious now."

With a grin, I rolled out of his arms and retrieved my brush. I knelt behind him on the bed and brushed his hair, slowly and gently, the way I liked mine to be brushed. Mom had brushed it a lot for me over the years, because sometimes I hadn't cared enough to do it myself and it had helped to relax me.

"Mmm . . . you're right. It's almost as good as foreplay," Tristan said with a shudder.

I chuckled. "I never thought about it like that. Of course, I guess if *you* were doing it . . . well, any touch from you is like foreplay."

"Really? You're that easy, huh?" He trailed his fingertips up and down my calf, the electric current giving me goose bumps. I squirmed from the tickle.

"Only for you," I said softly, kissing his ear.

I ran my fingers through his hair again and it felt soft and silky, like Dorian's. I smoothed the strands down and pulled them all into a ponytail, then yanked on it to pull him back against me. I draped my arms around his broad shoulders and he clasped my hand over his heart again.

"Thank you for coming back," I murmured. Like earlier, it didn't sound like enough, but I felt the need to tell him anyway.

"I'm sorry I ever left," he replied quietly. I wondered if he had felt a similar need to tell me that. The apology was good to hear, to be honest. Because there had been times I'd wondered over the years, when I dwelled in my darker hours, if he'd known exactly how bad it would be and went anyway. And, in my darkest of dark hours, if he had purposely left, his assignment with me finished.

"Me, too," I whispered. A tear slid down my face and dropped onto his bare shoulder.

"Don't cry, my love. We're together now."

I wiped my wet cheek against his hair. "Forever this time?"

"Forever. I promise."

I rested my chin on his shoulder, our cheeks pressed together, and closed my eyes. I breathed in his delicious scent and was reminded of motorcycle rides to Gasparilla Island when we first got together. I felt like I could sit here with him forever, never having to let go again. But then that strange, burning sensation started coursing through my veins and muscles. The energy began to build again and I tried to fight it. My body wanted to move, but my heart didn't.

Tristan finally broke the silence and made the first move to get up. "I don't know about you, but I'm starving."

I shrugged. "Not really. I actually feel like going for a run or something."

"You need to eat. And then *I* will give you a workout," he said with a smile.

"Oh, yeah? You planning to teach me Aikido?"

"Hmm . . . I guess I could. But . . ." He bent his head down to mine and ran his mouth over my jaw and neck. ". . . I was thinking of a different kind of workout."

"Ah, even better."

We went out to the kitchen to find something to eat. Guilt stabbed my heart when I saw the package of steaks on a plate in the refrigerator.

"I should cook those for you and Owen tonight," I said. "I owe him."

"Were you two planning a special dinner?" Tristan asked, raising an eyebrow.

I frowned and made myself busy, pulling meat, cheese and mustard out of the refrigerator to avoid his eyes. "The pretense was a celebration for finishing the last book, but I really just wanted him to go to the store and away from here long enough so I could leave last night."

I felt him eyeing me. "What were you thinking anyway?"

"About you," I said honestly as I started making sandwiches. "I wanted to find you. And I needed to save my family. When you went to them, they left us alone until now. I thought if I went to them, they would leave the others alone. And we could be together again. If my family would be safe, then I'd rather be in their hell with you than in my own hell alone."

He sighed heavily. "I'm sorry I made you so miserable."

I finally looked up at him, holding the mustard-covered knife in the air and jabbing it with emphasis. "*You* didn't make me miserable. Your absence did."

He stepped behind me and wrapped his arms around my waist. "I know what you mean, my love. Life is nothing without you."

"Exactly."

I finished the sandwiches and handed him one and half of mine. I really didn't feel hungry; my stomach felt too knotted to eat. The phone rang as we finished and I ran into the bedroom to grab it.

"Hi, Mom!" I answered, falling backwards onto the bed.

"You sound good," she said.

"You don't. You sound tired."

"Fourteen hours of air travel and another two on land and sea with a six-year-old is exhausting."

"Sheesh, where are you? I thought you were just going to a safe house."

"No, we came to Rina's. We just arrived. I wanted to see how you were before I hit the hay."

"I'm great! I really couldn't be any better."

"How are you feeling? Tristan said you were hurt pretty badly."

"I'm fine. Everything's healed up perfectly."

"How's Tristan?"

"Beautiful. Sweet. *Here.*"

"Does he seem . . . okay?" Worry filled the question. I could hear her concern clearly across the thousands of miles separating us.

"Yeah, he's fine, Mom. Actually, more than fine. He's

absolutely *divine.*" Even through the phone, Mom's chuckle sounded hollow, empty of humor. "Why?"

"I don't know. I'm just concerned about him . . . and you. We don't know what they've done to him. I'm sure they've left something behind."

"Well, there are some . . . residual . . . effects. But it's not anything we can't work through. He loves us, Mom. He loves me. We'll be okay."

She sighed and apparently accepted my assessment because she changed the subject back to me. "How are you doing? Anything going on with you?"

"If you're referring to any changes, I don't think so. Of course, I've been a little preoccupied."

"I'll be there in a couple days. I guess, in the meantime, just be careful. If something happens, Owen's there to help."

I thought about that and smiled to myself. It seemed, just like many years ago, I only had to worry about Tristan during sex and I felt pretty sure I wouldn't want Owen's assistance then. *Owen, help! I don't know if that was a moan of pleasure or a real growl!* Nope, wasn't happening.

But I simply said to Mom, "Yeah, I know."

"We need to get to bed, but Rina wants to make sure you tell Tristan to begin working on the plan. He'll know what she means." She paused and I heard what sounded like Rina speaking to her in the background. "Dorian wants to talk to you."

"You didn't tell him about Tristan, did you?"

"No, honey. That's your surprise. I wouldn't ruin it."

"Thanks, Mom. You're the best. I love you."

"I know you do. And it's nice to hear you so happy again. Hold on a sec while I get Dorian."

I motioned to Tristan to come lay next to me, putting my finger to my mouth. We'd already agreed he shouldn't "meet"

Dorian on the phone, but he could listen. We lay on the bed, our heads close together, the phone between us.

"Hey, Mom!" Dorian said. Tristan squeezed my hand as soon as he heard his son's voice. My own heart soared when I heard it. Just last night, I thought I never would again.

"Hey, little man. How are you?"

"I'm great! Do you know where we are?" he asked, wonder filling his voice, as if he'd never been anywhere so cool.

"Tell me!"

He told us all about Rina's ginormous rock house with the fires everywhere, even on the walls, and about the planes and the pretty flight attendants and the movies and everything else he could think of, moving from subject to subject without interruption, barely pausing to breathe. Tristan beamed by the time Dorian finished.

"Mom, when will I see you again?" he asked, the enthusiasm replaced by longing. "I miss you. A lot."

"I miss you sooo much, too, little man," I said. "But I don't know when. Soon, though. And when you do, I'll have a really big surprise for you."

I waited for him to gush about getting a dog for his upcoming birthday, not ever expecting the bigger and better surprise we had in store for him.

"Did you find Dad?"

What? Tristan and I stared at each other wide-eyed, mouths open. *How does he know?!*

"Dorian, why would you say that?" I finally asked.

"Because you left in his car and you've been gone a long time and now you're really happy."

I couldn't answer him. Tears filled my eyes and I thought even Tristan's eyes were moist.

"Mimi says I have to go now, Mom. I love you."

"I love you, too, little man."

I snapped the phone shut and we laughed and cried in amazement.

"I told you he's smart," I said, "but that blew me away."

"He's unbelievable . . . even better than I ever imagined," Tristan said wistfully. Then his lips spread into the really fabulous smile, the one that always made my heart melt and the rest of my insides turn to mush. "I think we need to try for that little girl."

He rolled over and pinned me on the bed, kissing my neck and my chest and . . . lower. Good thing we hadn't dressed—our clothes would have been shredded in renewed desperation. When his eyes blazed and he seemed to be losing control, I just had to tell him I loved him to bring him out of it. Our love served as the antidote to whatever lurked beneath his surface, whatever they'd planted in his subconscious.

We lasted slightly longer this time—long enough to break the bed in the middle, creating a bowl I had to climb out of.

"I liked that bed," I said regretfully. "It was . . . comforting."

"There are two more just like it in this house."

I didn't expect him to understand. While I lay on that bed, a bawling lunatic savoring our memories, I finally started climbing out of my dark pit. It was almost symbolic, having to climb out of the pit of the broken bed.

"We're staying in this room, at least."

"Well, help me move the beds. Or I can ask Owen?" He grinned.

My eyes widened. "Oh, no. I'll do it. That'd be too embarrassing."

He laughed. "Not for me."

Men, I thought with a shake of my head. Then I thought about Vanessa seeing this and knew I would feel the same way.

Tristan didn't really need help moving the beds. Although

he probably could have lifted them with one hand, he didn't even bother. He simply used his power, making me wonder if I would ever be able to do that. He said telekinesis was a basic power and even the weakest of our kind could move a bed. Then he said I would be so powerful, I would probably be able to move skyscrapers if I wanted. I laughed at the absurdity.

"Maybe we need to get a rock house like Rina's," I said, rubbing my hand over all the dents in the wall above the new headboard. I laughed. "You think that's why she has a rock house?"

"From what I've heard about Rina, I wouldn't be surprised. I hear you come by it naturally." His eyes danced in jest.

"Oh, I see. Now I know the *real* reason you came looking for me all those years ago," I teased.

"Nah, it's just a nice little bonus." He wiggled his eyebrows. "But I don't think Rina's house is what you're picturing. She lives in the ancient Amadis mansion, made of marble and limestone."

I envisioned Rina in her fancy dresses, gliding around an impressively large, resplendent house of marble. "Ah, that fits better."

"I do like Dorian's description, though." He flopped down on the new bed. It moaned in protest. "Even if we have a rock house, it won't help the furniture."

"No, it won't. We'll have to figure something out or the kids will be wondering why we need a new bed all the time. And can you imagine when they're older? They'll be mortified."

"They'll probably hate us for having such a great sex life," he said and we both laughed. He pulled me onto the bed and we lay in each other's arms. Just one day earlier I would have never guessed I could be so happy again. And here he was, my sun pushing the darkness away and lighting up my life once again. Discussing the future with him—including a daughter—was priceless.

Chapter 11

"What—the—hell—were—you—*thinking?*" Owen fumed as soon as he walked in the door that evening.

I backed away from him, until my back pressed against the counter. "I'm sorry."

"*Sorry?* Alexis, do you have any idea how I felt when I came back and you were *gone?* Do you know what Rina and the council would have done to me if . . . if . . . ." He couldn't finish. "And Sophia . . . she would've *killed* me."

"I'm *sorry*," I repeated with deepest sincerity. "I know I took advantage of you. And I understand if you never trust me again. I thought I was doing what was best."

"And *exactly* what did you think was best?"

"Surrender to the Daemoni so they would leave everyone else alone." Both Owen and Tristan groaned. "They want *me.* Not Mom. Not Rina. And not Dorian. And I knew you'd never just *let* me go."

"Of course not! That was incredibly stupid. And if Tristan

hadn't been there, you'd be in the Daemoni's hands—or *dead*—and he'd be here. How do you think all of us would feel about *that*?"

I couldn't answer, knowing how horrible the consequences would have been for them. I just stared at the floor, which swam through the tears I blinked back.

So he turned on Tristan. "And if *you* could have just let her know you were okay, she wouldn't have gone in the first place."

"I know. I take full responsibility for it," Tristan replied gruffly. "But you shouldn't have left her. What were *you* thinking?"

Owen raised his eyebrows at Tristan's accusing tone and went on such a rampage, I never would have thought him capable of it. He threw his hands in the air as he advanced on Tristan.

"What was *I* thinking? I was thinking she could stay put for ten minutes and keep herself safe! I was thinking she'd been through *hell* the last seven-and-a-half years and she actually wanted to celebrate something for the first time since. I was thinking I saw a glimpse of the old Alexis who no one has seen since that day we left her at the damn safe house begging you not to go! I was thinking I didn't want to disappoint her, even with such a little thing, after all the big disappointments she's had to suffer!"

"Ah! Like me leaving her? Of not being able to get back because I sat in my own *hell*?" Tristan leaned forward, their faces less than a foot apart. His voice rose. "Say it, Owen. Say it like it is. It's my fault she suffered. Say what you're thinking!"

"That's *not* what I'm thinking!" Owen bellowed, his hands balling into fists at his sides. "It's *my* fault! *I* didn't bring you back to her. *I* didn't keep you safe. *I* had to come back and tell her I thought you were *dead*. And ever since, I've had to see her misery, hear her screaming in her sleep from the other side of the house, watch her fall apart at the seams and know it's *my* fault. I've had to look at her and know she wished *I'd* been the one who didn't come back!"

I stared at him, my eyes wide with disbelief and confusion. *How had he twisted it into this?*

"Owen, stop it." I tried to put emotion behind the words so he would hear me and come to his senses, but my voice sounded small over the lump in my throat. He ignored me, still glaring at Tristan.

"You don't know what it's like to have her look at you and feel like you're the person who made her whole world fall apart."

"I do know what it's like!" Tristan barked. "I've watched it for the last week!"

Owen's jaw dropped. "A *week*? You've been back a *week* and made her go through that? Do you have any idea just how bad this week has been for her?"

"No, I don't fully know. But *you* have no idea what it's been like for me. To see *you* be the one who can take care of her . . . to see *you* at the park with *my* wife, playing with *my* son, because I don't know if I'll be overcome with the urge to *kill* them!" Tristan pounded the counter, adding yet another crack to the granite. I felt like he'd hit me, like I'd been punched in the gut with his words.

"Stop it! Both of you!" I finally yelled. "This is nonsense. I'm standing right here. Stop talking about me like I'm not. And stop being so damn stupid."

They both finally shut up and looked at me as if they just remembered I was even in the room.

"Owen, you're completely wrong. Yes, I was pissed off. I was pissed off at everyone—at Tristan, at Mom, at myself, at the Amadis, at the whole damn world! But I knew the *blame* was all on those bastard Daemoni who killed Stefan, who took Tristan, who took my whole life away." I swiped at the tears and drew in a ragged breath. "But, really, I just want to be over it. Tristan's back. We'll be with Dorian soon. Just let me be happy. I'm *happy* now, okay?"

I stomped into the bedroom and threw myself on the bed.

After a few minutes, Tristan sat next to me and pulled me into his arms as I continued to cry.

"You just said you were happy," he said quietly.

"I *am* happy, damn it!"

He chuckled. I did, too, through the tears.

"So why are you crying?"

"Because I feel absolutely horrible for both of you. I never meant for Owen to feel like I blamed him. And I had no idea what you saw at the park and how that must have made you feel." The cold, hard feeling from last night started working its way in again. "I *hate* them. I hate them for ruining our lives. I hate them for doing this to us."

"*Ma lykita*," he murmured, "they haven't ruined our lives. Not as long as we don't let them. We've had to live through hell for a while, but we don't have to let that ruin everything. We have many years ahead of us still. Many more than what they've taken."

We sat in silence for a minute or two. Well, he sat silently. I sniffled and pulled in noisy breaths, trying to stop the tears.

"How do you do it?" I finally asked.

"Do what?"

"Keep living through horrific shit like this and still be able to say that?"

"Ah." He kissed the top of my head. "Because it's been proven to me time and again that it can and does get better. After all, I have you. Again."

I sighed heavily and caressed his cheek, trying not to let the anger well up again as my fingertips slid over the nasty scar. "I love you."

"See? How can I hold onto anger when I get to hear that from your lips?"

I wiped the tears off my face, inhaled deeply and headed back to the kitchen.

Owen still stood where he had been, his head bent over,

looking at me through his lashes. He reminded me of Dorian when he had to tell Mom and me he'd been in another fight—guilty for disappointing us but not for the actual action.

"Sorry, Alex—" he started, but I held my hand up to stop him.

"*I'm* sorry, Owen," I said. He opened his mouth to say something, but I went on, needing to relieve him of his unnecessary guilt. "I'm sorry I ever made you feel that way. I admit I sometimes wondered how you made it back and not Tristan. But I didn't blame you for any of it. *Of course* I wished he'd come back and probably more than any of the others. But he's my husband, Owen. He was—is—my *life*. He'll always be my first concern. That's just how it is. But that doesn't mean I wished you'd never come back. You're like a brother to me. Stefan was like a dad. I wished none of you ever left in the first place, but you did and shit happened. It's done now. Over with. Tristan's here. You're here. I get two out of three. Let's just put it behind us, okay?"

Owen studied my face for a moment, looked at Tristan and then back at me. He finally relaxed and slumped back against the counter.

"Okay. It's in the past." He pretended to pick up some imaginary object and throw it over his head, behind him. Then he looked at Tristan. "We're good?"

"We're good, bro," Tristan said. Owen showed Tristan the latest male bonding handshake—the fist bump.

"So . . . what's up, little sis from a different miss?" Owen asked me, back to his normal self.

"A real celebration dinner?" I offered. "We have these beautiful steaks and all . . . ."

He smiled. "I'll accept that."

I blew out a sigh of relief and got to work. Owen and Tristan stayed in the kitchen with me, Tristan helping me cook and Owen updating us on the consequences of my escapade last night.

"The Daemoni are really going ballistic now that the two of you are back together. I guess that blonde vampire chick went on a rampage. Apparently, your blood, Alexis, is like a super-potent energy drink for vampires. It made her more powerful than usual and we had to do some damage control."

I didn't really want to know what he meant and I appreciated that he didn't explain.

"Do they know we're here?" Tristan asked.

"No, they still don't know about this house. But as soon as they can get to one or both of you, they will. And they know once they've got one of you, they've got the other now. Rina wants us to go to your house in Atlanta. It's probably safer there than here."

Tristan stopped slicing onions—he'd always taken that job because they didn't make him cry like they did to me and he'd naturally resumed it, just like old times—and stared at the counter for a few seconds. Apparently, he was exploring and weighing the options. Then he nodded.

"That'll work perfectly with the plan," he said, expertly moving the knife again.

"The plan Rina wants you to work on?" I asked. I'd passed on the message earlier, but I'd been too distracted to ask him what plan.

"Yeah," he answered distractedly, focused on whatever he had brewing in his mind. "There will be a fire. We'll have to make sure it's complete, so when they find no bodies, they still could think they were burnt to ashes. Maybe an explosion."

I stopped in my tracks, holding the plate of steaks in front of me. "*What?* You're going to blow up my *house?*"

"After the *Ang'dora*, A.K. Emerson can no longer exist," he said simply, as if this fact were obvious. He took the steaks from me and headed outside to the grill. I just stared after him.

It should have been obvious, that I could no longer be

the author. Not with the changes I would go through. But I really hadn't thought about everything that far. It bothered me how he said it so easily. Of course, he probably wouldn't ever understand how much I had needed to be A.K. Emerson, how important that part of me was. He hadn't been around for any of her existence.

I shook off the troubled feeling. Logic told me we would have to kill her—fake my death. Tristan would know the best solution because that was one of his abilities. And I'd been ready to give her up last night. With the last book complete, I could let go. Apparently, I would *have* to let go. Besides, I enjoyed the writing—not actually being a famous author.

"With no bodies, we leave the possibility open of a disappearance, just in case anyone recognizes you in the future," Tristan said when he came back into the kitchen. "However . . . we *will* have her reunited with the father of her son and married first."

I felt my face light up and opened my mouth but Owen shook his head before I could say anything.

"Too dangerous," he said. "Just moving you two to Atlanta will be bad enough."

"Just some pictures and a slip to the media right before we have to disappear," Tristan said. He looked at me and grinned. "We'll make those assholes eat their words."

I smiled back, but then sighed. "But she'll never get to be Mrs. Tristan Knight."

"Why not?" Tristan asked.

"Because then we can't use that name later, right?"

He shrugged. "It's just a name. You know it doesn't mean anything. I picked it as a kind of tongue-in-cheek thing."

Owen and I both looked at him expectantly, neither of us getting it.

"Tristan, the knight who fell in love with the one he could never have," Tristan said.

"Tristan and Isolde?" I asked, stifling a laugh. "That's where you got your name?"

"Just the Knight part. I chose Tristan for a reason, but the last names come and go." He lifted one shoulder in a half-shrug. "So if you want the author to be Mrs. Tristan Knight, then we'll do it. You will always be Alexis Ames, anyway. I can even be Tristan Ames."

I laughed. "I know that makes sense, since you really are an Ames anyway, but it's not happening. To me, you are Tristan Knight and I've waited forever to be your Mrs. I'll keep Alexis Knight for myself. So you'll need to be someone different for the author."

He wrapped his arms around me and whispered in my ear, "Whatever you want, my love. To me, you'll always be *ma lykita*."

"So . . . pictures," Owen said, obviously as a reminder of his presence. "We'll take care of those tomorrow, before heading to Atlanta. I'll need to get a camera."

"We'll need to go to Miami, too," Tristan said.

"Dude! Did you not hear me? Getting you two to Atlanta is bad enough. That's all."

"Rina's orders. Didn't she tell you?"

Owen exhaled a frustrated sigh. "She just said to make sure you got your affairs in order. I didn't know it meant a stop in Miami."

"That's where a lot of my affairs are," Tristan said. "It won't take long. We'll go tomorrow. You can take pictures of the author and her beau while we're there. Then we'll head to Atlanta the next morning."

"This will be fun," Owen muttered, the sarcasm heavy. He shook his head slowly. "Sophia and Rina will meet us in Atlanta. I think they're leaving in the morning and will get in late tomorrow night."

"That's ludicrous!" Tristan growled. "They should stay at the island. Do they realize how much danger they're putting themselves in?"

Owen nodded. "I know, but they want to be here. And we're going to need all the help we can get . . . just in case . . . ."

He glanced over at me.

"This is so absurd," I said. "They shouldn't be coming if they're putting their lives at risk—from me or anyone else. I thought the whole point of me being here is to keep me away from them."

"Sophia was coming no matter what. She never meant for you to be alone for long, but she wanted to make sure Dorian was safe first," Owen said. "And I guess Rina's decided she needs to be here, too."

"So we just lay low in Atlanta for another couple *weeks*?" I asked, remembering Mom saying the *Ang'dora* takes several weeks to complete. "What about Dorian?"

"Dorian's in the safest place he could be," Owen answered. "And Rina's not sure about it taking that long. From what I've told them, they think you're going faster than usual. That's why they're coming so soon."

Once they settled on a plan, they both started talking enthusiastically about my abilities and the *Ang'dora*. According to my ancestors' experiences, I should have been gaining power gradually, but as far as I knew, I couldn't do anything I couldn't do before, except see farther and run faster.

"You can flash, right?" Owen asked. "That's how you got back last night."

"Huh?" I asked, confused.

"No, I brought her back by myself," Tristan said.

"You can flash with someone else?" Owen sounded impressed.

Tristan shrugged. "Never have before, but I guess so. It was necessary and it just happened."

"Huh. Cool. Alexis, have you even tried?"

I looked at him as if he'd just asked me to fly. He may as well have—for me, flashing seemed nearly as impossible. "I don't even know what to do."

"Just think of where you want to be and let yourself go. If the desire to be there is strong enough, it just happens." He nodded at the balcony. "See if you can get out there."

"I thought the shield prevented flashing."

"We can flash within it, just not through it. No going in and out."

I furrowed my brows and narrowed my eyes, concentrating hard on wanting to be on the balcony, but nothing happened. I felt like an idiot.

"Guess not," Tristan said with a chuckle. I shot a look at him. "But you look adorable trying."

He winked at me and I forgave him . . . I couldn't remember the problem.

"We'll try some things in the morning," Owen suggested. "You might have powers you just don't know about yet and it would be good to know before we go on this idiotic trip to Miami. Of course, we'll all have to go. I'm not leaving either of you alone."

Neither Tristan nor I argued with his point. Only a major catastrophe could split us up right now. We weren't willing to take the chance of another long-term or permanent separation.

Tristan retrieved the steaks from the grill while Owen and I gathered the rest of the food and took it out to the balcony. With plans made, Tristan and Owen slipped into a lighter conversation, discussing topics requiring a Y-chromosome to understand, or at least, to care about. I couldn't keep my eyes off Tristan while they talked. I still couldn't believe he sat right here next to me.

And Tristan constantly touched me—my hand, my leg, my back, *somewhere*—as if he, too, wanted to be sure I really sat by his side.

Owen caught Tristan up on all the things that had gone on in the human world . . . well, mostly the sports world. Then they talked about the newest cars. Tristan's eyes lit up when he discussed what he should get to replace the Ferrari. Owen had brought the car back from Key West this morning, he said, but the Daemoni had left it in ruins.

"I'll take the damaged goods," Owen offered. "There's nothing I can't fix."

"I think we can work that out," Tristan said, glancing at me and back at Owen. "It's the least I can do."

"I *like* that car," I protested. Tristan fingered the key on my necklace.

"As long as you have that key, we can get whatever you want." He winked again. He knew how to make me forget to argue with him.

"Cool. That car's a chick magnet," Owen said, grinning.

"Yes, it is." Tristan chuckled. He seemed to be remembering something that didn't include me because he gave me a guilty look. "Although . . . I found motorcycles attract the best ones."

"We definitely need to get a new Harley," I said with a laugh.

Owen shrugged. "I think I can make-do with the Ferrari."

I looked at him and chuckled. Although I'd never considered him as attractive as Tristan, he was far from ugly. He could be pushing a shopping cart around as his only wheels and a number of girls would jump right in. He could probably get just about any girl simply by existing. Not only because he was good-looking, but because he was just so *good*. "Owen, you can't seriously have any problems attracting girls."

"Attracting isn't really the issue." He sighed. "I just haven't found the right one."

"Never? That's kind of sad. And you're how old?" I could be that way with Owen. He *was* like a brother—the older brother I'd always wanted, someone to stand up to the kids who teased me because I wouldn't do it myself.

"I'm only sixty-eight."

"*Really?* I thought you were ancient like everyone else." *Oops!* I threw my hand to my mouth and looked guiltily at Tristan. He just chuckled. "You don't look sixty-eight, of course, but you do look a *tad* older than when I met you. By a couple years, anyway."

"Yeah, well, unlike you guys, I still age. Just very slowly."

"You just don't seem like you're almost seventy, though. Mom doesn't seem like her real age, but she *feels* older than she looks. So does Rina. You know what I mean? But you don't."

He pondered my question for a moment. "I look it at this way—if I get to look young, why not enjoy it and act like it, too? I have the looks, the body and the expectation to live carefree like a twenty-five-year-old bachelor. I'll eventually have to act older and mature to match my looks, and I'll be old and decrepit one of these days, so why not make the most of it now?"

"That's what I'm talking about." Tristan held his fist up and they bumped knuckles again. I rolled my eyes.

"*You're* not a bachelor," I reminded Tristan. "And you have a family. You have to be mature *now*."

"Ah, just a little . . . and just for a few years. Then you and I can go back to living like young newlyweds." He grinned and gave me a squeeze.

And that's when it hit me—the whole not-aging thing. I was changing over and that meant I would look and feel like I was perpetually in my mid-twenties, based on how I looked right now. Experience would develop my mind and my emotions, but my body would never change. I'd always thought

I would be like Mom and Rina—mature yet timeless. Owen and Tristan had a great outlook on the situation, but . . . they were male. What male ever wants to grow up? They had a life men dream about—to know what they do at sixty-eight, or even two-hundred-sixty-eight, but be allowed to live the life of a twenty-two-year-old. Of course, I had a man every woman dreams about—worldly and wise, considerate and loving, yet forever young. And devastatingly gorgeous, of course.

"Hmm . . . we don't ever have to *stop* living like newlyweds," I said, smiling impishly at him. And nearly forgetting Owen was even there.

"Oooh-kaay . . . time for me to go," Owen said, pushing himself away from the table. "Thanks for the steak, Alexis. I have to admit, I was a little worried. I'd forgotten you even knew how to cook."

Tristan looked at me with his eyebrows raised. I just shrugged. I hadn't cooked anything except hot dogs, macaroni and cheese, and eggs since he had left. I'd been a little worried myself as I prepared the steaks and roasted potatoes, hoping I hadn't forgotten how to cook a real meal.

"What? Did you think I'd burn the house down or something?"

"Nah. Just food poisoning. But I'm still alive. And it was even delicious."

I threw my arms around his waist. "Thank you, Owen. For everything."

"It's good to see you happy again," he said, hugging me back.

"Am I forgiven then?"

"Hmm . . . yeah, I guess." He chuckled. "It's not like I could hold a grudge against *you*. Just, uh, do us all a favor—don't *ever* do that again."

I frowned. "Sorry, but I can't promise that. Considering

the circumstances, I'd do it all over again, even if I knew the outcome would be different."

Owen shook his head. "You *like* making my life difficult?"

"I thought I kept it interesting," I teased.

"I don't like *that* kind of interesting."

"Well, I might have saved an innocent girl from a horrific ending."

They both looked at me expectantly, so I quickly gave them the whole story. I shivered at the thought of what would have happened to her if I hadn't been driving by that particular alley when I did. Then I realized those vampires had probably had their meal anyway, maybe not with her but with someone. My stomach rolled with that thought.

"If it's the girl I think it was, she's not so innocent," Owen said.

"What do you mean? They were pushing her around, treating her like . . . like dinner. She was scared to death."

"Oh, she was scared, all right. But she was one of them. They were pissed at her for . . ." Owen clamped his mouth shut, pursing his lips together. Then he shrugged and finished. "For whatever reason they think they have."

"But she wasn't a vampire." I stopped to think about it, but now found it difficult to know for sure. After all, these things were still new to me. Maybe I hadn't seen her as clearly as the others. "I don't think, anyway."

Owen shook his head. "No, not a bloodsucker. A Were."

I inhaled sharply and blew the air out with an "Oh!" and then "Wow!"

"Yeah. That rampage they all went on—they took most of it out on her."

I stared at him, blinking several times. I didn't know whether to feel sorry for the girl now or not. I couldn't believe the Daemoni would turn on their own kind, but then again, they were evil. How could I ever understand them or explain their actions?

"Just wait until you've changed before you try to be a hero again," Owen said, his hand on the latch of the screen door. "For my sake."

"I *can* promise you that. But I sure wish I'd known if I had any powers, like you think. I really would've loved flattening that bitch against the wall after what she said about my mother."

Owen still laughed as he walked out to the brush and disappeared.

Chapter 12

After Owen left, Tristan and I sat on the balcony while I caught him up on my life. I told him about being bed-ridden for several months while pregnant and he asked about the delivery. I explained as best as I could. Dorian had been a preemie, arriving after a long, painful labor and birth—I passed out for part of it—followed by the heavy disappointment of no baby girl. Tristan pulled me into his lap and held me while I cried about it again.

I'd cried a lot today for someone who was supposed to be so happy now. My emotions ran wild, almost like Swirly still messed with me from a distance. But I had a feeling that either the situation or the *Ang'dora* itself really caused the havoc.

Once the tears dried, we talked about my books—he said he'd read them all in the week he'd been back in the real world—and all the events that went along with them. I couldn't tell him a whole lot, but he asked questions to jog my memory.

"Your fans love you and the books. There are tons of sites on the Internet," he pointed out.

"Yeah, I guess. I haven't paid much attention to them in a long time. Sometimes they were rude and insensitive and I couldn't take it. There was this one girl, though—her name is Sonya, if I remember right—and she was my 'biggest fan.'" I wiggled my fingers in the air to mark the quotations. "She followed us to every signing, release party and interview. I never had any particular bad vibes from her, but she worried my agent and publicist, so they took out a restraining order against her."

"I saw her posts online. She doesn't hold it against you. She's still very fond of you."

"Really? Well, that's a relief. I always felt kind of bad about the whole thing."

"Don't feel too badly. She *is* a little . . . fanatic. Her posts greatly outnumber everyone else's, which is why I remember her. And she's determined your characters are real. She's more fascinated with the lore than you are."

I groaned. "I hope she doesn't dig too deeply and find out just how right she is."

He chuckled. "I wouldn't worry about it. People have been interested in vamps for centuries. The bloodsuckers tend to stay away from them."

"Really? Why? I thought it would be the opposite—they'd want to get rid of the curious."

He shrugged. "They can't get rid of them all and they tend to be friends. So as soon as there are signs one has been the victim of a vampire, there are humans out looking for them, either wanting to become one or wanting to kill them. They make life a little difficult for the vamps . . . the hunting is easier, but that just brings more attention."

"Oh. Well . . . I guess that's good for Sonya."

He nuzzled his face against my neck. "Can we change the subject back to you?"

I thought for a minute. "I don't know what else to tell you. My memories are all pretty dim."

"Then stop talking." He kissed me on the mouth to make his point, his lips warm and delicious, and I responded immediately.

I moved around in his lap to straddle him. He took my face in his hands and crushed his lips to mine. I opened my mouth to let his tongue in, tasting his deliciousness with my own. My pelvis ground against his as his hands made an electric path down my sides, to the bottom of my dress. He lifted it over my head and dropped it on the ground. His hands circled my breasts, gently squeezing while his thumbs rolled my hard nipples. He leaned down and I arched my back as he took a nipple into his mouth, sucking a line of pleasure straight from my groin. I rocked my hips against his hardness, still imprisoned in his jeans. He finally stood and carried me inside.

We made love throughout the night, not able to get enough of each other. The first two times, earlier in the day, were just pressure relievers—letting us release just enough pent-up energy by meeting our most primal needs before we both exploded. Now, with that edge off, we could truly get reacquainted. No, it was more than that. Having been newlyweds for only two weeks, we hadn't even had a chance to really get to know each other in the first place, not intimately. We'd been allowed to smell the bouquet, to taste the flavor, even to enjoy a full glass, only to have the bottle taken away. Now, another bottle was brought out, same year and vintage, but with time and separation, the flavor tasted new, yet at least recognizable. And more intense . . . so much more intense.

We started slow, rediscovering places we'd been before but with new appreciation. Feeling at once familiar, yet unknown and exciting. It didn't take long to become more comfortable, less inhibited. We quickly moved on to explore and discover and learn with and from each other. And we made every effort to make up for those missing years. Well, at least one or two of them.

Several times I had to tell Tristan how much I loved him when he seemed to be losing control. At one point, he downright frightened me.

Using his paralyzing power, he pinned me against the wall, a couple of feet off the floor. It was an exciting game to see how long I could let him touch me without being able to move or respond with anything but my eyes or mouth. We'd only tried this experiment once before because it was a dangerous game— he had to maintain control or his power could literally crush me to death. The risk made it all the more thrilling.

He placed his hands on each side of my head and started by kissing my lips, then my cheeks, then along my jaw, his loose hair trailing over my skin like a feather. His lips moved down my neck and, his hands still flat against the wall, to my breasts. He kissed and sucked and rolled my nipples with his tongue. I could do nothing but let him. I desperately wanted to reach out and slide my hands over his perfect chest or press my body against the full length of his. I shivered with the combined feeling of anticipation and helplessness as his hands finally caressed my body.

Starting at my shoulders, they moved slowly down my arms and back up again while his lips and tongue trailed along my collarbone. Then he slid them down my torso, over every curve and every indent. They explored my breasts and my tummy and my hips. They ran down the outside of my legs and trailed electricity back up the inside. One came back up to my neck, while the other stayed in between my legs and a finger slid inside me. I could only respond with a moan of pleasure.

Tristan's mouth came back to mine again and I looked into his eyes. They exploded with fire. A long, feral growl rumbled through him as he kissed and sucked on my neck, one hand squeezing my breast and the other still between my legs.

"Tristan," I whispered breathily, "I love you, baby."

He growled again in response. Then it seemed like his hands were suddenly everywhere, fervently rubbing all over my body. His lustful gropes became rough, not his usual, careful caresses. Every place his mouth landed, he sucked hard, as if trying to devour me. And then I felt his power intensifying, pressing in on me, squeezing me from the outside in. My heart, already racing with excitement, throbbed even harder, as I felt a loss of control. I was paralyzed—unable to reach out and grab his attention. The shivers changed to trembles of fear.

"Tristan, please," I pleaded. "Look at me."

He ignored me. He panted with desire as he yanked me off the wall and into his powerful arms, holding me firmly against his hard body. One hand gripped tightly at the back of my neck and the other pressed into the small of my back as he carried me to the bed. His power was released from me, but now he could have easily snapped my spine or neck with just one unintentional squeeze or twist and I didn't know if I could heal from such an injury. I normally wouldn't have worried about him going so far, but I'd never seen him with such little control. His eyes burned brighter and panic rose in my chest as my heart tried to pound through it.

I braced his head in my hands and forced him to stop and look at me.

"I love you, Tristan. Please, baby." I sounded desperate and I didn't know if the distressed pleas would make the situation worse. But not knowing what else to do, I simply repeated the three-word sentence he'd been so eager to hear earlier and hoped it would get through to him before he did something rash.

I continued staring into his eyes as the fire finally died

down and his grip on me loosened. A look of horror spread across his face as he realized what he'd almost done and his eyes darkened completely with regret as he sat on the bed with me still in his arms. He shook his head and opened his mouth to say something.

"Shh," I said. "It's okay. We're both okay."

He fell backward on the bed and closed his eyes. I leaned over him and kissed his mouth, pressing his arms to the bed with my hands.

"Just let me do it now," I whispered.

I didn't have the power to keep him still, but he lay there as if I did. His hands clawed at the bed—and only the bed—as I took over. I leaned down further, pressing my breasts against his chest, while I kissed his face. My mouth moved back to his and I pushed my tongue inside, tasting his tangy-sweetness. I pulled on his lower lip with my teeth, then moved lower. I slid my hands and mouth over his neck and then his chest, kissing and licking and sucking. Continuing downward, I kissed and stroked every inch of him until he trembled with anticipation, just as he'd done to me. He didn't move until I straddled his waist and sunk down onto him.

I was ripe and ready for him and I moaned as he filled me completely. He finally lifted his hands and rubbed his palms against my hard nipples, then gently squeezed my breasts. I leaned over again and planted my mouth on his. His hands slid down, over my butt, then to my hips and they gently rocked me, slow at first, getting into our rhythm, then faster and hotter and deeper. I cried out when that last stroke went deep, hitting just right. I squeezed him as every muscle in my body contracted and I plunged into oblivion.

It had to be nearly dawn when we finally fell asleep from exhaustion. The end of my memory-dream played—the one that wasn't a memory at all, just a figment of my semi-accurate imagination. Tristan in the desert mountains, writhing on the ground in front of the Daemoni. Then his face clearly filled my vision, the scars bright red and fire filling his eyes. He growled loudly and deeply and then dove for my throat.

OH! I sat up, gasping and wide-eyed. My breath came out raggedly as I looked around, trying to get my bearings. *No desert. No mountains. Just a dream.* I sat on the floor of the Caribbean room, wrapped in a sheet, the room completely destroyed. Tristan lay on the floor next to me, his hand tugging my arm, pulling me to him.

"You okay?" he mumbled, squinting at me in the bright morning light.

"Yeah," I breathed, collapsing into his arms. "Nightmare."

"Mmm." He nuzzled my neck. "Want to tell me about it?"

The visions tried to come back into my mind. I shoved them out. "No. It was nothing."

I relaxed into him and we lay there lazily for a while.

"How come you don't have nightmares?" I finally asked, rolling over to look at him. "I think if I were you, I'd be afraid to even sleep."

He frowned. "It's a practiced art, but I've learned to cut off that part of my mind."

"Your subconscious? You can cut it off?" I asked with disbelief.

"Cut it off, close it down. It took a hundred years or so to learn how, but if I hadn't, you're right. I would have never made it this long."

"So, you don't dream at all?" I lifted an eyebrow.

"Only if I want to allow it . . . and when I do, I take the risk of reliving some horrors I've tried to forget. But while I was gone,

I allowed it, hoping to dream of you. And I did, every night."

My heart squeezed. "What did you dream about?"

He smiled. "Mostly our memories . . . the good times we had. But, sometimes, I got *really* lucky."

"What do you mean?"

His grin grew. "I dreamt of times like last night."

"You dreamt of dinner with Owen?"

He laughed, then nuzzled my neck again. "I think you know what I mean."

"Wow . . . you did get lucky. I never had dreams like that. Well . . . actually, I did dream of our wedding night."

"Yes, that would be one of them," he murmured against my ear. Goose bumps rose on my arms. "One of my favorites."

"But if you allowed those dreams . . . didn't you open yourself up for the bad ones?"

He sighed. "Yes, but it was worth it."

I sighed, too, remembering how I relished the memory-dreams, even the bad parts. "I know what you mean."

His eyes changed quickly, from dark to sparkly, and he smiled. "But now I get to wake up to you by my side every morning."

"Yeah . . . to all the beauty of my ratty hair and morning breath."

He chuckled. "I love it."

"I know you do. For now, anyway. After a hundred years or so, I'm sure you'll get tired of it."

His brows furrowed, as if he thought hard about this possibility, then he smiled again. "Nope. Don't think so."

He pulled me close to him and we lay in each other's arms again until I finally had to get up for the bathroom. My body burned and I assumed it was healing itself. My skin looked purplish-green with partially healed bruises covering almost every inch. When I came out, Tristan just stood in the middle of the room with the white sheet wrapped around his waist, looking around with an amused expression. His torso also appeared to be purple and green.

And our room . . . the poor Caribbean room. The white chaise lounge in the sitting area lay on its side, broken in two, cotton and spring intestines pushing through the torn upholstery, and its purple throw-pillow now just a pile of feathers. Splintered pieces of the wooden table lay strewn across the floor. The window treatments over the sliding glass doors barely hung from one corner, the jewel-colored fabric torn in several places. The bed stood as it should, but pillow-top stuffing exploded from the shredded mattress. Pieces of the headboard rested on the bed and surrounded the remains of a turquoise pillow. The walls looked like they'd been tattered by shrapnel and chunks of drywall littered the carpet. The dresser seemed to be the only piece to survive, although the mirror hanging over it now looked to be a puzzle of jagged pieces.

"I think Hurricane Alexis hit our Caribbean island." Tristan wrapped his arms around me and kissed the top of my head. "Did you have fun?"

I smiled. "Despite the results, yes. Last night was unbelievable."

He chuckled. "I agree."

"But it could have been Hurricane Tristan."

"Nope, first of the season. It has to be Alexis."

I tilted my head to look up at him. "So tonight will be Tristan?"

He grinned. "Can you handle it? Because it'll be a category five."

I laughed. "You already blew me away last night. I don't know how much worse—or better—it can get."

"Ah. I love a challenge."

We showered together, too sore to do anything *but* shower. He sat outside with a cup of coffee by the time I dressed in one of the sundresses. Owen knocked on the front door as I came out of the bedroom. He followed me through the kitchen and family room as we headed for the balcony. I yanked the bedroom door shut, but not before Owen caught a glimpse of the mess. He pulled me to the side and his eyes fell on the last of the bruises on my arms when I cringed from his grip.

"Are you sure you're okay with him?" he whispered, as if Tristan couldn't hear him anyway.

I rolled my eyes. "I'm fine."

"Alexis, I saw your room. And the bruises. Did he do that to you?" His eyes showed genuine concern.

"Don't worry about it."

"It's my job to worry about it. What happened? Did you two get in a fight?"

"No. It's really none of your business." *Please don't push it, Owen.* But he did.

"I'm supposed to protect you. If he's hurting you . . ."

"Geez, Owen, if you really have to know, we were just . . . making up for lost time."

I gave him a significant look. The bewildered expression on his face told me he still didn't get it. I groaned with frustration.

"We went balls to the wall fucking the hell out of each other! Got it now?!" I clapped my hand over my mouth. *Oh! Did I really just say that?*

"Oh," Owen said flatly. Then realization finally overcame him. "*Oh!*"

I heard something about Hurricane Alexis muttered from the balcony. I threw Tristan a look through the glass doors. He shook with laughter. Owen looked at Tristan, then at me and then at the bedroom door. He shook his head slowly.

"I need to get a motorcycle," he muttered.

I didn't know if I'd ever heard Tristan laugh so hard.

Chapter 13

As soon as we all sat out on the balcony, the guys hounded me about what I could do, briefly taking me back to my old school days when kids called me a freak for healing in front of their eyes. But, of course, to Tristan and Owen, what made me freaky was my *lack* of powers. In addition to what I could always do, I could only think of the heightened senses.

"So can you see that boat way out on the water?" Owen asked.

The only boat in our view appeared to be a small fishing vessel about a half-mile away.

"The one with the white hull and blue stripe?" I asked.

"Nice." He sounded impressed.

So something *had* changed over the last few days—not even two nights ago could I see so far.

"Can you read the name or the numbers?" Tristan asked.

"No. I can see that they're there, but I can't distinguish them," I answered. "Can you?"

"It's called the 'Trojan Horse,'" he said.

"It's kind of an odd name for a boat," I said.

"Makes you wonder why they'd name it that."

"Maybe it's not really a fishing boat," Owen said and then he quickly grew excited. "They must be hiding something bad. Maybe they're pirates. Or maybe there's a bunch of Cubans or Haitians in there, escaping to the States. Or maybe they're drug traffickers. There you go . . . that's it. Tristan, you wanna have some fun with a drug bust?"

Owen was obviously joking, but Tristan shook his head and answered anyway. "I just got back from hell. I'm not really in the mood to deal with automatic weapons and lunatic drug dealers."

"Well, I can hear a guy talking, and his words don't make any sense, but I'm pretty sure he's talking about fishing anyway," I said.

They both stared at me, their eyes wide and their mouths slightly open, apparently forgetting Owen's theories.

"You can't hear him?" I asked. Owen shook his head.

"I can hear him moving around," Tristan said, "but not any words."

"Huh." My brows furrowed as I tilted my head. "I don't know who he's talking to. I can't hear anyone else. And he keeps interrupting himself with incoherent and irrelevant words."

It wasn't just *what* he said that seemed strange. The quality of his voice sounded odd. His words kind of echoed or reverberated, as if spoken through a wrapping-paper tube.

Tristan peered out at the boat.

"I only see one guy. I think he's alone." He paused, looking at me, then back at the fisherman and back at me. "I wonder . . . It's a unique gift, but just maybe . . . "

"What?" I asked with trepidation, not liking his tone or the look in his eye.

"You might be hearing his thoughts."

"Nah," Owen guffawed, leaning back in his chair and lacing his fingers behind his head. "Rina's the only one who can do that. Besides, how can she hear his and not ours?"

"Maybe she's not trying and doesn't have control."

"There's no way," I said, shaking my head.

Tristan continued to peer at me, his eyes full of curiosity. "Try me."

I raised an eyebrow at him. "This is crazy. I can't read your thoughts, Tristan."

"Just try," he urged. "You *are* unique."

"Of course I am," I muttered.

"Remember that connection you spoke of yesterday?" he asked.

"I didn't hear your thoughts, though. If I did . . ." *Well, life would've been quite different while he'd been gone.* Our connection, if I was right about it in the first place, didn't exist through the mind, though. We were connected through our hearts or our souls . . . or our blood.

"No, it would have been too much of a distance. But it could be some kind of a precursor," he said.

I glanced at Owen. He apparently dismissed Tristan's idea. He stared off into the distance, seemingly lost in his own world, not paying attention to us. Good thing—our conversation had become a little too personal for comfort. I looked back at Tristan. Anticipation lit up his face.

"Fine, if it'll make you happy," I said with a sigh. "How do I do it?"

"I'm not exactly sure. Telepathy's an ability they couldn't give me—never theirs to give. My guess would be to open your mind and just listen."

I closed my eyes and tried to clear my mind of all my own thoughts. That's harder than it sounds. As soon as you tell yourself to not think, you're still thinking. So I gave myself something to think about: a black, empty space, like a big cloud of nothingness. And then I grew that cloud so it seemed to expand beyond the confines of my own head. I pushed it out farther and let it spread out on its own, eventually drifting out to enshroud the guys. Thoughts of it not working started to poke into my cloud and I almost gave up. But then I heard Tristan's voice singing an old rock song loud and clear in my head, sounding almost like his real voice. *"Here I am . . . rocked you like a hurricane."*

I burst out laughing. *I thought I rocked him.* Now he laughed. *Oh! He heard me!* He nodded.

Then a vision appeared as if I imagined it myself—the destroyed Caribbean room wavered into view. And then images of a naked woman and man in the heat of passion, their arms and legs entwined. They weren't Tristan and me, though. They were Owen and . . .

"*Owen!*" I gasped. I didn't even want to know the identity of the woman. It was bad enough to see *him* in the vision when I thought I'd been seeing Tristan's memory.

Owen jumped with surprise. He squirmed in his chair with obvious discomfort.

"Sorry. I didn't really think you could," he said. "I didn't even know you were trying."

"I wasn't *trying*. It was just *there*," I said, exasperated. "Ugh! I need to learn *control*."

"Yeah, you do," he muttered.

"Trust me—I don't like it anymore than you do. I don't want to go through life like this." I shook my head, trying to erase the image of Owen's fantasy as if my mind was an Etch-a-sketch. "That's really scary."

Tristan's eyes bounced back and forth between us. He lifted his eyebrows. *Hurricane Owen wants to visit our Caribbean island*, I tried to tell him with my thoughts. He grinned. He apparently "heard" me.

"Rina controls it so she only hears thoughts when she wants to," Tristan said. "She can teach you how to tune the rest out."

"I hope so," I muttered.

"Yeah, me, too," Tristan thought and Owen's thoughts echoed his.

I pressed my forehead against the table and put my arms over my head, trying to make the "voices" go away. I imagined sucking the cloud back in and making it disappear. Either both of their minds went blank or I was able to close my mind to them. I couldn't hear the guy out on the boat anymore, either.

"I am never doing that again," I finally said.

"Yeah, let's try something different," Owen said, jumping at the chance to forget the whole thing. He looked around. "We'll start with the easy stuff. See if you can make the chair move."

"Uh . . . *how?*"

He shrugged. "I use magic, so I can't explain it for you."

"*Magic?*"

"Uh, yeah, warlock," he said, flipping his hands toward himself, as if this title was as obvious as the blond hair on his head and I was blind. "Warlocks use magic."

I felt my eyes bug out of my head. "You're a *warlock?*"

He chuckled. "You didn't know? Thought you would've figured that one out."

I closed my gaping mouth and tried not to stare in disbelief. *But holy crap! Owen—my Owen, who I've known for years now—is a freakin' warlock!* My mouth opened again, but I was too stunned to speak. I pulled in a deep breath and composed myself. Apparently, these were things I would have to get used to.

"That's, um . . . unexpected. So, you're not really Amadis?"

He threw me a dirty look. "Sorry I don't get it yet. I mean, were you converted?"

"Third generation *good*," he said, proudly smacking his chest with his fist. "Rina's mother converted my grandparents. All I've known is the Amadis way of life."

"Wow . . . a warlock." I shook my head, still amazed. I knew, of course, that Owen wasn't normal, that he could do things regular humans couldn't, but I'd assumed he was Amadis in the same way Mom, Tristan and Rina were. I thought shielding was one of his quirks, like my sixth sense or Tristan's paralyzing power or Rina's telepathy. Never had I expected actual *magic*. "That's really crazy, Owen. So that's why you didn't stop aging—you don't have Amadis blood like Tristan and me?"

"Right. I'm warlock through and through. We get really old, though, so I'll be around at least as long as you."

"Is that a threat?" I teased.

He smiled. "Nope. It's a promise."

"So, do you have a wand or a staff or anything?" I almost laughed at my own question. It sounded outrageous when I said the words out loud.

"Have you ever *seen* me with one?" He asked with a snort. "Those are for witches, wizards and sorcerers. I just use my hands."

"Witches, wizards and *sorcerers*?" I stared at him in disbelief again. These creatures all existed in my books, but in real life? I wondered if a line between fiction and reality even existed. It seemed to all be blurring together now. Apparently, *my* fiction *was* reality. "What's the *real* difference between you . . . you . . . ?"

"Mages," he said. "We call all magical people 'mages'."

"Right. Mages."

"You were pretty much right on target in your books," Owen said. "Wizards and witches—the same thing but wizards are dudes and witches aren't—are your everyday magic people.

Don't get me wrong, though. They can be pretty powerful. But sorcerers and sorceresses have the greatest magical power and they're able to boost it by pulling more energy from the world and the atmosphere. We don't have any in the Amadis. They're loners, so no one has been able to get to them and they're probably too power-hungry anyway. And then there are the warlocks. We have more power than witches and wizards and we're physically built to fight—stronger, tougher, faster."

"Are warlocks just guys then?"

"Nope. They're both. Some of our best warlocks are chicks. And my mom."

"Your *mom*?" How come I never thought of Owen as having a mother? I'd known him for nearly nine years and was just now learning all these things about him.

"She's an awesome fighter. Our most powerful magic comes out when we're fighting."

"So that makes warlocks ideal protectors."

He grinned. "Yep. And you happened to get one of the best."

"One who caves into a pretty face and a steak dinner," Tristan muttered.

Owen scowled.

"Please don't," I said.

"No, he's right," Owen said, his voice heavy and the lines appearing between his brows. "I should've known better. And I do take full responsibility for it."

"It's in the past, remember? Can we get back to business?" I suggested. My eyes darted between them until I felt the tension release. "So, what do I use, if not magic?"

"It's just power," Tristan answered. He held his hand out and drew a line in the air with his finger. With the scraping sound of metal against concrete, the empty chair slid across the balcony floor. "Just concentrate your mind on what you want to do. If you have the power, you can do it."

I imitated his hand movement and focused all my mental energy on making the chair move. It wobbled and I did a dance in my own chair, shrieking with excitement. Owen laughed and made the chair do a flip in the air. My enthusiasm deflated.

"Show off," I muttered.

"Yours will strengthen," Tristan said.

"So what's the difference between power and magic?"

I'd accepted that Tristan and I—and Mom and Rina—had powers years ago. What I didn't realize was the magic behind them.

"Our powers are basically based on the will of the mind and we're not supposed to be born with them," Tristan said. "We come into them when it's time for us to receive them, like with your *Ang'dora*. Of course, you and I both had some powers before then, but they were weak. Owen was born magic, but he has to learn how to use it."

"You've been given enough magic to do certain things—abilities—but the power of your mind is how you use it," Owen added. "I have magical powers, but I have to learn how to use different spells and reagents to make the power useful."

I tried to make sense of their explanations. "So, Tristan and I, our magic is limited to the abilities we're given and we control them with our mind. But you, Owen, can do all kinds of magic, if you know the spells or have the right tools or materials?"

"Right. You got it." Owen grinned at me. "And your abilities are more physical—you might have to use the mind, but the power affects physical objects. I can conjure magical things out of nothing, like the protective shield over this place."

"What about this ability to get into people's heads?" I asked. "People's minds and thoughts aren't physical objects."

"Which is why it's such a rare gift," Tristan said. "Even in the Amadis."

"Of course, *I'd* be the one to get it," I mumbled. It was one gift I really didn't want.

He smiled. "It means your mind is strong enough to control such a unique power. It's a good thing."

I thought about Owen's fantasy and grimaced. "I don't know about that."

"Let's see what else you can do," Owen suggested, changing the subject as if he knew my thoughts. Perhaps he did. I wasn't positive I controlled my new "gift" very well.

They flashed and I walked to the edge of the property, by the trees and brush. Tristan and Owen took turns showing their strength by pulling out bushes with one hand and knocking over trees. They seemed to be trying to one-up each other. Of course, Tristan won on all accounts.

"All right, you've proven your point," I said. "Any more and you two will ruin our privacy."

"You try," Owen said. "Here, start out small."

He indicated a knee-high palmetto bush. I grabbed it at the base and tried to pull it out with both hands. The plant didn't budge.

"Guess I still have to be pissed off," I said. *Or getting it on with my sweetie.* I didn't have to hear Tristan's mind to know he thought the same thing. The small smile on his lips and the twinkle in his eyes told me. It was an inviting look and I so wanted to take him up on it. But we had things to do and places to go. I distracted myself by looking up at a tall coconut tree standing near us. "I won't even try knocking over a palm tree, so don't ask."

"I have an idea, though," Tristan said, following my gaze. He searched the ground and picked up a handful of small rocks, then looked up at the trees. "Try to hit the coconuts on that one."

He pointed to another tree thirty yards away, the coconuts twenty feet high. I missed by several yards on the first try. Tristan stepped behind me and showed me how to aim properly.

The electric pulse when he touched my hand brought back a memory, when he'd tried to show me how to shoot darts on our first date. Unlike those of the last seven years, this memory came bright and clear. I wondered if he remembered.

"I thought you weren't going to do that anymore," he reminded me, his voice in my head.

I looked at him guiltily. *Sorry. It's a nice memory I wanted to share.*

"Thank you for it." He raised his eyebrows. *"Now please get out of my head."*

I grinned sheepishly and tried to close my mind by focusing on the tree. But suddenly all I could see was an image of many trees and brush stretching high over my head, as if I lay on the ground in the middle of a forest or overgrown vegetation. The vision disappeared as quickly as it came. I shook it off, dismissing it as nothing but a quick thought. I just didn't know if it belonged to me, Tristan or Owen. And that annoyed me.

Owen and Tristan still watched me, both of their brows raised with expectation. I refocused on the tree and imagined a line the rock would follow between my hand and the coconut. I let the rock fly. *Oh!* I hit the seed dead on. And after doing so once, it came easily. I *couldn't* miss.

"What else?" I asked excitedly, wanting to move on to the next thing. Now that I found something I *could* do, the tests were getting fun.

"Do you think she has enough power to project?" Owen asked thoughtfully.

"We'll only find out if we try," Tristan answered. He demonstrated by holding his left hand out toward a tree trunk about fifteen feet away, twisting his wrist and spreading his fingers in a flicking motion. A fireball shot out of his palm, singeing a hole in the bark. I jumped in surprise.

"Crap, Tristan, you never showed me that one!"

He chuckled. "I don't like to use it. I can aim the fire perfectly, but it's hard to control once it starts spreading. Besides, it's much more effective to paralyze the enemy—or take them out completely with one shot."

I stared at him, realizing I never completely understood just how powerful he was.

He raised his eyebrows. "Your turn."

I looked down at my hands—my normal, human hands. They had performed all kinds of tasks over the years, from typing to changing diapers, from cleaning to throwing things, from punching a dirt-bag in the nose to caressing my baby's cheek. Normal, human hands—amazing all on their own. I certainly didn't expect them to ever shoot fire.

"C'mon already," Owen moaned, apparently growing bored.

I lifted my left hand and made the same motion as Tristan had. I felt a strange tug, as if a thin thread was being drawn through my veins and out the center of my palm, pulling toward the tree. As soon as it—*something*—hit the tree, the feeling disappeared. A small wisp of smoke rose and a black dot marked the bark, but nothing singed. And, although I'd experienced a physical feeling, nothing visible projected out of my palm.

"Hmm. Let me see how strong it is," Tristan said. He walked about ten feet out and stood in front of me. "Try me."

"*What?* I'm not doing that!"

He laughed. "If that's all you can do to the tree, I can take what you have."

He crossed his arms over his chest and stood in a stance that showed he wouldn't budge. I sighed and twisted my hand at him.

"Huh . . . that's interesting," he said. His lips pulled into a grin. "I felt an electric current. A shock."

"Oh! It was always *me*?!" I stared at my palm as if it had turned into some mutant shape, but it still looked the same.

Tristan laughed again. "Guess so. I guess I pulled it out of you. Now try with your other hand."

I did. I didn't feel anything.

"Hmm . . . I felt a little warmth," Tristan said. "Try again, but with your palm straight out."

He demonstrated by holding his arm out and his hand up, as if motioning me to stop. I mimicked him and focused on pushing energy through it. I felt a ribbon of . . . something . . . a warm and soft feeling . . . flow through my arm and out my hand.

"Yeah, warmth. Ah." He smiled. "Amadis power."

"*Really?*" I asked. I bounced on the balls of my feet with elation. "Like Mom and Rina?"

"Not quite. It's still pretty weak, but I can feel it."

I looked at Owen and he nodded approvingly. My insides squirmed with excitement.

Chapter 14

Owen fixed cheesy eggs for brunch that he and Tristan inhaled while I picked at mine. I wasn't hungry at all, my stomach feeling as if I'd already eaten a plate of worms. Anxiety for the afternoon ahead of us writhed inside me. As soon as he finished eating, Owen disappeared.

"Why are we doing it this way?" I asked Tristan as we left the house. "I mean, why don't we just flash all the way to the bank?"

"Because we need to be cloaked the whole time and Owen can't keep us cloaked when we're flashing. If we appear in the wrong place at the wrong time . . . there are Daemoni looking for us everywhere."

"So, this is probably another stupid question, but why can't we just flash into the vault where the safety deposit boxes are and flash back here when we're done?"

"Because we need the bank's key that matches our key to open the box." I was about to point out that he could easily open it himself if he wanted to, but he caught onto my thought. "It's against the rules to use magic or powers to gain access to a bank vault."

My brows furrowed together. "Whose rules?"

"The Amadis. No using powers or magic for personal gain."

"Oh." I remembered many years ago, when we'd run into Ian, who had left the Amadis for the Daemoni. He'd complained about all the rules and control the Amadis had over him and now his dissatisfaction made a little more sense. "But this isn't exactly personal gain. They're your belongings, right? It's not like we're breaking into steal a pile of gold bars or someone else's money."

"We're not allowed. That's how it is." He abruptly stopped in the brush and lifted my hand in front of me. The air itself seemed to waver, like it does when heat rises from a hot asphalt road. "That's the shield. Can you see it? Can you feel it?"

I nodded, though I only saw it because the air vacillated when I touched it and I felt nothing.

"As soon we cross it, we have to flash immediately. I need to concentrate, since I've only done this once before."

The worms in my stomach wriggled again. The memory of Vanessa and the others flashed in my mind, followed by the pseudo-memory of Tristan writhing on the ground in a foreign land. We had been safely confined within Owen's shield around the beach house. The estate had served as our refuge. Now we were about to leave its safety, risking our lives or separation again. I felt sick and imagined throwing up worms. Sweat beads popped out on my forehead.

"It's okay, *ma lykita*. We'll be okay." Tristan lifted me into his arms.

"Just don't let them separate us, Tristan," I whispered. "I don't think I could live through it again."

"Never, my love. But we'll be fine. We're just going to the bank." He winked at me, calming my fears. It's hard to be scared when your mind goes blank. "Ready?"

I nodded and tucked my face against his chest. He took two steps, then flashed us both. The air was sucked out of my lungs, as if a vacuum mask had been applied to my face. In a second, everything changed around us—the feeling of the air, the smells, the sounds. I automatically inhaled deeply, trying to fill my lungs again.

"You did it!" Owen said with a note of triumph. He stood next to a black Mercedes sedan with tinted windows, parked behind a small, brick building. I could see the words Key Largo Christian Church hand-lettered on a sign by the street. Owen had come ahead of us to lease the car because the Ferrari was too small for the three of us and too beat up anyway . . . and because the Daemoni knew to watch for the conspicuous sports car.

Tristan set me on my feet and Owen started rubbing his hands together.

"Wait," Tristan said and Owen stopped, lifting an eyebrow.

Tristan took my necklace off, fished the key off the chain, then returned the necklace to my neck. He handed the key to Owen, who stuffed it into his jeans pocket. Then Owen rubbed his hands together again and thrust them at us. If Tristan still hadn't been holding my hand, I would have assumed he had flashed. I could see myself perfectly, but there seemed to be nothing but air where Tristan just stood, although the sandy ground indented where his feet were planted. Owen had cloaked us. He ushered us into the back of the car, then jumped in the driver's seat and drove us farther north.

The key I'd been wearing with my pendant all these years opened a safety deposit box at a bank in Miami. Owen pulled the car into a parking garage beneath the building. We followed him inside, staying close to Owen to prevent anyone from bumping into us. The stiff, commercial-grade carpet inside didn't register our footsteps. As long as we remained silent, no one would know we were there.

I felt uneasy, though. My sixth sense—the one that told me whether a person's overall intentions were good or bad—didn't seem to be working. Nobody registered, not even the neutral people. Instead, a low humming sound filled my head. I hoped the *Ang'dora* wasn't removing that sense. I'd come to rely on it, especially the alarms the Daemoni set off. Now I felt as if I'd lost one of my connections to the outside world, almost as bad as losing my sight or hearing.

With that loss, the feeling of vulnerability slid over my shoulders and down my arms, as if an actual cloak were falling to the floor and exposing us in the midst of the enemy. The feeling was irrational, of course. So was my fear. After all, one of the best warlocks and the most dangerous creature on Earth protected me. Nobody could even see us anyway and, like Tristan said, we were just making a trip to the bank. Daemoni wouldn't attack now, not with all these people around. I hoped.

Nonetheless, the worms wriggled in my stomach again while Owen showed the banker the key and gave her the safety-deposit box number. The hum in my head intensified, becoming more like a buzz now. Tristan squeezed my hand, as if he could sense my distress.

The woman led us down a narrow hallway to the vault, where she stopped and pressed her hand against a pad attached to the wall to the right of the door. A little light over the pad flashed green, then yellow. She motioned to Owen. Owen held his hand up toward the pad and I felt Tristan shift slightly. The light turned solid green. I assumed Tristan had slipped his hand under Owen's to provide the correct biometric reading.

The banker didn't even notice how Owen hadn't pressed his palm flat against the pad. Just a few days ago, I probably wouldn't have noticed either. Realizing there were so many things we could do with these magical powers made me also realize the Daemoni could do the same. In that moment, I gained a new perspective of how some criminals got away with their crime sprees undetected— they didn't work alone. Or they weren't quite human.

With a hiss and a swish, the vault door slid open automatically, opening into a room about the size of a standard hotel room. Rows and rows of safety-deposit boxes lined the walls, from floor to ceiling, corner to corner, making the room feel as if it was covered in stainless steel. A chest-high, stainless-steel table stood in the center of the room. The woman led Owen, and us, inside the vault, selected a box and slid it out of its designated space, placing it on the table with a thunk. She and Owen both stuck their keys into the end of the box and it made a clicking sound. She slid the lid just a hair's width to ensure it was unlocked. Then she stepped outside and closed the door to the vault to give Owen privacy.

Owen waved his hands at us and there Tristan stood, right next to me, already reaching for the box. I held my hand out in front of me, flexed it and opened it again. I did a quick visual check of Tristan's whole body, hoping my own looked just as real and *there* as his did. We'd been cloaked much longer than I'd been the other day, when Owen drove me out of Key West. I hadn't felt any different while cloaked—then or now—but I supposed some part of me worried both of our bodies might have disappeared forever.

Tristan lifted the lid of the box to reveal several stacks of hundred-dollar bills, a pile of white envelopes, some documents laying flat and a host of keys littering the bottom. He placed the envelopes and documents on the table and started picking through the keys.

"London, Athens, Hong Kong . . . ," he muttered under his breath as he chose specific keys, each approximately the same size as the one that had hung on my necklace. He looked up at me. "Sydney?"

"Sydney what?" I asked stupidly.

"Do you think we might go to Sydney?"

"Australia? Oh, yes! Definitely! But not to live. I want to live here, in Florida, if possible."

"It might be a while before we can come back, but we will." He selected a few more keys and stashed them into his jeans pocket. He also stuffed several bundles of cash into his pockets, and then mine and Owen's, too. Then he picked up the stack of envelopes and started flipping through them. I peered over them, noticing the flaps weren't sealed. I could see passports and driver's licenses and realized they were various forms of identification. Tristan stopped at one. "How about Nikolai Skovorsky? Is that the father of Ms. A.K. Emerson's son?"

I lifted an eyebrow. "How would she meet a Russian, especially at nineteen?"

He shrugged and continued through the rest. He stopped on the second-to-last one and grinned mischievously. "Owen Allbright."

Owen grabbed the envelope and pulled out the documents. "You trying to steal my identity?"

I looked at the identification pieces—a Montana driver's license with Tristan's picture and Owen's name. Tristan chuckled.

"Just for an emergency. You never know. But, sorry, you're not marrying my wife." He snatched the papers back from Owen and stuck them back in the pile. He looked at the last one. "It looks like Jeffrey Wells. Does that work for you? A.K. Wells?"

"As long as it's not Tristan Knight, Owen Allbright or some ridiculous name that makes no sense, I don't care. I just want to get out of here." My fingers pressed against my temples. I didn't know if the vault's stagnant air or the tension of the day caused it, but my head thrummed, creating a dull ache.

Tristan put everything away and Owen cloaked us before calling for the banker. When she opened the door, she looked at Owen, then around the room, as if expecting to find someone else in here. She must have decided she'd been hearing things, because she turned on her heel and led us back to the lobby.

The drone in my head increased and the sound itself multiplied, becoming several different buzzing sounds, each with its own quality and volume. It felt like bees actually flew around inside my head and grew agitated with no way to escape. The sounds grew louder and more intense. A panicked feeling started to rise in my chest with the onslaught, making it difficult to breathe. I fought the urge to cover my ears and shut my eyes, as if that would silence the ruckus. A moan that would likely become a scream lodged itself in my throat. I'd never had asthma, but I thought I knew what it felt like now. My chest burned as I tried to draw in a breath, but couldn't. I felt Tristan's arm slide around my waist and he pulled me against him. I didn't realize I'd been trembling until I stopped as he comforted me. We finally left the busy lobby and entered the garage. The hum quieted, leaving only the ache.

Once in the backseat of the car, I leaned my head against Tristan and curled my body into his. I instinctively knew right where he was and how to fit myself within his contours, even when I couldn't see him. It had already become second nature again, as if we'd never been separated. His lovely scent and calming touch soothed away my anxiety. As Owen drove onto the highway, the headache dissipated.

"I have no idea what came over me," I finally said. "My head sounded like a beehive. And it kept getting louder, especially in the bank's lobby."

"Where there were more people," Tristan said, and then added, "more thoughts."

"You think all that noise . . ." I didn't finish. Of course, he was right. The buzzes, each with their own unique sound, were others' thoughts trying to enter my mind. My heart sank at the realization of what it meant. "I can't ever be around people again. It's too painful!"

Tristan gave me a squeeze. "You just need to get used to it and learn better control. Rina can do it. I know you'll be able to."

It wasn't a question of whether I would be able to. I didn't know if I *wanted* to.

Owen drove us back to Key Largo. He didn't drive as fast as Tristan did and I could feel Tristan's impatience. He didn't say anything, though, and just held me, for which I was grateful. I felt a strange tension hovering just beyond us, as though waiting for Tristan to let go of me so it could seize control of my body.

Before we separated so Tristan could flash us back to the beach house and Owen could return the car, we drove down a dead-end street, to a small beach in Key Largo. The sun hung in the western sky, still more than an hour from setting, providing a perfect back drop for pictures of the author with her long-lost lover. Owen turned the car off and we all just sat there for several long moments.

"It's as good a place as any," Tristan finally said.

Owen turned around in the seat and waved his hands at us. I felt relieved to see Tristan again. I decided I didn't particularly like this cloaking device. It was convenient and even necessary, but it had been too long since I'd seen my love's face for it to keep disappearing.

I wished my sixth sense would fix itself or return or do whatever it needed to do so I could rely on it again and feel a little less vulnerable. It was near dinnertime and the beach appeared to be deserted. A pier with a grass-roofed gazebo at its end jutted over the water, but no fishermen dangled rods from its edge. There was no one around to sense their intentions or for their thoughts to buzz into my head. Yet I felt exposed, as if someone—or some*thing*—watched from out-of-sight.

"They don't need to be good pictures," Tristan instructed Owen as we walked out to the sand. "In fact, people should have to look closely and just assume that it's her. The vaguer and blurrier the photos are, the less likely they might recognize us in the future."

Tristan and I walked up and down the small beach, Owen staying behind us to catch our profiles and nothing more with the camera. Though I hadn't made any public appearances for a few years, we didn't want to take any chances of recognition. Tristan and I held hands, walked arm-in-arm, kissed a couple times and even pretended to play at the edge of the water. It shouldn't have been hard to look like the reunited couple we really were, but my nerves were on edge and I couldn't completely play the role.

When we finally turned to cross the hundred yards to the car, the beehive grew in my head again. Just a low hissing sound at first, but the noise quickly grew louder, into a hum and then a buzz.

"*Him.*"

"Who?" I looked up at Tristan. We'd been walking in silence. Why would he suddenly blurt that out?

He peered down at me. "What?"

I realized that though the word had come clearly, the voice was unrecognizable. Not Tristan's.

"*They're here.*" Again clear, but an even different voice.

My heart picked up speed as I looked around. I saw no one. But I knew we weren't alone. The buzz grew louder and I clamped my hands over my ears to block it out. It didn't do any good, of course. The sound came from within.

"Alexis, what's—" Tristan didn't finish his sentence. He stiffened and his eyes scanned our surroundings. He sensed their presence. "Owen!"

As soon as Tristan called out his name, the buzzing exploded into different voices and random words and phrases, as if that one word had broken some kind of dam holding everything back.

"—*I'll wait*—"

"—*yes*—"

"—*she'll come*—"

"—*maybe we should*—"

"—*no*—"

"—*stupid moron*—"

"*Ha! How lovely!*" Even drenched in sarcasm, the words sounded like a breeze caressing silver chimes. A musical voice. A voice I'd already come to know too well.

"Vanessa," I whispered. "She's here."

On the other side of the car, under the shade of a clump of mangrove trees, a white figure emerged. She remained in the shadows, but I could feel her evil eyes on us. Her stone-white lips stretched into a grin. Then I noticed the other figures behind her. Vanessa stayed in the cover of the trees, but the others started moving toward us.

"Go!" Owen yelled. "Before they get too close!"

He thrust his hands out at the approaching Daemoni and one of them collapsed to the ground. Someone laughed. Then a blur of a figure shot toward us.

The next thing I knew, Tristan had me scooped into his arms. Then I felt that pull on the air in my lungs and a fraction of a second later, I sucked in a chest-full of air. Before I could take another deep breath, Tristan leapt several yards. Then he set me on my feet and pulled on my hand. I stumbled over wild ferns and other brush, scraping my arm against a palmetto's fronds. Our beach house stood thirty yards away. We were within the safety of the shield.

"They're back! But not Owen. I don't smell him. Where is he? I need him!"

Panting, I leaned over, my hands on my knees and my elbows locked to support me, as I tried to figure out what was going on. The words made no sense. I didn't recognize the female. Nobody should even be here. Was I confused? Was the adrenaline shooting through my veins messing with my head? Had Swirly decided to return?

"If Owen doesn't get here, Seth will kill me!"

I shot up and stood perfectly straight, frozen in place. Only the Daemoni called him Seth.

Chapter 15

A string of profanity flew out of Tristan's mouth. He didn't need to hear the female's thoughts. He knew she was there. His nostrils flared. His eyes sparked. He crouched in front of me, in a protective stance. I didn't know if my mind put up some kind of wall to block her thoughts out of fear, if her mind went blank or if she'd disappeared, but the female's thoughts fell silent.

I opened my mouth to ask what happened to Owen, then clamped it shut when an unfamiliar scent wafted below my nose, the odd mixture of honey, mesquite and dirt. Then I saw movement in the brush about ten yards away and froze. The top of a sapling wavered. Something snapped, the sound of a thick branch breaking under a heavy weight. Then a face appeared next to the rough bark of a palm tree. My heart sputtered. I blinked several times. The figure wasn't human. It wasn't even an animal that belonged on this continent, except in a zoo.

Large, yellow cat eyes stared back at us, framed with black and white stripes. A long, orangish-tan nose ended in a rounded muzzle with whiskers poking out of the sides. Round, black ears, pointed backward, twitched and then rotated forward. The huge feline head dipped down, but the eyes never ceased their careful watch on us. An orange paw as big as my head moved forward. Tristan soared at it.

"Tristan! That's a freaking tiger!" I shrieked.

He landed on the big beast's back and his arms wrapped around it. They rolled twice and stopped with Tristan on top. His muscles bulged as he squeezed the barrel chest. The cat struggled under him. Long claws dug into the dirt. Its tail whipped side to side. Lips pulled back, revealing curved fangs as long and nearly as thick as my index finger. But the tiger never growled or lashed out at Tristan.

"Tristan, wait!" Owen yelled from right behind me and I spun on him in surprise. I hadn't even noticed his return, too worried about Tristan. His blond hair stuck out everywhere and black smudges marked his face. A slash in his jeans gaped open just above his knee.

I turned back to Tristan and the beast, just in time to see the big cat begin to shrink. The orange, black and white fur appeared to retract into its skin. The limbs narrowed and transformed. The claws became fingers. Tristan jumped to his feet, landing fifteen feet away, his palm faced toward the morphing shape.

"Easy, Tristan," Owen said, taking a few steps toward them. "It's okay. She's with me."

The figure became a naked woman, long and lean, thin but with well-defined muscles. She lay on her stomach, her long, dark hair shrouding her face. Bruises covered her body—some new, probably from Tristan, but others a greenish-gray. She didn't move and for a moment I thought she was dead. But it was Tristan holding her still with his paralyzing power.

Tristan kept his hand toward her, even as Owen rushed to her side. He pulled his shirt off, knelt beside her and lay his shirt over her, trying to tuck it in under her.

"What do you mean, she's with you?" Tristan growled. "She's a fucking Daemoni!"

The woman whimpered.

"Can you at least let her sit up?" Owen asked.

Tristan's eyes blazed, but he must have let up. The woman rolled into a sitting position and tucked herself into a protective ball. She slowly lifted her head to look up at us and I recognized the young woman's face. Her brown eyes were full of the same fear I'd seen in them the other night in Key West, when the vampires were threatening her. But then she froze and I assumed Tristan paralyzed her again. Her head twitched, as if she'd tried to move but couldn't against Tristan's power.

"She wants to convert," Owen said. "She doesn't want to be one of them."

Another growl rumbled in Tristan's chest.

"Please help me," she whispered, her eyes pleading with us.

"It's a trick, Owen!" Tristan barked. "What the hell are you thinking?"

"No," she said, her eyes looking wild with protest. "Please. I don't want to be them. I never did. What they did to me . . . I hate that life. *You* have to know, of all people."

Tristan's hand never moved, but his eyes exploded in flames. "Of all people, I know the trick of *pretending* to want to change."

"And you *did* want to change, Tristan," Owen reminded him.

"She's not me!"

Owen stood to his full height, only a couple of inches shorter than Tristan. His eyes looked hard as sapphires as he glared at his best friend. "You're not the only one who hates that life. We've converted *thousands* who never wanted to be like them, but were forced against their wills."

They stared at each other, as if in a stand-off. I couldn't

take my eyes off of the woman. Her stringy hair draped around a dirt-smudged face. Her high cheekbones and angular jaw might have given the impression of strength at any other time, but right now she looked scared and weak. Actually, she looked downright pitiful. I could hardly believe that just a minute ago she'd been a deadly beast.

"This is what we're supposed to do," Owen finally said to Tristan, breaking the silence. "This is part of being Amadis. It's our obligation to help her, to save her soul."

"It's not what *we* do, Owen!" Tristan bellowed, making me jump and pulling my attention away from the girl. "Not you or me. That's what Rina and Sophia and some of the others do. Not us! We can't do it! And you're putting Alexis's life on the line. *Your* job is to protect Alexis!"

Owen's eyes darted to me, to the woman and then back to Tristan. "She's been here since yesterday morning. She's had plenty of opportunity if she wanted to do anything."

Tristan's eyes narrowed as he leaned toward Owen. "I don't know what you're trying to pull here, but I would have sensed her."

"I had her under a separate shield, blocked from you. But I couldn't guarantee both shields would hold while I was gone, so I put her under this one right before I left."

Tristan responded with a long growl deep in his chest. His anger frightened me. If he lost control, he might do something he would regret later. He had every right to be angry with Owen, of course. This Were's presence could have posed a danger to us . . . if she weren't so damn pathetic looking.

Tristan rocked back on his heels.

"You could have warned us," he finally said to Owen, anger still in his voice but not as heated as it had been. "I still think it's a trap."

"He'll never believe me. Night's coming. They'll come looking for me. I'd rather him kill me than go back to them."

I continued watching the young woman as she trembled on the ground, Owen's light blue shirt fluttering around her. Her eyes turned to me and focused on mine. She seemed to plead with me for understanding.

"Tristan, I think she might be for real," I said quietly.

"Yes! She'll do it! She can change me!"

"Alexis—"

I held my hand up to stop him and tried to indicate with a lift of my eyebrow that I heard more than our spoken words. I wanted nothing more than to block out this woman's thoughts. I was already tired of people entering my brain, with no way to control it. I didn't know why some thoughts were so loud and clear and others were annoying hums and buzzes. I really wished it would all go away, that I could at least turn the ruckus off at will. But I couldn't. And this woman didn't know I could read her mind. She wouldn't be trying to get to me through telepathic lies. Her thoughts were real.

"Please help me," she whispered, her eyes still holding mine. *"Please say she believes me. Please, please, please!"*

"We're supposed to help her, right?" I asked, looking at Owen. I knew little about the Amadis, but Rina once said the Daemoni tried to destroy human souls and our job was to protect them, to save them. Owen nodded. "How?"

His body noticeably relaxed. "I hoped you could—"

"Have you lost your mind?" Tristan growled. "She can't do anything! She's not ready!"

My eyes went wide and I shook my head. "Owen, I don't . . . I can't . . . ."

I didn't know what he expected me to do. I had no idea how to convert souls. I knew Mom used her power of persuasion and I also knew the physical actions she used to lead people to do as she said. But I didn't know how she actually persuaded them. I didn't have that power. At least, I didn't think I did.

"She just needs Amadis power right now, to keep her subdued," Owen said. "I'll call for Amadis help when we leave for Atlanta in the morning. For now, just share your power."

I stared at him with disbelief. The girl's eyes jumped back and forth between us, her expression mixed with hope and fear. I felt bad for her and wanted to help her. But what Owen asked . . . I didn't know if I could do it.

"She's not strong enough," Tristan said and I looked at him.

"You said you could feel it," I reminded him.

He shook his head. "Not enough to do what this . . . this *thing* needs."

"Please," the girl said. "Just try. Anything."

I looked at Owen and he nodded. Then I looked at Tristan. The fire in his eyes had died down to just sparks. He was coming around.

"She's not a thing. She might not be exactly human, but—"

"She's evil!" Tristan said.

"Which is why I have to try," I said to him and then I looked at the girl. "What's your name?"

"Sh-sh-sheree."

"I make no promises, Sheree," I said. "I have no idea what I'm doing. And if you try anything, these two will stop you in an instant. Understand?"

Her head twitched again, but she still couldn't move it. I wasn't willing to take the chance of asking Tristan to lift his power. He might be right. This could truly be a trick. I just took the twitch as a nod of understanding. I raised my right arm and turned my palm toward her, pushing that warm energy out of it.

"AAAAHHHH!!!" She screamed. Her body convulsed as if in agonizing pain, even against Tristan's power. I jumped back, jerking my hand to my chest.

"No! Don't . . . stop!" She begged through panted breaths. "It hurts . . . but . . . it's working. I can feel it."

I tried again, but even I could tell the energy came weakly. I barely felt the pull through my arm and out my palm. Sheree trembled, her face twisted in pain, but the quivering quickly slowed. Tears fell down her cheeks. I strained, pushing harder, but nothing more came. I, too, began to shake, all of my muscles feeling like jelly.

"That's all I have," I said weakly. "I'm sorry."

"That's all you can project," Owen said. "It's harder from a distance. Maybe if you touched her, held her hand, like Rina does . . . ."

"No!" Tristan roared. His free hand twitched and I soared into the circle of his arm. He held me tightly against him. "You're not going anywhere near her! She could kill you, Alexis. Hell, for all we know, you could kill her."

"I don't care," Sheree said, her voice rough and pleading. "They're going to kill me anyway, after this. I'd rather die trying than die . . . *evil* . . . damned to Hell."

Her words struck me like a mallet hitting a gong, reverberating throughout my body and into my soul. If she died right now, would she be damned to Hell? I didn't know the answer, but that wasn't a risk we could take. We had to help her. Her soul lay on the line.

"You can handle her easily if anything happens," I said to Tristan.

"You have no idea what the process is like," he said through clenched teeth. "It's draining. It sucks your energy dry. Both of yours. And you're already unstable as it is."

"But between the three of us, we can at least help her fight it," I said. "You can help me."

Tristan looked at Owen. "Why don't you just call for someone right now? Someone who can handle this better?"

"The Amadis are all fighting. There are attacks everywhere, remember? The closest ones are finishing the battle I just left to make sure you two were okay."

Tristan swore under his breath. He looked down at me and I raised my eyebrows in a silent plea. He gave in with a groan.

"Let's get out of the damn trees, at least. Owen, take the Were to the balcony. And Owen . . ." Tristan paused until he knew he had Owen's full attention. His voice came low and threatening. "I swear, if anything happens to Alexis, you will live a long life full of painful regret. I personally guarantee it."

Owen inclined his head in acknowledgement, then helped Sheree to her feet. Her knees knocked together and I was surprised she could hold herself up. She looked so weak. She pulled the shirt tightly together in the front, but she was so tall, Owen's button-down shirt barely reached far enough to cover the important lower parts.

Tristan strode off toward the house, his hand wrapped around mine, tugging me along with him. He slammed the door as soon as we were inside.

"I can't believe this," he growled. "This is senseless."

"It's not for long. We'll get help," I said. "Right?"

"I just don't get it. This is not like Owen. He wouldn't jeopardize your life like this. What is he *thinking*?"

I gently pushed on Tristan's chest, backing him against the kitchen counter. He slumped down and pulled me into his arms. I placed my hands on each side of his face.

"He's thinking like an Amadis," I said.

"No. He's thinking with his dick."

"Tristan!"

"There's no other way to explain it." He put his own hands on the sides of my face and pulled it up toward his. His lips pressed down on mine, but he broke off too soon. "I think we're too much for him."

"I wasn't done kissing you." I'd felt something besides normal desire when he kissed me, so I crushed my lips on his. The longer we kissed, the stronger I felt. His love boosted my Amadis power. I finally pulled back, though, before I passed out from lack of oxygen. I forced myself to remember how to breathe. "That's how we're going to do this. She needs to feel love again."

"Then let Owen give it to her. We're busy." His lips left an electric trail down my chin, around my jaw and down my neck. His hands slid over my back, one traveling lower, squeezing my cheek. My hands glided along his head to the ponytail and pulled him back.

"I don't think it works like that," I murmured over the pounding of my heart. "She needs *love*. Not lust."

"Mmm . . . it makes me feel better." A small smile tugged at his delicious lips and, to be honest, I wanted to let him take me right there on the kitchen counter. Apparently, he wanted the same thing because his thought of lifting me up and yanking off my panties floated in my mind. But Owen paced the balcony outside, making impatient sounds with each turn. Tristan sighed and gave a sideways glance out the sliding glass doors. "At least he put some clothes on her."

I peeked out the window. Sheree sat on the balcony floor, her knees pulled to her chest in a ball. Seeing her human form in a different setting made it even harder to believe she shifted into a killer cat. She still wore Owen's shirt, the sleeves rolled up to just above her wrists, and she now wore a pair of red-and-blue-plaid boxer shorts, as well. I couldn't have provided any better. Not only were nearly all of my clothes dirty, but she was tall and thin. I was short and, at least when I came here, fat. My own shorts only fit me by rolling the waist several times or with a pin. They would fall right down to her ankles.

"Is that what started this? Her being naked?" I teased.

He chuckled. "No, my love. Seeing your naked body

through that little dress is what started this."

I raised my eyebrows. "Is that another power you haven't told me about? X-ray vision?"

"No. I don't need x-ray vision to know what you look like under there." He tapped his temple with his forefinger. "I have the memory firmly locked in right here. A very nice memory."

"A very distracting memory."

He shrugged in concession. I moved to break free of his embrace, but he tightened his arm around me. With his other hand, he lifted my chin to look me in the eye. The green of his eyes was clear and deep, but the gold sparked, on the verge of flames.

"You don't have to do this," he murmured. "In fact, I really prefer that you didn't."

"Tristan, what would you have done if you had decided to leave them, but my mom hadn't been there for you right away? You'd already made the move, they knew what you were doing, but you were there with no immediate options."

"I would have fought them when they came."

"Exactly. And you would have crushed them. Don't you see she can't do that? You can see how weak she is. And all those bruises . . . they've already beat the hell out of her. She thinks they'll come looking for her."

"If they're all fighting right now, she's the least of their worries." He sighed and leaned his forehead against mine. "I guess that means it's the best time to do this. But you must know I won't hesitate to kill her if she does anything to you."

"I know." I kissed the tip of his nose. "I'm counting on that."

I took his hand and led him to the glass doors.

"But only if there's no hope for her," I added. He sighed with resignation.

Chapter 16

As soon as I opened the doors and stepped onto the balcony, a wave of cold air blew over me, causing a chill to run down my spine. It wasn't because the air temperature had become nippy. Early April in the Keys provided ideal temperatures with highs in the low eighties and even now, with the sun beginning to set, it had to be at least seventy-eight degrees. That cold blast came from Sheree.

This was the closest I'd been to her yet and I felt the evil energy surrounding her. The feeling wasn't my sixth sense sounding my Daemoni alarms, either. This was a physical feeling, as if malevolence emanated from her every cell and froze the air around us.

Owen sat next to the young woman, their backs against the railing bars, his arm around her shoulders. I almost thought Tristan might have been right about Owen's motivations, but the look on Owen's face told me he didn't hold her out of sexual want. His eyes were filled with sorrow and his nose wrinkled in disgust. His mouth twisted, as if he were suffering deep internal pain. He looked like he wanted nothing better than to let go and flee from her as far as possible.

Sheree's body quaked uncontrollably with more than just the loud sobs, groans and growls escaping her throat. Her eyes were squeezed shut and her face puckered in concentration, like someone does when they're trying hard not to physically lash out at someone else. I didn't know if she fought the Daemoni power or the Amadis power Owen tried to give her.

"Will she shift if she loses control?" I asked. The Weres in my books would and since I'd been right on so many other things, I had to know.

"Possibly," Tristan said.

My heart pounded with the thought of a tiger bursting out of her body in this small area. Even if she didn't mean to, a wild paw could severely injure any of us. Tristan and I would probably be okay, though it might slow our ability to fight back while we healed. But not Owen. He didn't have the same level of healing ability we did.

"I'm ready if she does," Tristan added, his palm already facing Sheree.

I nodded and took a deep breath, thinking about exactly what to do. I remembered how Rina could just take my hand and I would feel her Amadis power wash through me. Mom could do the same, though her power wasn't quite as strong as Rina's. Mine was still very weak, but it might be enough to at least get Sheree through the night. I sat down in front of her and started to reach out for her hand.

Pop! Pop! The sounds were muffled, but unmistakable.

Owen jumped to his feet. Sheree's body slackened, as if released from some unendurable agony. She pulled in a deep breath, her first in a long time, and exhaled with relief. Until the musical voice rang across the property. Vanessa's voice. We both started shaking. Tristan and Owen just stood there, at attention, their eyes scanning the landscape.

"There," Tristan said quietly, lifting his chin toward a giant entanglement of bushes, vines and mangrove roots near the water's edge, but not on our property. Two white figures stood in the dark shadows.

"They can't get in," Owen said.

"Th-they're here for m-me," Sheree said, her hoarse voice full of terror.

"Don't flatter yourself," Tristan muttered. "But thanks for bringing them."

"There's no way they'd know," Owen said. "I've been careful with the shields."

"Then how did they find us?" Tristan seethed through clenched teeth. "I knew this was a bad idea. It's stupid, Owen. You should have never brought her here."

Owen dropped his head and his shoulders sagged. He crossed his arms over his chest. His body language contradicted itself, as if he acknowledged Tristan was right but still defended his actions. He remained silent, his mouth drawn into a scowl.

"We need to leave now, before more come," Tristan said. "Morning will be too late."

Owen lifted his head and opened his mouth, but before he could speak, his pocket rang. He dug the cell phone out and flipped it open, walking toward the other end of the balcony as he spoke.

Tristan stared at Sheree, his normally full lips pressed into a hard line.

"Please don't make me go back to them. Kill me first," she pleaded. "Just don't send me back."

Tristan's eyes narrowed. "You don't know how tempting that is. You'd be a nice distraction for them while we attempt to leave . . . but it's not going to happen. I'm Amadis now. Only *they* would do something so despicable."

"Is it even safe to leave?" I asked. "We're protected in here, right? Can't we just stay?"

"Looks like we'll have to," Owen said, returning to us, his phone already put away. "That was Julia. Atlanta's not safe. The house is surrounded."

"Who's Julia?" I asked, momentarily distracted by the unfamiliar name.

"One of Rina's council members, her closest advisor after Solomon. She went ahead of Rina and Sophia to check security. Good thing, too."

Movement in the brush caught all of our eyes. All four of our heads twisted at once. We watched Vanessa and her brother walk the perimeter of the shield, testing it every now and then. Eventually realizing they couldn't get through anywhere, they sunk into the shadows.

"Call Rina and Sophia and make sure they know," Tristan said. "And try to get some soldiers here immediately." He jerked his head toward Vanessa and her brother. "They won't leave without a fight."

Owen pulled his phone back out and headed to the other end of the balcony as he dialed. Tristan paced our part of the balcony, his eyes constantly moving from Sheree to me to the darkness outside. He mumbled under his breath, wondering how Vanessa had found us. Again.

Owen finally came back. "I couldn't reach Sophia or Rina, but I did talk to Solomon. Rina and Sophia boarded the plane from London to New York hours ago. I'm sure they'll call as soon as they land. Solomon's sending soldiers, along with Julia. But there's no one close by to help Sheree. Not until Rina and Sophia get here."

"They can't come here!" I shrieked. "It's too dangerous. Especially now that *they* know they're coming."

I flipped my hand toward the last place we saw Vanessa and her brother.

"Someone can slip them in or I'll go out to cloak them myself. And they—" Owen nodded toward the same place "—can't hear us, so they don't know anything. The shield silences us. We can hear them, but they can't hear us."

None of his explanations calmed me. I didn't know if I could rely so completely on magic, something I hadn't believed truly existed until just this morning. Though he'd proven himself repeatedly, for some reason, Owen's powers felt different to me now . . . less *him* and more something else I didn't fully understand. My own sixth sense had been a part of me for as long as I could remember, something I could rely on more than any of my other senses because it had never been wrong. Thinking Owen's shield was similar must have allowed me to trust it so much, but knowing now that magic lay behind it all . . . that we trusted our *lives* with something out of fairy tales . . . it was just a lot to try to accept in one day.

I could almost feel Vanessa's eyes boring into us, whether she could actually see us or not. I didn't see how Mom and Rina would ever get past her. I didn't know why they would even want to try. They weren't reckless by nature . . . which meant they *did* trust Owen's magical capabilities. And if they could, I needed to. I really had no choice right now anyway.

I took a few calming breaths, trying to blow the anxiety out of my body. At least, the anxiety about Mom and Rina. I still had this task in front of me. Literally sitting in front of me, her eyes wide and her lower lip trembling.

"Let's just focus on this," I said. I looked into Sheree's terror-filled eyes. "We already know it's going to hurt. Tell us if you can't handle it. If you wait until it's too much and you do something harmful—to me or anyone else, including yourself—I don't know what these guys will do to you, but I'm sure it won't be good. Understand?"

She nodded and her voice came out in a rough whisper. "Just help me or kill me. That's all I ask."

I inhaled deeply and exhaled slowly. Then I lifted both hands toward her. Just as I was in reach, an electric current shot out of my left hand. I hopped backward on my butt. Sheree had nowhere to go, her back already pressed against the railing, but she shrank away as far as possible.

"Sorry," I muttered, scooting back toward her.

Tristan stepped right behind me, placing a foot on each side of my hips and standing over me. His forearm came into my vision, over my head, his palm facing Sheree. "This is a really bad idea."

"You already said that," I said.

"And I still think it is." The words came out as a snarl. "There are better solutions—like waiting."

I twisted my head to look up at him. "Haven't we learned that the *best* solution is not always the *right* solution?"

He tugged his eyes from Sheree to look at me. The green bands were dark and the gold sparkles dim as his eyes held mine, filled with concern. He exhaled a surrendering sigh and nodded just slightly. Then he looked back to Sheree, his body coiling, ready for action.

I raised just my right hand this time, reaching out toward Sheree. She hesitated. Then she lifted her own hand and clasped her fingers around mine.

Piercing needles of pain shot through my hand. A toe-curling scream wailed from both of our mouths. Her hand was glacial and it felt as if my own froze in her grasp. My blood went cold, ice traveling through my arm, up to my shoulder, into the bones. But we held on tightly to each other.

Owen dropped to his knees next to Sheree, his hands moving around her but not on her, as if afraid to touch her. Tristan stood over me, his palm still facing Sheree. He was prepared to shoot her if and when necessary. I almost begged him for the warmth a fiery ball would provide as the icy sensation continued rushing through my blood. The bitter hatred from the other night started overcoming me again, turning my vision red. My throat felt like I swallowed sandpaper and I realized I still screamed. I clamped my jaw shut, forcing myself to stop.

Various images popped into my head, like the slideshow of my dreams before Tristan's return. But these weren't familiar visions. They were Sheree's memories.

I felt her painful transition into a tiger the first time she'd shifted and saw the full, white moon in a clear sky. She had no idea what happened to her and terror overwhelmed her. Then appeared an unfamiliar face talking to her, his mouth moving, but I couldn't hear the words. Then she was traveling and I knew we were seeing through tiger eyes. The perspective seemed lower than it would be from her height, but taller than if she crawled, just a little taller than me.

We stalked through the woods, the stranger beside us. Tall pines reached for the night sky. A lake in front of us reflected a full moon. A couple sat by the water's edge. Our stomach growled with an emptiness as if we hadn't eaten for days. The man slid a collar off our neck and hissed. The sound incited something within us. We ran for the couple, letting out a roar just as we attacked.

I screamed out loud. Sheree let out a mournful sob.

An image of frozen terrain flashed and then we were in caves. My heart settled its frantic pace. This image I knew. I'd just envisioned it yesterday, when Tristan told me about his imprisonment and escape. How had I pictured this place so perfectly?

"*Because it's home. Your other home,*" a voice inside my head whispered. "*Your* real *home.*"

The voice didn't belong to Sheree. Not to Owen or to Tristan. It belonged to me. It was the cold, evil one I'd heard before Tristan's return. The one I thought had disappeared when my own sanity returned. Evil Alexis.

No! I silently protested, shutting that voice down. *I know it from Tristan.*

Then I realized that was exactly why the image had been so accurate. I hadn't imagined the caves when Tristan told me about them. I'd actually seen what he saw in his mind's eye as he told me. I just hadn't known I could read minds then. Just yesterday. And now here I was, seeing Sheree's visual memories.

As she remembered, she unintentionally shared with me the dark caves where she was free to roam inside, but could never leave. We went to Tristan's space. Various images of him in there over time—sometimes sitting, sometimes standing, sometimes pacing and sometimes curled into a ball—flashed across my vision. She'd been watching him.

The scene abruptly changed to Key West and I saw myself walking down the alley, from her perspective. The image changed again. The time must have been later. Vanessa, her brother and their friends were back, kicking Sheree in her human form, then throwing her around, as if they played a game of hot potato. I saw the wall coming toward us. I heard her thought, "*I'm not going to shift. I won't be like them,*" just before slamming against the wall. Then blackness. Then Owen's face. The cold voice inside me hissed.

A new vision popped into my head. I saw through Sheree's tiger eyes again. But this wasn't a memory. This image had a different quality, a different texture to it. Her current thoughts flooded my mind and I almost pulled away from her. She stalked toward me in her mind, just as she'd done with that couple by the lake. And then she jumped at me. Her sharp claws dug diagonally across my face.

"No!" I said aloud. "Stop it!"

"What?" Sheree wailed. "I can't stop anything!"

"*I want it. I want it so bad,*" she thought. "*I want to rip your throat out. I want to taste your sweet blood, devour your tender meat.*"

But her hand remained tightly clasped around mine as she fought the urge.

"*You want it, too. You know you do,*" my own cold voice said. "*You want to fight her. You want to kill her.*"

"No!" I cried. "No, no, no!"

My whole body suddenly went frigid. I started trembling all over.

"*Yes, yes, YES! Fight her! Kill her! Watch the life force drain from her eyes.*"

I could no longer tell the difference between Sheree's inner voice and my own. They both taunted for a killing match.

"*Find out what it's like! You want to. Admit it. JUST DO IT!*"

Sheree's body vibrated, her edges becoming a blur.

"Don't do it," Owen warned with a low, firm voice breaking into the internal argument. He wrapped his arm around her shoulder. His face contorted with his own pain. But Sheree calmed down. She gained control over the shift.

Evil energy coursed through my body, as if it had been pent up there forever and was now finally free. Free to take control. I squeezed my eyes shut but the images filled my mind. My own visions of lashing out, hurting, killing these very people around me.

No! I won't! This isn't me. Don't let it take me.

But that other part of me gained more control. The

slideshow played again, but now it was my own—yet not the one I'd dreamed. These were all the horrible images. Tristan leaving the safe house and twitching his hand to shut the door behind him, closing me in. The battle on the mansion's lawn. Tristan disappearing. His body writhing in agony on the cavern floor. Figures—some human, some not so much—beating him. And suddenly my fists pounded on him. Then I gripped something in my hands over my head. I slammed it down toward him. A sword pierced through his heart.

"*No!*" I screamed. "*Tristan! No! Tristan!*"

"Shh, shh," Tristan whispered against my ear, bringing me back to the balcony, back to reality. I hadn't noticed him sit down behind me, his legs on each side of mine, his arms around me. My throat felt raw and I realized I'd been screaming his name aloud until he quieted me. The cold began to subside as I allowed his love to rush in. "It's okay, *ma lykita*. I'm right here."

"*He doesn't really love you. It's all a hoax. He wants to kill you. He hates you!*"

I ignored that other voice, knowing it lied. Deception. The enemy's most powerful weapon. Instead, I pulled on Tristan's love harder and felt it boosting my Amadis power again. My body quaked with the change in energy, shaking the hell out of Tristan and me and I knew we would both have bruises everywhere our limbs collided. Sheree's arm jerked like a whip as I pushed the positive energy into her. She groaned and flopped onto the ground, her body going into convulsions. She kept a firm hold on me as if I were her lifeline, not just on my hand, but on my energy. On my soul. She pulled on what little love and goodness I still had within me, draining me of all of it, leaving only evil for both of us.

"This has to stop," Tristan said. "You're killing her."

A growl rumbled in my chest, underscoring his revelation.

I didn't know if he meant I was killing Sheree or she was killing me. It didn't matter. He was right. If we continued, we would end up killing each other.

Tristan pried Sheree's fingers back from mine, forcing her to loosen her grip. He yanked my hand away from hers and in one swift motion, had me in his lap in the far corner of the balcony, too far for her to reach. Owen tried to calm her, but her body still seized.

"I can take it, Alexis," Tristan said and I felt another energy pull on my body. My blood frosted over and I shivered in his arms. I realized what he was doing.

"No, Tristan," I whispered. "You're not stable enough."

"I can handle it."

He continued pulling and his power was too strong for me to fight it. I fell limp in his arms as I felt the evil energy leaving my body. I no longer felt cold. I no longer felt anything. Numbness encircled my heart. I didn't even know if it continued beating. The feeling began to spread throughout my body and all I felt was overwhelming despair. Loss. Hopelessness.

"*This is almost as good,*" the evil voice hissed.

My mind clouded over and the balcony disappeared. I found myself standing in a meadow, mountains on each side of me, a lake reflecting more peaks lining its far shores. The waist-high grass made a muted whispering sound as it waved in a breeze I didn't feel. I thought this place might have been beautiful, if there had been any color. Instead, everything was in different shades of steel-blue and gray, even the sunless sky and the wild flowers in the field. I noticed the flowers changing—wilting and shriveling. I smelled nothing but stale air, even with the breeze still stirring.

I realized the mountains were the same ones I'd sat on while watching the slideshow of images in my dreams. And I now stood in the same meadow I'd run through in my dream the other night, after Tristan saved me. But this world had been bright and warm then. It had made me happy. Now I felt nothing, no concern for where I was or how I got here.

Not even curiosity for the four bodies in front of me, lying under a gray tree whose leaves fell all around them. They were our bodies. They lay completely still with their eyes closed, but I could hear their heartbeats, very faint, very weak. I noticed how Tristan's hand held mine. I stared at our hands clasped together, waiting for something to stir within me. But it never did. The scene meant nothing. I felt nothing for any of them. I just watched them, for lack of anything better to do.

I couldn't tell if any time passed. The light didn't change. Nothing at all changed. The clouds in the gray sky didn't transform or even move, though the breeze continued. The scene remained constant, making me think of a computer screen-saver, with the waving grass and falling leaves the only action.

"Oh, dear God! Are they dying?" The voice came from all around me, yet from nowhere. It should have echoed off the mountains, but it just fell flat. The voice was a familiar one and I thought I should know it, but I didn't look around for it. I didn't feel a need or a desire to.

Dying? It seemed as though that word should mean something to me. But still I felt nothing. Nothing at all. I was completely numb.

"No, not dying, but they are not well," said another familiar voice with a heavy accent. "They need us, Sophia. Quick!"

Sophia . . . another word that seemed like it should mean something. I still couldn't grasp at what.

I stared at the bodies in front of me, the tree's leaves still falling, though it appeared to be losing none. I didn't know what this all meant. And I realized I didn't care if it meant anything at all. I. Didn't. Care.

But I did wonder . . . .

What happens to a soul when all the goodness and badness are removed? Is anything left behind? Or does the soul die or disappear, leaving just a body with no humanity at all? No emotions. No feeling. Just . . . some kind of soulless existence. Even evil and hatred means you *feel* something. That you have passion within you. That you still have a soul. I didn't even feel that. I felt absolutely nothing. Just an existence in this strange world that never changed.

The scene suddenly flashed yellow, as if the sun had decided to make an appearance in the gray world, colorizing everything for a split second, then vanishing again. I even felt its momentary warmth.

Then out of the corner of my eye, I saw something changing. Color slowly started bleeding into the grayness. A warm yellow seeped into the sky, as it does when a storm cloud moves away, revealing the sun a little at a time. The tall grass started turning green. The flowers reversed their earlier actions and bloomed across the field. I felt the breeze now, whispering across my cheek. I sucked the air in, as if I hadn't taken a breath since finding myself here. Perhaps I hadn't.

"Alexis, darling," said the accented voice. I could hear the relief in it. And I knew what relief was! An emotion. A feeling. It all meant something to me again!

A powerful wave of warmth entered through my heart and washed over me, like a splash of warm water. Something inside me instinctively pulled at the warmth, drank it in with large, thirsty gulps. My body reacted immediately. Goodness and strength began to refill every cell. I could feel my heart again. My limbs tingled as the numbness lifted away.

But I felt cold. So cold.

I blinked several times, grateful to leave the gray, meaningless world and to find a gorgeous face hovering over me.

"Rina?" I whispered as she pushed another wave of warmth into me.

"Do not worry. You are okay now."

"D-did . . . did I . . . ?" I swallowed what felt like a dagger wedged in my throat, its edges slicing all the way down with the thought. "Did I k-kill her?"

"No. She is very weak, but I think she will survive."

"Tristan?"

Her eyes flitted behind me, then back to my face. The corners of her mouth turned down as her eyebrows pushed together and lifted. "I am afraid he is not doing well."

Oh, no! I twisted around and his arms fell off me, to the balcony floor. His head lolled against his shoulder. Rina kept one hand on his arm, pushing more Amadis power into him, but we saw no signs of it doing him any good. I threw my arms around his chest.

Another onslaught of images filled my mind. Landing a blow to a stranger's head with a powerful fist, looking and feeling as if it were mine. But it was too big. Then an eighteenth-century village blazed with fire, people running amuck, screaming with terror, and a hand held palm-out in front of me. I knew then Tristan's memories swarmed through my head like another slideshow. Our blood-covered hands and a body slumped on the ground below us. Then faces, their hair or hats or bonnets indicating various eras and cultures, from traditional Japanese and Chinese to American hippies. Face after face after face. All of them twisted in agony or horror. And the *screams*. The blood-curdling screams of men, women and even children as they lost their lives to us.

My stomach rolled with nausea and my heart squeezed with sorrow.

"Tristan, stop it!" I was surprised at how forceful the

command came out because I just wanted to curl into a ball and hide from the depravity and suffering.

A low growl rumbled in his chest as the images kept coming. So I fought them with my own.

I remembered our early days, trying to push each of my own images into his head without knowing for sure if I even did it right or if I could do it at all. Or if it would do any good. But I had to try to replace his old, bad memories—the ones he would never talk about, never deliberately share with me—with our good ones. I pictured us sitting on the beach for sunsets, our first kiss, riding on the motorcycle, our wedding . . . even the joy of waking up in his arms yesterday morning. I felt my own good energy rising with the thoughts.

"Think of us, Tristan, our love," I said. I tried to help Rina by pushing Amadis power into him, but I was still too weak. I had too little to give. So I kissed him all over his face, thinking if I couldn't give him Amadis power, I could at least give him love. It had to be at least as good.

Then I couldn't see his memories anymore or even read his thoughts. My mind went blank.

"If I'm going to have this stupid gift, it could at least be reliable," I muttered.

"You have done well, Alexis," Rina said. "He is coming around."

I looked up at Tristan's face. His lips twitched into a small smile. His eyes opened. The gold sparked, but at least there were no flames. He seemed to drink me in with his eyes and the sparks died into just gold flecks.

"I told you it was a bad idea," he said.

Chapter 17

"I had no choice," I said. "I had to try. But you shouldn't have . . . ."

"I shouldn't have helped you?" Tristan murmured. "I should have let you fight that by yourself and watch the depravity consume everything I love about you? I had no choice either, my love."

He swept a thumb across each of my cheeks, wiping away the wetness. I hadn't even realized I'd been crying. Then he folded me into his arms and I collapsed against his chest, his heart pounding a steady rhythm in my ear.

"You should have waited for us," Rina said, "or at least for someone with more experience and power."

I looked up. Her face puckered with concern.

"She needed us, Rina. Owen said—"

"Owen needs to focus on his responsibilities." She shook her head. "He never could resist a damsel in distress, though."

A quiet noise rumbled in Tristan's chest—so quiet, probably only I heard the I-told-you-so tone to it.

"He just has a big heart," I protested.

"Yes, he does," Rina agreed, "but he also has big curiosity. He has a desire to test the boundaries, to see how far they can be pushed. He is often just a little late when you have needed him, no? He has always wanted to know how much you could withstand on your own. What any of us can withstand. He enjoys testing our abilities. He would never purposely put you in grave danger, but sometimes he overestimates our powers . . . or underestimates the enemy." She shook her head slowly and let out a soft sigh. "I will need to speak with him if he is going to continue as your protector. Our world is changing and he cannot be so reckless. He must be more judicious or he *will* put you in serious danger."

The weight of her tone quelled any more protest from me. We sat in silence as Rina gave another dose of power to Tristan and me, and then she rose to join Mom at the other end of the balcony.

Mom hovered over Sheree and Owen, probably pushing her own power into them. Sheree lay on the concrete balcony floor, her body convulsing in a seizure. A mix of sobs and groans sounded like they escaped from her every pore. Mom and Rina held their hands tightly against her writhing body. Rina's face took on that expression it does when she assesses me—her eyes still bright and alert to her surroundings, but her mouth pursed in concentration.

"She suffers greatly. She needs us," Rina finally said to Mom.

"Owen get them inside," Mom said, tossing her head toward Tristan and me without removing her hands from Sheree.

Owen stood, strong and sturdy on his own legs, his full strength already restored. He helped Tristan and me up as if we were one body and ushered us inside. Tristan sat with me on the couch. I still trembled against his side.

"*We are going to help you. You want to convert, no?*" Rina's voice sounded in my head but I knew she "spoke" to Sheree.

I closed my eyes, needing a moment of quiet, really

wanting to sleep. But trying to block out Rina seemed to take more energy than I had right now. The image of Sheree on the balcony, as seen through Rina's eyes, just simply appeared, without my trying. Sheree had stopped convulsing. She stared at Rina and Mom, her eyes like a wild animal's. Her answer to Rina's silent question came in a weak nod.

"You have to voice it," Mom said in a hushed tone.

"I want to convert," Sheree whispered.

"Why?" Mom asked. "You must convince us."

"I-I-I d-don't want be like them," Sheree whispered. "I hate them. They're horrible. *Evil.* They did this to me. M-m-made me a . . . a . . . a *monster.*"

"*You do not have to be a monster. We can show you how to live with what you are but without harming people. Is this what you want?*" Rina asked.

Sheree nodded emphatically. "Yes, oh, yes. That or to die."

"We won't let you die," Mom said. "But this will not be easy. What is your name?"

"Sheree."

"How did this happen to you, Sheree?"

The young woman gulped and her face screwed up as she forced herself to remember.

"I went to Africa, for a mission trip. We built a school and taught some of the orphans in this little village. On the last night we were there, I snuck out for a walk. It was stupid, being out by myself in the dark, but I couldn't sleep. I felt bad leaving those kids, you know? They had no one to love them and take care of them, and here I was, going back to my comfy life. With a real bed, hot food . . . a *shower.* All those things that are just there for us, but not for them. You know what I mean?" She sighed softly and then shook her head. "I'm not sure what happened. I remember hearing a growl, kinda like a cat but . . . different.

Lower, like it was bigger than just any ol' mouser. Then there was this awful pain down my back, like my skin was ripping apart. I passed out, and when I woke up, it was morning and time to go. I had scratches all over me, but they weren't deep, so I didn't worry about them. By the time we got back home, they were almost gone. I thought I'd been jumped by one of the smaller cats out there. There are all kinds they warned us about. I blew it off as just a stupid mistake. And it seemed like no big deal, once I was home and getting back to my normal life. Until the first full moon . . . ."

Sheree continued with her story of a Daemoni watching her transform the first time, seizing the opportunity to loop a collar around her neck while terror and confusion immobilized her. He told her he knew what was happening to her and he could make her better. He filled her with other broken promises and lies of hope. Then he took her away. She hadn't seen her family since.

They kept her captive in the same place in Siberia where they'd held Tristan. They told her they would release her when she accepted what she had become. After that first time . . . killing the couple by the lake . . . her senses returned and she vowed to never do that again. She refused to shift for the Daemoni except when the full moon forced her and then she wouldn't eat until the moon waned and she returned to human form. Because, for the three days of each month's full moon, they only provided human flesh.

She figured they'd been holding her there for about nine months before Tristan unknowingly helped her escape.

"They told me stories about Seth," she said.

"Tristan," Mom corrected.

Through Rina's eyes, I saw Sheree's brows furrow with confusion.

"We call him Tristan," Rina said. "You will call him Tristan now."

"Um, okay, stories about Tristan, the traitor who they got back and were torturing to death. 'That's what we do to those who try to leave,' they said. They were trying to scare me, but it just gave me hope that there must be another way for this . . . life, if that's what you call it. I heard him fighting them, trying to get out, and I snuck behind him, nobody noticing me in all the ruckus. I followed him all the way as he flashed back to the States, but I knew I couldn't go home. I was—am—a nasty, *horrible* beast. What would I do to my family if I lost control? I thought Seth, I mean, Tristan, might help me, if he knew what I wanted, but I couldn't bring myself to get close to him. He's, um, kinda terrifying, you know?"

She explained how she continued following him, from Atlanta to Key West, always maintaining a safe distance. Then Vanessa and her friends found her. They were supposed to scare her into submission. I interrupted them the first time. Owen found her next to the Ferrari the second time, after they'd beaten her to near death. She described the pain and fear they inflicted on her, her words seeming to hang in the thick air, followed by a long silence.

"You are very new to this. Do you still remember what love is?" Mom finally asked.

An image of the African orphans flashed in Rina's and my minds. Wide, white smiles against dark-skinned faces, emaciated with hunger. Their heads looked too large for their skin-and-bone frames. But they grinned at us nonetheless. And then other images of an older couple who must have been her parents and faces who were no doubt her siblings—the resemblance showed clear in her memory.

"She remembers," Rina said.

"Good," Mom said. "Remember that love, Sheree. Hold onto the memory tightly. Remember how love feels in your heart—warm, big, all-consuming."

Sheree stiffened as Mom and Rina pushed stronger Amadis power into her. At least she didn't seize this time.

"You can love again," Mom said, nodding her head and stroking Sheree's arm with one hand while holding her other hand around the Were's wrist.

"*Remember how it feels to hold them next to you, to comfort them, to provide for them in need,*" Rina added silently.

"You can do this," Mom encouraged.

She and Rina continued a sort of mantra, reminding Sheree of what love felt like. Eventually Sheree's body relaxed and she seemed to succumb to their power.

I pulled my focus from them and back inside and looked up at Tristan. His head leaned back, on the top of the couch cushions, his eyes closed. He opened them slightly, apparently feeling me looking at him. He frowned. My own brows knitted together and my bottom lip pushed out.

"What?" I asked, uncomfortable with his expression.

His eyes opened wider as he examined my face for a long moment. Then he sighed and closed his eyes again.

"You saw my thoughts, my memories, didn't you?" he finally asked, his voice quiet as a whisper. But I could still hear the pain and the shame in his question.

I dropped my head and leaned closer against him. I took his hand in both of mine.

"Yes," I whispered with my own shame. "I'm sorry."

He chuckled, but the sound fell flat with the lack of humor in it. "*You're* sorry? You can't help it. Especially with how intense everything was."

"Then why do you sound angry?"

"I'm not angry at you. I'm frustrated with myself. I should have been able to handle the power, to control it." He sighed again and his voice became even quieter. I could hear his disgust increase with each word—disgust with himself. "I never wanted you to know those things about me."

My heart squeezed with his pain and self-reproach. I swallowed the lump in my throat as I tried to think of the right words to comfort him. I didn't know what they were, though.

"I know you didn't," I finally said. "But you didn't honestly think I had no clue, did you? I mean, after watching that battle . . . when you left . . . I saw some pretty horrible stuff then, Tristan. By both sides. I had an idea of what you were like and I've had years to imagine all kinds of things."

"But it couldn't have been as bad as reality."

This time I chuckled with no humor. "I'm a writer. My imagination is pretty twisted."

He didn't reply. After a while, though, I felt him watching me. "And you still love me?"

I looked up at him with surprise. "Of course I do! What I saw doesn't change who you are now."

"It changes what you know about me. That must change what you think of me."

I rolled onto my knees and his arms fell away from me. A cold shudder consumed me as soon as his warmth was released. But I had to look him in the eye so he would know what I said was not made up to make him feel better, but was the full, heartfelt truth. I placed both of my hands on the sides of his face and held it firmly.

"You know what else I saw tonight? She doesn't know it, but through Sheree, I saw you in those caves. I saw your pain, your agony at being there. Your desperation of wanting to escape, to get away from them. I saw you fight them. You came back to *me*, Tristan. You came back to us, the Amadis. You yourself said earlier today that you're Amadis now. Your memories . . . that's your past life, remember?"

He closed his eyes, breaking their hold from mine. He opened his mouth to protest. I held my hand over it.

"*Nothing* can change the way I feel about you," I continued. "I know there was a time when you were . . . were . . . ," I couldn't say "evil," not about him, ". . . one of them. But that's in the past. You are Tristan Knight now. You are *my* Tristan and nothing will change that. I love you forever. No matter what. Understand?"

His eyes opened and searched mine, as if trying to find something besides honesty.

"After all this time, if you can't believe that . . . ," I started. But he didn't let me finish. His hands embraced my face and his lips crushed against mine.

"I'm sorry I doubted you," he said after pulling back.

"You're forgiven." I kissed him again. "At least . . . *I* forgive you. But, Tristan, somehow you need to find within you the ability to forgive yourself. If you don't, you'll never be able to completely let go of it all."

His brows furrowed. "Easier said than done."

"You've asked God for forgiveness, right?"

"Of course. It's part of converting to Amadis . . . but He's more merciful than I am." He obviously had enough talk about his past, because he pressed his forehead against mine and changed the subject to one of his favorites—my well-being. "How do you feel?"

I turned and pressed against his side again. My mouth stretched into a wide yawn. "Tired. Really tired."

"That's understandable. It's been a long day." His hand stroked my hair. "You should sleep."

"I want to, but I don't think I can. Not until I know she's okay."

"That could be a while." He wrapped his arms around me and gave me a squeeze. "You were great. So strong already."

I snorted. "I almost killed us all . . . or we all almost killed each other . . . or something like that."

"You held on for a long time, though. As long as you needed to."

"Barely. If Mom and Rina hadn't shown up . . . well, it's a good thing they did. How did they get here so fast anyway? Is it possible to flash off a plane?"

He chuckled. "Yes, but I'm sure they flashed from New York. You fought it for a couple hours."

My eyes opened wide. "A couple *hours*? It didn't feel so long."

"You were in an alternate state of mind. I think, by the end, we all were. I told you the process is draining." He yawned, too, as if to emphasize his point.

"That's not even the entire process. She's not converted yet."

"No. It takes a long time. First, you have to remove the evil energy and the pain is excruciating. Rina and Sophia are finishing it, but you started it. Next time you'll be strong enough to finish it, too."

I shook my head. "There won't be a next time. I failed her and I'm never risking that again. I'll leave it to Mom and Rina from now on."

His arms around me released their tight hold. He lifted my chin with his fingers and caught my eyes with his. "This is what you're made to do, *ma lykita*. Protecting and saving souls is your purpose for existence."

His eyes held mine, conveying deep meaning to his words. He raised his eyebrows, as if questioning whether I understood. My own brows knit together. Because I didn't understand.

"I thought my purpose is to write these stories for whatever it is the Amadis have planned. And to have a daughter so the Amadis could continue. And to eventually lead them."

"Those are all part of your duties, part of your purpose. But your true reason for being here is to save and protect souls. There are only certain people who can convert others. When

~ 232 ~

you have your full powers, you will be one of them."

I tried to shake my head again, but Tristan held my chin. "If this is what I'm meant to do . . . we're all in big trouble."

His lips pushed into a small smile. "You did fine. You just don't have enough power yet. But you will."

Not enough Amadis power, anyway. It seemed the Daemoni power in me had been plenty strong . . . almost strong enough. If Mom and Rina hadn't shown up when they did, I would either be dead or the Daemoni blood would have won. Then all hell could have broken loose. Literally. I would have rather been dead. And nobody knew if I would always have to fight that Daemoni power, even after the *Ang'dora*. The chance of the evil power winning next time wasn't worth taking. Sheree's was the first and last soul I would try to save. They would have to find something different for me to do. Surely there were other roles I could serve.

"How do you feel?" I asked, taking the cue from Tristan and switching the focus from me and my shortcomings.

"Hmm . . . not great. But better than I was. Don't worry about me."

But I did worry about him. His eyes should have returned to their normal beauty by now, but the gold still sparked and the green remained dark and disturbed, like a murky pond rather than bright emeralds.

"I'm fine, too, in case you were wondering," Owen piped up. He stood in the kitchen, munching on a handful of crackers.

"Yeah, I can tell," I said and I lifted an eyebrow. "But how can you eat?"

"I'm refueling. You guys should eat, too. Food equals goodness." He grinned, his sapphire eyes shining brightly.

My face twisted in a grimace. Right now, just the thought of food equaled sick stomach. When I glanced at the clock on the wall behind Owen, though, his hunger made sense. It was nearly eight o'clock. We'd completely missed dinner.

Mom slipped inside then and sat on the coffee table in front of Tristan and me. She took each of our hands and pushed more Amadis power into us. After about a minute, I pulled my hand from hers.

"He needs it more. Give it all to him," I told Mom.

She wrapped both hands around Tristan's. The sparks in his eyes finally returned to just gold flecks. They didn't shine brightly yet, but he looked better. I still shivered next to him, but not quite as violently.

"That should help until we return," Mom said.

"Where are you going?" I asked.

"We need to get Sheree to a safe house." She studied my face, but she mistook my fearful expression. "We'll return as soon as possible. You'll be okay until then."

"But why do you have to leave? They're out there, waiting for you. For any of us," I said, my voice rising an octave with panic.

"No one's out there right now, honey. They apparently left when our first soldiers showed up."

I hadn't even realized we had fighters out there, I was so consumed with everything else. "So we're protected?"

"Of course." She patted my hand, then stood and stepped back to the sliding glass doors to return to Rina and Sheree.

"Mom?"

She turned to look at me.

"Dorian's okay, right?"

She smiled. "Yes, honey. He's in the safest place he could possibly be."

I nodded, then slumped back against Tristan.

"We'll be back soon. I promise."

I cringed. The promise sounded too much like the one Tristan had left me with. Things hadn't turned out so well that time. *They'll be okay. They're well protected.* I found it difficult to convince myself, though. After all, there were real monsters out there, out in the world. And one monster right there with them.

I watched through the glass doors as Rina lifted Sheree and placed her limp form in Mom's arms. Her heavy weight didn't affect their graceful movements. They glided toward the stairs and then disappeared out of sight. I said a silent prayer for all of them—for Sheree's successful conversion and for Mom and Rina's safe return. I knew I would need them. I just didn't realize how soon.

Chapter 18

Tristan and I sat on the couch in silence for a while as Owen rummaged around the kitchen. I hadn't been to the market since the day after I arrived and hadn't purchased enough to feed me for more than a few days, let alone all of us. When I'd sent Owen the other night, he only bought steak and trimmings. So the cupboards and refrigerator were fairly empty.

"Not much here," Owen complained.

I still didn't know how he could be hungry, my own stomach still in knots. Of course, he'd probably been through similar situations many times in the past. The experiences were all new and overwhelming to me and add in the change of the *Ang'dora* that crept through my body, no wonder I felt so tense. Tristan had apparently recovered, too. He left me in the family room and joined Owen in the kitchen, in search of food.

"Can't you just conjure something?" I teased Owen as I finally rose from the couch, too.

"Not food, not without something to start with," he said,

as if there was absolutely nothing in the house. I knew better.

"Hmph, a lot of good you are." Even if I didn't feel hungry, they obviously needed to be fed. "Watch *my* magic."

I started pulling ingredients out of the cabinets and fridge—leftover steak, a can of black beans, salsa, the last of the eggs, cheese and tortillas. In no time, I whipped up some breakfast burritos, while Tristan sliced a tomato and an apple for us all to share. They dove into their food with enough vigor you'd think they hadn't eaten for days. The drain of helping Sheree certainly left us feeling as empty as if we hadn't, but I had to force-feed myself a third of the apple. Even the tiniest bit felt like a boulder in my constricted throat and my stomach was too tied up to make room. It didn't feel like it had earlier, as though worms filled it. Now it just felt tight and tiny, as if it had squeezed itself into the size of a walnut, too small for even a slice of apple. But that seemed to be all I needed, anyway.

Renewed energy suddenly overtook my body. Those synapses ticked through my nerves again, making my muscles twitch with the need for exertion. I couldn't sit still. After cleaning the kitchen, I paced around the living room, wishing I could run. I felt imprisoned inside the house.

"Can we go for a swim?" I asked. "If we stay within the shield?"

I just needed to get out, to go. I didn't care what lurked beyond, as long as I could *move*. Owen and Tristan exchanged a glance, then Owen shrugged.

"It's just as safe now as it was this morning. I don't see why not," he said.

I rushed into the destroyed Caribbean room and changed into my suit. We raced to the water's edge, all of us there in a split second, although they still managed to beat me. The water proved to be exactly what I needed. The tension washed off like a coat of grime and the waves carried it away. After swimming several laps, I lifted my legs and floated on my back, staring at the quarter-moon.

The moon's phase brought new meaning to me now, knowing Weres roamed the world out there, barely able to control themselves during a full moon. I wondered what they did during those three days each month. Did they hide? Did they go hunting? What did they hunt? I remembered Sheree's vision of the couple by the lake and a shudder overcame me.

Then I wondered how she was doing. I didn't know what came next for her or even how close she was to being converted. It seemed Mom and Rina still had much work ahead of them, removing all of the evil energy. *Then what?* I didn't know. Yet. And I didn't want to think about it. If Tristan was right, if saving souls was my purpose, I would eventually have to learn. But not right now. Thinking about it only reminded me how much I'd failed . . . how close I'd come to ending our lives.

Realizing the space around me had been quiet for some time, I up-righted myself and tread water, looking around for Tristan and Owen. Water dripped from my hair and into my eyes and I wiped it away to be sure it wasn't blinding me. *Nope.* They were nowhere around. My heart stuttered. *Where are they? Are they . . . gone?* I spun around in the water, my throat tightening with each pounding heartbeat. Even in the night's darkness, I could see almost perfectly, as if the moon shone nearly as brightly as the sun. But I couldn't see them.

Several thoughts ran through my mind. *Protectors are keeping watch out there. I could call for them. It's too quiet for them to be there, though, and why can't I see them? Can I just try to find their thoughts, if they're still here? If I only had control and could make real use of my power . . . .* The ideas raced too fast to even focus and settle on one as panic began to overwhelm me. *Stupid. This was so stupid. Why had I even asked to do this?*

Then Owen's head popped out of the water right next to me, making me squeal.

"Holy crap! You scared the hell out of me!" I shrieked. "Where's Tristan?"

Owen lifted his hand out of the water and pointed. "Down there."

The breath whooshed out of me. Of course. He could hold his breath indefinitely.

"I was wondering how long you could go now," Owen said. "Probably longer than a normal human. Maybe even as long as Tristan."

I raised an eyebrow. Owen gave me an encouraging grin.

"We're still safe, right?" I asked.

"I'm not an idiot. You wouldn't be out here if you weren't."

"Okay." I took a deep breath and plunged downward.

The salt water didn't bother my eyes at all and I could see almost as clearly under the water as I could in the moonlight. Owen moved his hands beneath the surface and his head appeared in front of mine. He held his hands over his mouth for a few seconds and then he grinned, pointed ahead of us and led me a little farther out, where Tristan swam along the bottom. Owen must have used some kind of spell for himself, because he stayed under far beyond the minute or two an average human could tolerate.

I could remain under water for a lot longer than humanly possible, as well, but not nearly as long as they could. After about fifteen minutes, I came up for a breath and dove down again. The guys were still at the bottom, apparently wrestling. I rolled my eyes and looked around for any fish life. Many years ago, Tristan and I had snorkeled here. There hadn't been a ton of life, but there had been some. More than there seemed to be now. I wondered if fish slept at night.

Then I saw movement farther out. My heart leapt. The figure seemed to be at least as big as a human. But when it came a little closer, a long, rounded nose pointed at me, I realized what it was. *Holy crap! A freakin' dolphin!* I took off after it, leaving the guys to their childish antics. I wanted to see how close the animal would let me get. I really wanted to touch it, to feel its skin, but I didn't expect it to let me. The creature didn't swim away, though. It seemed just as intrigued with me as I was with it, watching me as I approached. It turned slightly and I reached out my hand to touch its fin.

Water rushed past me. Then cool air, as if I were in a wind tunnel. And then I stood on my feet in the sand, on our little beach. Owen leaned over beside me, his hands on his knees as he gasped for breath. Tristan appeared right next to us.

Followed by a *Pop!* and then a splash of water way out from the shore. A head emerged from the water, her wet, blond hair shimmering like liquid silver in the moonlight.

"What the hell, Owen?" I demanded. "I thought we were safe!"

"We . . . are," he panted. "As long as . . . you stay . . . in . . . the shield."

I gulped. I hadn't realized I'd swam out so far. Vanessa's head bobbed on the water at least two football-fields away, at the edge of the shield. Which meant I'd swam about one-hundred yards in only a few seconds and Owen had taken less than two to bring me in from where Vanessa was now.

"I'm sorry," I said. "I didn't realize . . . ."

"It's my fault," Owen said, having caught his breath. "I'm supposed to be watching you. Not screwing around."

"It's not like you can control my every move."

"So I'm learning," he muttered. "Exactly why I should be watching you more closely."

"Let's just get back to the house," Tristan said, taking my hand.

He turned his head toward Vanessa and growled over his shoulder. I laughed under my breath. Petty, I knew, especially because she couldn't hear us behind the shield, yet still satisfying. Several *Pops!* sounded across the water and I turned to watch as Amadis protectors swarmed on her. She disappeared again. The Amadis stayed in the water, ensuring she didn't come back, as we returned to the house. By the time we climbed the stairs to the balcony, I could barely lift my legs or hold my own weight. My flesh and bones felt as though they'd turned into a leaden gel.

"That swim took a lot out of me," I said, falling into a balcony chair. "More than I realized. More than it should have."

"You need to eat something," Tristan said. "You didn't touch your dinner."

"No, Owen did for me." I yawned. "That's not it, anyway. I still don't think I could eat right now. I just feel really *tired* again."

I probably could have fallen asleep right in the chair, except my body wouldn't stop shivering. I went inside to change out of the wet bathing suit and thought a hot shower was exactly what I needed. I let the heat of the water and the rising steam envelop me. But when the water started running cold, even with the knob turned all the way to the H, I still shivered. I finally gave up. I dressed in sweatpants, an old, long-sleeve t-shirt and socks. I dragged the torn comforter and the only intact pillow out to the living room and curled up on the couch. My body felt heavy with exhaustion. I just wanted to sleep, but I couldn't stop shaking.

"You okay?" Tristan asked when he and Owen came inside.

"I don't know. I'm *freezing*." My teeth rattled noisily against each other.

"Is it still from earlier?"

I shook my head. "I don't think so. I felt a lot better when we were swimming. Now I feel like I'm getting sick."

Tristan held his palm to my face and then wrapped it around my hand. It felt like a heating pad. "You're like *ice*. Colder than you were with Sheree."

He and Owen exchanged meaningful looks.

"I'll call Sophia and Rina," Owen said.

He stepped outside and Tristan disappeared into our bedroom. He came out a few minutes later with wet hair and wearing cargo shorts, instead of swim trunks. He must have taken a quick shower. I felt bad—it had to have been freezing because I used all the hot water.

Owen returned at the same time. "I couldn't get either one of them but finally got a hold of Julia. She's with them at the safe house. They're still working on Sheree, but they want to know if anything happens with you and the *Ang'dora*, so Julia said she'd tell them."

"Is this normal?" I asked. "For the *Ang'dora*, I mean?"

Owen shrugged. "You're asking the wrong person. But there's not exactly anything *normal* about you, Alexis."

He was teasing, but absolutely right.

I pulled the comforter tighter around me, closed my eyes and tried to focus on making the shivers go away. The attempt proved pointless. Tristan lifted my head and shoulders and sat down, laying me down in his lap and rubbing my arms and shoulders. If his shower had been cold, I couldn't feel it on him now. He felt nice and toasty. He asked Owen to get more blankets from the back bedrooms and a minute later I felt the added weight, but they didn't do much to warm me.

"Sh-sh-sheesh, I-I-I'm s-so *c-c-cold*," I chattered. Tristan was right. This version of cold felt much worse than it had with

Sheree. My whole body felt like it had been plunged into a tub of ice water, the ache going right to the bone, everywhere except around my heart. Warmth cocooned it. *At least it won't freeze. Has to be a good sign, right?*

I closed my eyes again and tried to imagine pulling the warmth from my heart into the rest of my body. Then I tried not to focus on how cold I felt at all, but on something different. I pictured Dorian's face. My heart warmed more, but nothing else. So I imagined being held in Tristan's warm arms, close to his warm body. The thoughts seemed to be working until a violent shudder racked my body. Tristan moved to get up.

"No, p-p-please d-d-don't leave."

"I'll be right back."

When he returned, he placed a hot, wet washcloth around the back of my neck. Then he removed the back cushions from the couch and lay down behind me, wrapping his arms around me, the whole length of my body pressed against his. The shivering slowed and then finally stopped. I closed my eyes and deep sleep overcame me.

I didn't remember dreaming, but I did remember a disembodied face staring at me. I thought it belonged to the man who'd taken Sheree, but I couldn't be positive. I'd only seen her kidnapper's face for a brief time and through the haze of her memories. The face watching me floated in front of me, his hair and a goatee white as snow, his eyes like blue ice. Though the hair gave the impression of old age, no wrinkles lined his face. His lips pulled into a devious grin, exposing icicles for teeth. The face observed me and I thought he might be patiently waiting for me to do something. Nothing ever happened, though.

When I awoke much later, chills racked my body. Through the sliding glass doors, I saw the moon hanging low in the sky, as if strung on a necklace between the trees over our beach.

I had no idea of the exact time, but I felt sure midnight had slipped by while I slept. Tristan had left my side. He came back when he saw me shaking and lay next to me again.

"S-s-sorry," I said. "I-I-I kn-now it's n-not comfortable."

He had to scrunch his legs up just to fit on the couch.

"Do you want to go to the bed?" he asked.

"N-n-no. N-not now. I c-can't move."

My body felt like a slab of marble—too heavy to lift and cold to the touch—and I wondered if death felt like this. Tristan eventually warmed me enough again that I stopped shivering. I just wanted to lay there like a rock. Not a log—I felt too heavy to be a log. I was definitely a cold, heavy rock.

"Did Owen leave?" I asked.

"He's just making more calls. Trying to find out when Sophia and Rina will be back, but they're still working with Sheree. Do you need me to get you anything?"

"No. Just stay here, please. You're really warm."

He kissed my cheek and neck. His lips felt like hot matches striking against my icy skin. Pulling on every ounce of energy I could muster to move what felt like twice my body weight, I turned over to face him. I pressed my face against his chest and inhaled his warmth, his mouthwatering scent coating the back of my throat. He rubbed my back through the layers of blankets. Sleep overcame me again.

The next time I awoke, the sky was pitch-black and it felt like that time just before morning, when the whole world seemed to be dead. The coldest and darkest hour of the day. I couldn't even see the moon from my position on my back. It had probably set by now. There were no lights on inside and I should have been blind in the complete darkness, but I could see perfectly. Owen slept sideways in the chair, his legs dangling over the arm. Tristan slept next to me, his arm and leg thrown over me, pinning me down. My clothes stuck to my skin, making me realize they were drenched in sweat. I had the sudden need to escape from all the heavy blankets, feeling as though they were made of iron and weighing me down. I kicked and thrashed, not able to get Tristan and the blankets off of me fast enough.

"What's wrong?" Tristan asked, quickly awake. Owen stirred in the chair and peered at me through slit eyes.

"I'm so *hot* now," I panted, finally unwrapping myself.

I stood up and pinpricks of light danced in front of my eyes. My legs trembled, feeling like cooked noodles under my weight. Tristan held his hand to the small of my back before I toppled back on him. Once I steadied myself, I headed for the bedroom, peeling the sweat-soaked clothes off of me. I wanted to lay naked, spread eagle on the cool bed, but stuffing still bulged out of its shredded top. I took another shower instead, this time letting the cool water run over me. I had to change the pressure on the showerhead to a gentle spray—anything else felt like thousands of needles piercing me. I felt every single drop patter against my skin, like the fat drops at the beginning of a rain storm hitting me one-by-one, but these were small and thousands at a time. It was a strange feeling.

Clean clothes at a minimum, I put on a tank top and pajama shorts, my only other choice being one of the fancy sundresses. The clothes rubbed harshly against my skin, feeling more like paper than cotton. The fabric even sounded like paper scraping and crinkling against itself. Tristan and Owen both eyed me when I came out of the bedroom.

"How do you feel?" Tristan asked. I flinched and covered my ears with my hands. He sounded like he nearly yelled.

"Except that everything feels, looks and sounds so intense, a lot better," I whispered. "A little shaky, though. I'm really thirsty . . . and hungry."

They both sighed with relief and the rush of air sounded like two train whistles. Being thirsty and hungry must have been a good sign. I drank a big glass of ice water and it cooled my insides, but not enough to radiate outwards to my feverish skin. I fixed another glass, retrieved the last of the crackers and sat next to Tristan on the couch. My muscles twitched, like they did when I wanted to run.

"That was weird," I said, still whispering. "I was so cold and tired. Now I feel really warm but energetic. I feel like I could go for a ten-mile run."

Tristan chuckled quietly and, thankfully, kept his voice low. "I don't think so. You take it easy."

Electricity pulsed through my body, though. I wasn't sure I *could* sit still. A cell phone rang shrilly. I jumped and covered my ears again. Owen muttered, "finally," as he stepped outside, lifting the phone to his ear.

I turned sideways on the couch and lay my legs over Tristan's lap. He brushed my cheek with his fingertips and his touch felt so soft, but pleasurably shocking. Goose bumps spread down my neck and arms. He smiled and he looked absolutely sublime, his features even more perfectly sculpted than I'd ever noticed—if at all possible—even with the scars. My heart swelled with the immense love I had for him and a smile spread across my own face.

"Thanks for keeping me warm," I whispered.

"My pleasure." He leaned over and brushed his lips across mine, sending another delightful shock.

"I love you."

He smiled again and my heart flipped. "I'll never understand why you love me, but I will take every bit you give."

"You have it all."

"And you have all of me." His fingers brushed my cheek again and I shuddered. He leaned in for a long, loving kiss and it felt like he'd never kissed me before. His lips felt soft and full against mine and silky smooth, and I could taste real mangos, papayas and lime on my tongue. A sudden desire rose and I had to fight the impulse to rip his clothes off and jump him right here on the couch. I settled for wrapping my arms around his neck and pulling him hard against me as he continued to kiss me.

Owen interrupted us.

"Sophia and Rina are on their way back," he said, keeping his voice low. "I'm going to meet them outside to make sure they get in with no problems."

He eyed us. Tristan disentangled himself from my hold.

"Don't get crazy. I won't be long," Owen added with a shake of his head.

"I wish we had more time," I said after he left. "I'm quite enjoying these new sensations."

"We'll have plenty of time soon, my love."

"I just don't know how long these heightened senses will last."

I stroked his face and found myself surprisingly amazed at the texture—I'd never noticed just how velvety his skin felt. Except for the scars. They weren't soft and spongy like normal scars. These were hard, rigid. I suddenly didn't like touching them. An icy sensation flowed into my fingertips when I did, like hundreds of tiny icicles pricking my skin. I hadn't noticed that before either. The feeling made the hairs on the back of my neck stand up.

So I ran my fingers over his lips instead, which felt much better because they reminded me of Dorian's cheeks when he was a baby—smooth and supple, inviting me for a kiss. Tristan cupped his hand around my face, stroking my cheek with his thumb. My skin warmed even more and tingled, the feeling spreading throughout my face, up into my scalp and down through my neck. Goose bumps rose and I shivered.

"Are you cold again?" he asked, his brows furrowing with concern.

"No, not at all. Just . . . *tingly*." I shivered again.

He smiled with understanding. "Hmm . . . I wish we had more time, too."

He winked and I fell back against the arm of the couch, my insides softening so I couldn't hold myself up anymore. He leaned over and kissed me again, his hand trailing lightly down my neck and shoulder and arm, electricity spreading in a web across my skin.

I instantly felt overheated. My blood simmered. I had to push him back.

"Okay, maybe not. That's too much," I breathed.

I fanned myself with my hand. He blew lightly on my face, his cool, tangy-sweet breath filling my nostrils and into my mouth, overwhelming me. My heart started racing and I thought my temperature shot up three degrees. My blood no longer simmered—it boiled. My skin crawled from my scalp to the tips of my fingers and toes. I jumped off the couch, panting.

"It's too much! I can't take it!"

I grabbed the glass of ice water and drained it. The liquid felt like hot tea by the time it hit my stomach. I went into the kitchen, filled the glass again and chugged it. I splashed cool water on my face and neck and then leaned over the sink, forcing myself to take slow, deep breaths. None of it helped. My heart continued to race and my skin prickled and burned.

"Son of a witch, I feel like I could jump out of my skin," I panted. Tristan came into the kitchen and my skin tingled and crawled with just the anticipation of his touch. I held my hand up when he came within three feet. "I think you'll send me into cardiac arrest if you come any closer."

"Alexis . . . are you okay? You're so pale." He still whispered but it sounded so *loud*.

I turned to look at him. Not a light shone in the house but I had to squint because the room looked so bright. All of my senses seemed to be crashing with overload.

"I don't know," I whispered.

Then several things happened simultaneously. The front door flew open with what sounded like an explosion. Owen, Mom, Rina and another woman appeared in the kitchen doorway. The air swooshed over me like a raging wind. I dropped the glass I held and it shattered on the floor. The shrill sound pierced my ear drums. My heart contracted painfully and burned white-hot. *No, not my heart burning. Above it.* The skin of the Amadis mark scorched, like it had been pressed with the mean end of a branding iron. Pain ripped through my chest. I screamed in agony and my fingernails clawed into my breasts.

Tristan's eyes burst into flames. He growled—a terrifying, heart-stopping resonance—and crouched as if preparing to lunge.

And Owen flew across the kitchen.

"*Tristan, NO!*" he roared.

Chapter 19

"Julia, go!" Rina ordered and the strange woman disappeared.

My vision grayed out as I collapsed to the floor.

The next thing I knew, Mom and Rina carried me into the back bedroom, to the only surviving bed. Their hands felt like iced braces as they held me tightly because I writhed uncontrollably. They lay me on the bed and my back arched against the hard, scraping sensation of the sheets and my clothes.

"Mom, what's happening?" I screamed, the sound deafening to my own ears.

"It's okay, honey, it's okay," she soothed.

Rina placed her hands on me, one on the burning Amadis mark and one on my forehead, and closed her eyes. I felt her energy flow into me and it calmed my nerves enough so I could lie still on the bed. The Amadis mark still felt white-hot, blistering and sending throbbing heat throughout my body. Mom took my hand and I gripped hers tightly.

"It's happening so fast," Mom said to Rina, unusual concern filling her voice.

"She can handle it." Rina remained calm as she kept her hands on me. "We just need to keep her temperature moderated. We need some ice."

Mom pulled away from me.

"Don't leave me!" I cried.

"I'll be right back, honey."

She returned in a second with towels, ice and water. She slipped an ice cube into my mouth and rubbed water on my face with her hand. The cold on my skin and in my mouth contrasted sharply with the heat in the rest of my body, making me shudder. She placed a cool, wet towel over my forehead and eyes. It was comforting.

I slipped in and out of consciousness. Every time I blacked out, the ice-man's face watched me again, and every time I came to, Mom and Rina sat right by my side, their hands directly on my skin. I felt new energy flowing through every cell of my body, twisting and turning and swirling through my veins and nerves.

"Something's terribly wrong," Mom said to Rina one time when I came to. She sounded anxious, but relatively calm considering the statement. She looked at me, saw my eyes open and didn't say anything more. I blacked out again.

ଏ୬

"Where's Tristan?" I asked another time.

"He's with Owen, honey," Mom said.

"Why isn't he here? I *need* him." I blacked out again before hearing her answer.

ଏ୬

"Mom?"

"I'm here, honey," she answered.

"Tristan?"

"He can't be here," she said. "I'm sorry, honey."

I struggled against something holding me to the bed. I couldn't feel any straps or bindings, but I couldn't move either. I thought maybe the dead weight of my own body held me down.

"Did he *leave* again?" I asked.

She didn't answer me for a long moment. "No, honey, not exactly."

What does that *mean?* I didn't have a chance to ask, though. I slipped out of consciousness again.

❧

"I think I've got him contained for now, but I don't know how long it'll hold," Owen said from the doorway another time.

"Who? What's going on?" I asked. Panic rose in my mind. I heard the bedroom door close.

Mom's face moved over me. "Shh. Nothing for you to worry about."

"How are you feeling, Alexis?" Rina asked.

"I don't know. Scared." I tried to take an assessment, but I couldn't feel much. Every part of me just felt heavy and deadened, like my body had died but forgot to tell my brain. "Kind of numb, actually."

"Do you feel hot or cold?"

"No, nothing. Nothing at all. Am I okay? I feel almost *dead*."

I could hear and talk and see, and I could *sense* something was wrong. It seemed as though I had no sense of touch anymore, no feeling. I consciously focused on trying to lift my hand but if it even twitched, I felt nothing. *Am I paralyzed?* I wondered if and how such a thing could have happened.

"I think your body is just resting, preparing for the next wave," Rina said.

I blacked out again.

❦

When I came to, I first noticed the variety of intense smells. Freesia, lemon and vanilla first. Mom's natural scent. Then orange blossoms and fresh rain. Rina. From farther away came pine and sea air—Owen. And then mangos, papayas, lime and sage. I smiled inside, knowing Tristan was still here. The smells of coconuts, salt water and stale sex also lingered on the air.

Next, I noticed all the sounds. The blood and energy pounding and whirring through my head came loudest. I could hear the whispers of fabric rubbing against itself and two heartbeats, besides my own, in the room. From the background came a low, rumbling growl, like a faraway train, and heavy breathing from somewhere else. And from even farther away, I could hear the waves on the beach.

I briefly opened my eyes. The dim light in the room made me think it was day time and the shades were drawn. Then it became painfully bright, as if a strobe light hit my face. For one surreal moment, I thought someone had taken a picture with a flash to commemorate this horror I suffered. I squeezed my eyes shut. The reverse images of Mom and Rina's heads glowed on the backs of my eyelids.

The sense of touch and feeling came last. My skin burned, everything against it feeling arctic, even the air. I felt each thread of wet terrycloth and each droplet of cold water on my arms, around my neck, across my face and forehead as Mom sponged me. Rina's hands felt like blocks of ice on my chest. Her breath felt cool on my face.

The energy traveling through my body earlier began to build and separate at the same time. My muscles felt on fire and the nerves twitched under my skin. Electricity charged through my veins, currents jumping from cell to cell. The gradual coming on of my senses escalated to a high crescendo, everything—the smells, the sounds, the touches—intensifying to an unbearable level. My ears rang and throbbed. My heart pounded. My breathing became shallow. My body trembled from the onslaught.

"Something's happening," I gasped.

Every single muscle, every tissue fiber tensed at once, pulling at each other in opposite directions. My body convulsed, every muscle pulled taut. Lightning shot through my veins and I felt as though I was being electrocuted from within.

An angry, moaning sound ripped through the room. It came from me.

Rina's icy hands pressed harder and I thought my skin would freeze and crack under them.

Then I felt the two streams of power—fire and ice—flow up through my limbs and course through my body, both rushing to my chest. Two angry rivers raging toward each other. Agonizing pain exploded through my chest cavity as the two energetic powers crashed against each other. I screamed with the pain. My back arched uncontrollably, throwing Rina back. The two forces twisted and pushed at each other, tearing through my lungs, ribs and muscles as if splintering them into pieces. A warmth surrounded my heart, like a shield, while the energies clashed ferociously. The Amadis mark seared and blistered painfully.

"Oh, my God, it hurts so much," I cried. "Make it stop!"

"What's happening?" Mom gasped.

"It seems the two forces are battling," Rina answered. She

sounded like she stood at the other end of a long tunnel. "We have to let this happen. There is nothing we can do."

And then the bedroom vanished.

༄

Perhaps I passed out again. I didn't know what happened. I just knew I was no longer there. Not in mind and spirit anyway.

I felt a sense of both familiarity and disorientation at my new surroundings. *Where am I?* I sat up and found myself in that strange meadow again, surrounded by mountains, and the lake in front of me. But the place looked and felt different once again. Not a warm, happy place, nor steel-blue-gray and desolate. I slowly rose to my feet as I focused on the tree with the constantly falling leaves.

But only half of it possessed actual leaves. Golden petals filled the branches on the right. They sparkled and glinted as some fluttered to the ground. The branches on the left half, however, were barren of any leaves, any life. Instead, that half looked as if an ice storm had come through, wrapping every branch and twig in a coating of crystal. Snowflakes floated to the ground, as if falling from those branches.

My vision pulled out and I realized I aligned perfectly with the center line splitting the tree between ice and gold. And I realized the whole world was split in half. To my right, the tall grass waved in a warm breeze that caressed my right leg, right arm, right half of my face. Green pines covered the mountain and the sun shone in the sky, reflecting off the lake. Flowers bloomed and turned their faces toward the sun. Birds chirped from their hiding places in the tree branches and I heard soft footsteps of wildlife on the forest floor.

To my left, snow blanketed the field and the trees on the side of the mountain. The left side of the lake had the pseudo-

~ 255 ~

transparent look of water frozen solid. A lone white wolf sat near the base of the tree, watching me carefully, though I didn't feel afraid and it didn't look concerned. The left half of my own body felt cold, but not uncomfortable. In fact, there was nothing chilling at all about any of the scene. It was a beautiful, wintry landscape, just as lovely as the other side, but in a different way.

I considered the strangeness of my environment. *How did I get here? What am I doing here?*

"You need to decide," said a familiar, accented voice. Unlike last time, when it had sounded flat, it now resonated across the field like soothing music. I peered to my right and saw Rina and Mom standing far off, near the base of the mountain.

"Decide what?" I asked. I didn't yell, not feeling the need to, although they were several hundred yards away. I somehow knew they would hear me even if I whispered.

"Which way you want to go," said another voice, this one unfamiliar. A male voice with a different kind of accent. With surprise, my head twisted to my left. A man, perhaps in his late twenties, stood almost directly across from Mom and Rina, at the base of his mountain. His hair and goatee were snow-white and his eyes ice-blue, the same face I'd seen earlier in my mind. But now it came attached to a body, clothed in black slacks and a tight-fitting black shirt that emphasized his powerful build. He smiled, but his teeth now looked bright but normal, not icicles as I'd imagined. In fact, the beauty of his smile stunned me. "You can come with us . . . ."

"Or with us," Mom said from the other side.

"Well, that's a no-brainer," I muttered. I took a step to the right, toward Mom and Rina. As if in response, the warm, yellow tone of the right side shifted more to the left, taking over part of the winter scene . . . increasing its area.

"Such a quick decision for an intelligent person such as yourself, Alexis," the man said, halting me in mid-stride as I started to take another step. "There is much for you over here, too. Isn't it beautiful?"

He swept his hand through the air and the snow sparkled as if he'd just scattered diamonds over it. I shifted my weight and when my foot finally came down, it landed back to the left. The wintry side regained the ground it had lost from my first step.

"You can rule the world," the man said. He waved his hand again and, like the slideshow of my earlier dreams, pictures hung in the air between him and me, but these were different— pictures of palaces and wealth and servants catering to me . . . and to Tristan and Dorian. I moved another step toward that side to get a better look. The scenes changed to even more people following us, worshipping us, then to Tristan and me standing at the top of stone steps, waving at a crowd of people that stretched farther than the eye could see.

"Power or love, Alexis?" Rina called from the other side. I turned toward her and Mom. They waved their hands and more pictures hung in the air, of Dorian and Tristan, of Mom, Rina and Owen. They moved their hands again and warmth flowed over me. Again, the decision came easily. I had little use for power, but I needed love. I took several steps in their direction.

"You can have it all over here," the man called out. "Power, love, wealth . . . everything you ever wanted. Everything."

I glanced over there, his side much smaller now after the steps I'd taken to the right.

"Lies, Alexis," Rina said. "Remember that they deceive. They do not know love."

The man shrugged. "But isn't this what you want?"

More pictures appeared, all filled with Tristan, Dorian and me, involved in different activities, all of us looking blissfully happy.

"Only with us can you all be together, can you have it all," the man said. "Otherwise, you lose."

He snapped his hand back, as if snatching something from the air. A small boy suddenly appeared in the crook of his left arm. Dorian.

"No!" I started running toward them, feeling the cold side taking over the warmth, creeping closer to Mom and Rina. Every step pushed a ripple of frozen ground into their space, like a loose carpet being pushed back with the force of my feet. But I didn't care. He had my son.

"Dorian is safe, Alexis!" Mom yelled. "He's with us. He's safe. Don't believe their deception."

"They lie, too, Alexis," the man said. "They can't give you everything you want."

"We give life and love," Rina countered.

"We give power and wealth and everything the heart desires," the man said.

I continued running toward him as Dorian struggled in his clutch. Rina and Mom spoke of love, life and goodness . . . all those things I believed in so strongly. But I had to ignore them. Something told me that if I went to them, I would lose Dorian forever.

"That's right," the man said, as if reading my mind. "Come with us and you can have those most important to you."

Tristan suddenly appeared on his knees, in front of the man. He struggled, too, as if bound by something unseen.

"No, Alexis! Come back to us," Mom cried out.

"That's it, young one, come to us. We'll take care of you. You'll have it all," the man taunted.

Though I kept running, I never reached them. It was like those dreams, where you keep running and running toward a door at the end of a hall, but the hallway grows longer with each step, so you never make it. I glanced over my shoulder. The snow had crept more than half-way to the other mountain. Mom and Rina stood their ground, though, waving their hands, trying to push warmth toward me. I felt just a slight movement of air. Their power was not enough.

"They're pathetic," the man said. "They can't stand up to us. You're making the right decision. The best decision."

Dorian and Tristan stopped struggling. In fact, now they suddenly seemed to be perfectly fine, happy even, on that side, smiling and waving me toward them. *It can't be that bad. It's the best decision.* I had no problem believing this to be true. I saw a glorious life with the three of us together, safe, because no one hunted us now. They already had us. Why had that seemed like such a bad thing before? Knowing they had us and what we could do for them, they would treat us like royalty. We wouldn't be prisoners. They wouldn't even care about another daughter. We could live life the way we wanted, spending our days together doing whatever we felt like. No more fear. No running from danger. If we were with them, we would have peace. We would be together forever. We would be happy. Everything I ever wanted. It made all the sense in the world. Right?

Then another figure appeared next to the man. This one made my blood turn to ice. For the first time since arriving in the strange field, I felt cold. Freezing. And hateful.

Vanessa. *Daemoni*, my mind reminded me, as if I'd forgotten. *Evil. They are evil.*

The urge to kill her overcame me. I envisioned lunging at her, wrapping my hands around her throat, even clawing and biting at it. I imagined tearing her to shreds and her blood spraying me. The taste of it filled my mouth and I liked it. I ran at her, my hands in front of me, already curled like claws in anticipation. *I will kill you.*

The ground around me suddenly gave way to empty blackness, as if I'd stepped off the edge of the world. Air whipped and roared, spinning into a tornado, but instead of debris, pictures of faces swirled around me. Tristan. Dorian. Mom. Rina. The icy man. Vanessa. Owen. Sheree. Vampires. Werewolves. Other frightening creatures.

"You want to kill?" the man's voice called. "We'll let you."

"No, Alexis! Love!" Rina yelled.

Their words dwindled into chants of "kill" and "love" as visions of fighting, embracing, killing and loving whirled around me. Fire and ice filled my body again. Churning. Swirling. Clashing. Battling.

"*Come home,*" my own evil voice called above the ruckus. "*This is what you want!*"

"No!" I said. "I don't!"

I realized I could no longer hear the others. Their voices were gone and I was left to myself. Images kept flashing in front of me, like the slideshows once again. I saw Tristan's old memories, but his blood-covered hands in front of me shrunk into my own hands. I saw myself in the midst of battle, people falling, dying at my feet. Then Dorian's face. Then Tristan's face. Then me attacking Vanessa. And then she transformed into Tristan.

"No, no, NO!" I yelled. "I love!"

"*You hate,*" the evil voice said and a flash of Vanessa's face appeared.

"NO! I refuse. This is not who I am. I am Amadis!"

"*You are also Daemoni!*"

"Fuck you!"

"*See? You're not them. You'll never be perfect like them.*"

"I don't have to be perfect. But I *am* good."

"*You cannot deny your evil side.*"

"Yes, I can. I'm supposed to choose. I can choose!"

"*And?*" the voice taunted.

"I choose Amadis. I choose goodness, love . . . life."

"*Are you sure?*"

"Yes, I'm sure!" I sucked in a deep breath and yelled at the top of my lungs. "I. AM. *AMADIS!*"

The voice fell silent.

The bedroom returned.

And so did the physical pain.

I thrashed in the bed against the unseen pressure holding me there, my legs kicking and my arms flailing. My chest felt like it shattered open as the power violently pushed through and up, bursting outward, pulling my back off the bed with its force. Icy-hot energy charged painfully from the tips of my toes and fingers and the top of my head, through my body and up and out of the crater-sized hole in my chest.

One horrified scream ripped through my throat.

An answering roar resonated from somewhere else.

My heart stopped beating.

My lungs stopped breathing.

My body hung in the air.

Then I was falling . . . falling . . . falling forever . . . until darkness overcame me.

Chapter 20

I lay perfectly still with my eyes closed for several minutes as I assessed myself.

No shivers. No burning. The air didn't feel frozen around me. My body temperature finally felt perfectly comfortable. The luxurious cotton sheets felt satiny against my bare skin and I knew I was naked. I also knew I'd returned to the physical world, *my* world, not that eerie soul-sucking place. I prayed to never return there again.

My heart beat a normal, steady rhythm. The Amadis mark no longer burned, but the skin felt slightly taut. My chest and lungs felt good as I breathed naturally. I sucked in a deeper breath. *No pain, no hole.* The feeling of my chest ripping open had been so real, I was almost surprised I now felt no damage.

The scents came clearer than ever before and I determined the people in the house hadn't changed—Mom, Rina, Owen and Tristan. Strange sound bytes of conversations over the last—*last what?* I had no idea how long I'd been in that room—hours or days reverberated in my mind, reminding me of Tristan's absence. *But he didn't leave. He's still here.* I comforted myself with that thought.

My hearing was better, too, but the sounds were not painfully loud. Footsteps paced against hard tile in the kitchen. The two hearts close by beat steadily, while one in the kitchen pounded harder. The other out there raced, as if pushed to its physical limits. *What are they doing out there?* I could still hear the rumbling train, too, but it sounded deeper and faster now. *What is that?*

I opened my eyes. The room seemed bright for an instant, but my eyes immediately adjusted. I stared at the ceiling and I could see every little swirl and divot in the textured paint as if looking through a magnifying glass. I looked around and the vibrant colors astounded me—colors I'd never seen before. Mom sat on the bed on my left, and I noticed how her hair was not simply auburn or chestnut, but a million different shades of browns and reds, each strand slightly different from all the others. It was breathtaking.

On the far wall behind her hung an African safari painting, keeping with the theme of the room's décor. I saw each brush stroke and the tiny initials "TK" in the bottom corner. Tristan must have painted it many years ago. Now I noticed all the little details he had captured—the different colors of the desert sand, the ridges of giraffes' hooves, the pond's ripples. Had I not noticed before because I hadn't paid enough attention? Or because now I could see so much more clearly?

The painful sensory overload had disappeared, leaving my senses exponentially more powerful.

That potent energy still ran through my blood and muscles and nerves, but not the icy or burning forces. Just pleasant warmth. *This is good energy. This is Amadis power.* I had no doubt.

And an odd but delightful feeling filled my entire body, every cell, deep into the very core of my being. Into my *soul*.

Is it over?

"*Yes, dear, it is over,*" Rina's voice answered in my mind.

She sat on the bed to my right, looking majestic and glorious, although she didn't wear the usual formal gown, but a black shirt and black jeans, just like Mom. Only Mom wore a cotton scoop-neck T and Rina wore a shimmery silk tank. Rina took my hand and closed her eyes. I could feel her power, but not as strong as it used to be—at least, not relative to my own. I could tell she assessed me.

"Simply amazing," she said aloud.

"Magnificent, as you always said," Mom agreed, giving my other hand a squeeze. "How do you feel, honey?"

"Um, *good*." My voice surprised me. I expected the words to come out in a croak or even just a whisper after everything I'd been through, but my voice came clear and strong. "Is Dorian okay?"

I had to be sure. Doubt lingered from the bizarre experience. Things might have changed since the last time I'd been fully aware of everything.

"Of course he is. He's at the Amadis mansion. He's in good hands," Mom said.

I wanted to hold him and know for sure. And I couldn't wait for the three of us to be united, but I also knew he was safer there than here right now.

"What about Sheree?"

"She's stable," Mom said. "One of our best counselors is working with her now."

"So she's not converted yet?"

"Conversion can take weeks or months . . . or longer," Rina said.

"Oh." I had no sense of how much time had passed, but it seemed it'd already been a long time since they'd left. I felt as though I'd slept for days. "How long was I out of it?"

"We returned about seven hours ago. Not long," Mom answered.

"That's *it?*"

"It happened very fast," Rina confirmed.

I sat up in the bed, holding the sheet to my chest to cover my nakedness. The door remained closed and only Mom and Rina were in the room, but their eyes stayed glued to me, making me self-conscious.

"What, exactly, happened?" I asked.

"You've completed the *Ang'dora*," Mom answered simply. "You want to see?"

She and Rina helped me out of bed, but I really didn't need any assistance. My body felt perfect—strong, healthy, full of power. As we walked into the adjoining bathroom, though, I was glad they were there. Because I staggered with shock when I saw myself in the mirror. They both beamed.

"Tha-that's . . . that's *me?*" I breathed. Of course, it had to be. Who else would be standing naked between Mom and Rina with that shocked look on her face and the bright red Amadis mark on her chest? It took me a moment to make sense of the vision.

I was . . . *beautiful.*

Not pretty. Not even gorgeous like a model or a movie star. But *beautiful.* Like Mom and Rina and Tristan beautiful.

My features hadn't really changed—my eyes were still the same almond shape and mahogany brown and my nose, lips and chin were still shaped the same. They were all just . . . *better.* I couldn't pinpoint exactly what looked different, but there was definitely something. My skin looked like golden silk, perfectly smooth. And my hair shone vibrantly like Mom's in a million shades of reds and browns. And I'd aged backwards even more. It would be hard to pass for much older than twenty. *It's like I am nineteen again. Like I've gone back to where my real life left off.*

My body had changed, too. Unfortunately, I hadn't grown at all. I was still small. But my muscles were more defined, yet in a feminine way. And I was . . . curvier.

"Wow," I breathed as I lifted my boobs in my hands. They were fuller than they'd ever been, even bigger than when I'd been pregnant. Mom and Rina chuckled.

"Exquisite," Rina said.

"Stunning," Mom added.

"*How?*" I asked, running my hands over my body, still trying to grasp that the reflection in the mirror actually belonged to me.

"We revert to the single point in time when our bodies were physically, mentally and emotionally strongest," Rina explained. "Then the Amadis power multiplies those strengths. The beauty comes from within—our faith, hope and love shining through."

Love. The pleasurable feeling I couldn't pinpoint earlier flowing through my body and soul. More love than I thought any person—or being—could possibly hold. In fact, it overflowed and I wanted to wrap Mom and Rina within it. If I weren't naked, I would have pulled them into me.

"So this is where I stay forever? Looking like this?" I asked.

"Pretty much," Mom answered.

"How? Are we like vampires?"

Mom chuckled. Rina shook her head.

"No, not quite," Rina said. "We are not frozen in time. Our hearts still beat, blood still flows through our veins and we still need oxygen, although we can regulate how much we need when necessary. The explanation is connected to our ability to heal, which is essentially the regeneration of cells and tissues, yes?"

She looked at me as if expecting an answer, so I nodded my understanding.

"Sleep allows our bodies to completely heal from the day's effect on them," Mom said. "Every organ, tissue and cell regenerates, making our bodies exactly as young and healthy as when we first awoke that morning."

"But I could heal before . . ." I stopped as the realization hit me. "Oh, but only injured cells."

"Correct," Rina said. "It is the Amadis power that regenerates *all* cells. Every night, while we sleep, our bodies return to their strongest. Every day is, indeed, a fresh start. Because we heal quickly, we do not need as much sleep as normal humans."

No wonder Mom and Tristan always seemed to get more things done in one day than many people could accomplish in a week. I couldn't wait to start this new life.

Although I didn't look like I'd been to Hell and back and I certainly didn't feel it now, I remembered enough of the phases of the *Ang'dora*—freezing, burning, sweating—to feel the need for a shower. The feeling of the water pouring down on my skin enraptured me, but I showered hurriedly. I wanted to see Tristan. Just the thought of him made my soul sing.

"I see you've been a little too busy to do laundry," Mom said as I dried myself off. "You only have one outfit left."

She laid the brightly colored sundress on the bed. It was my favorite one, which is why I hadn't worn it yet. Metallic gold outlined the abstract design in jewel tones—ruby, sapphire, amethyst, emerald and topaz—against a black background. The dress seemed too showy for hanging around the house. Now I had no choice but to wear it. When I pulled it on, the silk slid softly against my skin, like the brush of soft, smooth lips.

"Where's Tristan?" I couldn't wait to be in his arms again, now that I'd finally gone through the long anticipated *Ang'dora*.

I'm finally more like him.

Neither Mom nor Rina answered me, but they exchanged meaningful looks. Impatient with their silence, I headed to the door.

"No!" They both cried, but not aloud. They were in my head . . . or I was in theirs.

I turned around.

"What?" I asked.

Neither answered. But their faces said it all. Something was wrong.

"What's going on?" I demanded. I dimly remembered those bits of conversation, but none made sense.

And then the voices raged in my head all at once.

"He's going to kill her," Mom thought.

"She is strong enough. She can handle it." Rina's thought.

"I can't hold him much longer! I need reinforcements now.*"* Owen.

"Kill the little bitch." A frightening, deep-throated growl. *"No mercy. Just kill her."*

The feeling, whose ever it was, came so strong it filled my head until I thought my brain would explode. No images appeared except an angry swirl of reds and deep oranges, pulsing and growing until the mass pressed against my skull. I threw my arms over my head as if they could stop the onslaught.

"Go away! Make it stop!" I shrieked.

"Alexis!" Rina said sharply, grabbing my attention. My head snapped up and my arms fell to my side. "Focus on my voice and nothing else. That's it—focus on me, on my words."

I looked her in the eyes and listened specifically to her voice. The others' thoughts dimmed in my head, just background noise now. The colors faded away and the pressure ebbed back.

She spoke slowly and softly, like a hypnotist. "There you

go. Just remain focused on me. Now, imagine a black wall in your head and the only sound on this side of the wall is my voice. Yes?"

I nodded. I closed my eyes and imagined pulling a wall up in my head, dividing that black space or cloud, separating her voice from the others. The jumble in the background went completely away.

"Now, can you hear me?" Rina thought.

Yes.

"Anyone else?"

No. I opened my eyes.

"Good. You are doing beautifully. You are very powerful." She smiled, then she said aloud, "Sophia, think about something you *want* Alexis to hear."

Mom nodded.

"Now push my voice behind the wall and focus on your mother's thoughts," Rina directed.

I tried, but the wall fell.

"He's going to break loose! I can't hold him!" Owen's thoughts roared.

"Kill. Her. Kill! Her!" Images of crimson blood against grayness flashed in my mind.

"Who wants to *kill* somebody?" I cried aloud, frightened and offended by the thought. "Who else is here? I can't tell!"

"Alexis! You *must* focus," Rina ordered.

"How can I focus with that? It's *horrible!*"

"That is *why* you must focus. You have a very powerful and rare gift, but you need to learn to control it. The world is full of horrible and you will not be able to handle your power otherwise. Trust me."

I took some deep breaths to calm myself, then I focused on putting up the wall again.

"Do you have a wall?" Rina asked.

I nodded.

"Now, concentrate on your mother's voice. You know her voice very well. Listen only for it. Do not try to move the wall or try to take a piece of it out. It must always remain there intact. Just concentrate on the voice you want."

I envisioned the cloud again. It enshrouded Rina, but the wall blocked off everything else. I imagined the cloud reaching out to include Mom.

"You can do this," Mom's voice reverberated in my head. I nodded.

"Can you still hear me?" Rina asked. I nodded again. *"That is good if you want to hear us both, but you need to focus on just one. Block me out."*

I tried pulling the cloud away from Rina.

"Rina is right. You are amazingly powerful. I can feel it above my own." Mom kept on with the pep rally as Rina's voice died away.

I tried the opposite and I could hear Rina again and not Mom. Rina must have sensed me.

"Now tune out everyone and listen only to yourself," she instructed.

I focused on shrinking the cloud until it became nothing in my mind, nothing but my own thoughts. But my thoughts still worried about the other voices and the wall started to crumble. I concentrated on holding it there, beads of sweat popping out on my forehead from the intense focus. The wall finally held. I relaxed my mind slowly and the wall remained.

"Control will take much practice," Rina said aloud. "Just hold the wall up and the rest will come in time."

I mentally assigned one part of my brain to hold up the wall and tested the rest to wander. I thought about Tristan. The wall remained—no one's thoughts came through—even with the swelling of love that felt nearly overwhelming. It felt strange to be able to hold one part of my brain there on its own. The capacity of my mind felt larger and I could use more parts of it at once. I continued thinking about Tristan, kept the wall up and used a different part of my mind to think of Dorian. *Wow! This is incredible!* I kept those three thoughts running and tried communicating with Rina.

Rina, I think I can do this.

She smiled. She heard me. And Tristan's and Dorian's faces held, as did the wall.

"I knew you would be good," she thought.

I suddenly realized how tense my muscles were, as if I physically held the wall in place. I relaxed one muscle group at a time, working my way down from my neck to my feet. The wall held.

"So who's here?" I asked aloud. "Who is that terrible person or . . . *thing*? I don't *sense* evil. Why would anyone here want to kill someone?"

Mom and Rina exchanged glances again.

"You do not sense evil?" Rina asked.

"No. *Should* I?"

"That is interesting," she said. "That is good."

Mom shot her a pointed look. "Don't *you* sense something?" she asked Rina.

"It does not matter what you and I sense, Sophia. Alexis will be more highly tuned to it than us. She has a connection that we do not. We need to rely on her in this situation."

At the same time as that conversation, I thought about the voices, trying to identify that horrible growl. I'd heard Rina, Mom and Owen in my head. But not Tristan. I still smelled his mouthwatering scent, so I knew he was in the house. *Is he sleeping? Or . . .*

"Oh, no!" I cried. "What's wrong with Tristan?"

"Honey," Mom said, "we have a serious situation we're going to have to deal with as soon as you open that door."

"What's going on? Was that *him*?" I started for the door, already knowing the answer.

"Alexis, wait!" Mom barked. I stopped with my hand on the knob and turned to look at her.

"He needs me, Mom. He needs my help." I opened the door and the growl—what had sounded like a train—became a terrifying roar.

"Alexis, you can't just go out there!" Mom cried. "He wants to kill *you*!"

Chapter 21

"That's ridiculous, Mother!" I started down the hallway and she grabbed my shoulder, spinning me around. The roar quieted slightly to a loud rumble while footsteps hurried back and forth in the kitchen. "He loves me. He just needs my help."

"That is not *your* Tristan, Alexis. That is Daemoni. They got to him, honey, and all he's wanted since we returned is to kill you. Owen can hardly hold him back."

I pulled away from her grip and continued down the hallway. "He *is* my Tristan. I don't *feel* Daemoni. And I was with him for two days. I think I would know. Owen knows, too. He spent the day with us yesterday. You even saw him last night."

"And he wasn't doing so well," Mom reminded me.

We'd come into the kitchen. Owen paced frantically, shaking his head.

He spun at me. "He's snapped, Alexis. Something's made him completely lose it."

One part of my brain heard him, but the other part focused on the scene.

"Holy *hell.*" My hand flew to my mouth.

He didn't *look* like my Tristan. His back pressed against the front of the refrigerator, and he struggled forcefully, the fridge moving back and forth as if tied to him, I assumed by magic. His muscles bulged and strained against his clothes. He growled at me, his lips peeled back from his teeth like an animal. *And his eyes.* There were no whites, no green or gold. Just fire against blackness.

"Why do you have him tied up like an *animal?*" I cried, tears of anger and compassion burning my eyes.

"Because he's a beast!" Mom said. "Stay away from him!"

"How did this happen? Did *I* do this to him? Is it because he took all that evil energy from me last night?"

"We are not sure," Rina said. "Last night probably did not help matters, but I believe the Daemoni planted dark magic in him. Something to respond to you only. I think the energy change in you has set it off. Your Amadis power won, Alexis. You overcame the Daemoni force and when it left you . . ."

"He took it again, didn't he?" I asked.

Rina's dark expression answered my question. "Not like he did last night, no. I believe it found him, as a . . . how do you say . . . an already open vessel. And now Tristan is losing."

As Rina spoke, I wondered if Tristan was in a place like my meadow, fighting himself for his soul. Although my life had been far from perfect, I'd always been surrounded by love and goodness. Overcoming the evil temptations came relatively easily to me. But Tristan had known only evil for hundreds of years. And now he'd been separated from the Amadis, not receiving that regular dose of good power for so long. He'd been unstable when he came back and last night could have only made it worse. But I knew he *wanted* to be good. If he were in that strange meadow, part of him would still be fighting. The part that needed me.

"I can't hold him much longer," Owen said, his voice strained with effort. "We need help."

"When you lift the shield, there will be Daemoni, too," Mom warned. "They'll hear him."

"I *know*," Owen said. "Protectors are waiting to get in, though. We just have to hope there'll be enough."

While they debated this, I took a few timid steps toward Tristan. My heart picked up speed as a part of me feared for my life. His power rolled off in waves from his tensed body, the energy crashing over me like a hot, violent sea. And his eyes absolutely terrified me.

But I knew *my* Tristan was in there. He had to be. And I had to bring him out. So I gathered my courage and held up the wall in my mind while reaching out to him with my mental cloud. I focused intensely on his mind, saying what had always worked before.

Tristan, it's me, baby. I love you. I trust you.

He struggled wildly. The refrigerator slammed against the walls, the drywall cracking and big chunks crumbling to the ground. The floor quaked and the kitchen cabinets shook. Their contents rattled and crashed. A cabinet door swung open, popping the bottom hinge, and the door continued swinging, the corner of it crashing into Tristan's temple. He took no notice of it.

"*You disgust me. I've been waiting a long time to tear your throat out and watch you die,*" his thoughts growled. Not his voice at all, but a wretched, throaty sound. *A devilish sound.* My mind filled with images as seen through his eyes—him attacking me, snapping and crushing my bones with his power, my body going limp as his teeth dug into my throat.

Tristan, stop it! You're not going to kill me. You love me!

The muscles in his face and neck strained, purple veins popping out, the scars severely red. He snarled ferociously, a wild beast threatening its prey.

I thought he just needed to feel my touch, to be reminded of me and our love. I reached my hand out and it trembled fiercely. I held it in mid-air for just a second, terror almost forcing it back to my side. I trusted my senses he was still in there, that he wasn't Daemoni. But he was much more powerful than I'd ever realized and even the slightest movement could possibly kill me. *I'm stronger now.* Yes, the *Ang'dora* made me less fragile and I had my own powers. I doubted they were anything close to his, but I had to do something for him. So I moved my hand closer and just barely touched his arm with my fingertips.

Electricity zapped between us. It broke the magic. A lion-like roar rattled my bones as he lunged at me.

And then I somehow stood in the family room.

I must have flashed because Tristan hadn't touched me and I'd felt nothing push me there. I stood in the kitchen in front of him and then I didn't. The suddenness disoriented me and I lost my balance, falling into the chair.

Tristan bowled through the kitchen island, smashing through the wood and granite as if they were hollow props. He stood where the island once had, the fire-eyes on me, his muscles twitching and jerking. Mom and Owen stood in fighting stances, their hands held out toward Tristan. They had some kind of power on him. I didn't know what, but knew it couldn't be good.

"Stop it," I yelled, jumping to my feet. "You're hurting him!"

But Tristan's face showed no pain. Only fury. He flicked his hand casually and Mom and Owen flew backwards several feet, their powers released from him. Tristan flashed into the family room, less than five feet from me. He started to lift his hand toward me.

"I have to do it," Owen yelled. The air in the room whooshed upward, followed by popping noises as four more people appeared. They immediately crouched, hands and wands out, focused on Tristan.

"*NO!*" I cried, throwing myself in front of him, my arms held out protectively. "Don't hurt him!"

Tristan roared again. More popping outside and then cackling. *Daemoni!* My old sixth-sense alarms weren't sounding. I had a feeling my new "gift" replaced that other sense. Instead, I identified the Daemoni with an instantaneous conviction. I could physically *feel* their evil energy nearby. The noises outside momentarily diverted everyone else's attention. Tristan took advantage of their distraction. He snarled ferociously and his arm suddenly snaked around my waist, pinning me to his body.

Evil! Good! Evil! Good! Again, not my sense, but a physical feeling of the powers battling within him. I remembered the pain I'd suffered as the same forces had battled inside me only hours before. I had to help him win. I had to bring him back to us.

The protectors' eyes flew from Tristan to me to the glass doors. The popping outside continued like popcorn in a hot pan.

"Go!" Mom commanded the others. "Outside! Owen, we need more help!"

"Already on it," Owen yelled.

"*Alexis, you can do this,*" Rina thought calmly. "*His heart is yours. His soul is yours. Use your Amadis power.*"

Confidence filled her silent voice. Confidence that felt unworthy. I knew the truth in what she said about his heart and soul. They belonged to me. Or, at least, they had. I didn't know what, if anything, remained. The evil energy—the demon, the Daemoni force, whatever raged inside him—was so strong. Even if I could beat it, I couldn't help but wonder what the evil power had already done to him . . . what would be left of him . . . if he would still be my Tristan.

The energy in him is so strong, Rina. Stronger than Sheree's. I can't do this. You and Mom have to.

"*Use your Amadis power,*" she repeated.

It's not strong enough. I'm not risking our lives again. I can't do it, Rina!

"*Yes, you can, darling. Your power is stronger than even mine. You can do this, Alexis.*"

Tristan put the debate to an end. He flexed his bicep and forearm, squeezing me tighter so I could barely breathe. One more move like that and he would crush my ribs. Maybe even snap my spine. But because he hadn't done so already, I knew he still fought for us. Somewhere deep inside, he resisted.

"*Trust me, Alexis. I am here if you need me, but only you can reach Tristan.*"

I closed my eyes, inhaled as deeply as possible and focused on harnessing the Amadis power. I could feel it concentrating and then expanding, creating a bubble within me. Then I heaved the air I'd been holding and forced the bubble outwards from my core. A growl rumbled in my own throat as I impelled the Amadis power away from me. The bubble exploded from my body.

Electricity zapped between Tristan and me, violently separating us. I flew into the shelving against the wall. Glass shattered around me and rained to the floor. Tristan flew to the opposite wall. He crashed onto the couch, which broke with a crack under his force. He raised his hand. His power pinned me against the wall as he stood up. I remained motionless for several moments, knowing from previous experience that his power paralyzed his victims. But I realized I wasn't completely paralyzed. *I* am *strong enough.*

I lifted my left arm and twisted my hand at him. The power surged through my arm and out my palm—not a thin thread anymore, like yesterday, but now a thick rope pulling through my veins. Blue lightning shot out, hitting Tristan in the chest. His shirt sizzled and fell to the floor in pieces. I pulled back slightly, for some reason afraid I could actually hurt him. I made the current strong enough to hold him still as he continued to hold me with his own power.

Owen and Mom both moved to take advantage of the opportunity.

"No," Rina said. "Alexis needs to do this."

"*Mother!*" Mom gasped.

"She can do it, Sophia. She *needs* to do it. She is the only one who can."

"And what if she can't? She won't be able to kill him."

"Her powers are very strong already," Rina said.

"Even if she could *physically* kill him, she doesn't have it within her. She won't bring herself to do it."

"What are you talking about? *I'm not going to kill him. We don't kill!*" I shouted, confused and astonished at what my own mother said.

"See, Mother?" Mom seethed. She turned her eyes on me. "Alexis, if it's your life or his . . . you'll *have* to kill him."

"She will not have to," Rina said. Her voice remained amazingly calm. "Alexis, you can do this."

"We'll do it if she can't," Owen muttered. "But it'll take all of us."

Pain shot through my chest as my heart squeezed. "Nobody's killing him!"

Even while this whole debate went on, even while I held the current on Tristan, another part of my mind assessed the situation outside. The popping noises had stopped and I heard fighting, but no one made their way up to the house. The protectors held the Daemoni back . . . at least for now. I had to keep Tristan away from them, keep him with us. Because if they had any influence on him, I might really lose him forever.

Mom was right—I could never kill him. Even if I lost him again. In fact, I thought I would just follow him this time and make everyone's lives easier.

But what about Dorian? The Amadis?

They needed me and I needed him. I *had* to fight for him. He *had* to still be in there.

Tristan, listen to me, baby. It's me. Your Lexi, your wife, your soul mate. You love me. You don't want to hurt me.

He growled and increased the pressure on me. I could barely hold the current on him.

Tristan, you don't want to do this. I love you. I trust you. I know you're in there and I know you love me. Please, baby, come back to me.

My love and trust had always worked before. Mom and Rina even emphasized love when working on Sheree. But it seemed to only anger Tristan—or the monster within him. I could feel his power gaining on me, pressing my flesh tighter to my bones. I started to panic and lost control of the current. It jumped, singeing a hole in the wall. The break was exactly what the monster inside Tristan needed.

He lunged at me again.

I wasn't quick enough this time.

He coiled his arms around me as if tackling me in a football game. We flew through the air, crashing head first through the sliding glass doors, through the railing and over the edge of the balcony. We landed hard on the ground below—hard enough to loosen his hold. I rolled free. We both jumped to our feet, facing each other. He let out a roaring bark and threw a flame of fire at me. I jumped out of the way and shot electricity at him.

Mom and Rina leapt from the balcony, landing to my right with the soft sound of bending grass blades. Owen followed with a harder thud, but still landed on his feet, his hands out and ready to throw magic. I noticed all this out of the corner of my eye while keeping my main focus on Tristan.

Everyone else had stopped fighting, holding each other at

bay while watching Tristan and me. White noise, like static, buzzed in my head—everyone's thoughts agitated and louder than normal with the promise of bloodshed. My wall started to crumble and I had to make a point of keeping it up. But the attention to the wall made me realize that if I could keep it up and focus on Tristan, not on talking to him, but listening to him, I would at least know his next move.

It was a good defense. Every time he moved at me or tried to use a power, I eluded it. He lunged. I stepped to the side. He shot a fire ball at my legs. I dodged it with a hop. He shot another, but higher. I dropped to my knees and leaned back, my shoulders nearly touching the ground as the flame soared over me. From my upside-down viewpoint as I looked behind me, I watched Mom extinguish the fire with a shot of water from her hand. The shock of never knowing she could do that consumed my mind, but my body moved on its own, jumping back to my feet to face Tristan. My evasions infuriated him and his chest rumbled angrily. His thoughts filled with frustration and we stood in a stand-off.

I didn't know what to do. Reading his mind protected me from his attacks, but it wasn't a good offense. I didn't want to hurt him, if that were even possible, but I had to do something to reach him—the Real Tristan imprisoned by the monster trying to kill me. I'd never fought before. I'd never even *thought* about fighting. This part of my life had arrived so soon and so quickly and no one had prepared me. I didn't even know what powers I had, how to use them or their strength.

And I fought the person I loved most in this world, the person I could not live without, my own husband, my Tristan.

No, not my Tristan. The demon within.

Chapter 22

I had Amadis power and love and those would have to be enough. *But are they?* I just didn't know. Whatever the Daemoni had planted in Tristan proved itself powerful. He was the mightiest creature on Earth and he couldn't control it on his own. He needed my help. He needed my love. After everything we'd been through—everything we'd both suffered because of our love— surely it was strong enough to overcome this. *Isn't it?* Tears stung my eyes with the possibility that the answer was "no."

Owen's words from just a couple of days ago echoed in my mind: "We *always* win." *Good always wins over evil, right?* I'd lost my faith in that belief over seven years ago. And then Tristan came back . . . or so I thought. *No, don't think that. He is my Tristan. I just need to pull him out, help him beat the demon.*

A strong gust of wind blew through the grounds. My hair whipped around, slapping my face, and my dress thrashed at my legs. I glanced up for a split-second, the wind watering my eyes.

A storm cloud formed directly over us, though the rest of the sky was the clear blue of a Spring day. The cloud reminded me of our wedding, right when Tristan took his vow to the Amadis. A strange, angry storm had hovered over us then, too. Like that one, this dark cloud swirled and twisted and lightning shot across its belly. Evil brewed above us, preparing to strike at the opportune moment.

Tristan and I watched each other carefully. His muscles bulged with power, his hair blew wildly and his eyes blazed with fire. He looked like a beautiful but enraged god of darkness. Everyone's eyes remained transfixed on us as we moved side to side in a macabre dance. I monitored his thoughts and a series of profanities flew through his mind. The monster was pissed. It couldn't beat me. *Yet*. I wondered how long it would take for the monster to completely take him over. *Can it take his soul? Will the gray meadow imprison him in its lifelessness? Will his soul be lost forever? What will I do then?*

I snapped out of the pensiveness with the sound of a *Pop!*

A long-legged, white-blond female, clad in her usual leather, appeared about ten yards behind Tristan. Her red-blue eyes, almost lavender in the daylight, shifted from Tristan to me and back to him. Her lips peeled back in a wicked grin.

Damn it! Can we ever get a break?

The Daemoni cackled and cawed around us. For the first time, I noticed the white-blond, male vampire from Key West—Vanessa's brother. Just to his right stood the vampire who'd threatened me in my room. *How can they be out right now?*

"Uh-oh. Are we having a little squabble?" Vanessa sang as she sauntered over to Tristan's side. She chuckled, the musical sound ringing in the air. "Looks like you finally came to your senses, lover."

"Glad you could join the party," her brother said. An Amadis protector snarled at him.

"The party's just getting started. My Seth is finally coming back to me," she crooned as she strutted around Tristan—too closely for my liking.

Tristan paid her no notice, but I was distracted. For a second too long. His power overtook me before I could react to the thought and he held me in place. I could barely deliver the electric current, especially as the blond vampire bitch ranted on. She ran her hands over Tristan's bare shoulders and arms, her eyes on me, mocking me.

"Are you going to kill her, darling? Or do you want me to do it for you?" she purred.

"C'mon, Seth, just do it!" one of the Daemoni jeered. "What are you waiting for?"

Some of the others followed with their own taunting, the last thing we needed right now. I just had to hope he ignored them as much as he ignored the snow-white bloodsucker hanging all over him. Granted he was trying to kill me, but at least I had his undivided attention.

But seeing Vanessa touching him revolted me. The emotions—combined with Tristan's intensifying power—started to weaken my resolve.

I can't do this. I can't hold him.

"You love him, Alexis. You can do this," Rina thought.

I'm not strong enough. I'm going to lose him! I'll kill us both.

"Use your love and your Amadis power. I told you. You are strong enough now."

I didn't understand why she couldn't help, but once again I followed her instructions. With effort, I tuned out Vanessa and my emotions—all but my love for Tristan—and dragged my right hand up, palm out toward him. I focused on pushing the power through. That warm, soft ribbon, wider and stronger now, streamed through my body and along my arm and surged out of my hand. I felt it connect with his chest, right at the mutilated Amadis mark, penetrating into his heart.

I love you, Tristan. You and me together forever. That's how it is. You and me, baby. Think of our love, Tristan. Think of your son's love.

Tristan growled, the corner of his lip lifting in a snarl. I could feel the evil energy building inside him, gaining force to fight my Amadis power. And I thought it might be too late—I might already be fighting Daemoni.

So now what?

I couldn't kill him. Even if I wanted to, he was virtually impossible to kill. The Daemoni had tried all their different ways and they couldn't even take his heart. *Because it belongs to me.* Did that mean I *could* do it? Was I the only one? Is that what Rina meant after all? My stomach clenched into a sickened knot.

But even if that's true . . . he's Tristan. *My one and only love.* Mom was right. I couldn't kill him. I would let him kill me first.

"Do it already, darling. Kill the little bitch," Vanessa taunted. "Then we can finally be together. Oh, the things we will do . . . ."

She draped herself around his non-responsive body. My heart squeezed.

Get your raunchy hands off him!

I hadn't meant for her to hear me, to reach into her head. The idea disgusted me. But she laughed aloud as if I had. Appalled, I returned my focus to what mattered.

No, Tristan! Remember our LOVE. Remember Dorian.

His growl deepened and grew louder.

"We can have so much fun, now that she'll be out of the way. Come on, lover, just do it," Vanessa sang. Then her voice became a snarl. "*Or I will!*"

"Do it, Vanessa!" her brother shouted. "Fuck Lucas!"

"Shut the hell up!" I yelled.

The fury gave me the strength I needed to fight Tristan's power. I turned my left hand on Vanessa, while holding my right on Tristan. I didn't realize the extent of my power until I unleashed the electricity on her. She couldn't handle it like Tristan could. She twitched and seized, her face twisted into a pained grimace.

"Easy, Alexis. We do not kill unless there is no hope. She is a soul that can be saved," Rina reminded me.

Are you freakin' kidding me? She's ready to kill me!

But I knew in my heart Rina was right. Overwhelming love still filled my body and I could feel a twinge even for the vulgar vampire bitch. I also knew Owen and the others wouldn't let her kill me. I let off the current and Vanessa collapsed, her once beautiful blond hair standing on end in patches, what remained only an inch long. Purple smoke rose off her blackened skin.

"*You little*—" she screamed. She lunged at me, but then she soared thirty yards backwards. Out of the corner of my eye, I could see Mom and Owen magically restraining her.

I paid for the distraction. In an instant, Tristan's power pressed on me more forcefully than ever. I now knew exactly why they considered him the ultimate warrior. His power was unbeatable, literally able to squeeze the life out of somebody. It compressed my body into itself, squishing my bones as if they were made of putty. My chest pressed into my spine, my heart flattening, my lungs about to collapse. My veins and arteries constricted, the blood flow slowing. My head felt like it would implode.

And I couldn't bring myself to fight him. I couldn't do whatever I needed to do to save myself. I couldn't even think straight about it. I couldn't save him and I couldn't kill him.

It's happening. Evil is winning. He's actually killing me.

All those times he'd been so worried about accidentally

killing me and I'd never believed he would do it. Now he was. And I was letting him.

But my death would leave the Amadis without hope for another daughter. It would leave Dorian without a mother. And it would leave Tristan—if there's still soul left that would even care—to live out his existence knowing he'd killed me.

I'd promised him several years ago I would never let him do that to himself. I would never let him have to live with that. I would never let him kill himself over it. *This is Not. Going. To. Happen!*

There was only one thing to do. I prayed.

Dear God, please help me. You are so powerful and I can't do this without You. I need You. He needs You. I offer myself as a tool. Use me however You need to. Just please save him. Please, dear Lord, save Tristan.

A voice answered in my head and it didn't belong to Rina. This voice came as quiet as a whisper, yet I could feel the immense power reverberating through it.

I am here for you, My daughter. His soul is already Mine, Alexis. When he gave it to the Amadis, he gave it to Me and nothing can change that. But until I bring him home, his soul needs protection against the demons. I have already given you what you need. Use the power I have gifted to you, My daughter. This is My plan for you. This is your purpose.

And I understood. I knew then what I was made to do. My purpose in life, just like Tristan had said. I was never meant to be normal. I knew it all along, despite all the lies I told myself, despite the ruses I attempted to make life normal. But that was never really me. That wasn't Real Alexis. I was Amadis. More than that. I was Amadis royalty. The books, a daughter, eventually leading the Amadis . . . those were part of my duties. But Real Alexis was created to be the fierce protector. My main purpose in life was to defend souls from evil.

And Tristan's was my first.

"NOW, Alexis. You can *do it!"* Rina's voice loud in my head.

I won't let you do this to yourself, Tristan! I yelled into his mind. *We will WIN!*

I struggled against his power, panting and sweating with effort. I heard Rina and Mom praying. A rush of otherworldly power washed over me, poured over my skin and seeped into my pores, filling my body with strength and force. I gathered all of that force, pulled it from every cell in my body and directed it through my hand to Tristan's heart, focusing only on the power God had given me and my love for Tristan.

I know you're in there, baby. We can beat this together. We can do this. Please, Tristan. Come back to me. Stay with me!

My thoughts escalated as desperation grew. I pushed with every bit of strength I had. And I watched as the scars around his heart began to dissolve and the fire in his eyes dimmed.

That's it, baby. Come on. We can do this. You love me. You want to be with me. You and me forever, *Tristan!*

His hold on me weakened. I continued pushing the full strength of Amadis power on him.

Love, Tristan. You WANT to love. You LOVE me. You LOVE Dorian. We love you! We need you!

DO.

NOT.

LEAVE.

ME.

AGAIN!

And his power released me.

I felt instantly free. His body convulsed violently and a painful moan replaced the growls. Then he fell to his knees as I kept Amadis power focused on him. The skin around his heart smoothed and the Amadis mark, now whole, began to brighten. The fire in his eyes died and then disappeared.

The now hazel eyes, full of pain and regret and love, penetrated my own eyes.

"Alexis," he whispered. I took a half-step toward him.

"*NO!*" Vanessa screeched, making me freeze, the sound more terrifying than a long-nailed finger scratching against a dark window. "*Get her! Get them both!*"

She ran at me. Chaos erupted as everyone responded. The Daemoni sprang toward Tristan and me. The Amadis protectors fought them back. Vanessa, still at least fifteen feet away, jumped and flew through the air toward me. She moved so fast, just a blur of white and black. I didn't have time to react. Just as she came close enough to feel a rush of air on my neck, she suddenly flew sideways. Her back cracked against a steel post supporting the balcony. The post vibrated with a twang as she crumpled to the ground. My eyes wide with terror and surprise, I swung around to see whose force had saved me. Tristan's hand still faced toward her.

He lithely jumped to his feet and, in martial-arts style, he turned, seemingly in slow motion, his power hitting the Daemoni one at a time as his hand swung around in an arc. One-by-one they fell to the ground. Then they each disappeared with a *Pop!* The storm overhead rapidly shrunk, then vanished.

We all stood there in the stillness, breathing heavily, looking around to make sure they all disappeared. I could hear every single heart pounding with adrenaline. Then we let out a collective sigh of relief.

Tristan turned back toward me, agony all over his face.

"Alexis," he whispered again.

I ran for him and jumped into his open arms. He held me tightly as I kissed him all over his face and he kissed me back.

"I love you, Tristan," I gasped between desperate kisses and tears. "I love you so much."

He squeezed me against him. "I love you, Lexi, my beautiful, brave Lexi, *ma lykita*."

I held his face in my hands and looked into his eyes and they filled with love, the gold flecks sparkling brightly.

"I'm sorry, so sorry."

I placed my finger over his lips. "It wasn't you. And it's gone. It's just you and me now."

His lips found mine and kissed me with fervent love. Then we just looked into each other's eyes as I held his face in my hands and stroked his cheeks with my thumbs. I felt a light rippling under my right thumb. Something changed in his skin.

"Oh!" I continued stroking and then kissing the scar stretching diagonally across his cheek. It gradually dissolved away and he shuddered when it had completely vanished. I did the same to the one around and under his eye and it, too, dissolved. I erased the one on his chin and kissed him all over his beautiful face, each little scar disappearing. I slid my hand over his cheek. No icy ridges. Nothing but soft, velvety skin. "They're gone. The scars are gone!"

Keeping one arm tightly around me, he rubbed his other hand over his face. He smiled warmly.

"The dark magic is gone," he said. "Gone for good, because of you. You saved me again."

I threw my arms around his neck.

"We save each other," I said. "We *need* each other."

He nuzzled my hair and murmured, "Yes, my love. Our souls are bound together. Forever."

Chapter 23

"Owen, take care of this." Rina waved her hand at the destruction as we headed up the stairs and into the house. The shield had already been replaced and the Amadis protectors had walked beyond it and disappeared, except for Julia, who remained at the shield's edge. Whether she stood guard or simply waited for Rina, I didn't know.

Owen rubbed his hands together, as if they were cold and he warmed them, and then thrust them out in front of him. The pieces of the balcony and screen flew back together. As we stood back and watched, he made the movement again toward the glass doors and then with the interior—the furniture, the walls and the kitchen island returned to looking like new. I had to snap my jaw shut, amazed at what I'd just witnessed. *As if everything else today is perfectly normal . . . .* I snorted to myself.

"Get the bedroom, too," Mom said. I cringed and stared at the floor in embarrassment. Owen seeing it was bad enough. *Now Mom and Rina, too?*

"Don't know why I should bother," Owen muttered as he headed into the bedroom.

Tristan squeezed my hand and a guilty smile tugged at the corners of my mouth. I wondered why Tristan hadn't had him fix it before. Perhaps, like Owen, he didn't see the point of it.

Rina sat in the chair and signaled for me to sit on the couch. Tristan sat next to me, not letting go of my hand, and I felt a pull of energy through my arm and into his. He strengthened his goodness with my power. Knowing I could do that for him felt strange yet comforting. I gave his hand a squeeze with my own.

"May I?" Rina asked Tristan, holding her hand out to him. He reluctantly let go of my hand and took Rina's. She closed her eyes for several long moments, her face tense with concentration. I held my breath as she assessed him. Finally, she relaxed and a smile spread across her face. "Excellent, Tristan."

He let go of her hand and picked mine up again, kissing the back of it before clasping it between both of his. I pushed my energy into him, knowing what he needed.

"Thank you," he murmured and I had a feeling he meant that for both Rina and me.

Rina looked at me with her large, mahogany eyes. Less than two weeks ago, both she and Mom could have nearly passed as my daughters. Now we could all be sisters, rather than three generations spanning over a-hundred-and-fifty years. But Rina's eyes would almost give her away. Not for her age, but for her wisdom.

"You have waited a long time to hear your story, no?" she asked.

"Way too long," I said. My stomach fluttered with anticipation.

"You have been very patient, I know. And now that you have your full Amadis power, everything will be revealed. There will be no more secrets."

Finally.

Rina sighed. "Unfortunately, I must ask you to wait a few days longer."

What?! Are you kidding me?

"Sophia and I must return for a debriefing from the council immediately," Rina continued. "This is not over. In fact, it has just begun. The council must be made aware of everything that has happened and discuss our future. In the meantime, before you can come, you and Tristan, with Owen's help, need to prepare to start a new life. You have five days to do what needs done and to travel to the Island. Tristan, you have a plan for A.K. Emerson, no?"

"I did," Tristan said, "but it included destroying her house in Atlanta. Is it still unsafe there?"

Rina pursed her lips for a moment. "No, the situation there is under control, but I would rather not lose that property. It may be useful for us."

Tristan nodded and considered other solutions. Anxious about the demise of my author's life, I reached for my pendant, for the calming effect it gave me. I gasped, my fingers feeling only the bare skin of my chest. Tristan's head snapped toward me.

"Mom, please say you took off my necklace in the back bedroom," I said. Tristan disappeared.

"I don't see it!" he called from there.

"No," Mom said. "I know you don't ever take it off."

"Oh, no! Not good!" I jumped to my feet and frantically searched around the family room, not able to remember now exactly where we'd been when Tristan tried to kill me.

"It's not there," Tristan said, now back in the family room. Mom and Rina exchanged a meaningful look with each other and then with Tristan.

"Maybe when we flew off the balcony?" I asked. Tristan,

Mom and Rina disappeared. I heard them outside on the ground. I tried flashing, too. *I did it!* And, sucking in air, I fell on my butt when I appeared. It really was disorienting to be in one place and suddenly somewhere else. Owen laughed from the balcony and I shot him a look.

"You'll get used to it," Mom said, lifting me up.

I walked around a portion of the yard as we each sectioned off areas to search. I could see every blade of grass in twenty different shades of green, little bugs of all shapes and colors and the tiniest specks of dirt and sand. But no necklace or pendant.

"We have four sets of the best eyes in the world. We *have* to find it," Tristan muttered.

"Owen, can you summon it?" Mom asked.

I looked up at Owen, wondering why he hadn't tried by now. He waved his hand and I looked around, I guess expecting it to be flying through the air or something. But there was nothing. He shook his head. Mom's and Rina's shoulders slumped.

"It's nowhere around here," he said with a shrug.

He obviously didn't understand its importance. Mom and Rina seemed to understand, though. In fact, it seemingly held more significance to them than it even did to me. Once again, they traded pointed looks with Tristan. They all seemed as upset as I felt over its loss, but I was sure for different reasons. To me, the pendant was Tristan's first gift to me, made by his own hands, and it had served as a lifeline at times. But their expressions gave me the feeling it was more than just a pretty piece of jewelry. I rubbed my bare neckline, feeling partially naked without it.

"Don't worry. We'll find it," Tristan promised with a squeeze of my hand as we went back inside.

"As I was saying," Rina said once we were settled again, "we will hold council on the sixth day and you both will need to be there. Make a plan for Ms. Emerson, Tristan."

"I have it now. We still submit the photos to the media, announcing her marriage to her son's father. Then they go to Greece for a honeymoon." Tristan winked at me and I could barely follow the rest. I was happy to know that hadn't changed with the *Ang'dora*. Even if it made me stupid for a moment or two, I didn't ever want to lose that effect he had on me.

"Very good. Five days, no more." Rina stood up, but then she paused, looking at me. *"We will keep your new gift a secret for now."*

I blinked at her, not understanding. *Didn't all those fighters just . . . hear . . . me, though?*

"I monitored their thoughts. You controlled your wall very well. Nobody knows. I would like to keep it as such for the time being. Your gift might be useful in discovering information about the email and the video."

Someone knocked on the door. Rina looked toward it, then back at me, her eyebrows raised in a question. I nodded. Then she must have silently invited the visitor in, because a tall, pale woman with long, black hair came through the door and into the kitchen. The same woman who'd accompanied Mom and Rina inside last night, just before I collapsed. Julia gave a slight nod to Rina, Mom and even me, then she just stood there, eyeing me. She made me uncomfortable and I had to look away.

Something about her felt . . . different. Owen had said Julia was Rina's closest advisor, after Solomon, so surely she could be trusted. But she just didn't feel right to me. The thought of peeking into her mind occurred to me, but I didn't think I had enough control. Rina would probably end up telling her, if she really was her close advisor, but since I'd just promised Rina not to reveal my gift, I couldn't take the risk. So I was grateful when Rina finally made the move to leave and Julia moved back toward the door.

Tristan and I walked them outside. Rina told Owen to accompany them to the airport, as an extra precaution. I had a feeling she would use the opportunity to reprimand him for his lack of attention to his responsibilities. I felt bad for him. Though what Rina said made sense and I could definitely see the truth of it in Owen, a lot of our mishaps were also my fault.

"Give Dorian hugs and kisses for me," I told Mom before they left. "And please save our surprise."

"Of course, honey," Mom said as she hugged me. "You work on your powers. Learn what you have and how to use them. Be prepared for anything."

Owen snorted.

"Anyone who can handle Tristan the way she did can handle *anyone*," he said. "I thought I did good just to hold him for so long. But, you, Alexis, you literally brought him to his knees."

"Ah, Tristan's easy. I know his weakness." I saw Owen was about to ask. "But that's *my* secret."

Tristan squeezed my hand as we watched Mom, Owen, Julia and Rina walk down the driveway, into the brush, and disappear.

❦

Tristan and I sat on our beach for the sunset. Until now, I hadn't purposely watched a sunset since our honeymoon. I kneeled behind him, kissing and rubbing the scars away from his back. He'd shuddered several times, but had otherwise been quiet and withdrawn. My own thoughts had been reeling over everything that had happened in the last twenty-four hours.

"How can Vanessa and the other vampires come out in daylight? Is that just a myth?" I asked, breaking the silence. His back free of scars and dark magic, I moved to sit in front of him, between his legs, just like the old days.

He chuckled. "With all the questions you must have, you're still focused on vampires?"

I shrugged. "I *have* been writing about them for the last six years."

I'd been curious about this since yesterday in Key Largo, but I really asked now because it was the most trivial of all my questions. I felt the need to lighten the tension hovering over us. It worked— or, at least, distracted him from his heavy thoughts. He wrapped his arms around my shoulders and leaned his chin on my shoulder.

"Can't your vamps come out in the daytime?" he asked.

"*My* vamps have no limitations. They're the ultimate predators."

"And so are real vamps."

A seashell in the sand caught my eye and I reached out for it. It came to me without my touching it. I did it again with another one.

"Whoa," I breathed.

Tristan chuckled again. "You'd better be careful or you'll create bad habits. Next thing you know, you'll be at a restaurant and the salt shaker moves across the table in front of the waiter."

"Good point. But I'm supposed to practice."

I made the shells play leap frog with each other. Then I tried to levitate a shell; I couldn't hold it. A different shell rose and hung in the air, but not by me. I watched Tristan's hand, but it just looked like he held it out, waiting for someone to shake it. I tried to imitate him, but my shell only hopped up and down.

"I thought *you* were the ultimate predator," I said. "If they have vampires, why did they need to create you?"

"I'm a warrior, not a predator. There's a difference," he said darkly. He made his shell fly into the water. I tried levitating mine again and was able to hold it in the air. "Vamps have their own problems. You can get the scoop from Solomon in a few days."

"Solomon?" I tried picturing Rina's mate. I hadn't seen him since the day Tristan had disappeared, when they left for the battle. In fact, I'd only seen him twice in my life—the only other time in Mom's cottage in Cape Heron, when I'd first met Rina, too.

"Sure. He is a vampire, after all."

"Solomon's a *vampire?*" The shell fell with my astonishment.

"What'd you think he is?"

"I don't know. Didn't really think about it." From what I did remember about Solomon, he looked to be of African descent, but with very pale skin, and he *was* exceedingly attractive and quite scary, actually . . . but I didn't remember fangs, like Vanessa and the others. Of course, I hadn't known vampires were even real at the time, so I wasn't exactly looking for them. "So, we have vampires on our side, too?"

"Of course. That's what Amadis do, remember? We save the souls of the so-called damned."

"That's an oxymoron. How can we save souls that are already damned?"

"That's exactly it. There are some who willingly gave their souls up long ago, but for most, they're not entirely lost causes. If they've been bitten, turned against their will, they can continue to hold onto some humanity. They can hold onto their souls. As long as there's any hope, Amadis power can lead them to goodness. Like they did with me. Like *you* did with me."

"They started it. *Mom* started it."

"You finished it," he murmured as he tightened his arms around me in a hug.

"Can you feel that it's gone? I mean, I actually felt the dark power leave my body."

"The evil force? Most of it, yes. And with each scar you remove, I feel the last traces disappearing. But the strength of our powers mostly comes from Daemoni magic. It's part of our DNA."

I shuddered. "I hate that part."

"It's pointless to hate it. There's nothing you can do about it. Something I realized a long time ago. But we can use it for good and you have a lot of strength you can do good with. I think you may be more of an ultimate warrior than I am."

I laughed. "Yeah, right."

"I'm serious," he said and his voice held no hint of humor. "Owen was right. No one else could have done what you did with me."

"Like I told him, I know your weakness. You told me a long time ago."

He pressed his lips against the side of my neck. "You."

"And our love."

"Our love is a strength." He sighed, the warm air fluttering the tiny hairs at the base of my scalp. "My biggest strength *and* my biggest weakness."

I remembered being ready to give myself up to the Daemoni for love. "Yeah, probably mine, too."

We sat in silence as the sun sank behind the water. The heavy tension returned with each heartbeat of dead air. My attempts at conversation hadn't lifted Tristan's mood at all. I sighed, knowing what simmered in his mind.

"You're brooding," I finally said.

"Hmm . . . ?" he asked distractedly.

"You're wallowing in regret and you need to stop."

He confirmed my suspicion by not responding for a long moment. When he finally did, his voice came out in a pained whisper. "I almost killed you today, Alexis."

I shook my head. "No. Not you. *You* protected me. The monster tried to kill me, but you were still in there, too. Preventing it."

"I couldn't control it, though."

"I'm still here, aren't I?"

He sighed. "You give me too much credit."

"I wish you would stop beating yourself up," I said with a groan of frustration. "If you really wanted to kill me, Tristan, you would have. But you didn't. You couldn't do it. You overcame the monster."

He shook his head. "God overcame it."

"God gave me the power and I gave it to you to strengthen the *real* you. Because we knew you were still fighting. I would be dead right now if it weren't for Real Tristan . . . *my* Tristan . . . keeping me alive."

He fell silent again for a long time. I hoped he accepted my point.

When he finally spoke, his voice was much lighter. "Well, keeping you alive *is* in my best interest. And I'm selfish like that."

I snorted. "You are one of the most *un*selfish people I know."

"Hmm . . . when it comes to you, you have no idea how selfish I can be."

I smiled to myself. "Well, I forgive you for that, too. Since it's also in my best interest."

"Thank you," he murmured. His kisses behind my ear and the lighter feeling in the air told me he no longer mulled over this afternoon's events. Happy to move beyond the gloom, I trained my thoughts on the blaze over the water.

"Can I ask you a question?" I asked, turning sideways to see his face.

"You can always *ask*," he teased, pulling out one of my old lines, from when we first met. I smiled at the memory . . . and at the fact that his attitude had genuinely improved.

"What is it with you and sunsets? You never told me why you like them so much."

"Ah." He shrugged. "They're just beautiful, aren't they? The perfect piece of art, each one unique."

"That's it?" I'd always thought there was something more to it—he'd always made such a point of watching them.

"Well . . . not exactly. I like to watch the sunrises, too, but you're never awake for them." He paused. "See, the vamps may be able to come out in the day, but they prefer the night and the cover of darkness. All the Daemoni do. Humans fear the unknown and anything beyond the light is unknown. The Daemoni feed off that fear. I once lived for the night, too, but now I appreciate the light and all its various forms. The colors it produces that can't be seen in its absence. The way it bounces off the clouds and the water when it's on the horizon. Sunsets are a little extra special because they mark another day I've been able to live in the light. They only mean anything when I'm with you, though."

He glanced down at me, then quickly looked away, as if embarrassed by this secret he'd just divulged. The pinks and purples and golds—so many more than I'd ever noticed before—swam out of my vision as I took in an even more precious sight. If at all possible, he appeared even more exquisite now than he'd ever been before. And, if at all possible, I loved him more this moment than ever before.

I took his face in my hands and kissed him. It became the first passionate kiss we'd had since the *Ang'dora*. It blew me away. His lips felt even softer and smoother than they had last night, like silk against mine. I caressed my hands over his face, feeling the new smoothness, and slid them back, twisting them into his hair and pulling him closer. I separated my lips and his tangy-sweetness tasted delicious.

He lay me down in the sand, cradling my head in the crook of his arm, and moved his mouth along my jaw, down my neck and across my shoulder and then followed the path back up again. The electric current underneath my skin charged more intensely than ever and felt more exciting than our first touches. His free hand trailed down my side, over my hip and around my thigh. He slid it under the bottom of my dress, up along the inside of my leg. I shuddered with overwhelming excitement as his fingers trailed along the edge of my panties.

"This is unbelievable," I breathed.

"Mmm . . . it's a good start," he replied, still kissing me. Then he picked me up and carried me into the house, our lips moving together the whole way. The results of the *Ang'dora* magnified every sensation of making love to him by at least one hundred times compared to before. I lost any control I'd ever had. And he did, too . . . but not in the way that made his eyes blaze. In a good way. A blissful way.

I knew because when I lost control, the wall in my mind fell and I could hear his thoughts. And I felt the sensations and experienced the excitement for both of us. Overcome with euphoria, my mind exploded and reached into his, sharing what I felt.

"Oh . . . *Lex*," he moaned pleasurably as we both flew over the edge.

I apologized later, as we lay on the floor, the bed in shambles again. "Sorry for getting into your head. I couldn't help it."

He grinned widely, the gold flecks in his eyes dancing. "Don't be sorry. That was . . . *mind blowing*."

I slept peacefully—for the first time in over seven years, I didn't have a single dream.

Chapter 24

We spent the next two days doing what needed to be done, as Rina had put it. Tristan used my computer to move money around our various accounts. Owen met Julia, who delivered identification for him and for the new A.K. Emerson-Wells. We also worked on my powers.

By our last day there, I could move objects—even Tristan—with my mind, control my electrical charge at different levels of power and flash without falling. We practiced flashing together, too, Tristan holding my hand and leading me. I found this even more disorienting than flashing by myself, because I went with him but didn't know where. The "destination" I had to concentrate on was simply "wherever Tristan is." We must have done it fifty times before I could land without falling, Owen laughing at me every time. Although I learned to sense Tristan's flash trail, the guys decided against my learning how to follow it yet. Apparently, following a trail was more difficult than I had time to practice.

We also searched for my pendant. We never found it.

Our flight from Miami to London, where we would connect to Athens, left in the afternoon of the third day. My emotions were mixed as we prepared to leave the beach house, where so much had happened to me.

"Will we ever be able to return?" I asked Tristan.

"I don't know. I hope so."

"Me, too," I said with a sigh.

From my honeymoon to grieving to the *Ang'dora*, this house had seen the best and worst of me. It would forever hold a special place in my heart. We shared one final kiss in *our* house and then Tristan looked down at me and smiled.

"Ready to go home?" he asked.

I felt sad to leave but excited for what was to come, even with the danger we could face on the way. "I guess. Let's do it."

He took my hand and we walked down the driveway, into the brush and flashed. I'd become accustomed to the absence of air by now, but I still sucked in a huge breath when we appeared, a natural reaction.

Owen had gone ahead to drop the photos in the mail and to transport our luggage because we couldn't flash with it and we'd look suspicious flying without any. He waited for us in the long-term parking lot at the Miami airport.

"So much for the Ferrari," Owen muttered sadly as we abandoned the sports car and headed for the terminal.

"I thought you were getting a motorcycle," I teased to cheer him up. It worked.

His face brightened and he smiled. "Oh, yeah."

We traveled with no problems from the Daemoni. Tristan had been concerned they would stage a terrorist attack, but apparently they weren't ready to go that far with the humans. When we arrived in Athens, we had to go our separate ways. The Amadis mansion occupied a private island in the Aegean

Sea. Owen took the Amadis boat with our luggage, but Mr. and Mrs. Wells checked into a hotel room and then rented a boat for the day, leaving a paper trail for the authorities and the media.

The boat trip was unbelievably beautiful. The sun shone brightly, dancing on the azure water and warming the air, although the wind held a slight chill. I was glad to finally be able to let my mind relax—being in crowded places was difficult. It had taken every ounce of mental energy to keep my wall up on the airplane, knowing I couldn't escape the voices if it fell. Owen and Tristan took turns "singing" and "talking" to me, just to give my mind something to tune into. Now, with no one around but Tristan, I didn't have to hold the wall at all.

After about an hour, Tristan idled the engine and pointed at an island about three miles away, barely visible on the horizon. "That's where we're flashing to first. I'll lead. Then we'll have to swim to the Amadis Island. It's shielded, of course, so we can't flash onto it."

"Okay," I said, although I didn't feel okay at all. My insides squirmed with anxiety.

Tristan twisted his hand and shot a bolt of fire at the boat's engine. It ignited, large flames building on the fuel. No turning back now.

And then we both heard another boat engine approaching quickly. Too quickly.

"They'll go by—I hope," Tristan muttered. We had little time with the flames growing larger by the second and we certainly didn't need someone coming to help before we flashed.

"*Got 'em,*" the horribly familiar yet beautifully musical voice chimed in my head. I felt the blood drain to my feet.

"Vanessa," I barely croaked.

Tristan spun around and eyed the approaching boat. He swore under his breath, his fists clenching at his sides.

"Now what?" I mouthed, unable to get the words out.

His body relaxed as he turned to me. "Stick to the plan. She won't be able to get us."

"Will she follow us, though?"

"She won't know where we're going and she won't get close enough to follow our trails." Tristan's eyes cut to the fiery engine. "We have to go."

He grabbed my hand but I couldn't bring myself to stand up. I watched the other boat approach from the back and swing around to the front of ours.

My insides contracted tightly with panic. *What if I screw up and don't go with Tristan? What if I get stuck here alone? Can I fight her?* I thought I could, but I wasn't positive. And Vanessa had back-up. Her brother drove the boat.

"Come on, *ma lykita*, we'll be okay," Tristan said softly. "Trust me."

Those last two were the words I needed to hear. I stood up and nodded. Holding hands, we ran up the bow and jumped.

Barely in time. The boat engine exploded.

Vanessa stood right below us at her bow, grinning as she looked up at us. Her brother stood behind the wheel, also gazing at us. They seemed to be waiting for us to land right into their laps.

And then we flashed.

But not before I caught the gleam of the sun hitting a silver circle with a red stone in the center, dangling from Vanessa's gloved hand, as if taunting me.

We landed on the island and I sucked in a deep breath as Tristan surveyed our surroundings.

"We're good from now on," he said.

I turned around, though, and started stomping away as if that was the way back to Vanessa. "Stupid, evil, thieving vampire bitch."

Tristan's arm immediately encircled my waist, holding me motionless. "I know, my love. I saw it, too."

"Then let's go get it!" My anger overshadowed the fear I'd just felt when I first heard her thoughts.

"Don't worry, we will. Just not right now. We need to get home." He pressed me tighter against him.

I stopped struggling. As strong as I was now, intensified more by my anger, I was still no match for Tristan. And he was right. There would surely be plenty of opportunities to get my pendant back in the future. Because she—and the Daemoni—would not give up.

Which became obvious immediately. I heard her thoughts again first and then her boat as it quickly approached the little island.

"Son of a bitch," Tristan muttered.

"How does she always know where we are . . . ?" My voice trailed off as I realized the answer. "Oh! Oh, no! Tristan . . . my blood. My blood is in her!"

His arm dropped from my waist and I slid to the ground.

"*Shit.* Why didn't I think of that?" He kicked a boulder the size of a soccer ball and it sailed across the water before dropping with a *ker-plunk*.

"How far until we're safe?" I asked.

He took me back into his arm and walked to the edge of the water. He nodded at another island, again about three miles away.

"The shield goes one mile out from that island."

"Can we flash into water?"

"*I* can, but I don't know about you," he said. "It takes practice—you can't inhale like you do or your lungs will fill with water. And we have to get the distance just right, close to the shield, because they'll be right on top of us. There's no room for error."

Vanessa's boat came around to our side of the island,

slowing down as it approached the beach, aimed for right where we stood.

"Then we fight or we try. Unless you have any better solution?" I asked.

Vanessa stood at the tip of the bow, ready to jump. The adrenaline coursed through my veins and my heart picked up speed.

"We'll give it a try," Tristan said as he lifted me against his body. He spoke quickly while wading into the water. "We'll do both. I'll hold you. You keep them back. When I say, take a deep breath and I'll flash."

"Can you do it *with* me again?" Flashing with someone was very different—and nearly impossible—than leading someone, as we had practiced.

"I've done it twice now. We're going to try. Ready?"

"I'm not getting my pendant, am I?"

"Sorry, my love, but not this time. We *will* get it back, though. It can't be in their hands."

Vanessa jumped right for us. I shot an electric bolt at her, sending her back to the other side of her boat. Tristan held me and swam. Vanessa's brother seemed to be lost, his head swiveling between her in the water and us.

"Get them, you jack ass!" Vanessa screeched.

Suddenly they were both in the air, about to land on top of us. I started to reach my hand out, remembering at the last second that I could move objects with my mind. But it was already too late.

"Now!" Tristan bellowed. Forgetting my necklace for now, I shot wildly at them while inhaling my last breath.

We appeared in deep water, the light of the sky far above us. I fought the natural urge to inhale after flashing and continued to hold my breath while kicking upwards.

"Nice job," Tristan said when we surfaced.

I looked around as I tread water. "Are we close?"

"Not really. We'll have to swim from here, though. And fast. I hear them coming."

"Alexis, I got them. You two get to shore." Owen's voice shouted in my head.

"No, it's not them. It's Owen! He's going after them."

"Then swim!"

So I swam. The sea felt cold but it didn't bother me—my body adapted and maintained my normal temperature. We swam fast and I didn't tire at all, but it seemed to take a decade. Especially after Tristan said we'd crossed the shield and were safe, because then the excitement built up inside me. I was going to my real home. I was about to see my baby. He was about to meet his daddy. And I was about to finally learn the secrets kept from me my entire life. My heart raced, not from exertion, but from anticipation.

As soon as the water became shallow enough to wade through and my feet touched the ground, an intense feeling of power and magic overcame me. Tristan took me in his arms and kissed me.

"Welcome home," he murmured. We walked out of the water hand-in-hand.

Mom and Rina stood on the beach waiting for us with towels and robes, both smiling warmly. My wet skin chilled in the cool breeze—a feeling I noticed, although it wasn't exactly uncomfortable, just there. Still, I welcomed the warmth of the thick, soft robe. As I rubbed the towel around my hair, something crashed through the trees lining the top of the beach. I expected an elephant to break through.

"Mom!"

Dorian burst onto the beach, running full speed. I ran to him and swept him into my arms, spinning around and kissing him all over his sweet, little face.

"I missed you so much!" I said, squeezing him tighter. I buried my face in the crook of his neck and inhaled his tangy little-boy scent.

"Wow, Mom, you got strong!" Dorian mused. He touched my face, then kissed my cheek. "And very beautiful."

I laughed at his observations. "And I think you got much bigger."

I squeezed him tighter as I spun him around again. I stopped us to face Tristan. He watched us, a mixed expression of love and trepidation on his face. Dorian became quiet and stared at him wide-eyed.

"That's my dad," Dorian whispered in my ear. It wasn't a question.

"Yes, it is, little man," I whispered back.

He sucked in his breath noisily. He looked at me, his face lit with the brightest smile, and then jumped out of my arms and ran as fast as he could into Tristan's. A huge grin spread across Tristan's face as he scooped Dorian up and held him tightly. I ran over and wrapped my arms around both of my guys. We fell to the ground, all of us laughing and crying at the same time.

At some point during all of this—I hadn't even noticed when—Owen returned and came to shore.

"Uncle Owen!" Dorian shouted, jumping to his feet and running into Owen's arms.

"Hey, little buddy." Owen returned the bear hug.

Tristan and I stood up and brushed ourselves off, then Tristan took my hand and pulled me close to him.

"Uncle Owen, my dad's here!" Dorian flew back to Tristan, who scooped him up in his free arm. Dorian wrapped his arms around Tristan's neck and planted a kiss on his cheek. Tristan squeezed my hand and I could feel his joy. My heart would explode if it grew any bigger.

"Hey, Alexis?" Owen said.

I tilted my head. "Yeah?"

He looked at Tristan and back at me. "We *always* win."

He stood with Mom and Rina and they all grinned and nodded. I looked at Tristan and Dorian and they beamed, too. And I realized this was my family—Owen, Rina, Mom and my two men. The people I loved. And I was finally Real Alexis, with my Real Tristan. We had suffered through the darkness and emerged into the light, our lives drastically changed forever. But we were all together. Finally.

We *did* win.

Epilogue

Silence filled the Amadis mansion as Tristan and I headed downstairs after changing into dry clothes. It felt like a museum at night. Well, an ancient museum—the two-story foyer was dark, with the only light coming from torches on the stone walls.

Mom? I didn't know where to find Mom and Rina, and I didn't think calling her name aloud would be appropriate. She appeared in one of the three arched doorways off the foyer. Tristan and I followed her into a stately sitting room, where Rina waited for us, holding two leather-bound books in her lap. We sat on a brown leather couch in front of the fireplace while Mom sat on another couch next to Rina.

Mom and Rina both smiled warmly at me and Rina began.

"We start with ancient history. As your mother has taught you, in the very beginning, there was rebellion in Heaven. God permanently cast the Archangel Lucifer and a third of the Angels out of Heaven, sentencing them to Earth and Hell. There has been spiritual warfare waging ever since.

"The outcast Angels, now called demons, take many forms and most take no form at all, but are evil spirits. The spirits frighten humans, plant evil thoughts in their minds, tempt them with immorality and sometimes even possess the human body to do their evil deeds. Their goal is to bring human souls to Satan and Hell. God and the Angels work through priests, ministers and counselors to cast these demons out and keep them away." Rina sighed. "Sadly, most humans do not realize there is this ongoing battle for their souls."

She paused and closed her eyes. I wondered if she prayed for those souls.

After a couple of moments, she continued. "A much smaller number of demons take some kind of human or animal form, such as mages, vampires and shape-shifters. These are the Daemoni. Their purpose is to harm or kill humans, disregarding their souls. They continuously seek more power and, therefore, more members. Growing their army requires human sacrifice— the humans may not actually die, but their lives are forever changed and their souls are at risk.

"Those created demons are the souls the Amadis are responsible for. We cannot do anything about the original demons, the Ancients, but we can still win over the souls of the rest of the Daemoni. We show them how to live responsibly with their abilities and powers and how to control their desires without hurting humans. We bring the goodness out of them and, hopefully, we can lead them to the decision to ultimately save their souls, giving them true immortality. And I believe you know how that is accomplished?"

I nodded. "But how did this become our responsibility? I mean, why us? Who are we?"

"In short, we come from Angels. We are the result of the Daemoni infecting a half-Angel and half-human woman named Cassandra. Although infected, she still only knew love and goodness and she started the Amadis at the direction of the Heavenly Host of Angels."

"So, we are Angels, but we are also essentially Daemoni?"

Rina shook her head. "Not exactly. There are the Angels, including the original Daemoni, and there are offspring of Angels. We are the offspring. We have Angel blood and we have Daemoni powers. But we are their exact opposites. We are inherently *good*."

"And we can bring goodness out of them," I said, glancing at Tristan.

"Yes, if there is any soul left, we can affect them," Rina answered.

"And . . . if there is no soul left?" I asked. I wasn't sure I wanted to know the answer.

Rina sighed.

"If they are a threat to humans or ourselves . . . well, sometimes we have to kill them, honey," Mom answered.

"So the ones at Tristan's house in Cape Heron that one day, during the storm, you wanted to kill them. They had no souls left?"

"No. Unfortunately, Edmund had given his soul to the Daemoni and they completely destroyed it," Mom said, her voice heavy with grief.

"Remember when we discussed the rogues back then?" Tristan asked. I nodded, though I barely remembered. "The rogues usually have destroyed souls, which is why they can't be controlled."

"So how do you know if they still have a soul?"

"You will learn to sense it," Rina answered. "If you can feel any love or compassion toward them, they can be saved."

"And if they show anything like mercy or love, there is hope," Mom added. "Like Vanessa. She showed feelings for Tristan."

"Hmph," Tristan grunted.

"I think that's lust," I muttered.

"I don't know about that. She has a desire to be with someone else, so she still has a soul," Mom replied.

"And the vampire that threatened me . . . since he showed mercy, he still has a soul?"

"Yes," Mom answered. "That's also why he left when he sensed me and then Owen. He didn't want to take the chance of us converting him."

"He brings me to the subject of my books. What is their purpose?"

"Ah, good question," Rina said. "We will start with more history. You see, up through the eighteen-hundreds, the Daemoni ran rampantly in the human world and humans were very aware and fearful of them. This fear strengthened their faith and helped protect them from being lured into the evil world. Unfortunately, however, the humans killed many innocent people who were not evil or possessed at all. Even those who were real Daemoni were not usually rogues. They still had hope. You would be most familiar with the Salem witches, no?"

I nodded.

"There were many similar incidents around the world. Heaven lost innocent humans, the Amadis lost the ability to convert the souls and the Daemoni lost many of their soldiers. The Daemoni decided to become more covert then. We have an obligation to keep the existence of our people secret, which means keeping the Daemoni secret, too."

"So what changed? Why did you decide to break that obligation?" I asked.

Rina shook her head. "We have not broken the obligation. We have not revealed their existence. When the Daemoni went underground, humans felt safer and became complacent. We have just reminded humans there could be a *possibility* of their existence. You see, over the last century, with advances in science, humans have lost their belief in, and therefore, their fear of the creatures we know as the Daemoni and evil in general. They only see evil in each other, perpetuating wars among themselves. With this loss of fear has also come a loss of faith."

Rina stopped and looked again as though she worried for humans.

"You're an excellent writer and your readers want to believe your characters are real," Mom said, picking up for Rina. "For them to believe the good ones are real, they must also believe the bad ones are, too. You've made humans more aware of the *possibility* of their existence. They can better protect themselves, by increasing their faith."

"You see," Rina said, "the Daemoni truly desire to take control of the world and rule over humans. They are growing restless and angry with their limitations and are preparing to fight. The union of you and Tristan has exacerbated their anger. We believe you have changed over so soon—so young—because we will need as many generations of Amadis daughters as possible. The Angels are preparing for major war. Our hope . . . our plan . . . has been that your books will help prepare the humans. The humans will need their faith and knowledge of how to protect themselves as spiritual warfare will re-enter their realm in the near future."

"Why don't I just write our story—mine and Tristan's—then," I muttered. I meant it rhetorically, not at all desiring to tell the whole world about us.

"I hoped you would say that," Rina said, smiling. "You, of all people, could write it so people think the story is fiction, but it seems like it could be very real."

I stared at her in disbelief. Out of the corner of my eye, I could see Tristan shaking his head slowly.

"I wasn't serious!"

"But it is something to think about," Rina said, a gleam in her eye.

"I think I've done enough damage already. It was risky to write those stories. Now the Daemoni feel justified in killing us."

"Any risk is worth saving humans," Rina said pointedly. "But the Daemoni really do not have Provocation because we did not break the obligation. We did not really expose them. And, now that we know Tristan escaped, we believe they used Provocation as an excuse to come after you. If they could get you, they could get Tristan back."

"They'd already planned it before I escaped," Tristan said. "That's why I made the move when I did, because she was in danger."

"Yes, they have been discussing this for some time. They have been giving me ultimatums to make her stop since she wrote her second book," Rina said. "But they knew they did not have real Provocation. They were empty threats. If they came after her at all when they still had you, it would be to have you both. So the books were really irrelevant to their desire to attack her. They served as an excuse."

"And I wouldn't have known they were lying," I said. "I would've fallen for it. I *did* fall for it."

"Yes, we know we made a mistake in not telling you sooner," Rina admitted.

"So why couldn't anyone tell me? Why has Mom always had to keep this from me? I'm twenty-seven years old and just now learning who I am and what it means!"

Rina sighed. "I understand your frustration and I appreciate your patience. There were many reasons for your not knowing the whole truth. First, there was a trace of doubt about the power of the Daemoni in you—enough doubt that we had to be cautious in protecting our secrets. Second, our secrets are always kept hidden until the woman goes through the *Ang'dora*.

We all lived normal, human lives until then.

"You, however, are unique. You had powers before your *Ang'dora*, so you knew something was different from a young age. For the rest of us, our mothers left us to return to the Amadis just before they changed over and we continued living normally until our turn came. You, however, saw and understood that your mother does not age. Sophia was so concerned for your safety, she would not return to us when you became too old for her to look like your mother. Then Tristan came to you and you deserved to know at least some of the truth so you could build a solid relationship with him. So, you actually knew more than any of us did before the *Ang'dora*.

"Finally, as your gift of writing became apparent along with your interest in creatures you thought were mythical, we knew you could serve a great purpose. You would not have done so well if you knew it was not fiction, no?"

"No, I might not have written them at all," I admitted. I thought I'd been creating—and losing myself—in my own world.

"So we still could not tell you *everything*, even when you already knew so much." Rina placed one of the books she'd been holding on the table between us and slid it toward me. "Read your history, Alexis. You will learn everything you have been waiting to know."

I picked up the heavy book. The title was embossed in gold on the cover:

The History and Life of

Alexis Katerina Ames Knight

"It will give you the insight you seek," she promised.

I ran my finger over the title and then opened the cover. The inside cover depicted a family tree—well, more like a vine—starting with someone named Andrew at the bottom and ending with Dorian at the top. *Holy crap!*

"Mom . . . you're a *twin*?" I'd never known that before. She'd never mentioned it once, not that she had a brother and definitely not that she was a twin. But depicted on the family vine next to her leaf was another—Noah.

She and Rina both looked a thousand years old, full of a thousand years of heartache, as they both nodded. I opened my mouth to ask what happened to him, but Mom gave a nearly imperceptible shake of her head. Rina stared at the flames in the fireplace, though she didn't seem to actually watch them. Her mind was far off, lost in distant memories. I'd brought up a difficult subject. Noah must have met a terrible end and I had inadvertently brought it to the forefront of Rina's mind.

I wanted to tell her I was sorry, to hug this woman who always displayed control and power, but seemed so despondent and broken now. But my intuition told me the best thing to do was to simply give her a moment of silence. So I returned my attention to the book and became engrossed in the first couple of pages, which were about Andrew, a fallen Angel, his twin children, Jordan and Cassandra, and a potion that forever altered our DNA. Tristan tapped his finger on the page.

"They used a similar potion to create me," he murmured.

I flipped the pages and saw text only partially filled the heavy book. The majority of the pages were blank. I looked questioningly at Rina, who seemed to have recovered from the pain inflicted by the reminder of her son, her attention returned to me.

"The rest will fill in as you go through your life here on Earth," she explained.

"And when the pages run out?" I asked.

"That is when you either die or ascend," she replied.

"Ascend?"

"When your purpose is fulfilled here and your daughter is ready to take over as matriarch, you will ascend to a different place, joining our ancestors and the Angels in the Otherworld."

"Assuming I have a daughter," I muttered.

"I *know* you will," Rina answered confidently. "We do not yet know the purpose of Dorian's lone arrival. But the messages I have received from the Angels indicate there will be another Amadis daughter. This is something we will need to discuss with the council. As you know, our very existence relies on a girl in the next generation."

"And if there's not? Dorian can't rule the Amadis?" I asked.

"We are a matriarchal society, Alexis." Her tone was firm, as if that were answer enough. As if it could never be changed.

"What if he has a daughter? Can we skip a generation?"

Now they all—including Tristan—sighed heavily, it seemed with despair. I looked at him in surprise, thinking he would support this thought. He pursed his lips and just barely shook his head.

"Read your book, Alexis," Rina said, "and you will understand."

I flipped through the pages of the book again. My story, starting with my conception and ending with my travels to the Amadis Island today, used only a few pages, compared to the number of blank ones.

"Well, I will either have a very long or a very full life."

"I believe you will have both," Rina said, smiling now. "But the pages cannot be counted—the number is protected by the Angels and they can add more or take some away, so we have no idea how long you will actually live."

She placed the other book on the table. "Tristan, we have yours, too. We did not include any history. You probably do not mind, no?"

"Absolutely not," he said, picking up the book with his Amadis name on it.

"Good. It starts when you saved Sophia, your first step in becoming Amadis."

I looked at him in surprise again. "You saved Mom? I thought she saved you."

"He saved me first," Mom answered for him. "Once I had him convinced there was enough good in him, he fought Lucas, who tried to kill me. Actually, I was unknowingly already pregnant, so he saved both of us."

I inhaled sharply. *Even then we needed each other.* I pushed the thought into Tristan's head. He smiled at me.

"We always have," he thought. *"Maybe I somehow knew you were in there and we already had that connection."*

I like *that thought.* I smiled back at him. *You and me together forever.*

He thumbed through the hundreds, perhaps thousands, of blank pages in his book—about as many as there were in my own. *"Forever."*

Mom and Rina left the room so Tristan and I could read the Amadis history. I curled my legs under me and snuggled into him, opening my book between us to the family vine. I traced my fingers up the branch as I scanned the names and then searched for the meaning of the brown leaves and asterisks. Small print in the corner provided the explanation.

"Oh, *no!*" I gasped, tears springing to my eyes. "All the males!"

Tristan squeezed me closer and his voice filled with sorrow. "I know, my love. That is why Dorian cannot rule or even produce an Amadis daughter."

No, no, no! Not my son!

For the first time since the *Ang'dora*, tears flowed freely. I clutched at my chest, forgetting again that the pendant—my life saver—was gone. *Not my Dorian! Not my son!*

"Is there anything we can *do* for him?" I cried aloud.

Tristan leaned his head against mine. "We will do everything we can, my love. Everything in our power."

We'd already won so much. We'd fought our personal demons to be together—the ones we created in ourselves, such as the inabilities to trust or to love and be loved; and those implanted into our DNA and by our enemies. Our love was strong enough to overcome those obstacles. Good had won over evil.

But is Owen right? Does good always win? And is our love strong enough to overcome all the obstacles still ahead of us? There are so many battles still to fight . . . for us, for our son, for the Amadis . . . for all humankind. How do we face it all?

I hadn't realized my mind was still connected to Tristan's and I shared these desperate thoughts with him until he responded. I could hear the confidence—almost cockiness—even in his thoughts.

"We fight together, ma lykita, side by side, hand in hand, souls bound as one. The ultimate warrior and the fierce protector." I looked up at him and he grinned. *"Bring it on!"*

Then he winked and I smiled through the daze.

Yeah. Who can beat us, right?

It was a question with an answer only God knew . . . and only time would reveal as our purposes unfolded before us.

About the Author

Photo by Michael Soule

Kristie Cook is a lifelong, award-winning writer in various genres, from marketing communications to fantasy fiction. Besides writing, she enjoys reading, cooking, traveling and riding on the back of a motorcycle. She has lived in ten states, but currently calls Southwest Florida home with her husband, three teenage sons, a beagle and a puggle. She can be found at www.KristieCook.com.

Connect With Kristie Online

Email: kristie@kristiecook.com
Author's Website & Blog: www.KristieCook.com
Series Website: www.SoulSaversSeries.com
Facebook: www.Facebook.com/AuthorKristieCook
Twitter: www.Twitter.com/#!/KristieCookAuth
Tumbler: www.Tumblr.com/tumblelog/KristieCook
Google+: Kristie Cook

An Excerpt from *Devotion*, Book 3 in the Soul Savers Series, Coming February 2012

Devotion

I stood in the sitting room of the ancient Amadis mansion, stared at the giant tapestry spanning the entire stone wall and wondered how I could change the future it told for my son. A long vine, embroidered in gold and green thread with leaves on each side, wound and climbed its way up and across the wall-hanging, a golden name on each leaf. These were the names of my ancestors. The Amadis Family Vine only showed the mothers and their children, the fathers deemed irrelevant in our matriarchal society—most had died young, long before their widows even knew their real heritage.

Silvery-green thread outlined most of the leaves—the ones with female names, the daughters—but some were brown and separated from the vine. The names on the brown leaves were all male, a twin to a green-leafed sister, and each had an asterisk next to it—a seemingly insignificant little symbol ominously marking the fate of each boy. The meaning looked disproportionately large on this huge hanging: *CONVERTED TO DAEMONI.

A much smaller rendition of the image spread across the inside cover of the leather-bound book I hugged to my chest: The History and Life of Alexis Katerina Ames Knight. My history. The one I'd just finished reading, where I learned that not only did Angel blood course through my veins, but so did the blood of vampires, Weres and mages—the magical race that included witches and wizards, the more powerful warlocks and the strongest of them all, the sorcerers. We gained their best qualities when my earliest ancestors consumed a powerful potion, often called Jordan's Juice, which infused the creatures' DNA into ours. The *Ang'dora* brought their endowments, as well as powers given to us by the Angels, into full effect. The book was full of fascinating history and explanations and I'd read it beginning to end in one sitting.

I stared at the enormous vine in the wall-hanging, though, because it better reflected the magnitude of my feelings than the tiny one in the book. For at the top of the Family Vine, just above my leaf, scripted in gold like all the others, was the name Dorian, my son. His leaf, unaccompanied by a female twin, an anomaly in itself, was brown, though not separated from the vine. Not yet, anyway.

I had no idea what I would do to keep it that way. I was too new to this Amadis life. But I vowed to do something. I could not let my son fall into the hands of the Daemoni, our innate enemies, servants to Satan himself.

"*Ma lykita*," murmured a smooth, sexy voice from the doorway, "staring at it doesn't change anything."

Tristan stepped behind me and wrapped his arms around my shoulders, sending electric currents under my skin.

"I know," I said with a sigh. "I'm just thinking about what we can do that *will* change it."

He kissed the top of my head. "We'll figure something out.

Fortunately, we have a few years."

"According to the book and history, yes. But if he's anything like me or you, unique in so many ways, he could go early."

"But not tonight or tomorrow or anytime soon. Right now, we have more pressing matters to worry about."

"More pressing than our son's life?"

Tristan sighed. "Nothing is more important than Dorian's life. But there's a difference between important and urgent and, for now, the issue isn't urgent. We have time. But tomorrow morning—in just a few *hours*—we have a council meeting and I expect it'll be intense. It's late and I know you have to be tired. You need some rest."

My body did feel heavy with exhaustion, not surprising with the combination of jet lag and a lack of sleep. The fear of being overwhelmed by my new mind-reading ability caused sleep to allude me on the flights from Miami to Athens. The anticipation of learning my heritage didn't help, either. I'd been awake for nearly forty-eight hours. I didn't think I could shut my mind down right now, though. Between all the information I just learned about my history and my genetic make-up and figuring out what to do about Dorian, there was just too much to think about.

"How am I supposed to sleep?"

"You might be surprised once you let yourself relax. And, if you can't relax," he kissed my ear, giving me goose bumps, "I can help with that, too."

"That's stimulating, not relaxing," I said, my body already trembling for his touch.

"Hmm . . . good. After all, we do have that other pressing matter and the council will want to know that we're working on it." He nuzzled his face into my hair, pressing his lips against my neck. As always, my body immediately responded to his touch.

I couldn't help it—he'd always been irresistible to me.

"We do need to keep trying," I conceded with a smile. "And it *has* been a while."

"It's been *way* too long." He took my hand and led me up the stone stairs, lit by torches affixed to the stone walls.

Two days certainly felt like a long time, for us, anyway. Until now, we'd never gone more than twenty-four hours without making love—if you didn't count the seven-and-a-half years while he was held captive by the Daemoni. Our eight-year anniversary was less than four months away, but we were still newlyweds in a very real sense, having had a total of three weeks together as husband and wife. We also had a mission to accomplish: we needed a daughter for the survival of the Amadis—my family, our society. And if the Amadis didn't survive, neither would humanity. It would be lost to the Daemoni.

"Can't we just flash to our room?" I asked as we continued up the stairs to the third floor.

"If you flash everywhere, you'll get lazy and I won't have a lazy wife," Tristan teased. "More importantly, you don't want to create bad habits. We'll have to mainstream soon and you can't be flashing all the time in the human world."

"I know. But I'm not being lazy." We weren't alone in the mansion and I didn't know who might be nearby, so I finished the rest as a thought, sharing it with him telepathically. *I'm just horny.*

"*Ah. Why didn't you say so?*" He picked up the pace and we practically flew through the long hall.

I slowed down as we entered our wing. A door on the left led to Mom's suite and I knew she was still awake, probably reading. I stopped at the door on the right—Dorian's room.

"I stayed until he was sound asleep," Tristan whispered, but

I cracked open the door anyway, needing to see him. A little-boy snore rattled in the darkness and his dream appeared in my head—he was swimming with his dad…and happily fighting sharks. I could only imagine the bedtime story Tristan must have told him. I closed the door with a smile.

We entered the front room of our suite at the end of the hall and as soon as Tristan closed the door, I was in his powerful arms, locked into a kiss.

"Not in here," I reminded him as we yanked each other's clothes off.

When Mom had first shown us to our suite, she'd warned us about the antique furniture in the front sitting room. The bedroom, however, was specifically designed for our kind, completely bare except for a large, stone platform with a two-foot thick pad and lots of pillows—the bed. A stone pillar stood at each corner and blue gossamer hung in curtains between the posts. The bedding was either easily reparable or easily replaced—a necessity considering our kind tended to destroy things in moments of passion.

Tristan lifted me with one arm and carried me to the bed, his satiny lips never leaving my tingling skin. Making love with him had always been intense, but since the *Ang'dora*, my heightened senses made it so much more sensual and our powers made it so much more *fun*. As usual, it wasn't long before Tristan took me over the edge. The loss of control crumbled the mental wall I so carefully held up to block out others' thoughts . . . and to protect my own.

It all flooded in at once. Thankfully, Dorian still dreamt of sharks, but Mom stiffened in her reading chair then shook her head, thinking, "*Alexis!*" Solomon and Rina, in their own bed, exchanged knowing looks. Owen felt surprised and confused and . . . *excited?* The sheet over his lap began to rise. *Oh, shit!*

My mental wall flew up, feeling more solid than ever, in fact, solid as steel. I could almost hear a metallic clang as it slammed into place, like the thick, heavy door of a vault. Everyone's thoughts disappeared. Mine were my own again. I panted, my body as rigid as the steel wall in my head, as I still clung to Tristan, who was pressed against the ceiling. I forced myself to relax and let go, fell to the bed and just lay there on my back.

"Oh, shit?" Tristan said as he joined me on the bed, his expression a mix of satisfaction and amusement. "That's a new one. I think I prefer 'Don't stop' or 'Right there' or even 'Love you, baby' to 'Oh, shit.'"

"Did I say that out loud?" I asked hopefully.

"Mmm . . . no."

I groaned, automatically reaching for the necklace that no longer hung around my neck. Playing with the ruby pendant Tristan made for me had been a nervous habit for years and now it was gone. Vanessa the evil vampire bitch had it.

Tristan rolled onto his side, facing me. He took my hand from my neck and kissed the back of it. "What's wrong? I thought that was pretty great myself."

"Of course it was." I brushed his hair, still long and darker than usual, back from his face, to see the gold in his hazel eyes sparkling brightly with my affirmation. I dropped my hand with a sigh. "And that's the problem."

He lifted an eyebrow. "That's a problem?"

I threw my arms across my face, trying to hide. "Everyone in the mansion just heard me!"

He chuckled. "Their hearing isn't *that* good, especially through stone walls."

"That's not what I mean. You just heard me, right? But in your head?"

"Ah," he said with understanding. And then he laughed.

"Tristan, this is so *not* funny! I'm . . . *mortified*."

He kept laughing, though. I dropped my arms from my face and stared at him. I wanted to hit him. He must have seen it in my eyes because he finally stopped.

"Lexi, there's nothing to be embarrassed about. They all expect it. In fact, they *want* us to do it. They want a daughter, too."

"But, Tristan, you know how I can make you feel what I'm feeling through my thoughts? I just did that with them!"

"Then I'm sure they enjoyed it." He flashed my favorite smile, then pulled me into his arms. "I bet Rina and Solomon are having their own fun now, and Sophia and Owen . . . well, at least they'll have good dreams."

I didn't know about anyone else, but I didn't sleep long enough to dream. Although exhausted, I tossed and turned throughout the night, my mind unable to turn off. The words of my history book churned in my head, particularly those that kept pointing to the fact that we would lose Dorian. Every male of the direct Amadis bloodline went to the Daemoni. Every. Single. One. Since the beginning, when Jordan, the first male twin purposefully sought them out. He abandoned his twin sister, Cassandra, and hunted for the demons, believing himself to be one of them. He joined them in terrorizing humanity and gained the demons' admiration and trust, eventually becoming leader of the Daemoni army. Obsessed with the idea of gaining immortality and any other powers he could have, he and Eris, a witch, created the potion, Jordan's Juice, that forever changed the Daemoni and, by giving it to Cassandra, unintentionally started the Amadis.

Ever since, all of the boys followed Jordan's path to the Daemoni. With Tristan born and raised by them and my own sperm donor one-hundred-percent evil, Dorian had a lot more Daemoni blood running through his veins than he did Amadis. Everything told me he was doomed—nothing in the book provided any kind of escape clause or even the mention of one—but I just couldn't believe it. I rolled over again. *There has to be* something *we can do.*

❧

I procrastinated in our suite as long as I could the next morning, not wanting to face everyone. If I had any chance of talking to Rina, my grandmother and the only other telepath to exist in many centuries, I would have been the first one downstairs, asking her to teach me better control. But with the council meeting, I knew she wouldn't be able to help much today.

"Alexis, I don't know about you, but I'm starving," Tristan said. "Can we please go eat breakfast? This meeting could last all day."

I stood at the doorway to a small balcony wrapped with wrought iron, a white sheer curtain puffing around me in the spring breeze and the hem of my dated sundress—one of the few items of clothing I owned—fluttering against my thighs. Our suite was on the third floor of the mansion and the mansion on a hill, so I could just barely see the blue-and-white-capped Aegean Sea beyond the ancient cypress treetops.

"Go on and eat. You don't have to wait for me," I said without moving.

He placed his hands on my shoulders and turned me to look at him. The wide ring of emerald green in his eyes shone brightly, the gold sparkles around the pupils glinting. His skin seemed to glow, like it had on our honeymoon the morning after our first time. He was happy. This place was good for him. He'd literally been to Hell and back and he needed the Amadis power—you could feel the energy pulsing from the island itself—to strengthen his goodness.

"I know what you're doing," he said with that devastating smile that made my heart flip. "You have to face them some time. Do you really want to do it by yourself or would you like me next to you?"

"Of course I'd like you next to me. Always. But . . ." I hesitated.

"But what?"

I dropped my head, staring at the floor. "But you think this is funny. I can already hear the jokes."

"Hmm . . . yeah, I'm not the least bit ashamed of what I can do to you." He lifted my chin with his fingers, brushing his thumb across my lower lip. Then his hand trailed down my neck, between my breasts, along my stomach . . . and lower. I shuddered. He smiled proudly. "So I guess I'll just go downstairs now and we can all have our laughs without you."

He kissed me and winked, then turned and walked out the door. I stared after him in a daze and when the fog cleared, I hurried after him.

"Don't forget I can do the same to you," I said when I caught up to him.

He chuckled. "Trust me, I'll *never* forget that. And I'm not ashamed of it, either. But I do promise to behave."

He took my hand, his touch automatically calming me, but just before we entered the dining room, I stepped behind him.

"Dad!" Dorian bounded from his chair at the table and leapt into Tristan's arms. "I've been waiting *forever* for you to wake up!"

He threw his arms around Tristan's neck in a tight hug.

"Guess I don't count for anything anymore," I said with mocked pain.

He peeked over Tristan's shoulder with the same hazel eyes as his father. "Hey, Mom. I missed you, too."

"Sure you did," I said, ruffling his blond hair. I didn't blame him for his enthusiasm for Tristan—yesterday was the first time they'd ever met. They had a lot of catching up to do.

Rina, Mom and Owen sat at the table, coffee mugs and breakfast plates in front of them. Their conversation we'd heard from the hallway fell silent as soon as we appeared. I barely glanced their way, just in time to see Owen turning his head, his face as pink as the half-eaten grapefruit on his plate. The image of the rising sheet popped into my mind and my face heated, probably turning darker than Owen's. I studied the tablecloth, wondering if anyone would notice if I crawled underneath it and stayed there the rest of my life. Or at least until Owen left. *How can I ever face him again?*

As soon as Tristan and I sat down, a woman who looked as old as the ancient mansion came through a door with a tray of coffee, mugs and condiments. She placed everything in front of us and I reached for the coffee pot, but she picked it up first, pouring our coffee for us. I wasn't used to this.

"Alexis, this is Ophelia," Rina said with her accent that I now knew was Italian. Though she was my grandmother and over a century-and-a-half old, she looked like she was in her late twenties, not much older than Mom looked. Her wide, mahogany eyes, nearly identical to mine and Mom's, warmed with appreciation as she looked at the elderly woman. "She has served the Amadis for over two-hundred years, since the days of my great-grandmother's rule. Ophelia, I'd like you to meet our Alexis."

Ophelia dipped into a curtsy while still pouring our coffee. I definitely wasn't used to that.

"Nice to meet you, Ms. Alexis," she said, her voice soft and smoother than I expected, looking at her severely creased face. She turned to Tristan. "Nice to see you again, Mr. Tristan. It has been a long time."

Ophelia looked back at me, her gray eyes surprisingly clear behind the many folds of her eyelids. Doing the math, I realized she was nearly the same age as Tristan. *Ew. That thought's . . . discomforting.* I banished it immediately.

"What would you like for breakfast, dear?" she asked me.

"What are my choices?"

She smiled. "Anything you'd like, Ms. Alexis."

"Anything?" I asked with surprise. "Chocolate croissants? And strawberries?"

She curtsied again. "Certainly. Mr. Tristan?"

I stared at him as he rattled off a list of eggs, bacon, sausage, biscuits and a couple other things.

"I told you I was starving," he said once Ophelia disappeared.

"I thought we were in a hurry," I muttered. "It'll take forever for her to cook all that."

But as soon as I said the last word, Ophelia came through the door again, another tray on her arm. I wondered if the kitchen always had food ready to go and then realized it was probably prepared by magic. And then I realized, with mild shock, Ophelia was probably a witch—she definitely wasn't an Amadis descendant or a vampire, so that left a witch, warlock or Were. She looked too frail to even be able to hold all the food—so definitely not a Were—and then I noticed she wasn't actually carrying it. The tray hovered just an inch over her arm. *Yep, a witch. Weird.*

Tristan dug into all his food, only stopping once, when his whole body seemed to freeze and his eyes became distant. Just as suddenly, though, he relaxed and started shoveling again. I could only figure he'd swallowed something wrong in his haste. I pulled my croissant apart, picking at it more than eating it. My stomach remained knotted with worry, not helped by the embarrassment for my loss of control last night. I couldn't have felt any more awkward than I did now, sitting in a room full of people who had all experienced my orgasm right along with me.

"Alexis, I need to talk to you about your gift," Rina's voice said in my head, sounding very nearly like her regular voice. Had she just heard my thoughts? I blushed. *"Yes, we will talk about that, but it will have to wait. I need to discuss a few things with you regarding the council meeting."*

Like this or in private? I asked her.

She rose from her chair. "The meeting starts in twenty minutes. Sophia, Alexis, please come with me, yes?"

I dropped the fist-sized strawberry I was eating onto the plate next to my half-eaten croissant and stood up.

"I'll stay with Dorian during the meeting," Owen offered. He wasn't a member of the council—just my bodyguard, though I thought of him more like the big brother I never had but always wanted. Similarly, he was like an uncle to Dorian. They adored each other. Dorian, who'd just been pouting because he wanted Tristan to himself all day, grinned at the idea of at least getting to hang out with Uncle Owen.

"No, Owen, I would like you at the meeting," Rina said. "You will continue to serve as Alexis's protector, so you need to know everything. Ophelia will take care of him."

"We'll go toad hunting," Ophelia called from the kitchen, just as Dorian was about to frown again. His eyes lit up. He jumped off his chair, gave Tristan and me quick hugs and ran for the kitchen.

I followed Rina and Mom out of the dining room and down a long hallway. Rina's deep-violet, floor-length gown swished around her as we entered what must have been her office. It was a large room, beautifully decorated and furnished with polished wood furniture, including a desk and ceiling-high bookshelves full of ancient-looking books and knickknacks. A leather sofa and two high-back chairs created a sitting area near the fireplace. Everything was antique.

"Alexis, use your mind to determine if anyone is nearby," Rina said after Mom closed and locked the door.

This was something she could do herself, of course, but I was sure she was allowing me to practice. I probed outwards with my mind, careful to keep my mental wall in place. I sensed no other thoughts nearby and shook my head.

"Before we go into the council meeting, you need to know that we have not disclosed your gift of telepathy to anyone," Rina said, moving to the chair behind her desk. Mom and I took the seats in front of her. "Only the three of us, Solomon, Tristan and Owen know and we would like it to remain so for as long as we can keep it secret."

I nodded. She had told me this before, back at the beach house in the Florida Keys, implying that it had to do with the video I'd received showing the Daemoni beheading Tristan. The video was, obviously, a lie and no one knew who sent it.

"I do not even want the council to know at this time," Rina said.

"Okay . . . but why? I thought you figured out that the Daemoni had hacked your email and sent the video to me—"

"That was a guess," Mom said. "It makes the most sense that they would send it, but we're still looking into it. Rina has reason to believe—"

"I would like you to listen to the council members' minds during the meeting," Rina cut in, her eyes hard as she threw a look of anger at Mom.

My eyebrows shot up. "Um . . . I could be missing something here . . . but isn't that a big invasion of privacy?"

"You *are* missing something," Mom said, leaning back in her chair and crossing her arms as she glared at Rina.

"What?" I asked, my eyes bouncing between the two of them.

"I—" Rina broke Mom's gaze and began shuffling and stacking papers on her desk. "I just need you to listen and tell me what you hear."

"But why me? Can't you do it?" I didn't mean to sound so demanding, but her request made little sense and made me uncomfortable. As did whatever was going on between the two of them.

Rina abandoned her papers and clasped her hands together. Her chest rose and fell with a deep breath and she shook her head slowly. I'd noticed yesterday, while she provided some of the answers I'd been waiting to hear for so long, a new sadness I'd never seen in her before. Something different—less confidence, I supposed, as if something had seriously shaken her. I thought it'd been my mention of Noah, her son and Mom's twin, but today it seemed even more pronounced. Her face looked tighter than normal and she held her shoulders at a more defined angle, as if she were tense.

"Someone might be blocking her power," Mom said when Rina didn't answer me.

"But not mine? Wait—they can *block* your power?" I asked, taken aback, nearly knocking my chair backwards with my sudden jolt.

Rina sighed. *What's making her so unhappy? What can I do to help?* I just wanted that look on her face to disappear.

"There is a possibility a mage might be able to shield me from entering his or her mind," she finally said. "A slight possibility, but a possibility nonetheless. I would have thought only a sorcerer would be powerful enough, but the witch, wizards and warlocks on the council are among the most powerful in the world, nearly rivaling any sorcerer."

"Then they could easily block me, too," I pointed out.

"Not if they don't know that they need to," Mom said. "The reason for keeping it secret."

"Well, there aren't any guarantees it'll stay secret. It's not like I have the best control." I anxiously pawed at the base of my throat, once again coming up empty, no pendant hanging there.

"I just need you to keep your wall up and listen—just *listen*," Rina said. She implored me with wide, pleading eyes and again, I wanted to make that look go away. *But could I do what she asked?*

I stood up and walked over to the fireplace, gnawing on my lip and staring at intricately designed glass eggs lining the mantle.

"Alexis, I would not ask you if I did not think you could handle it," Rina continued. "You have excellent control of protecting your own thoughts. I cannot even hear them without your allowing me to."

I looked over my shoulder at her and lifted an eyebrow, hoping it was enough to remind her of last night.

"Yes, well, that is a different matter," she said dismissively.

"You and Tristan won't be having sex at the council meeting," Mom said more bluntly.

"No, but what if something else happens?" I asked, throwing

my arms in the air and nearly knocking over one of the eggs. Thankfully, my reactions were much faster than before the *Ang'dora* and I was able to steady it before it fell. I turned and began pacing. "That many people . . . all those thoughts . . . I nearly had a mental breakdown on the planes over here. If Tristan and Owen hadn't been there . . . I'm just not ready right now. Can't it wait until I'm better at this?"

"No," Mom and Rina said in unison.

Rina stepped in front of me, forcing me to stop pacing. She took my hands into hers and looked at me with pleading eyes. "I need you to do it now, darling, or I would not ask you. It is quite urgent."

I blinked at her desperate words. "What's going on?"

She pursed her lips together as if trying to hold the words back. "I cannot imagine who . . . or why . . . I trust them all immensely . . . perhaps too much . . ."

"Who? What?" I asked, not following her.

"Just say it, Mother," Mom said with obvious impatience.

Rina sighed and I thought I could almost see tears building in her eyes. "I have received a message from the Angels. I can only interpret it to mean . . ." She cleared her throat, blinked back any moisture that had been in her eyes and lifted her chin. ". . . to mean that there is a traitor in our midst."

ↀↀ